Chestnut Hill

THE NEW CLASS

Chestnut Hill

THE NEW CLASS

by Lauren Brooke

SCHOLASTIC INC.

New York Toronto London Auckland Sydney
Mexico City New Delhi Hong Kong Buenos Aires

Special thanks to Elisabeth Faith

ISBN 0-439-73854-7

Chestnut Hill series created by Working Partners Ltd, London.

12 11 10 9 8 7 6 5 4 3   5 6 7 8 9 10/0
Printed in the U.S.A.   40
First printing, August 2005

*For Graeme,
my rock in all
things*

Chestnut Hill

THE NEW CLASS

CHAPTER ONE

"Dylan, we're almost there. Wake up, honey."

Dylan Walsh blinked her eyes open. Glancing out the window, she saw whitewashed fences lining lush green pastures. "What?" Dylan murmured. "Why'd you guys let me go to sleep?"

"We just got off the interstate a few minutes ago," her dad explained.

"You didn't miss anything." Dylan's mom looked over her shoulder into the backseat of the family SUV. "I thought you probably needed the rest."

Dylan rolled her eyes before she brushed her red hair behind her ears and turned her gaze back out the window. Dylan was relieved to know she'd soon be escaping her mother's overprotective ways. It was true that she hadn't been able to sleep a wink the night before. There had been too many things going through her head. She'd been looking forward to this day for so long — she was really on her way to Chestnut Hill! She searched the fields for any signs of horses, trying to gauge how close they were to the school. She wondered if all of Virginia was this picturesque.

Dylan followed the stretch of fence toward the horizon and her heart pounded when she saw the brick pillars that marked the entrance to the esteemed boarding school.

"This is it!" she yelled, recalling the first time she had visited the school. After the prospective-student weekend that spring, Dylan had been set on coming to Chestnut Hill.

She rolled down the window to get a better glimpse of the iron gates at the start of the drive. As her dad turned the car, Dylan's eyes focused on the Chestnut Hill crest. The chestnut tree (*what else*? she thought delightedly) with spreading roots and branches was worked into the ornate iron gate, along with the profile of a horse's head.

White rail fences continued on either side of the driveway, and Dylan shielded her eyes from the sun to scan the paddocks for the Chestnut Hill horses. She thought they were all beautiful, but she held her breath as she searched for one pony in particular.

Before she could find familiar brown-and-white coat, the car turned to follow the gravel driveway, and the rest of the grounds came into view. Dylan leaned forward as they approached Old House, the magnificent white colonial building that had been the original school over one hundred years ago. With its tall white pillars, it gave Chestnut Hill a look of great Southern tradition. Now Old House just held faculty and administration offices, and the classrooms and science labs were in classic red-brick buildings on the other side of the campus. Ever since the fourth grade, when she read about it in *Horse and Rider* magazine, Dylan had wanted to attend Chestnut Hill for its top-tier riding program. *I can't believe I'm actually here*, she thought, with a shiver of excitement. From the moment she had laid eyes on the campus that spring, she had been imagining this moment. Everything about the school was the best money could buy: the Olympic-size swimming pool, the indoor track, the art studio complete with ceramics workshop and kiln. And the school was known for high academic standards that prepared students for acceptance into the most competitive colleges, which pleased her parents.

Mr. Walsh took a left turn, following the signs to the dorms on the north side of the campus. There were six houses, where students slept, studied, and generally hung out. Dylan already knew that she was in Adams House, which, very conveniently, was the dorm closest to the stable yard. She slid across the leather seat so she could look out the other window and tapped a drum roll with her fingers as they passed the wooden stables. *I'm going to be able to walk to the barn in less than five minutes*, she thought. *I'll be the most dedicated rider at Chestnut Hill. Just wait until team tryouts!*

Inside, a girl was carrying two buckets to the end stall. As the girl opened the door, Dylan caught sight of a magnificent black horse and twisted around so she could keep looking.

"Honey, you'll get whiplash if you keep turning your neck like that!" Mrs. Walsh warned in a teasing tone.

Dylan straightened up, meeting her mother's eyes in the vanity mirror on the front passenger visor. "You need to brush your hair," Mrs. Walsh told her. "It's flipping up again." She reached up to smooth her own neat red bob, but her tresses were already sleek and perfectly in place. Dylan might have inherited her mom's hair color, but she sure didn't have the same patience to style and sculpt it.

"Maybe I'll just wear my hard hat." Dylan grimaced, running her fingers through her thick hair. "Then no one will notice." Her mom had been trying to persuade her to get bangs, but she preferred having it all the same length, even if she needed a clip or a ponytail holder to keep it from falling into her eyes. "Hey, Dad, if you stop right now, I can get my hat out of the back."

Mr. Walsh raised his eyebrows. "If we stop now, you'll disappear into the barn. Then you'd need a shower before you could pass your mom's inspection."

Dylan snapped her fingers. "You got me," she grinned. *Dad is so cool,* she thought, as she watched him pat her mom on the hand. *He totally gets me.* Her mom reached back and handed her a tortoiseshell hair clip. As Dylan reached for it, she switched off the DVD player built into the back of the front seat. She didn't mind not being able to watch the end of *Charlie's Angels*. Right now, real life was about one hundred times more exciting!

Dylan shifted to the middle of the backseat so she could look out the front window. The road ahead was almost completely jammed with sports cars, SUVs, and luxury sedans. There didn't seem to be any parking spaces close to the dorm.

"Let's just stop here," Mr. Walsh said, pulling over to the curb. "We can carry your luggage to the dorm."

Dylan had her hand on the door handle before her dad had even turned off the ignition. She jumped out onto the gravel path and took a deep breath. The air held a hint of autumn, but the sun, when it wasn't behind the clouds, was still at its summer strength. Everywhere Dylan looked, girls were getting out of cars, their arms full of garment bags and backpacks. Dylan followed her father around to the back of the SUV and pulled out the smaller of her two black suitcases. Mr. Walsh let out a groan as he tested the weight of the larger bag.

"Come on, Dad. Here's your chance to prove what your country club membership does for you," Dylan said with a laugh. She doubted her dad had ever even been to the club's gym. He pretty much belonged for the golf and tennis, which he always ended up playing with his business partners. Without waiting to hear his reply, Dylan headed up the sidewalk in the direction of the dorms. She paused at the bottom of the sidewalk that led to the front door and tipped her head back to take in the white four-story building. There were girls and parents on the steps leading up to the covered porch. Nobody had to wear the school uniform today, and everyone seemed to be taking advantage of that freedom. Like Dylan, lots of girls had on jeans and casual fitted tops, which was a relief. Dylan's mom had tried to get her to wear a pleated linen skirt with a cashmere tank, arguing that Dylan should try to make a good first impression.

The front porch cleared, and Dylan made her way up the steps and through the double doors. The foyer in Adams House seemed almost as busy as the unloading area outside — and twice as noisy. Dylan caught her breath. In front of her, on either side of the room, was a formal double staircase that swept upward in a swoosh of crimson carpet. At the top of the stairs, a Chinese-style vase with a colorful and elaborate arrangement of flowers sat on a polished antique table. Sunlight streamed in through a beautiful stained-glass window on the second floor, making Dylan squint. *I feel like I'm in* Gone with the Wind, she thought. She hovered uncertainly, not having a clue where she should go.

"Excuse me!" An older student carrying a cello case stopped right in front of her.

"Oh, sorry," Dylan said, embarrassed, realizing she was blocking the door. She stepped to one side and placed her suitcase on the waxed hardwood floor. *Way to go, Walsh. No better way to look like a first-year student than standing right in the doorway with a dumb look on your face.* She took a deep breath and noticed a lovely scent of jasmine in the air. She tracked the aroma to another arrangement of flowers, this one in a cut glass vase on a polished maple table, the top of which was dappled with light. Dylan glanced up to see a magnificent chandelier hanging above her, dripping with crystals. She couldn't believe this was campus housing. It looked more like an interior design showcase.

"Dylan Walsh?" A smiling woman with dark curly hair appeared beside her. She glanced down at a clipboard and then back at Dylan. "Welcome to Adams House. Don't worry," she said. "This is the only day of the year when all chaos breaking loose is officially allowed." She held out her hand. "I'm Mrs. Herson, your housemother. If you have any problems settling in, come see me and I'll try my best to help." Mrs. Herson's brown eyes twinkled as she handed Dylan a map. "Noel Cousins, our dorm prefect, will show you where your room is, if you're ready."

"That would be great," Dylan said, reaching down for her suitcase.

Mrs. Herson waved to a tall girl with wavy auburn hair who was just coming down the staircase. "Noel," she called. "This is Dylan Walsh. Can you take her up to Room Two?"

"Sure," the senior nodded, walking over.

"Noel is co-captain of the senior jumping team," Mrs. Herson told Dylan. "So you already have something in common."

"Co-captain? That's great!" Dylan said, standing up a little straighter as she made eye contact with the senior. "I mean, isn't that what everyone wants? If they're in the riding program, I mean." She winced. *What was going on?* Dylan was used to being so composed and knowing just what to say, but her words sounded all jumbled.

Noel smiled at the compliment. "I'd like to say it's not a big deal, but . . ."

"You don't want to lie, right?" Dylan relaxed enough to grin at the senior. She looked around for her parents, and, spotting them in the middle of the foyer, she waved for them to come over.

The Walshes followed Noel up the scarlet-carpeted staircase. Halfway up, the prefect paused and pointed down at a pair of doors leading off the foyer. "Before I forget, the seventh-grade common room and study hall are through there," she told Dylan. "I'm sure you'll log plenty of hours in those rooms."

As Dylan leaned forward to look down the corridor, a girl with her hair in cornrows started down the stairs, waving to someone below. She accidentally bumped against Dylan as she tried to get past. "Hey, watch it, Tanisha," Noel warned and gave Dylan an apologetic smile. "Typical upperclassman attitude. They forget they were rookies once, too!"

"I heard that," Tanisha called over her shoulder.

Listening to their banter Dylan bit her lip. Right now, it was hard to imagine she'd ever feel that comfortable around this place. It wasn't like her to be overwhelmed. She vaguely remembered her first day of kindergarten, and even then, she'd had a very practical, can-do attitude about taking on new things.

At the top of the stairs Noel turned left and walked down a hallway to a second, narrower flight of stairs.

"Your dorm room is up here," she explained. "You know, I started off in Room Two. I've always thought it's kind of lucky. Every year that I've been here, a first-year student from Room Two has made it onto the equestrian team."

"That's good news. I'm hoping to try out for the team," Dylan admitted, her heart beating faster.

"Yeah?" Noel glanced at her. "Competition's going to be tough this year, then. I know that Lynsey Harrison, who's rooming with you, is trying out, too." She paused to wait for Dylan's parents, who were looking rather out of breath. "Everyone gets used to all of the stairs after a while! There is a rickety elevator in the back, but Mrs. Herson gives us a lecture on the importance of exercise if she catches us using it."

Noel held open the heavy fire doors at the top of the stairs, then led the way down a broad hall, past open doors where Dylan caught glimpses of girls unpacking. Her stomach flipped again as Noel stopped. This was it! Her room at Chestnut Hill!

"Welcome to Adams Room Two," Noel declared, opening the door. "You're rooming with Felicity Harper and Lynsey Harrison. You have a couple of hours to unpack and have a look around and then, at five o'clock, the school will be meeting in the chapel for our first convocation of the year." Noel stepped aside to allow Dylan to enter. "If you need anything, you can head down to Room Five. We're all seniors. We're a little more sane than the underclassmen. They'll calm down, though. It's just because it's the first day."

"Oh, it's okay," Dylan said. "I can handle a little insanity now and then."

"That's good to hear." A dimple flashed in Noel's cheek as she gave Dylan's parents a courteous smile. "Later," she said with a wave before slipping from the room.

Dylan let out a sigh. She hoped she had made a good impression.

Her mother stepped past her, hanging Dylan's garment bag over a chair. "Oh, this is lovely! Your lilac bedsheets will look fabulous against those floral drapes." She went over to feel the material. "You really lucked out."

Dylan followed her mom and looked around. There were

three twin beds in the room, each with a matching cedar wardrobe and dresser with a pull-out desk top. The wood was the color of warm honey, glowing in the sunlight that poured through the window at the far end of the room. It appeared that the bed immediately underneath the window had already been taken. Four cognac-colored leather suitcases with the initials *LAH* were stacked next to it, and the bed itself was covered with shoe boxes and garment bags. Dylan set her own suitcase just inside the door.

Dylan's dad heaved the other bag over the threshold and straightened up, rubbing his back. "And I thought *you* packed too much. I pity whoever carried *her* luggage up those stairs," he joked, nodding toward the pile of bags by the window.

"That's right, Dad!" Dylan responded. "You should never take me for granted. See what an easygoing daughter I am?"

"Yes, an easygoing daughter who begged incessantly for three years to go away to boarding school," her dad replied in a slightly accusatory tone.

Dylan knew that her father had wanted her to stay at home. She was an only child, and her dad had always treated her as though she were a friend as much as a daughter. They would swap jokes at dinner, go fishing on weekends, and, once in a while, go trail riding together. Dylan thought it was ironic — her dad had given her his love of horses, and that love had made her want to attend a boarding school over four hundred miles from home.

She walked to the far end of the room and leaned her elbows on the windowsill. The view looked straight across campus, but more importantly, it had a great view of the stable yard, where she could see a beautiful bay gelding being led in from the field.

"Look at the lines on that Thoroughbred. I bet he can really jump, huh?" Dylan's dad said as he joined her at the window. "I guess we would take him at Riverlea."

Dylan and her dad liked to daydream that they would buy a ranch out West and name it Riverlea. They'd have a dozen ponies and horses and then some cattle. Dylan knew it would never happen — for starters, she was more focused on equitation and jumping than riding Western and driving cattle — but it was fun to talk about. They sometimes did it just to tease Dylan's mom, who would consider moving to a ranch only if she could fly her hair stylist out weekly and get Prada home-delivered.

Mr. Walsh pointed to a snazzy chestnut backing out of a trailer.

Dylan felt her stomach flip with excitement as she watched the everyday commotion of the stable: buckets, haynets, lead ropes, traveling wraps, horses, horses, horses! *Get me down there!* She couldn't wait to start pitching in. She'd spent most of the summer hanging out with her friends at the local stables, riding every day. Her instructor had let her try different mounts all summer, so it had felt as if she had half a dozen gorgeous ponies of her own. But the last few days had been filled with packing and sorting out her bedroom at home, so Dylan was anxious to get into the saddle again.

"Look at this set!" Mrs. Walsh exclaimed, eyeing the suitcases on Dylan's roommate's bed and running her fingers over the largest one. "I'm sure I saw one just like it in Takashimaya on Fifth Avenue."

"They must belong to Lynsey Harrison," Dylan told her.

Mrs. Walsh straightened up, beaming. "The Harrisons! Of course! I knew I'd heard the name. There was an article in *Vanity Fair* last month that mentioned Mrs. Harrison's last fundraising event. The banquet was held at their home, and it was such a beautiful house. I'm sure Lynsey will make a wonderful friend for you, Dylan."

"Mom! Like I'd choose her as a friend because her family has enough money to be featured in *Vanity Fair*!" Dylan said. *Why does mom always get so hung up on America's A-List?* She frowned.

Her dad held up his hands in a peacemaking gesture. "Whoa, I'm sure that's not what your mom meant. After all, any of the girls here are going to come from . . ." He looked left then right and dropped his voice to a whisper, ". . . moneyed backgrounds."

Dylan grinned and threw a pillow at him from the selection on the bed closest to her.

"Is that the bed you want, honey?" Mrs. Walsh asked. "We'll help you unpack."

"Um, it's okay, Mom. I think I can handle it. Anyway, I thought I'd wait until Felicity arrives so we can see who wants which bed." *In other words, I'm ready for you to leave so I can go check out the horses*, she translated silently, catching her father's eye.

"Come on, hon. I'm sure Dylan can handle it. If we linger too long, she might actually think about how much she'll miss us. We don't want her to do that."

"Dad!" Dylan didn't want them to think she didn't want them around at all, but her urge to explore was too strong to suppress.

He caught her up in a huge hug, planting a kiss on the top of her head. "You have your cell phone, so be sure to call us if you need anything," he told her. "And even if you don't."

"Sure thing," Dylan replied, her voice muffled as she pressed her head into her father's shoulder.

She hugged her mom next and, as Dylan inhaled the familiar Amouage perfume, a wave of homesickness gripped her. *This is going to be tougher than I thought.* It was going to be so weird being away from home for this long; this was way different from summer camp, where it was for just a few weeks, or from visiting her grandparents' house in the country. "Call us later," Mrs. Walsh told her, reaching out to tuck a strand of hair behind Dylan's ear. "And don't forget your Aunt Ali is here for you."

"Yeah, right. Me and two hundred other girls," Dylan

pointed out, but she smiled to show she was joking. Dylan hadn't known what to think when she had first heard that her aunt had taken over as Director of Riding at Chestnut Hill. Dylan's parents had already signed all her admittance paperwork, so it had been too late for her to change her mind. Dylan had always loved visiting Ali's stables in Kentucky, but this was different. She couldn't help but think that it would be awkward living on the same campus and having Ali as her riding instructor. *So much for my new independence!* Plus, Dylan didn't want the other girls thinking that she was going to get any favoritism from Ali. She wanted to make it at Chestnut Hill on her own. But right now, Dylan had to admit that the thought of a familiar face was sort of comforting. *Great. I'll be wanting a pacifier next.*

"I'll call later," she promised her parents. "Or you can call me when you get home." She walked to the door and watched them all the way down to the end of the hall. They turned and waved before disappearing through the double doors, and Dylan went back into the room. Suddenly it felt very empty. She sat down on the edge of the bed as a funny sensation, kind of like the butterflies she felt before a riding competition, hit her stomach. *Get a grip*, she told herself. *I'm at the best school in Virginia, which has an incredible riding program, and my favorite pony in the whole world is waiting for me down in the stable.* She lay back on the bed and closed her eyes. She had a framed photo of Morello, the paint gelding, in her backpack, but she could picture him just as clearly in her head.

She'd first met him that summer when she'd spent a couple of weeks on her aunt's farm in Kentucky. Dylan smiled as she thought back to how quickly she'd become smitten with the pony. He had the cutest personality ever! He was adventurous and mischievous — Ali had said that Dylan and Morello had a lot in common. The first time Dylan had seen him, Morello had been loose in the stables, snuffling at the feed room door. Ali had quickly caught him and put him back in his stall, playfully reprimanding the pony as she slid home the bottom bolt. Morello could undo the top lock with his teeth, Ali explained. Then she told the story about the time he wandered up to the farmhouse and was caught pushing his way through the kitchen screen door.

Morello could be a challenge in the stable, but he was a dream in the ring. He had a great rhythmic pace, and his jumps exploded with energy. Dylan had never known a pony that made riding such fun.

And, while Dylan didn't want to flatter herself, she thought Morello had been just as taken with her. By the end of her stay, he would whinny whenever he saw her and come to her at the paddock gate.

Dylan's apprehension about Ali being accepted as the

riding director quickly dissolved when she heard that Morello would make the move, too. Of course! He would be perfect for Chestnut Hill. And so would Ali. Her mom had made a big point about how this job was a great opportunity for Ali — a fresh start. Dylan knew her aunt was a talented instructor. Her students had dominated at the show they went to when Dylan was visiting.

Dylan thought about the photo of Morello in her bag. It had been taken at the Lexington Horse Show, where they had placed third in the Turnout class. Dylan had wanted to compete in a jumping class, but her mom insisted Ali would be busy enough with her regular students. Still, when Dylan claimed the yellow rosette, Mrs. Walsh had acted like she'd won a ribbon at a major competition — and on reflection, Dylan thought she'd done pretty well to get Morello's white patches as clean as she had, and her braids were always neat and tight. Not all judges would rank a paint that high against all the stylish ponies at an A-level show.

Dylan looked up at the sound of the door opening. She felt her heart jolt as she prepared herself for the fact that her parents had probably come back for more good-byes. Instead, it was Noel Cousins who smiled in at her before stepping back to let a petite girl with shoulder-length blond hair enter the room.

Dylan stood up and helped the girl drag in her suitcases.

"Welcome to Room Two!" she said, feeling like a veteran. Acting confident seemed to ease the butterfly battle in her stomach.

"Thanks." The girl smiled, pulling her hair back from her cute, heart-shaped face.

"Dylan, this is Felicity," Noel said. "I thought you could show her around. Just make sure you're both at the convocation."

"No problem." Dylan waited for Noel to shut the door behind her before turning to her new roommate. "How are you doing, Felicity?"

"I haven't been called that in ages," the girl replied, almost in a whisper. "It sounds so formal. You can just call me Honey."

Dylan blinked when she heard her new roommate's polished accent, but she didn't miss a beat. "Nice to meet you, Honey. I'm Dylan. I'm from Connecticut."

"Oh, I'm from . . . well, I used to live in London, in England. We've only just moved out here — my father is a professor at the University of Virginia," Honey explained. She nodded toward the suitcases on the far bed. "Are they yours?"

"No!" Dylan said quickly. "They belong to Lynsey Harrison. I like to think of her as BBB."

Honey turned and raised a thin blond eyebrow.

"Best Bed Bagger," Dylan translated, her face perfectly

straight. "I mean, I guess it's first come, first served, so I don't really blame her."

Honey smiled. "So we get to choose between the other two, then?"

"You go first, I'm cool with either one."

"Well, if you're sure you don't mind, I'll take this one." Honey pointed to the bed nearest the door. She skirted Dylan's bed and lifted up a stylish plaid backpack. She unzipped the front pocket and pulled out a stack of photographs.

"Hey, he's gorgeous!" Dylan exclaimed, spotting a picture of a showy chestnut pony jumping over parallel bars. "Is he yours?"

"He was," Honey confirmed with a wistful sigh. "His name's Rocky. My parents bought him for me when I was nine, but I had to leave him in England." Honey reached out to trace her finger across the glass in the photo frame.

"That must have been really hard," Dylan said sympathetically. She had never had a pony of her own, but she knew how difficult it had been saying good-bye to Morello after riding him for only two weeks.

She figured it would be kind of rude to head straight for the stable yard now that Honey had arrived. She started to unpack, almost wishing she had taken her parents' offer to help as she realized just how much she had brought with her — her school uniform, riding stuff, clothes for wearing around the dorm, clothes for formal dinners, not to mention books and photos. And at the bottom of the case, there was a stuffed panda bear named Pudding that her grandmother had knitted when Dylan was a baby. He was a bit squashed after being stuffed in the oversized suitcase, but she gave him a shake, pummeled his nose back into shape, and propped him on her pillow.

Honey glanced over and caught her eye. For a moment Dylan paused. *Is it totally babyish bringing a stuffed bear to boarding school?* But then Honey wordlessly took out a small brown bear and tucked him under the top of her duvet, before flashing a grin at Dylan.

"There was no way I was coming here without Woozle!" she joked.

Relaxing, Dylan unwrapped the layer of tissue paper from around the first photograph. It showed her dad holding up a sign for his engineering company's new branch, with his other arm around Dylan's mom. The next photo was one of Dylan standing next to Morello, the yellow ribbon clipped to his bridle.

"Oh, do you ride, too?" Honey asked, leaning over to look. "What a fabulous pony!"

"This is Morello. He's actually here at Chestnut Hill. He's a little spoiled. He'll probably expect a bunch of organic carrots off a silver platter when he sees me," Dylan told her. "I was about to go down to the stable before you got here. Do you want to head down together?" She glanced at her watch. "We've got lots of time before convocation."

Honey's brown eyes lit up. "That sounds good."

Dylan grinned, figuring things couldn't get much better — and she'd only been at Chestnut Hill for an hour. She sprang to her feet. "Let's go!"

CHAPTER TWO

The moment they walked through the barn's big white double doors, Dylan was hit by the familiar sweet smell of hay and grain. She inhaled deeply and, for the first time since she'd arrived, she felt really at home. *Just bring down my luggage and I'll room here!* she thought. Opening her eyes, she looked around. The barn had a wide center aisle, lined on either side with box stalls. Most of the ponies were still out in the paddocks, but at least five horses were looking over their doors with their ears pricked, hoping for a treat. Dylan smiled at Honey and they headed down the aisle together, taking it all in.

A group of girls stood by one of the stalls, admiring a handsome blue roan pony still in traveling wraps. Dylan hesitated when she walked past. She was sure she recognized the tall blond girl who was combing her fingers through the roan's long forelock. As if she had read Dylan's mind, the girl looked over, narrowing her gray-blue eyes.

Dylan frowned as she searched her recent memory to match the girl's face with a situation. At that moment the pony poked his head over the door, rattling his immaculate leather halter against the door frame. An engraved brass plaque on the cheekpiece caught the light, and Dylan squinted to read the pony's name: *Bluegrass*. She suddenly made the connection. She had met the pony's rider at a show in Rhode Island that summer. Dylan remembered the pony, but she couldn't recall the girl's name.

"Hi," the girl said. Her voice was cool but friendly. "Do we know each other?"

"Sort of. We were both at the Red Valley show last July. You were riding in the Large Pony class and I was in the Medium group. I think I loaned you some fly spray," Dylan recalled.

"Right! I remember now." The girl smiled. "You had Absorbine. It's the only brand I can use on Bluegrass. He's allergic to everything else."

Dylan nodded and smiled. The girl seemed pretty down-to-earth, but Dylan couldn't get over the fact that she was hanging out in the stable wearing a burgundy skirt-and-shirt ensemble that looked far more appropriate for a Parisian nightclub. As far as Dylan could tell, her roommate had been shocked into silence. Honey looked around at the girls with one eyebrow raised.

"Hey, guys, you've all heard the news, right?" Tanisha, the eighth-grader who had pushed past Dylan on the staircase, let herself out of a stall and walked up to the small group. The sound of a radio drifted from behind her, and Dylan heard girls chatting at the far end of the barn. Tanisha paused, making sure she had everyone's attention. "Elizabeth Mitchell left. She's going to be teaching at Allbright's this year!"

"That's old news. I hear our new Director of Riding, Ali Carmichael, is from out West," replied a girl who wore her dark brown hair in a sleek bob. "Somewhere in Kentucky."

"You've gotta be kidding, Patience," said Tanisha, opening her eyes wide. "They only turn out jockeys there!"

Kentucky isn't only for horse racing, Dylan thought, shifting her feet uncomfortably. *And it is hardly "out West."* She wondered whether she should stick up for her aunt. She didn't want to seem like she was picking fights already, but Ali deserved more credit than she was getting from the rumor mill.

The girl who had been at the Red Valley show untwisted a mint from its wrapper and fed it to Bluegrass. "I just hope she can cut it. My sister, Rachel, was the captain of the senior jumping team last year, and they won the Interscholastic championship. Rachel had nothing but praise for Elizabeth Mitchell, and now she's training our top rivals. Let's hope this new instructor doesn't think that the way to win medals is by galloping around with our stirrups too short." She gave a pretend shudder. "It'll take a lot more than speed to beat Allbright's. Kentucky might have the Derby, but Virginia is real horse country."

"You are so bad," Patience said as they all broke into laughter. "Don't worry. She won't be here long if she doesn't have what it takes. The headmistress will see to that."

Dylan felt her cheeks burn and forced herself to swallow her words. *Were they serious? How could they joke around about someone's job like that? They hadn't even met Ali yet.* Dylan knew that if she stayed a second longer, she might say something that either she or Ali would regret.

"Catch you later," Dylan announced abruptly. She turned to leave, noticing Honey glance from her to the other girls with a puzzled frown.

Dylan gritted her teeth and walked down the aisle, toward the far end of the barn, with Honey close behind. A gray mare tossed her head and pawed the floor, obviously hoping for some attention, but Dylan kept walking, scanning the stalls for Morello.

A familiar whinny greeted her from the end of the row as a handsome brown-and-white face looked out from the last stall. His forelock was standing up in a ratty tuft. Dylan guessed he'd been rubbing his head against his haynet again.

"Hello, boy." Dylan smiled. She held out her hand for Morello to smell before reaching up to pull out the strands of hay tangled in his forelock. "Up to your old habits, I see. Are you getting used to your new home?" She put her face against his neck and felt herself relax.

"Oh, he's lovely!" Honey said with an exaggerated sigh after she had stepped up to Morello's stall. "He's even cuter than his photo! You're so lucky to have your own pony here."

Dylan fumbled in her pocket for a horse cookie. Morello wasn't technically her pony, since he belonged to Ali, but she had forged such a strong bond with him over her summer visit that he felt almost as good as the real thing. Still, she wanted to be honest with Honey. She seemed nice, so Dylan figured she could trust Honey with the truth about her bond with Morello. But just as she was about to launch into the explanation, she heard another voice behind them.

"He's been looking for someone to give him some TLC all afternoon. I think he's feeling a bit homesick."

Dylan spun around to find her aunt looking at her with an uncertain expression in her brown eyes. Dylan turned bright red. *It must have sounded like I told Honey that Morello was mine*, she thought guiltily.

"I'm Ms. Carmichael, Chestnut Hill's new riding instructor." Dylan's aunt wiped her hand on her breeches before holding it out to Honey.

"I'm Felicity Harper — but my friends call me Honey," Dylan's roommate explained.

"I think you've already been introduced to Morello? I brought him along with my other horse, Quince. He's across in the other stable, looking even lonelier!"

Honey darted a confused look at Dylan.

Dylan groaned inwardly. How was she going to explain this without sounding like a compulsive liar?

"Are you both settling in okay?" Ali Carmichael asked, pushing her fingers through her short dark hair.

"Great, thanks," Honey said. "The horses are gorgeous!"

Dylan didn't reply. Her mouth felt as if it had become temporarily detached from her brain. She didn't trust herself not to blurt out something else that would get her in social turmoil.

"Well, if I don't see you sooner, then I'll look forward to seeing you when classes start on Monday." Ali smiled. "If I remember my schedule correctly, I'm assessing you then, right, Honey? We'll have to see which level of the riding program would be best for you."

Honey nodded. "I hope I make the intermediate program. I like jumping, but I'd really love to do some work on my dressage this year."

"Well, we'll soon see if you're up to the intermediate level," Ali Carmichael said, leaning over the stall door to straighten Morello's dark blue sheet. "Don't worry, the assessment isn't too difficult. But there's no point overstretching your skills in the first term, so I like to get a sense of where you'll learn the most. Okay, then, I'll see you on Monday." She walked back up the aisle, pausing to talk to one of the seniors who was just going into the gray mare's stall.

"She seems really nice," Honey said, breaking the silence. "I hope she's up to the other girls' standards."

"Yeah," Dylan agreed absently, her eyes still following her aunt. She knew Honey must wonder why Dylan had acted like she owned Morello — and why she had a photo of the new riding instructor's pony in her room. But Dylan also knew she couldn't set Honey straight without admitting Ms. Carmichael was her aunt, and that wasn't something she was ready to do yet. She had decided she wanted to be known first as Dylan Walsh at Chestnut Hill, not as Ali Carmichael's niece. She'd tell everyone eventually. By then, she was sure she'd have lots of loyal friends—and Ali would have loyal students and admirers.

"Let's go check out the other barn," she suggested over the sound of a horse's hooves approaching.

"Okay." Honey nodded as she crossed the aisle to open the door of the opposite stall. "I'll get that for you," she offered to a girl who was leading a broad-faced liver chestnut.

The girl clicked her tongue and gave the pony a pat as he walked into the stall. "Hey, could you do me a favor?

Can you go see if Rose's stable sheet is in the tack room? I asked for it to be put in her stall, but it's not here," she said. "You can just ask anyone in there if they've seen Paige Cox's stuff."

"We're on it," Dylan said, motioning to Honey. Dylan welcomed the chance to have a look around the tack room. She planned to know every inch of the stable yard before the weekend was over.

⟡

Dylan and Honey may have found their way around the stables without a problem, but they got lost twice in the dorm hallways before they finally made it back to their room.

"I vote we tie a ball of string to the doorknob and unravel it behind us next time we go out!" Dylan laughed, opening the door. "The horses would eat bread crumbs, so that would never work."

It took them a few seconds before they realized that their third roommate was there, filling the bulletin board with pictures of herself and a beautiful blue roan pony. She turned around, flipping her long hair over her shoulder with a practiced swish, and Dylan saw that Lynsey Harrison (a.k.a. BBB) was none other than the blond girl from the barn — the one who had questioned whether Ali Carmichael was up to the challenge of teaching at a

Virginia boarding school. Lots of the girls had voiced their doubts, but Dylan felt like Lynsey's tone had been particularly harsh.

"Hi, guys! You must be my roommates. I'm Lynsey Harrison. Didn't we meet earlier?" The girl greeted them with a gush of charm and none of the attitude from the barn. Dylan still felt suspicious of the girl but was determined to put the previous conversation behind her.

"We sure did," Dylan replied, introducing herself and Honey.

"So, what do you think of it here so far?" Lynsey asked, pinning up another picture — this one of her sunbathing on a pool recliner with a magnificent white antebellum mansion in the background. "Of course, I already know the campus like the back of my hand — both my sisters went to Chestnut Hill," she continued without giving them a chance to answer.

Dylan was distracted by the sound of the door opening. Patience, the dark-haired girl they'd seen in the barn, casually strolled into the room without even knocking. "Hi," she said. She nodded at the picture of Rocky on Honey's bedside table. "I was admiring that photo a few minutes ago, wasn't I, Lynsey? He's such a cute guy! Did you bring him with you?"

"If only." Honey smiled.

"We were about to go check out the tennis courts.

Why don't you come with us and tell us all about him?" Lynsey suggested, pushing a thumbtack down on the corner of a photo.

From Lynsey's detached tone, Dylan had a feeling that she wasn't all that interested in hearing why Honey hadn't been able to bring Rocky with her. Lynsey looked at Dylan. "You can come too, if you want."

"I'd be up for tennis," Honey admitted. "I loved playing back home. In fact, as a treat before we moved this summer, my dad got us all tickets for Center Court at Wimbledon."

"You're kidding!" Lynsey said. "I really wanted to do Britain while we were yachting in the Mediterranean this summer, but my mom insisted it would be too cold to go that far north." She shrugged. "I did get some great outfits in Monaco, and we stayed at an old vineyard in Tuscany, but there wasn't enough time to go to all the places I wanted."

"So you're from England?" Patience said, looking at Honey with genuine interest in her hazel eyes. "Wow, I've always wondered what it would be like living there. There's so much history all around. Do you know Prince William?"

"No, I do have a friend at Eton, but we're much younger than either of the princes," Honey told them, looking a bit awkward.

Patience shrugged. "My dad thought about sending me to school overseas," Patience added. "Wait until I tell him that there's a British girl on my floor at Chestnut Hill."

Dylan resisted the urge to roll her eyes. Lynsey and Patience were treating Honey like she was an exhibit in a museum or a freak show. *Come and see The Incredible Walking, Talking Girl from England!*

Lynsey looked at her watch. "Hey, guys, if we're going to go try out the courts, then we need to head down now. We have less than two hours before convocation." She held open the door and then tapped her forehead with her hand. "I forgot to mention . . . I hope you don't mind, Dylan, but I went ahead and moved some of your stuff into your closet. It was in my way. I guess that's the problem with your bed being in the middle of the room — you'll have to be careful that you don't leave things on the floor."

Dylan looked down at the empty area around her bed and then back at Lynsey. "Or, I can just leave things out and you can put them away for me." She laughed at her own joke, but Lynsey only gave her a blank expression in return. *Okay, so I guess I should lay off the sarcasm a bit*, Dylan thought.

"Are you coming with us?" Honey asked.

"I don't think so. I play tennis with two left hands," Dylan replied, making a face.

"Okay. See you later," Honey said, following Lynsey and Patience out the door.

"Later," Dylan echoed. She fell back on her bed — the one in the middle of the room — and put her hands behind her head. She wondered what she should do now that she had the room to herself. She savored the peace and quiet, guessing she might not get a lot of it with Lynsey and Patience around.

But twenty seconds later, she grabbed her paddock boots out of the closet where Lynsey had deposited them, pulled them on, took her hard hat in her hand, and headed out the door. Who needed peace and quiet when you had horses?

CHAPTER THREE

Dylan headed straight back to the stable yard, figuring she had over an hour to acquaint herself with some of the horses. First off, she'd take a good look at Bluegrass, since Lynsey was out of the way. The blue roan was one of the classiest ponies Dylan had ever seen. His speckled dark coat gleamed, and there were threads of silver running through his long silky mane and tail.

Bluegrass swung his head around and stared past Dylan, his small ears pricked at the sound of hooves. Ali Carmichael was leading a gray pony toward her. "I'm glad you're here, Dylan," she said. There was a warmth in her voice that Dylan hadn't noticed earlier. "Can you take a halter from the tack room and bring in Nutmeg for me? She's the small buckskin in the top paddock. She didn't want to be caught earlier, the little trouble-maker. It would be a big help. Kelly and Sarah need to

34

start the evening feeds, and I have three horses to lunge before I can get ready for convocation."

"Okay," Dylan said, guessing that Kelly and Sarah must be the stable hands. She was more than happy to ease her aunt's workload. It had to be a busy day, with all the students' ponies arriving.

"The tack room is at the far end, across from Morello's stall," Ali Carmichael called over her shoulder as Dylan hurried down the aisle. If Nutmeg was tricky to catch, then she didn't want to waste any time. *I can just see myself being late to convocation after chasing a stubborn pony for an hour,* she thought. Dylan cringed at the thought. She hated being late.

She jogged along the path that led away from the barn and slowed as a girl with wavy blond hair passed, leading a palomino gelding.

She looked at the halter slung over Dylan's shoulder. "Are you going to catch Nutmeg?"

"How did you know?"

"She's the only one left. Nutmeg's really sweet most of the time and will do anything for a cookie, but sometimes she decides not to play ball. . . ."

"Unless the game is dodgeball?" Dylan guessed.

"Exactly. And you're the ball," the girl confirmed with a laugh. "Good luck!"

"Thanks. It sounds like I'm going to need it. Are you Sarah?" Dylan asked.

"Close. I'm Kelly." She turned around and continued to lead the palomino in the direction of the stables.

Dylan tried to commit the name to memory, then looked toward the paddocks. She rolled her shoulders in circles like a boxer limbering up in the ring. "Okay, Nutmeg, prepare to meet your match," she announced. "This is one girl who doesn't take any monkey business from a pony — not even one with big-horse attitude."

She was surprised to see the buckskin mare standing just inside the gate with her head over the fence, her ears pricked forward as if she were just waiting for Dylan. As she came closer, Dylan noticed that Nutmeg had patches of dried dirt on her hindquarters. Her fingers twitched, and she wondered how soon she would be allowed to groom the ponies.

Dylan adjusted the halter so it was hidden by her arm and then climbed over the gate, talking to Nutmeg all the time. "Hello, girl. Aren't you gorgeous? Have you been rolling? How'd you get so dirty? I'll give you a good brushing if you come in. Your dinner will be waiting for you. I hear molasses is on the menu tonight." Dylan kept talking in a friendly tone as she reached into her pocket for a horse cookie. "You want a treat? Yeah, you're such a good girl — hey!"

With lightning speed, Nutmeg snatched the cookie off Dylan's palm and wheeled away at a brisk canter, kicking up her back hooves.

"Of all the rotten, ungrateful creatures," Dylan muttered as Nutmeg skidded to a halt and turned back to study her. The mare tossed her head up and down, and Dylan swore she was taunting her. She could almost hear the pony laughing.

Then Dylan realized that there was the sound of real laughter behind her. She spun around to see a girl with dark curly hair and sparkling blue eyes leaning on the gate. "I thought she was a gorgeous, good girl!"

"She obviously has a problem with authority," Dylan said with a defensive shrug, but she couldn't help laughing herself.

"Do you want a hand?" the girl offered.

"Well, I think it'll take about ten extra hands and a lasso, but if you want to give it a try, be my guest," Dylan replied. "I'm Dylan Walsh, by the way. I'm in Adams House."

"Malory O'Neil. I'm in Adams, too."

Dylan had assumed from the girl's worn jodhpurs and old yard boots that she was one of the assistants who had looked after the horses during summer vacation. She did a quick mental reassessment now that she knew Malory was a student — and dormmate. "So, do you have a plan?"

"I have an idea," Malory answered quickly as she reached out for the halter. "Come on." She flashed Dylan a smile and headed toward Nutmeg. The mare had dropped her head and was busy grazing.

Dylan guessed the pony was just pretending to concentrate on the grass. More than likely, she was watching their every move and calculating her next escape. When they were a short distance away, Malory paused and tucked the halter under her shirt. "Do you mind if I try something a little odd?"

"Go for it," Dylan urged, wondering what Malory had in mind. "I'm not sure anything less than a tranquilizer dart is going to work. That pony could teach Houdini a thing or two!"

Malory gave a low laugh. "Well, here goes nothing."

Dylan watched in amazement as Malory dropped onto all fours and began to crawl toward the paddock gate. Nutmeg's curiosity was obvious. The pony stopped chewing to watch Malory's small, hunched body move across the ground. *She looks like a giant turtle*, Dylan thought, biting back a grin. She had no clue how Malory thought she would catch Nutmeg by slithering in the opposite direction. Still, no matter how funny Malory looked, she had gotten Nutmeg's attention. The pony took a couple of hesitant steps, following Malory's path.

Go, Malory! Dylan gave a silent cheer when Nutmeg began to follow Malory in earnest, stretching out her neck as she got closer. At last, her muzzle bumped against Malory's back as the pony sniffed with curiosity. Then, very quickly, with smooth, gentle movements so Nutmeg wouldn't be frightened, Malory reached her arm around the mare's neck and pulled the halter over her ears, then securely clipped the strap.

Dylan let out a yell and jogged over to join them. "That was totally amazing — where did you learn that trick?"

Malory rubbed Nutmeg on the swirl between her eyes before leading the mare to the gate. "My old riding instructor showed it to me," she explained. "Where I learned to ride, we had to catch and tack up our own ponies. The trainer said it was an important part of learning stable management. I rode this horse named Ivan for a while. He refused to be caught, but he could never resist the crawling trick."

"I could have used that one in Connecticut!" Dylan admitted. "We had some stubborn ponies there, too, but none as wily as Nutmeg." She gave the buckskin a light pat on the neck. "Where did you learn to ride?"

Malory clicked to Nutmeg to walk up the path and seemed to hesitate before saying, "Cheney Falls Stables."

"So you live close by?" Dylan asked, recognizing the name of the town just west of Chestnut Hill. "Does that mean you're a day student?"

Malory shook her head. "No, I'm boarding. In Adams."

"Oh, that's right. You said that. Sorry." Dylan glanced over at Malory and got the impression she didn't want to say any more. Dylan decided to keep quiet so Malory would have the chance to open up if she wanted to, but the other girl stayed silent. Malory just concentrated on twisting the end of the lead rope around her fingers, her brown curls falling forward into her face. Dylan wondered if it had been something she'd said, but then she chalked it up to first-day jitters. *Besides*, she thought, *it's kind of nice to just walk with someone and not have to chitchat the whole time.*

The buckskin mare walked faster when she saw the barn, obviously anxious to get her nose into the promised bucket of molasses. At that moment, Ali Carmichael strode out through the double doors. "Great, you caught her," she smiled.

"Yeah, thanks to Malory," Dylan said. She didn't want to take credit for Malory's triumph — especially since Ali had already overheard her pretty much telling Honey that Morello was her very own.

"Good work," said Ali. "I'm glad you've met, since you'll be in the intermediate riding program together."

"Cool!" Dylan said enthusiastically. She hadn't been absolutely sure she'd get into the intermediate program, although she'd crossed her fingers when her mom had filled out the application. The intermediate program had separate modules for dressage, show jumping, and cross-country, using the professionally built course that ran through the back hills of the Chestnut Hill campus. There was also a brief unit when the girls had a chance to try different kinds of riding, like sidesaddle and Western. Dylan couldn't wait!

"Would either of you mind helping me out a little more?" Ali asked, taking Nutmeg's lead rope. "Colorado and Kingfisher still haven't been exercised today. I was going to lunge them, but if you could tack them up and bring them down to the ring, I could give you both a quick lesson. It will be just for a half hour on the flat — we can't risk being late for convocation — but it would be fun."

"I'm in!" Dylan said, exchanging a smile with Malory.

Ali pulled off her old blue sweatshirt as the sun came out from behind a cloud. "Dylan, I'd like to see how you go on Colorado. You'll have your work cut out for you, because he can be a bit of a mule. Malory, you take Kingfisher. I'll meet you down in the outdoor arena."

Dylan and Malory grabbed the horses' tack from the clearly labeled hooks before separating outside the stall doors.

"Hey, Colorado," Dylan said, pulling back the bolt. The handsome dun gelding ambled through the deep bed of straw toward her. His coat gleamed, and Dylan could see that she wouldn't have to groom him. Before tacking up, she held out her hand for him to sniff. The gelding lipped hopefully at her palm, flicking his ears back when he discovered that there was no treat.

"Maybe later, if you behave yourself," Dylan said with a laugh, slipping the reins over his head. Her spirits picked up when Colorado willingly opened his mouth for the bit and she neatly buckled the bridle on. *If only you were*

Morello, then this day would be perfect! But she was only half-serious. It was always fun riding a new pony, and Dylan was sure she and Morello would have their proper reunion soon.

"I'm all set. Are you ready?" Malory called over the adjoining partition wall.

"Sheesh, what have you got, six hands?" Dylan called back.

Malory laughed. "No, just two, but they move very quickly."

Dylan grinned and hurriedly slid Colorado's saddle onto his back. By the time she was ready, Malory had already led Kingfisher out and was mounted on the pretty bay.

Dylan checked her girth before swinging lightly onto Colorado's back and clicking her tongue for him to walk on. They fell in alongside Kingfisher and made their way to the outdoor arena. The first thing Dylan noticed was that Colorado had a much shorter stride than she was used to, and she had a feeling that she'd have to use her legs and seat strongly to get him to respond well.

Ali Carmichael was waiting for them in the center of the arena. She gave the girls a quick wave. Dylan thought her aunt looked right at home — her tall, lean figure made her seem commanding and confident. "Okay, spread out and trot a serpentine, please," Ali called.

Kingfisher burst into a lively trot, and Dylan waited a

few moments and then, with a squeeze, asked Colorado to trot. Immediately, the gelding stiffened and raised his head in protest. *Oh, no, you don't*, Dylan thought. She tightened her legs until the gelding broke into a slow trot, but for the entire serpentine he resisted Dylan's hand and leg signals, making it clear that he would rather be back in his stall.

"Bring them to a walk and come into the center!" Ali called after they had finished three loops. "You had Kingfisher going nicely, Malory. You rode him very sympathetically considering it's the first time you've been on him." She smiled. "But I'd like to see him be a little more responsive. I'd like you to use half-halts — light squeezes on the reins — so you have him really listening to you, okay?"

"Sure," Malory nodded, patting Kingfisher's neck.

"Dylan." Ali turned to her, reaching up to pull Colorado's black forelock free from his browband. "Colorado's not working for you. You have to use your seat and a lot more leg to get him to respond. He's not a push-button pony. He requires a strong rider. If you want to get him to go for you, you've got to give one hundred percent."

Dylan stared at her aunt. *Feel free to tell it like it is*, she thought. *Don't be easy on me because we're related. No, don't sugarcoat it to spare my feelings*. Dylan wondered why Ali had to be so harsh. She'd had no problem praising Malory.

Dylan hadn't been on Colorado more than four minutes. Ali hadn't even given her a chance!

"I want you drop your stirrups and trot him in a small circle at the far end," her aunt finished, stepping back.

Malory gave Dylan a sympathetic look as she rode past. Dylan made a face, hoping Malory wouldn't notice how frustrated she was. She twisted her ankles to dig her heels into Colorado.

"Make sure your signals are invisible," Ali called.

Luckily, Dylan's back was to her aunt, so she could roll her eyes as dramatically as she liked. At least she could put her frustration to good use by squeezing Colorado. She soon found that, to get the reluctant pony on the bit, she had to use her legs for every stride. She lost count of the number of times they circled, and her legs began to burn. Biting her lower lip, she felt a rush of delight when the gelding finally lowered his head and began to bring his quarters underneath him. *Good boy!* Suddenly the short, lazy stride felt powerful, and Dylan grinned, forgetting all about her aching legs.

"Okay, Dylan, come in," Ali called over her shoulder. Malory was cantering Kingfisher at the other end of the ring, and Ali's attention seemed to be totally focused on her. Feeling a little frustrated, Dylan uncrossed her stirrups and patted Colorado's damp neck before walking him into the center of the arena on a long rein. She had to admit that Malory had Kingfisher going in a beautiful, collected canter. Malory sat lightly in the saddle, supple at the waist to accommodate Kingfisher's long, bouncy stride, and her hands were completely still. Malory was much taller than Dylan, and her long legs added an elegant quality to her riding position. When she finally slowed Kingfisher to a trot, her cheeks were flushed and her eyes sparkling.

"You were right, Ms. Carmichael! The half-halts really made him listen!" she exclaimed.

"You did great," Ali told her.

"Dylan had Colorado working well, too." Malory smiled across at Dylan.

"Yes." Dylan's aunt nodded. "You got him to go on the bit, but you need to use your inside leg more to help him bend inward on the corners." Once again, all Dylan could do was give her aunt a dull stare. With one sentence, Ali had erased all of her positive feelings about her work with Colorado. She wasn't sure what to say in reply. She certainly didn't want to be too meek and agree with every single thing that Ali said — Malory was already doing enough of that for both of them.

Dylan felt her cheeks burn with guilt for trying to place blame on Malory. She looked down and fiddled with a piece of Colorado's mane.

"I think that's enough for today. Walk a few laps to cool

them off and then take them back in," Ali Carmichael instructed. "Don't forget that you have to change into uniform for convocation."

Dylan let the reins slip through her fingers so that Colorado was able to stretch his neck.

"It's nice to see you riding again." At first Dylan thought her aunt was talking to her, but as she glanced back she saw that Ali had her hand on Kingfisher's shoulder and was looking up at Malory.

Dylan turned to face forward again and frowned. *Malory must have ridden at Chestnut Hill at some point during the summer. How else would Aunt Ali have seen her ride?* It made sense, if Malory lived close by. Under normal circumstances, Dylan would have just asked Malory, but she remembered how reticent the girl had been earlier.

She couldn't help but be curious, but for now she had to hurry and untack. She only had twenty minutes until convocation — the official start of the school year!

Chapter Four

Dylan pulled her gray jacket on over the navy blue sweater and then glanced across at Honey. "Is that how they wear uniforms back in England?" She nodded at the price tag still hanging off Honey's sleeve. "Or are you trying to start a new trend? I don't really think it will catch on."

Honey glanced down at her sleeve. "Yikes! I can't believe I missed that!"

"I think there's a pair of scissors in my cosmetics bag," Dylan told her, starting to rummage in her nightstand.

"It's okay, I'm already on it." Lynsey had finished getting changed and was looking ultrasmart in her uniform, which somehow seemed better tailored than anyone else's. *How come I look like a girl in an oversized blazer and she looks like something out of an early Britney Spears video?* Dylan wondered. She wouldn't have been surprised if Lynsey

47

had her own personal fashion designer and tailor based in a wing of her sprawling white mansion. She felt like she knew the Harrisons' home better than her own after seeing the photo collage of the Harrison estate that covered the shared bulletin board.

Lynsey took a suede manicure case over to Honey. "There you go," she said, neatly snipping off the label and tossing it in the wastepaper basket.

"Let's go." Dylan took one final look in the full-length mirror to check out her appearance, taking a second glance as she noticed a strand of hay in her hair. "Thanks, you guys — you were going to let me cruise into convocation with half a bale of hay in my hair," she said.

"I thought you were trying to start a new trend," Honey said, straight-faced.

Dylan groaned. "Fine, I guess I deserved that one."

"Seriously, Dylan," Honey assured her. "I didn't see it. I would have told you if I did."

Dylan couldn't help but smile. Honey was so sincere.

"Are you ready yet?" Lynsey glanced at her Cartier watch and stepped into the hallway.

Dylan bent over and shook her head, running her hands through her hair. She flipped her head back and grabbed the doorknob. "Wait up!" she yelled down the corridor. "I'm right behind you!"

❧

They joined the groups of Chestnut Hill girls filing into the chapel through the massive arched wooden doors. The chapel was over a hundred years old and had a musty charm. The late-afternoon sunshine peeked through tall stained-glass windows, and pools of dazzling color danced like a giant kaleidoscope on the oak floorboards and polished pews. Dylan followed Honey and Lynsey toward the front rows, where the rest of the seventh-graders were seated. She straightened up when she noticed that the faculty members were already in place, sitting at the top of the sanctuary in pews that faced into the center of the chapel. She scanned the solemn faces until she found her aunt, who was on the end of one of the wooden benches, dressed in the same ceremonial black gown as the rest of the staff.

From the second row, Patience turned her head and motioned with a lift of her chin for Lynsey to sit beside her. Dylan bit her lip as she looked at the minimal space left on the bench. "We'll all fit," Lynsey announced, sliding down. "Scoot over some, okay, Patience?"

Sure enough, Honey and Dylan settled into the pew. Dylan crossed her ankles and took a deep breath. Almost immediately Lynsey gave a snort of laughter. "Check out the chic footwear on our esteemed Director of Riding," she whispered to Patience.

Patience peered at Ali Carmichael from under her lashes, and Dylan followed her gaze to see her aunt's dirty rubber boots poking out from underneath the shiny black gown. "Oh, they are sooo this season," Patience whispered back.

Dylan dug her fingernails into her palms. *Way to give them ammunition, Aunt Ali.* Even though she was still simmering with frustration from the lesson, Dylan still wished her aunt hadn't made herself such an easy target. Did she have any clue where she was? Dylan knew her aunt was laid back, but at least she could try to make an effort. As she shook her head, Dylan could feel Honey looking at her and didn't dare meet her glance.

"Where do you think I could get a pair?" Patience went on.

"Hicksville," Lynsey replied without missing a beat.

Dylan shifted uncomfortably as the muffled laughter traveled from girl to girl.

The whispers faded at the sound of footsteps echoing from the vaulted ceiling. The rows all turned in slightly to watch the principal, Dr. Angela Starling, walk down the center aisle. The sunlight highlighted glints of red in her long dark hair, which was swept up into a French twist. Her black gown flared with each long stride. She climbed the slate stairs into the pulpit and opened the heavy book resting on the antique lectern. Instead of reading from the book, she glanced up to smile at the seated girls. Her eyes swept over the sanctuary, and Dylan had the distinct feeling that the principal was looking directly at her.

"Welcome! I'm very pleased to be greeting you at the

start of a new year at Chestnut Hill." Her voice was low and melodious but still carried to the back of the chapel. "Before I give a reading, I'd like to welcome our new seventh-graders." An excited murmur ran through the rows, and Dylan felt a fizz of exhilaration at the thought of being a Chestnut Hill student for the next six years. Even the minor setbacks of the day couldn't take that feeling away. She glanced up at the wall behind Dr. Starling, where impressive maple plaques hung from the exposed beams. Long lists of scholars and academics who had attended Chestnut Hill were engraved in gold italic letters. Dylan didn't know why Lynsey and Patience were so hung up on English history and culture. There was more than enough history and tradition right here at Chestnut Hill!

"As you know, we have the highest standards at Chestnut Hill. As Virginia's oldest all-girl institution, we must strive for excellence in all our pursuits. Just by the fact that you are seated in this chapel, I know each of you has proven you have what it takes to make a lasting contribution to Chestnut Hill — and beyond." Dr. Starling paused before continuing.

"It's true that there is a lot to live up to at Chestnut Hill, yet this does not necessarily mean you should tread in the footsteps of those who have gone before. Each one of you will distinguish yourself in your own way. And it is our job, as the faculty of Chestnut Hill, to help you discover what you have to offer." Dr. Starling's gray eyes twinkled, and Dylan wondered how the principal had known just what to say to both comfort and inspire her. "Before we sing our first hymn, I'd like to welcome the newest member of our faculty, Ms. Ali Carmichael. Knowing the way news spreads around campus, I'm sure that many of you have already heard that she has replaced our previous Director of Riding, Elizabeth Mitchell." Dr. Starling smiled. "We have a fine tradition of equestrianism here at Chestnut Hill and I have no doubt that Ms. Carmichael is going to ensure that our riding teams continue to excel and, more importantly, that we don't let the Interscholastic Championship cup fall into the hands of Allbright Academy this year!"

Some of the seniors at the back of the hall let out a small cheer, and Dr. Starling smiled again.

"There's more good news regarding our equestrian achievements," Dr. Starling went on. "For the first time in seven years, we have a first-year student who has been awarded the prestigious Rockwell Award." Dylan felt Lynsey tense beside her and there was an outbreak of curious whispers. Honey raised her eyebrows inquiringly, but Dylan shook her head. She had never even heard of the Rockwell Award.

"I bet it's Lynsey Harrison," a girl murmured directly behind them. "She was champion at three A-level shows this year."

Dylan bit back a grin. *Somehow, I have a feeling that if Lynsey had won something, we'd know about it by now*, she thought.

"Fifteen years ago, Diane Rockwell represented the United States in the Olympic Games, and she's always insisted she owes everything to the riding instruction she received here at Chestnut Hill. She set up the generous grant to enable other girls to achieve their ambitions. Her grant has two essential qualifications: the recipient should have above-average talent and be just a little bit horse-crazy." Dr. Starling reached for a glass of water on the lectern and took a sip. "I would like to extend a special welcome to this year's winner of the Rockwell Award, Malory O'Neil."

Most of the girls in the chapel started craning their necks, trying to figure out which of the girls in the seventh-grade seating section was Malory. Dylan leaned forward and looked at the girl who was sitting at the end of her pew. Malory sat motionless, her eyes down and her cheeks bright red. Dylan guessed the award explained why her aunt had seen Malory ride before, but why hadn't Malory told her about the scholarship in the stable? If it had been her, Dylan wouldn't have been able to keep quiet about it! Maybe Malory hadn't wanted to sound like she was bragging, but Dylan couldn't imagine her coming off as arrogant.

"I never noticed her on the circuit, and I rode in all of

the A-level shows in Virginia this summer," Lynsey whispered to Dylan. "I'd love to know how she managed to catch Ms. Rockwell's eye, because I didn't see her."

Dylan shrugged. "Maybe she wasn't riding in the big shows."

"Then how did she win the award?" Lynsey shot back. "Unless she was on the Florida winter circuit — that's the only explanation." Dylan was relieved she didn't have to reply, because Dr. Starling had announced their first hymn. The organ struck the opening chords, and Dylan took the hymn sheet that Honey passed down from the end of the row. As she stood up to sing the first line, Dylan's heart swelled along with the raised voices. She was happy that Malory had snagged the prestigious award. Although she had to admit that she'd have been happy for anyone to receive it other than Lynsey; it was only the first day, but Dylan was already getting a little bored with her roommate's endless self-promotion. She could tell that there was going to be some fierce competition for the junior jumping team — and she hadn't even met any of the other intermediate program students yet!

🐎

Dylan hovered in the entrance of the middle school sitting room, smoothing her new Juicy Couture hooded sweatshirt. She chewed her bottom lip, wishing that she hadn't taken so long choosing between her hoodie and her sleeveless Fossil top. She had told Lynsey and Honey that she'd catch up with them, but she hadn't anticipated being the last one to arrive in the lounge.

"Dylan!" There was a shout from the far end of the room and Dylan saw Honey stand up and wave.

At the end of convocation, Dr. Starling had announced that, as a treat, all the girls would have pizza for dinner in their separate dorms. Usually the boarders would eat together in the student center cafeteria, but having their evening meal in the common rooms would give the dorm-mates a chance to get to know one another.

Dylan sat down on the cranberry-colored sofa beside Lynsey and Honey. Patience was sitting on the facing sofa with two girls whom Dylan had noticed in the chapel. To Dylan's right, Malory was seated on a high-back chair with one leg tucked beneath her, and a girl wearing stylish rimless glasses was on the matching ottoman.

"This is Wei Lin Chang," Patience explained, turning from Lynsey to the petite girl beside her.

"Hi there," Wei Lin said and smiled, revealing a mouthful of perfect white teeth. Her shiny black hair was cut into a sleek chin-length bob. "How are you doing?"

"And I'm Razina Jackson," said the other girl on Patience's sofa. "We're all in Adams Four. Nice to meet you." Her braided black hair swung down over her shoulder as she leaned across the low table to shake hands.

Dylan was impressed with Razina's presence — she made a point of looking everyone in the eye as she offered her hand. She seemed so mature, Dylan wondered what her story was. The others all took their cue from Razina and introduced themselves. The girl with the rimless glasses, turned out to be Malory's roommate, Alexandra Cooper.

"We're still waiting for Lani, our other roomie, to arrive," Alexandra added, pushing her glasses up her nose.

Dylan looked around at all the girls and wondered how she was going to remember the names. And this was just the first-year students in Adams. There were five other houses!

"Your last name sounds familiar," Wei Lin told Patience. "Are you from the Boston area?"

"My father is Edward Hunter Duvall," Patience said. She flicked her light brown hair over her shoulder and sounded bored, as if she'd been asked this a dozen times. "You know, the novelist?"

"Oh, wow!" Wei Lin snapped her fingers in the air. "That's amazing! I love his books! Do you think the English teacher could get him to give a symposium on writing?"

"I guess I could ask him," Patience said. She still sounded offhand, but Dylan noticed a subtle smile stretch across her mouth, as if she were enjoying the attention.

Dylan thought the name Edward Duvall sounded familiar, but she had never read anything by him.

"So, Malory," Lynsey said, leaning forward to take a
carrot stick from the coffee table. "You must have been
totally excited when you got the news about the
Rockwell Award. When did you find out?" She smiled
at Malory before popping the carrot into her mouth.

Malory glanced up from picking at a loose thread on
the cushion on her lap. "It came in the mail. Maybe in
July," she recalled. "I was stunned. I thought it was my
dad's idea of a joke when I opened up the letter."

"Is everyone here totally obsessed with horses?" Patience
asked.

"Not me," Razina said, pouring seltzer into the glasses.

"Me, either." Wei Lin shrugged. "It's not something
that's ever appealed to me. I'm more into the winter sports
scene — skiing and snowboarding. Although I play tennis, too, so I'll probably try out for that."

"Hey, I love skiing!" Razina beamed. "Every Christmas
my mom takes me to the Alps for a week, on our way back
from Tanzania."

Dylan took a sip of the fizzy water and looked at
Razina. "Wow! It sounds like you've traveled a lot!"

Razina nodded. "Yeah, I'm really lucky. My mom owns
a gallery specializing in South African art and cultural
relics. She homeschooled me for the last two years, so I

went with her when she scouted new sources. It was an amazing experience." Somehow, Razina didn't sound at all boastful, just impassioned.

"Pizza's here!" Mrs. Herson walked into the room, followed by a girl Dylan hadn't seen before. Their house-mother was carrying four enormous flat boxes, and as the smell of melted cheese and oregano wafted over, Dylan realized she was licking her lips. Mrs. Herson put two of the boxes down on the table beside the eighth-graders and then headed toward their group, artfully balancing their boxes on one palm.

"Ta da!" Mrs. Herson spun the boxes around on her hand before sliding them neatly onto the table. Dylan sus-pected that the housemother had some deep-dish pizzeria experience somewhere on her résumé. The seventh-graders laughed and burst into applause. Mrs. Herson grinned and waited for the noise to die away before turn-ing to the tall girl standing next to her. "Everyone, I'd like you to say hello to Lani Hernandez from Colorado." Lani smiled at them, her freckled nose crinkling. "I'm sure they'll all introduce themselves to you," Mrs. Herson added.

"How are you doing?" Lani grinned around, looking not at all fazed by her late entrance. *She looks pretty cool*, Dylan thought, taking in the girl's short dark bangs and warm brown eyes. She was wearing a long-sleeved T-shirt with a Canadian maple leaf design and slim-fitting jeans that covered all but the toe of her tan cowboy boots. "I missed my connecting flight in Chicago, but it looks like I've arrived in time for the most important part of the day." She eyed the pizzas appreciatively.

"I'm sure the girls will give you a rundown on what you missed at convocation," said Mrs. Herson. "If you need any other help, my apartment is at the far end of your floor. And, everyone, don't forget that you can always go to Ms. Sebastian and Mrs. Marshall, the assistant and high school housemothers, if I'm not available. Their rooms are on the second floor."

Lani nodded and waited for Mrs. Herson to go before taking a seat right on the floor. She rubbed her hands together and looked around the group. "Is it every woman for herself or is someone going to hand out some slices? I'm so hungry I could eat a whole cow!"

"What? You didn't bring one along with you from the ranch?" Lynsey asked sweetly. Beside her, Patience swallowed a giggle.

"Heck no!" Lani responded with an exaggerated western twang. "I tried to get me one of those steers onto the plane, but nothing doin'." Lani finished by slapping her knee.

Dylan was in the middle of taking a drink and, as she sputtered with laughter, it went down the wrong way. It was a relief to know that someone else actually had a sense of humor!

"Are you okay?" Lani asked.

"Fine, thanks." Dylan coughed as Honey hit her gently on the back.

"That's kind of a mixed blessing. If you'd choked, it would have meant extra slices for the rest of us," Lani teased.

By now Razina was handing around plates with giant slices of Hawaiian pizza.

"Delicious," Dylan sighed, taking a huge bite and dribbling some cheese down her chin.

"We were just wondering if *everyone* here is into horses," Wei Lin said. She raised her eybrows at Lani. "Don't tell me you're also going to be camping out in the barn?"

The newcomer dropped her pizza slice onto her plate to hold up her hands in mock surrender. "Guilty as charged."

"Did you ride Western where you live?" Malory asked.

Lani nodded enthusiastically. "It's pretty much all I've ridden since moving out to Colorado. My dad's a commander in the air force, so we move around a lot. I've done some English riding, too, so I'm hoping that I'll get into the intermediate program. I have to try out or something."

"I'm being assessed for that as well," Honey said, leaning forward to pick up her drink from the table.

"No kidding! Are you nervous?" Lani asked.

"A little," Honey confessed. "I had this dream last night where I showed up at the tryout wearing my pajamas. And then, when I looked down, I was riding a billy goat!"

"That's fabulous!" Lani announced. "I have this book on the symbolism in dreams. We have to look up the meaning of goats."

Honey gave Lani a sweet yet uncertain smile and took another bite of pizza.

Lynsey left her seat next to Dylan and squeezed in next to Patience. They immediately began discussing a party that Lynsey's grandfather, a senator in Washington, had held that summer. Wei Lin moved over to make room for Lynsey without breaking from her intent conversation with Razina, which sounded like it was about a safari.

Looking around the room, Dylan noticed everyone seemed to be involved in an animated discussion. Meeting new people was usually easy for Dylan, but for some reason she was content to eat her pizza and observe. She realized she had known a lot of girls like Lynsey and Patience back home — social, sophisticated, assertive. Some of those girls were her closest friends. *But minus the claws and cattiness*, Dylan told herself. Thinking of them, her mind drifted to the going-away party her mom had thrown for Dylan and all her riding friends. Each girl had received an unmarked box, and they all opened them on cue, releasing hundreds of gloriously colored butterflies. Mrs. Walsh had explained that the butterflies represented the group of friends: Each one would take a different course — each one was beautiful and vibrant. Dylan lingered on the thought of her old friends, and when she shook herself back into the present, she realized Malory was smiling at her. Then Malory turned back to Alexandra, who was talking about their syllabus for English that year. It appeared that Alexandra had done the literature reading in its entirety over the summer.

"I loved *To Kill a Mockingbird*," Alexandra enthused.

"Wait, you've already read it?" Malory asked.

Okay, Dylan thought, looking around the room in an attempt to assess the friendship possibilities. *Here's what I've got to work with in Adams. . . .*

Lynsey is no doubt the queen bee — she has zero competition. It couldn't hurt to chum up with her. But not if it's too much work. You can't forget she's got a great pony — extra points for that.

I'm not so sure about Patience. It looks like she's staked a claim on Lynsey's right side, so they might come as a pre-packaged pair. And Patience is quick with the cut-downs — maybe too quick. Still, she's a little like Jess from back home, who was a super loyal friend.

Now Razina's totally together and therefore totally intimidating. But I don't think she means to be. She'll probably claim one best friend and be on the fringe of the in-crew — that's what the mature ones always do.

Wei Lin is trickier. She might be a little too smart for me. But straightforward, which is good. And pretty genuine, I think. Great sense of style. No riding.

Malory seems pretty cool. She won the Rockwell Award — good credentials for a friend — which will impress my mom, no doubt. A little quiet, but still quirky. Kind of a suck-up to Aunt Ali, though.

Alexandra is way too smart for me. Talking about classes on the first day? No way. Nice, though.

Honey. As sweet as her name. Roommate. Rides. English. Probably thinks I'm a compulsive liar, yet still seems to like me. She has potential.

Lani — a shining beacon of hope in the humor department. Way goofy and pretty oblivious. Definite contender.

Dylan couldn't remember the last time she had been in this situation — new place, all new people. Even when she started kindergarten, she already had friends from play groups and preschool. *This is definitely new territory,* she realized, but she was up for the challenge.

When Dylan finally emerged from her character evaluations, Alexandra was still talking about English class and worrying about the caliber of the instructor.

"If it's Ms. Conroy, then we'll be quoting whole acts from Shakespeare before the week is out," Lynsey said, overhearing them and breaking off her conversation with Patience. "Some of the teachers here are totally obsessed with their subjects. Ms. Conroy is definitely one of them. The phys ed teacher, Ms. Feist, is an absolute taskmaster.

There practically has to be a hurricane before she'll cancel an outdoor practice."

"How do you know all this?" Razina licked her fingers as she finished her pizza slice.

"My sisters went here," Lynsey told her. "They gave me the full rundown."

"So tell us what the housemothers are like. Will we be able to get away with sneaking out for midnight feasts?" Lani's brown eyes sparkled and Dylan realized she had settled into the group more quickly than any of them, given that she'd only arrived ten minutes ago.

Lynsey smoothed out a wrinkle in her lilac Dolce skirt and looked around to make sure she had everyone's attention. "For one thing, don't be fooled by Mrs. Herson being so laid back today. She can be fun, but be careful. There's definitely a line that you don't want to cross. The high school housemother, Ms. Marshall, is the opposite. She's an absolute ogre if you break any of the house rules. She won't hesitate to report an infraction to Dr. Starling."

There was a collective murmur of dread, and Lynsey paused.

"But it's fine, because she sleeps like Rip Van Winkle. After nine o'clock, anything goes. We should all pity anyone in Meyer. Mrs. O'Connor wakes up at the slightest noise *and* does random night patrols. She should get a life." Lynsey's steely blue eyes flashed with disdain. "And everyone knows that the Curie dorm has the best deal with Ms. Ford. They could burn down the house before she'd interfere. We need to make some friends there, so they can host parties!" Lynsey finally ran out of steam and leaned forward to take a sip of seltzer.

Dylan picked up her own drink and eyed Lynsey. The girl did talk a lot, but she sometimes shared valuable information.

CHAPTER FIVE

"See you in study hall," Dylan called to Razina as she stuffed her Spanish books into her bag. Her first official riding lesson was next, and she was ready to run all the way to the stables. Razina waved as she headed in the opposite direction, toward the sports center.

Honey and Lani were looking pretty nervous when Dylan caught up with them. Their assessment for the intermediate program was in the indoor ring with Ali, while the riders already in the program had a lesson in the large outdoor arena with Aiden Phillips, the jumping coach.

"You'll be great," Dylan told them. "I'll come find you if we finish early."

"Oh, fabulous. The more public the humiliation, the better," Lani said. "Do you know how long it's been since I sat in an English saddle? I'll be lucky if I can bend my knees."

"Well, if you can't, at least it will help me look better," Honey offered with a smirk.

Dylan smiled, happy to see that Honey was feeling relaxed enough to joke about the tryout. "You'll both be great," she confirmed. Then, on seeing the group of girls gathering for the intermediate lesson, she felt her own stomach flutter with nerves.

⁀☙

Dylan had been disappointed when Kelly, the stable assistant, had announced the pony assignments. She wasn't sure she could wait much longer to ride Morello again. *At least I'm not stuck with lazy, cranky Colorado*, she thought. Dylan had to admit that Shamrock, a fourteen-hand dappled gray mare, already seemed more willing.

When Dylan trotted into the outdoor arena, Aiden Phillips was standing in the middle watching each girl as she flashed past. "Relax, everyone, this is not a firing squad," she said. "Soften your lower back and straighten through the shoulders."

Dylan allowed herself a small smile. Straight to work — she liked it that way.

"Trot a figure eight, please," called Ms. Phillips. "Malory, you cross first when you reach the far corner."

Malory looked just as natural on Flight, a pretty pure-gray mare, as she had on Kingfisher. When she reached the corner of the school, she turned straight across the ring, followed by the other riders.

Dylan changed the rein, keeping one pony-length behind Lynsey on Bluegrass, and sat for two strides to switch diagonals. Shamrock continued to trot smoothly, her head arched to accept light contact on the bit. Dylan found herself relaxing. Shamrock might not be Morello, but she moved like she was floating on air, with a smooth, even stride. This was what Dylan had been waiting for since fourth grade, and it was just day one.

Dylan fanned her cheeks with both hands as she walked away from the stable block with Malory and Lynsey. Even though it was late afternoon, the sun was still beating down. She was feeling good about her first lesson, and she guessed the other two were as well. From what she'd seen so far, Malory and Lynsey would offer the most competition among the new class for the junior riding team. Dylan knew she had a good chance, too. Except for one glaring mistake, her last round of jumps had been perfect. "I thought I was going to hit the dirt when Shamrock ran out at the oxer!" She sighed.

"You looked like a stunt rider, dangling over her shoulder like that," Lynsey agreed.

"Gee, thanks," Dylan said, giving Lynsey a gracious

smile. "I'm so glad to have provided the afternoon entertainment."

Lynsey shrugged. "Oh, come on. We needed some livening up. That course was so basic, Bluegrass could have done it blindfolded."

"And with you reading a copy of *Vogue*, no doubt," Dylan said sarcastically.

"Exactly," Lynsey replied with a sly smile.

Dylan looked at Lynsey in surprise. Were they suddenly swapping jokes? She considered the possibility for a moment. It was true that Lynsey and Bluegrass were in a class of their own, not even rapping a single fence in the lesson. Lynsey could probably read the entire *Encyclopedia Britannica* without missing a stride. But Dylan was more intrigued by Lynsey's reaction to her joke. If Lynsey had somehow developed the ability to laugh at herself, she would be a lot more fun to be around.

"Since we've finished early, do you want to go down to the indoor arena to see if Lani and Honey are still doing their assessment?" Malory interrupted.

"Oh, I promised Patience I'd meet up with her once we finished," Lynsey told her. Patience was doing the basic riding program, which had a session with Roger Musgrave, the equitation coach. "I guess I'll have to catch up with you guys later."

"Later," Dylan said, and Malory gave a quick wave.

As they headed down to the indoor ring, Sarah passed them, leading Bluegrass.

"Bluegrass is an amazing pony," Malory enthused. He looked gorgeous, his dark coat gleaming after being sprayed down to get the sweat off. "I loved watching him in today's lesson."

"But you've seen him before, right?" Dylan asked. "On the show circuit?" She had discounted Lynsey's comment about never having seen Malory at the best shows. After getting to know her better, Dylan realized it was a miracle Lynsey had remembered her from Rhode Island — and that was only because of the freakishly big flies at the Red Valley showground. Dylan was convinced that Malory would have to have been competing a lot to win the Rockwell grant.

There was such a long pause that Dylan thought Malory wasn't even going to answer her. Finally, she lifted her hands, palms up. "I guess we must have been in different classes."

Dylan felt a twinge of annoyance. *There she goes again! Why does she always clam up the moment I ask about anything personal?*

They had reached the indoor arena and saw that the big double entrance doors were closed. They walked around to the long side of the building, to a smaller entrance that led up to the viewing gallery.

Ali Carmichael was standing in the center of the ring,

watching Honey and Lani ride at a collected trot. Dylan recognized the pony Honey was riding as they thudded past. It was Hardy, who was stabled beside Morello in the barn. Honey looked relaxed as she sat deeply in the saddle. As usual, she looked immaculate. Dylan smiled. Only Honey would wear a pressed show shirt with an overcollar for the assessment. With her cordovan-colored gloves, beige jodhpurs, and polished boots, it was clear that Honey wanted to be taken seriously.

Lani was riding a horse that Dylan hadn't seen before, a pretty chestnut mare that looked to be about fifteen hands.

"That's Skylark," Malory whispered. "I saw Kelly schooling her yesterday, and she was being a real handful."

Dylan nodded. Skylark didn't exactly seem to be giving Lani an easy ride, either. She sidestepped along the edge of the ring with her tail kinked high. Lani drove her forward, the tassels on her chaps bouncing against her legs. Dylan didn't think that either Honey or Lani had noticed them, but as they both turned the far corner and began riding down to the mirrored end, Lani stuck her tongue out of the corner of her mouth and rolled her eyes.

Dylan turned at the sound of footsteps coming up the stairs. She scooted farther down the bench as Patience and Lynsey joined them.

"Oh, my gosh," Lynsey whispered, leaning forward and

resting her elbows on the balcony. "Check out Annie Oakley."

Dylan winced. She had thought it was kind of cool that Lani was wearing chaps.

"Okay, that's enough," Ali Carmichael called out to Honey and Lani.

Honey brought Hardy to a halt and leaned forward to pat his neck. When Lani tried to halt Skylark, the chestnut snatched at the bit and shot forward into a canter. The horse dropped her head, but Lani leaned back and closed her long legs against her, crossing one rein over her neck while giving and taking with the other. When Skylark came galloping around the corner, Malory gasped and closed her eyes.

"It's okay, she's still on," Dylan told her.

Lani started turning Skylark in decreasing circles, until the mare returned to a collected trot. Ali called, "Finish off with a serpentine, please, to show her you're the one in control."

"Talk about the Wild West!" Patience murmured.

Dylan ignored her and clapped when Lani finally halted.

"Thank you." Ms. Carmichael glanced up at the gallery. "You can go now, girls. I don't want to be responsible for making you late for study hall."

Dylan figured that her aunt didn't want to give Honey and Lani her decision with bystanders in the gallery. She hoped that didn't mean there would be bad news.

It would be so much fun if Honey and Lani made intermediate.

"Well," Lynsey said as they began to head down the stairs. "I don't think Lani's got much chance of getting into the intermediate program. If she can't even transition from a trot to a walk, how's she going to jump?"

"Maybe they'll draw up a new program just for her." Patience let out a low laugh. "I have a feeling lassoing would be her thing."

Dylan felt a surge of annoyance. Just because Lani didn't wear breeches and high boots, that didn't make her any less of a rider! "If you ask me, she deserves to get in just from the way she handled Skylark," she said hotly.

"That whole thing where she crossed her reins was pretty cool. I've never seen that before," Malory agreed. "And she has to have strong legs."

"That's what they teach them at the rodeo," Patience claimed.

Lynsey raised her eyes heavenward. "If she gets into the intermediate program, I'll eat my jodhpurs."

I'll remember that, Dylan thought, as Patience clutched Lynsey's arm, shaking with laughter.

The seventh grade had Ms. Marshall, the other Adams housemother, supervising them for study hall. Even though it was the first day of the semester and the girls didn't have any homework other than to learn some Spanish verbs, she insisted that, instead of getting out early, they had to read one of their assigned books for English literature. The minutes started to drag long before the bell rang.

Dylan stuffed her books into her bag and caught up with Honey and Lani, who were heading down the hallway with Malory. "Hey, you guys, wait up!" she called. "So, how did your assessment go? Did Al —" She caught herself just in time. "Did Ms. Carmichael let you know if you made it into the program?"

"She sure did," Lani grinned. "Honey, do you want to tell Dylan?"

"No, I think you should do it," Honey said.

"But you'd do it so much better than me," Lani replied, straight-faced.

Dylan raised her eyebrows at Malory. But Malory just looked up at the ceiling and began whistling under her breath.

"Aargh! All right, enough already!" Dylan shook a fist in the air.

"We both got in," Honey announced, her brown eyes shining. "She even told Lani that she handled Skylark well, that she's always high-strung after she jumps."

"Way to go!" Dylan exclaimed, giving them both a high five.

"Yeah, things really fell apart after you guys showed up. I'm lucky. Ms. Carmichael gave me a break."

"Come on, you deserve it. Dylan and I knew you'd

make intermediate," Malory said as they continued walking down the hallway to the cafeteria. "Now we'll all be riding together. I'm so glad Lynsey was wrong."

Dylan stopped as a thought occurred to her. "I've got to go up to my room for something. I'll see you all in the cafeteria." Before the others had a chance to say anything, she turned and hurried back to the stairs, holding back laughter as she devised her plan.

🐎

Dylan quickly chose salmon and new potatoes from the serving counter in the cafeteria before joining the other seventh-graders. Honey had saved her a place. As Dylan sat down, she glanced over at Lynsey. "I guess you've heard the great news about Honey and Lani," she enthused.

Lynsey refused to meet her eyes and instead rolled a cherry tomato around her plate with her fork.

"Aren't you hungry?" Dylan asked sympathetically. "Or maybe you're just saving room?"

"For what?" Caught off guard, Lynsey looked up at Dylan.

"Your jodhpurs," Dylan grinned. She pulled a pair of breeches from her shoulder bag, flapping them in the air before placing them on the spare tray she'd brought over. She pushed it across to Lynsey. "Do you want ketchup with that?"

Lynsey glared at Dylan, her blue-gray eyes smoldering.

"Whatever." She scowled and shook her head at Dylan, as if she thought her roommate should know better.

"You did say you'd eat your jodhpurs. . . ." Dylan reminded her impishly.

Lani leaned across and prodded the trousers. "Lynsey, I'm concerned that you might have an eating disorder."

Lynsey snatched up the jodhpurs and rolled them in a ball. "Very funny, Dylan. I owe you one," she responded sweetly before turning to Patience. "Did you get a chance to look at the bulletin board and see which movie we're getting tonight?"

"It's *Hidalgo*," Patience replied. "The Viggo Mortensen movie about the Pony Express rider who enters a race across the desert."

"Viggo who?" Lani looked blank.

"Um, Viggo Mortensen," Lynsey said, speaking slowly. "You know, as in the very cute guy from *Lord of the Rings*?"

"*Lord of the Rings* meets the Pony Express. The good folks in Hollywood are really struggling for original ideas, aren't they?" Lani said dryly.

Lynsey shrugged. "I've already seen it. My dad got it for our home movie theater, but I guess I could see it again."

"Oh, the cinematography is supposed to be great. I've been meaning to see it for a while," Wei Lin said, breaking off from chatting with Razina and Alexandra.

"You can sit with me and I'll explain the difficult parts,"

Dylan teased Lani as she squeezed some lemon juice over her fish.

"Or if you want to skip it, then you could come down to the stables with me," Malory chipped in. "I asked Ms. Carmichael if I could clean some tack or scrub buckets to earn some points for stable management before we get too busy with classes."

"That sounds more like it," said Lani with a grin. "I'm not in the mood to sit around tonight — too much pent-up energy."

Malory glanced across at Dylan. "You don't mind if Lani doesn't watch the movie with you guys, do you?"

Dylan blinked. "No, of course not," she replied, but she couldn't help feeling that Malory had intentionally given Lani a counteroffer. She told herself she was being over-sensitive. It wasn't like she was going to be watching this movie on her own, and, as much as she liked stable work, she felt she had earned a night on the couch.

Dylan squeezed in on the sofa between Razina and Wei Lin. "So," Wei Lin smiled, offering Dylan some popcorn out of the enormous bowl they were sharing. "Does the fact that I'm not into horses mean that I'm not going to understand one word of this movie?"

"No. You can enjoy all of the other parts," Dylan said,

throwing a piece of popcorn into the air and catching it in her mouth.

"Great," Wei Lin replied, snuggling farther back into the cushions.

"Like Viggo Mortensen all hot and sweaty and smelling like horses!" Dylan added, shouting with laughter as Wei Lin pelted her with one of the plaid throw pillows.

Tanisha Appleton walked over to dim the light before switching on the wide-screen plasma TV and clicking on the DVD remote.

Dylan took another handful of popcorn and handed the bucket to Honey, who was sitting at the end of the sofa. She caught her eye and smiled. So far, boarding school was like one giant sleepover — with the extra bonus of riding!

CHAPTER SIX

Dylan gave the saddle one final rub and admired the soft chestnut glow on the leather. She had passed up the opportunity to go on a shopping trip to the mall in Cheney Falls. It had been such a busy first week that she much preferred the idea of chilling out in the stable.

"Do you want a hand with that?" she asked Honey, who was wrestling with Hardy's bridle after taking it apart for a thorough cleaning.

"I'm fine, thanks," said Honey, without looking up from buckling one of the cheekpieces.

Dylan looked over at Lani and Malory, who were soaping saddles on the other side of the tack room. They had already been hard at work when Dylan arrived. Then Honey had joined them half an hour later, after writing a postcard to her brother. Dylan had the sneaking suspicion that they were all there for the same reason: They hoped they might be told they could ride, even though it was the weekend. Usually, weekend sessions were purely make-up or were scheduled in advance for a student needing help in a particular discipline. The Adams girls hoped cleaning tack would earn them points with the stable staff. "I'm going to get a soda, can I get you guys anything?" offered Dylan.

"I'd take her up on her offer — she doesn't make them that often," a voice said from the doorway.

Dylan spun around. "Nat!"

Her cousin held up his hand for a high five. His amber eyes twinkled as he dodged to avoid Dylan ruffling his fox-colored hair — it wasn't that hard, since he was at least eight inches taller than she was. "So you've survived your first week?" he teased. "I'll admit, I'm impressed."

"You should be." Dylan smiled. She turned back to the other girls, who were staring at Nat with open curiosity. "Guys, this is my cousin, Nat. He's a freshman at Saint Kit's. You know, the boys' school on the other side of Cheney Falls? The dark side."

"Just so you know, the bad sense of humor does not run in the family," Nat said solemnly. "How are you all doing?"

"You know, you sort of remind me of someone — and it's not Dylan," Lani said, squinting her eyes and screwing up her mouth as she took in Nat's high cheekbones.

"That would be my mom," he told her.

"How on earth would she know your mom?" Honey asked, dropping her sponge into the bucket at her feet.

"Um, Nat's mom is Ms. Carmichael," Dylan told them, feeling uncomfortable. "As in, Ali Carmichael." Dylan hadn't told anyone that she was related to the riding director, but now she was kind of glad it was out in the open.

"Oh." Lani paused for a minute. "She's your aunt? I guess that's pretty cool."

"That explains how you knew that paint pony!" Honey exclaimed, putting it all together. "You're so lucky. I'd love it if someone in my family was into horses. Whenever I started talking about Rocky back home, everyone's eyes sort of glazed over."

"Yeah," Malory said quietly. "She'd be a cool aunt."

"Do you know where she is?" Nat asked, glancing at Dylan. "Maybe you could show me around?"

"Sure. See you later, guys," Dylan said, following Nat out of the tack room.

"I think Ms. Carmichael is schooling Quince," Dylan said, leading the way out of the barn and onto the yard.

"It sounds so weird hearing you call her that," Nat said, sticking his hands in his jeans and kicking at a small stone. He glanced at Dylan, narrowing his eyes. "I hope I didn't make things tricky for you back there. I'd have thought by now your friends would know that you're her niece."

Dylan shrugged. "I didn't want anyone thinking that I was going to be getting any special treatment. I mean, your mom will be selecting the competition teams. I really want to make it, but only if I deserve it."

"Don't you think your friends would understand that?"

"Well, it takes a little bit to know who your friends are — who you want to tell, you know," Dylan tried to explain.

"That makes sense," Nat agreed. "They all seemed really nice back there. I'm sure your secret's safe."

"Oh, I don't really care anymore. I'm actually relieved you blew my cover."

"Anytime, Dyl." Nat gave her a playful jab in the shoulder.

They came to the outdoor ring and leaned on the gate to watch Ali riding. Quince was working at an extended trot across the ring, and Dylan thought the dappled gray mare looked fantastic, with her neck arched and her long silver tail streaming in the air like a banner. Quince was her aunt's competition horse, a Thoroughbred with an unpredictable stable temperament but outstanding manners in the ring.

"Hey, Mom!" Nat put his fingers in his mouth and let out a piercing whistle.

Ali looked their way and, seeing who it was, stood up in her stirrups and pushed Quince into a canter while she held the reins in one hand and waved with the other. Dylan grinned — this was the Aunt Ali she knew, goofing around, instead of Ms. Carmichael, Director of Riding.

It always amazed her that Ali was actually her mom's sister — she seemed to have more in common with Dylan's laid-back, horse-loving dad.

Ali pulled Quince to a stop and slid off, laughing as she hugged Nat across the gate. "You're early," she said as Dylan took Quince's reins, reaching up to scratch the mare's damp neck.

"Good to see you, too, Mom," Nat said. "I'll just come back next week."

"Don't you dare!" Ali said quickly. "I just need five minutes to cool Quince off and then I'll be ready. Dylan can take you up to my office, and I'll catch up as soon as I'm done, okay?"

"Sure," Nat said.

"Thanks, Dylan," Ali said, retaking the reins. "Nat and I are going to grab a bite to eat in town before I drop him back at Saint Kit's. Do you want to come with us?"

"That would be great," Dylan said.

"So you like snails, right?" Nat said, as they turned to walk back up the path. "We're going to this French restaurant, and if you don't eat the complimentary snails they serve as appetizers, the maitre'd gets really offended."

Nat was always playing pranks on her, and Dylan

wasn't going to get suckered again. "Sure, I like snails," she said, straight-faced. "Especially the small ones — they're extra slimy — a lot like warm snot."

"Gross!" Nat's face wrinkled. "I swear you should have been a boy."

"I swear you should have been one, too," Dylan snapped back.

It was a long-standing joke between them that Dylan wasn't a typical girl — not in the demure, polished ways her mom would like her to be. She had her dad's sense of humor and his athleticism. Dylan was more like her mom's sister, Aunt Ali, than she was like her mother. And Nat was the perfect stand-in big brother for Dylan, who was an only child.

"You'd do anything for a laugh," Nat said.

"It runs in the family" Dylan laughed as she reached for the doorknob of her aunt's office. Just then, a blue roan trotted past and clattered onto the yard.

Lynsey circled Bluegrass back toward them.

Lynsey certainly hasn't mastered the art of subtlety, Dylan thought, watching how her roommate swiftly assessed her cousin.

"Slipping into the director's office with an unannounced visitor, Dylan?" Lynsey questioned in a conspiratorial tone. "Well, this certainly improves my opinion of you."

"Don't let it," Dylan quickly announced. "He's my cousin."

"Oh, well." Lynsey pulled off her hat and ran her fingers through her hair, giving Nat a wide smile. "I'm Lynsey Harrison. I room with Dylan."

"I'm Nat Carmichael. My mom works here."

This news caused Lynsey to pause, but to Dylan's amazement, Lynsey didn't comment on the connection. She did, however, drop her riding crop.

"Oops," she said, looking at Nat and making no effort to pick it up.

You've gotta be kidding me, a voice in Dylan's head groaned, as Nat bent down to retrieve the crop. *Someone should just hit her with that thing. Knock some sense into her.*

"Ms. Carmichael is going to meet us here," Dylan said in a warning tone. "I'll come back in about fifteen minutes," she added, not wanting to hang around to see any more of Lynsey's overt flirtations. If Nat fell for Lynsey's fake 'n' bake charms, Dylan was going to be seriously disappointed in him.

Dylan decided to go to the student center to grab a bottled water and send some e-mails to her friends back home before meeting Ali and Nat for their lunch date.

"Hey, Dylan. Wait up!" She turned to see Malory jogging across the yard. "I told Kelly and Sarah I'd help with the mucking out. Do you want to pitch in?"

Dylan started to wonder if Malory spent any time

away from the stables. "I was just going to send some e-mails home before going out for lunch," she explained. "Any other time, and I'd be there."

"Are you going anywhere nice?" Malory asked.

"Some French restaurant," Dylan told her.

"*Très mal*," Malory said.

Dylan glanced at her. "Um, I think you mean *très bon*."

"Why, what did I say?" Malory pushed her hair off her forehead.

"'Very bad!'" Dylan grinned. "Although if I have to eat snails like Nat is threatening, you may not be too far off the mark."

"I guess I need to spend more time with my French book. I think there's a quiz next week." Malory looked a little bewildered. "Well, I'll see you later, then," she said, turning to head down the path that led to the barn.

But Dylan was only half paying attention. She was peering over Malory's shoulder at the pony being ridden a short distance away in the outdoor arena.

"I'm sure that's Morello." She frowned. She hadn't been able to ride Morello yet, so she was surprised to see him being worked on a weekend.

Malory looked toward the ring, shading her eyes. "Shouldn't there be a trainer somewhere?" she asked in surprise.

"That's exactly what I was thinking," Dylan agreed.

Students were forbidden to ride unsupervised in the arenas, especially if they were jumping.

They could see Morello trotting down the far side of the ring. As he reached the corner, his rider gave him a kick, which made him trot faster. The rider then shook the reins and kicked harder, driving him into a rocky canter. Morello swerved off the rail, and Dylan gasped. "She's going to jump him!" she yelled. There was a fence about halfway up the ring, nearly three feet in height. Without saying another word, Dylan and Malory hurried to the arena.

He looks crooked, Dylan thought. Even from a distance, she could tell that Morello was not straight. She held her breath, and at the last minute, the pony veered away from the jump. Thrown onto Morello's neck, the rider had to grab his mane to keep from falling off.

They were close enough that Dylan now recognized the rider. It was Emily Page, a seventh-grader from Curie House who was in the basic riding program.

"Bad boy," Emily shouted, yanking roughly on the reins. Morello pinned his ears and raised his head, shuffling backward several steps and flashing the whites of his eyes. He had broken into a sweat, and when Emily pushed him into a trot, his normally fluid stride was choppy.

"What's she doing?" Malory exclaimed.

"I don't know." Dylan shook her head in horror. Something had to be terribly wrong for Morello to refuse a fence, and she worried what Emily might try next.

As Morello neared where Dylan and Malory were standing, Dylan cupped her hands over her mouth and called, "Where's Ms. Phillips?"

"In the office," Emily replied, kicking Morello into a canter again.

"You'd better wait!" Malory shouted, but Emily ignored her and nudged Morello with her heel as he neared the fence.

This time the gelding evened his pace and made a brave try, even though the stride still wasn't right. But he took off too soon and hit the pole with his hind legs. Emily fell onto his neck, and when Morello landed awkwardly on the other side, she turned a somersault right onto the ground. She lay unmoving on the sand, in a small crumpled heap.

"Oh, no!" Malory cried. "She fell off!"

CHAPTER SEVEN

Dylan pulled open the gate and sprinted across the sandy arena with Malory right behind her. Morello was standing a few meters away from Emily, his reins trailing on the ground. As the girls came closer, the pony snorted and shied away.

Dylan's chest tightened. She knew if his legs got tangled up in his reins, he could hurt himself. Leaving Malory to see to Emily, she moved slowly toward the paint gelding. "Steady, Morello. Whoa, there's a good boy."

His whole body was tense, and his eyes rolled. He snorted and raised his head, but he didn't move away. Dylan took a step closer and slowly reached out her hand to catch his reins.

"Dylan! Run and get Ms. Phillips, now!" Malory's voice rang through the air.

Morello threw up his head, nostrils flaring, and sprang into a trot.

Dylan cursed under her breath. Morello's reins whipped around his legs, making him more scared as his trot turned into a canter. There was no way she'd be able to catch him now. She had to make sure he didn't get out of the ring.

She turned and raced past Malory, who had helped Emily sit up and was unbuckling her riding hat. "I can't catch Morello," she explained breathlessly. "I need to shut the gate."

"He'll be fine. You need to get Ms. Phillips," Malory shouted after her.

Is she crazy? Dylan thought. *Emily's the one who looks fine. If Morello keeps running and steps on his reins, he could fall and break a leg.* She reached the gate and slammed it shut. She spun around to look at Morello, who was careering around the ring. Suddenly he stumbled to a halt. Dylan froze. His foreleg was caught in the reins. Morello's head was lowered, the reins taut between his leg and the bit. Dylan knew that if he panicked he could get into real trouble. All she wanted to do was run over to him and help, but she knew he was nervous and volatile. The last thing she wanted to do was spook him. She looked toward the office, wishing that Ms. Phillips would appear around the corner. Emily was sitting up on her own now and talking with Malory, so Dylan made up her mind. She took slow, methodical steps toward Morello, being careful not to startle the pony.

She was so close now she could hear the gelding's noisy

breathing. She could see the tension in his neck, where he was straining against the reins. "Whoa, boy. It's okay. I want to help you," she said, trying to keep her voice calm. She reached out and placed a hand on his withers, and his muscles twitched. She gently ran her other hand down his foreleg. "Up," she said, leaning lightly against his shoulder, just as she had done dozens of times to pick his hooves. Morello shifted his weight slightly and carefully lifted his foot. Quickly, Dylan grabbed for the reins and unlooped them from Morello's leg. She straightened up with a sigh and rubbed Morello's forehead.

"Don't ever do that to me again," she told him, feeling wobbly with relief.

She led him back to Malory and Emily. "Everything's under control with Morello." She held out the reins, expecting Malory to take them so she could then get Ms. Phillips, but Malory was too focused on Emily. Dylan was surprised to see that Emily looked very pale, even though she was up on her feet. "Are you okay?"

"Where's Ms. Phillips?" Malory demanded before Emily could answer.

Dylan frowned. "I already told you. I needed to help Morello first. I'll go get her now."

"No, Dylan. It's too late for that. What if Emily had been seriously hurt? At the worst, Morello would have broken his reins. You need to get your priorities straight," Malory argued.

Dylan's temper flared in response. "My priorities? Look at how stressed he is!" She jerked her head at Morello, whose sides were still heaving. "None of this would have happened if Ms. Phillips had been here in the first place." She glared at Emily.

Malory shrugged. "Maybe, but you should quit acting like you're the only one who knows how to handle Morello. It's not like he's yours. He's here for everyone to use, and it's obvious that not everyone is going to ride him the same way as you."

Dylan felt like she'd been slapped across the face. Why was Malory suddenly the moral judge around here? And how did Dylan become the bad guy when Emily was so clearly in the wrong? She took a step back and slowly clapped her hands. "And the smugness trophy goes to Malory O'Neil," she declared, feeling her red-hot temper cool to ice. "It must be such a step down for you to be here at Chestnut Hill, since you clearly think that you are so much better than anyone else."

Malory's cheeks flamed. She stared at Dylan, not saying anything.

"I did what I thought was right," Dylan said plainly.

Malory narrowed her eyes. "I'm taking Emily up to the office. You can take care of Morello. I'm sure you want it that way." She slipped her arm through Emily's and led her in the direction of the gate.

Dylan stared after the two girls for a moment and then

turned back to Morello. "Did you get any of that?" she asked, spreading her hands out.

Morello let out a heavy sigh, as if their argument was way beneath him.

"Come on, boy," Dylan said. "Let's get you back to your stable. I've got a lunch date." But the last thing she felt like doing was going out to socialize. All she really wanted to do was curl up in the bed of straw in Morello's stall and figure out what had just gone wrong between her and Malory. She couldn't remember exactly what she had said to Malory. She had a bad feeling it might be something she would regret, but when she played the scene with Morello and Emily over in her head, she still felt she had made the right decision for Morello.

One thing's for sure, she thought ruefully as she patted Morello. *My priorities seem pretty straight to me.*

🐎

Dylan hadn't talked to Malory for the rest of the weekend, and from what she could tell, Malory hadn't told her side of the story to anyone else. So no one knew that something had happened between them, but it was obvious to Dylan. Malory was more reserved than ever around her — and that was saying something. She only seemed comfortable around the stable — or when they were all talking about riding — so it was upsetting for that to be where their problems had started.

For now, however, Dylan was able to focus on something else. It was their first full class with Ali Carmichael as instructor — and she had assigned Dylan to ride Morello. It was her first time on him since arriving at Chestnut Hill, and he was just as wonderful as she had remembered.

As they started on the course Ali had set for their lesson, she could hardly stop the big grin that spread across her face. But the grin faded as they came around the turn to the double. This was a serious fence!

Dylan slowed Morello's stride by straightening in the saddle and closing her fingers on the reins. *One, two, three*, she counted, then bent forward from the waist for the take-off. Morello sprang neatly over the first jump and put in two short strides to sail over the second. He thudded down on the other side and gave a playful buck.

"Good boy!" Dylan exclaimed as she trotted him to the other end of the jumping arena, patting him on the neck the whole way. She had been the last to jump in their lesson, and the ground had been a little torn up in places, but Morello had been a star. Dylan was relieved that the events of last Saturday hadn't seemed to affect him at all. He hadn't shown any reluctance or wariness after the Emily episode. She slowed the paint gelding to a walk as they drew nearer the rest of the class. There were thirteen intermediate riders in seventh grade, split into two classes. Today, both groups were practicing their jumping — Dylan was in her aunt's group, in the outdoor arena, while Ms. Phillips was working with her class indoors.

"Way to go," Lynsey said when Dylan halted alongside Bluegrass. "That was a great round, even if you did knock the wall."

Dylan looked at her in surprise. "Thanks!" she said. "It was all Morello. He saved me at the wall. I turned way too sharply. If I hadn't done that, we might have gotten a clear round." The fences at Chestnut Hill were far more sensitive than those at Dylan's old stable. It didn't take much to drop a pole or knock over some other element of a fence. Still, it seemed Lynsey managed a clean round almost every time.

"Oh, don't worry about a little thing like that," Lynsey said generously, and for a moment Dylan wondered if she needed to rethink her opinion of her roommate. "You're sure to make the junior jumping team with a performance like that. And with your aunt being the Director of Riding, I guess it wouldn't matter if you'd knocked down a few more." She gazed innocently at Dylan, giving her a bright smile.

"Everyone form a line, please," Ali Carmichael called before Dylan could come up with an appropriately biting response.

Still fuming, Dylan reined Morello back a few steps so Lani could turn Colorado and drop into the line.

"I wouldn't take any notice of our friend over there,"

Lani said in a low voice. "She's just mad because you rode the course better than she did — and on an inferior animal!" She delivered the last few words in a perfect mimic of Lynsey and then grinned. Her smile was so bright and wide, Dylan wasn't sure if she was still mocking Lynsey. Regardless, Lani always seemed to make Dylan feel better.

Dylan noticed Malory walking Hardy farther down the row as they lined up, and Dylan realized she was deliberately putting Lani and Honey between them. Dylan was beginning to see that Malory was every bit as stubborn as she was, and she wondered if their disagreement would come to an easy resolution.

"You all did great today. I'm seeing some real improvement. If I didn't know better, I'd swear you were trying to impress me!" Ali said, standing in front of the group.

The girls exchanged glances and slightly nervous smiles. It wasn't a secret that they all had the team tryouts on their minds. The trainers would select the junior jumping team in just a few weeks, and competition was already fierce.

Ali Carmichael looked at Dylan. "That was a solid round. It was a shame you tipped the wall — next time watch Morello's stride more carefully as he comes out of the corner." Dylan nodded, knowing that tight corners were one of her weak spots, especially when she was trying to maintain a faster pace.

"I know you've all tried a selection of ponies since you arrived," Ali continued, looking at each girl in turn. "We wanted to find the mount that best matches your individual strengths and style."

This is it! Dylan thought, certain that Ali was about to announce which ponies they would ride for tryouts. She crossed her fingers.

Ms. Carmichael hesitated. "I think the best thing is if you stick with the ponies you're riding now. I'm happy with the pairings from today, and since the tryouts are a few weeks away, you should have ample time to build a good bond. I wish you all the best luck."

Things were starting to look much brighter! Dylan was tempted to let out a whoop of joy at the thought of riding Morello exclusively for the next few weeks. Riding Morello would give her the best chance to make the team. It had been months since they last jumped a course together, and they were still totally in sync. She leaned forward to rub his neck and noticed Malory, farther down the line on Hardy, doing the same. In spite of their argument, Dylan was glad Malory was pleased with Ali's choice of pony for her.

"The team consists of four regular riders plus a reserve," Ali Carmichael told them. "And since you'll be up against the rest of the seventh *and* eighth grade, competition is going to be pretty tough. Most ponies will have two riders, and we'll draw names to see which rider goes first."

"I don't have to share Bluegrass, do I?" Lynsey protested.

Ms. Carmichael started to shake her head.

"That's just as well — he's very sensitive, and I doubt he'd go well for anyone else," Lynsey added before Ali could say anything.

"Well, if he's as sensitive as you say, maybe you should think about using one of the Chestnut Hill ponies," Ali returned evenly. "Keep in mind, if you make the team, your mount becomes part of the team. There are circumstances when others — sometimes even riders from other schools — would be required to ride your horse."

Dylan hid her smile behind her gloved hand. She couldn't imagine Lynsey being at all happy about someone else riding Bluegrass. Nor could she picture Lynsey astride a common school pony, but Dylan knew there was nothing common about Morello. *It's time to get serious*, she told herself. *You have three weeks to get good enough on Morello to make the team. Don't screw it up.*

❧

"Dylan!" Lani's voice called through the door. "If you don't come out right now, I'm gonna come in and drag you out by your hair!"

Dylan grinned and quickly finished running a tube of Gash lip gloss over her bottom lip. She tiptoed over to the door and yanked it open. Still holding onto the knob, Lani staggered into the room.

"Would you hurry up? I've been waiting for you forever," Dylan scolded, straight-faced. "It's not like I have a date with fifty boys every night of the week."

"Whatever, Walsh," Lani retorted. She picked up Dylan's comb and ran it through her hair. "Honey and I have already divided them between us."

There was an evening discussion for the riding students scheduled in the school auditorium, but the fact that the boys from Saint Kit's would be there had generated more excitement than the symposium itself.

"You guys, come on!" called Honey.

"After you." Dylan waved her arm at the door.

"No, after you, I insist," Lani grinned. "You're going to need all the help you can get tonight. But I doubt that a head start will do you much good."

"Hey!" Honey popped her head through the door, her blond hair worked neatly into a French braid. "If we don't leave right now, we'll get locked out of the auditorium altogether, and then we'll see how many dates you get."

Dylan and Lani looked at each other and burst into laughter, each taking Honey by an arm as they escorted her down the hall.

The campus was lit with yellow light spilling from Victorian lampposts. Dylan, Lani, and Honey hurried along the path to the auditorium, hoping they wouldn't be the last to arrive. The talk was on alternative treatments for horses, and Dylan was really looking forward to hearing Amy Fleming, one of the scheduled speakers.

"I remember reading an article about her," she said as they headed up the steps that led into the arts building. "She worked at this place called Heartland, and she practically ran it by the time she was sixteen. Can you imagine that?"

The others didn't answer, and when Dylan glanced up she saw why. On the top step stood Ms. Marshall, the Adams House high-school housemother, and she glared down at the tardy students as she held open the main door.

"You're late," she said, walking ahead of them down a hallway and pushing open another set of doors. "There are some seats on the left with the rest of the seventh grade. Please sit there," she whispered, nodding into the darkened auditorium.

As the girls tiptoed down the dimly lit aisle, they could hear Dr. Starling introducing the first speaker, Dr. Jeremy Haslum, who was a professor of veterinary studies at Virginia Tech.

"Sorry," Dylan whispered as she stepped on Grace Findlay's toe. The eighth-grade intermediate rider stood up to let Lani and Honey pass, clearly not trusting them to find their way to the spare seats without crushing her feet as well.

They pulled down their theater seats, and Dylan realized that she was sitting next to Malory. Malory stared straight ahead at Dr. Haslum, who was pointing to a diagram of a horse. Dylan wondered if Malory was ignoring her or just concentrating on the speaker. She wished she hadn't lashed out against her classmate, yet she wasn't sure how to take it back. Her words had no doubt been hurtful, even if they were just said in the heat of the moment.

Dylan peered at the right-hand side of the auditorium, where the Saint Kit's boys were sitting. Although the lights were dimmed, she could just make out their profiles.

"You're supposed to be here for the talk, not to ogle boys," Lani muttered out of the side of her mouth.

"Ditto," Dylan whispered behind her hand, noticing that Lani's head was also swiveled to the right.

There was a cute dark-haired boy in the third row who kept glancing in their direction. Dylan nudged Lani, but the boy must have seen her, because he quickly looked back at the stage and didn't turn around again.

"Who do you think he was checking out?" Dylan whispered.

"If you ask me, it was Mal," Lani muttered. She leaned across Dylan to ask, "Hey, did you see your secret admirer?"

Malory was silent for a moment. Then, when Dr. Haslum paused to move on to the next slide, she whispered back, "His name is Caleb Smith. I met him in the summer. He was riding at my stable."

"So he's your boyfriend?" Lani asked in a loud hiss, causing girls from the row in front to turn around.

"No!" Malory protested, still facing the stage. "He's just a friend."

Lynsey was sitting in the row behind them, with Patience, Razina, and a girl from Curie. She leaned forward. "Who did you say that guy is? Patience wants to know."

"Lynsey!" Patience gasped.

"Shh!" The warning had come from the upperclassmen's section, and the younger students quickly quieted down.

Dylan settled back into her seat and listened to the end of the doctor's lecture on conventional veterinary medicine. Dylan found just about any equine discussion interesting, but it was the next speaker she was really waiting for.

"I'm going to hand you over for the rest of evening to Amy Fleming," the professor announced at last. "She's not only a successful equine therapist, she also happens to be one of my students." He put down his laser pen and smiled at the slim girl with long, light-brown hair who stood up to join him.

"I wonder who her stylist is?" Dylan overheard Lynsey whisper. Amy's simple pantsuit fit her well but was clearly not from a Lynsey-approved boutique. As far as Dylan could tell, the only makeup she was wearing was mascara. She didn't really need any more. The young equine therapist had a very natural beauty that didn't require flashy clothes or two-tone eyeshadow. Amy Fleming obviously had more important things to think about.

"Hi." Amy spoke in a clear, pleasant voice. "I've been asked here tonight to tell you a little about the work that I've done to help horses, using complementary methods." She looked around the auditorium, her gray eyes glowing with enthusiasm and possibly a little apprehension.

She couldn't be any older than eighteen, Dylan realized, surprised that anyone that age could have enough experience to be speaking in a lecture.

"Complementary methods are also known as alternative therapies," Amy continued. "These are ways to treat a horse in addition to traditional medicine." She pushed a button, and a diagram filled the screen behind her. She explained that it showed various pressure points on a horse's body. "T-touch — a circular massaging movement — has been proven to increase relaxation of horses and other animals when pressure is applied to these areas. A horse doesn't even need to be sick to benefit from this procedure.

"My mother spent many years experimenting with various herbal treatments, especially Bach Flower Remedies," Amy went on. She glanced down at the floor for a moment. "She had this amazing notebook that detailed what each flower could do. I can't tell you how many horses that notebook helped save," she continued. Hearing a catch in her voice, Dylan remembered from the article she'd read that Amy's mom had died several years ago, leaving Amy to carry on her work alone. Dylan felt a tug of sympathy.

"Next, I'm going to show a short film about the join up — a technique we use at Heartland for gaining horses' trust," Amy said, picking up the remote control.

A long-legged, dark roan colt flickered up on the screen above the stage, trotting around an outdoor arena. "This is Spindleberry," Amy explained. Her voice softened, and Dylan wondered if she herself sounded so totally smitten with Morello when she talked about him. "He's being trained using all of the techniques I'm telling you about this evening. He arrived at Heartland extremely dehydrated. If we hadn't rescued him, he might have died. We used conventional and complementary methods to save him, and then we started emotional therapy. One of the ways we gained his trust was by using join up." The screen showed Amy standing in the middle of the arena, flicking a lead rope at the colt, to send him cantering around in circles.

Dylan frowned. *How could that encourage the colt to put his trust in anyone? It looks like she's just chasing him away.*

As if she'd read Dylan's thoughts, Amy went on to explain, "It might seem strange that I'm chasing him away from me, but it's the first stage to winning his complete trust. I keep driving him away until he acknowledges that I would make a great herd leader and what he actually wants is to depend on me for protection — for survival, even. This appeals to a horse's herding instincts." Moments later the camera showed the colt lowering his head, and then he started opening and closing his mouth as if he were trying to chew air.

"This is it," Amy said quietly. "This is his way of saying that he doesn't want to run from me anymore and that he trusts me to look after him because I'm tougher than he is. It's very interesting. All horses convey this with the same signs — the lowered head and the chewing."

Dylan sat forward on the edge of her chair. She didn't take her eyes off the colt as he slowed to a trot. His hooves brushed over the sandy surface, while his inside ear flickered toward the girl in the center of the ring.

"Watch what happens when I turn my back on him," Amy urged.

Hardly breathing, Dylan watched as Spindleberry turned into the center of the ring and walked up to Amy, eventually nudging her back with his nose. A spontaneous round of applause went up as the screen showed Amy walking forward, the colt matching her stride for stride as if they were attached with an invisible thread. "By deciding for himself not to keep running away from me, he's formed a bond between the two of us. That bond is based on mutual respect and trust — something that a whip and spurs can never bring." Amy turned back around to face everyone. "Any questions?" she asked when the lights were turned back on. She grinned, suddenly looking very young, and a sea of hands appeared all over the auditorium.

The questions ran overtime, and when Amy was finally allowed to sit down, the auditorium erupted with more applause. Dylan stood up, clapping hard, wondering if any of the Heartland methods would be incorporated into their own riding programs.

Lani put her fingers into her mouth and let out a piercing wolf whistle as the Saint Kit's teachers began moving down the aisle to escort the boys back to their bus. Dylan caught sight of Nat as he was leaving the auditorium, and he waved to her, then shrugged to show that he couldn't stay to talk. She wondered briefly why he'd bothered coming to the symposium — after all, he wasn't interested in horses, in spite of growing up around them all his life. *He must have come to give Aunt Ali some moral support for her first interschool event,* she guessed.

"I wish I'd had a chance to say hi to Nat," Lynsey commented as the girls walked back to the dorm. She looked at Dylan. "How can he afford to go to somewhere like Saint Kit's? I mean, his mom's just a riding instructor."

Dylan felt a slow anger begin to swirl inside her. She was sure there was a tuition-support arrangement between Saint Kit's and Chestnut Hill staff members, but she wasn't about to explain that to Lynsey. Instead she turned to Lani and stated in a loud voice, "Hey, did I tell you about Nat's dad? He's a big-time graphic designer. He just won some award for his work with Diamond Spring."

"Wow — I know that brand. It's like sparkling water and fruit juice, right? It looks like high-end stuff," Lani said, matching Dylan's forced tone but still sounding impressed.

"Oh, it is. They had it at my club," Lynsey said, as if Dylan had been including her all along. "Well, now that I know a little more about him, I can go ahead and get him to ask me out."

Now that you have a better sense of his financial pedigree, you mean, Dylan thought, furious. She glanced over at Malory, who seemed unfazed by the conversation. She had been quiet since identifying the curly-headed boy at the convocation.

"If that girl with all her *alternative* ideas hadn't run overtime, I'd have gotten a chance to talk to him tonight," Lynsey added, emphasizing alternative with air quotes.

Dylan was just about to defend Amy Fleming's methods, since they clearly got results, when Malory jumped in. Her blue eyes were shining, and there was a spot of color on both her cheeks, as if she'd been outside in the wind. "I think it was a great talk, and I wouldn't mind trying some of her techniques myself. Better to treat a horse with respect and understanding than to try and control him with a whip and fear. I'd rather work *with* a horse than *against* one."

"Absolutely. I know I'm still learning about horses, but her approach convinced me," Razina agreed.

Malory's unexpected outburst managed to silence even Lynsey. *I just never know which way that girl is going to jump*, Dylan thought in surprise.

CHAPTER EIGHT

Dylan was determined to work her heart and soul out. Whatever it took to get on that team with Morello, she was willing to do it. An extra practice session had been scheduled on Friday after morning classes, and she was thrilled with how well things were going — she and Morello seemed to share the same rhythm. Ali had set up a practice jump in one half of the arena for those waiting to take the course of jumps in the other half. Not only had Morello cleared the practice jump with a foot and a half to spare, he was now flying around the main course.

Dylan slowed Morello to steady him for the fence that every other rider except Malory had knocked down. "Take it easy, boy," she murmured, feeling him pull against her hands. Obediently, Morello slowed, and Dylan held him together as they rounded the corner. The fence was a tall upright that was particularly nasty since it was the first jump out of a fast turn. Morello cleared the gate without even rattling it.

"Good boy!" Dylan whispered. She turned him in a circle toward the parallel bars that marked the halfway point of the course. There was no way she wasn't going clear now!

"That's enough, Dylan. Bring him in, please." Ali Carmichael's voice rang across the yard before Dylan reached the next fence.

Dylan reined Morello in, staring at her aunt in confusion. She hadn't stopped any of the other girls partway through the twelve-fence course. "But I haven't finished," she argued.

"Now, please, Dylan. Morello's had enough." Her aunt's tone was clipped.

Shaking her head, but not daring to say any more, Dylan rode Morello out of the ring. Her face felt hot as she wondered whether Ali would have let another rider finish the round. She caught sight of Lynsey's smug expression and tried not to scowl.

I don't know why I was concerned that people would think I'd get special treatment because I'm the riding director's niece. If anything, it's the other way around!

🐿

"Hey, Dylan. Wait up!"

Dylan turned to see Honey and Lynsey hurrying down the hallway after her. She was on her way to study hall and had so far managed to avoid them since the riding session. She wasn't feeling up to any of Lynsey's wise-cracks about the way Ali had stopped her halfway around the course.

"Seems like your disappearing back is all we've seen of you today," Lynsey declared as they caught up with her.

"Obviously I need to perfect my technique a little more," Dylan said pointedly.

"I'm sure Ms. Carmichael wasn't singling you out," Honey said.

"She didn't stop anybody else before they completed the course," Dylan grumbled. "She said 'Morello's had enough.' What does that mean?"

"Maybe Morello's fitness level isn't as high as the other horses," Honey suggested.

"After all, this is his first year at Chestnut Hill." Lynsey smiled, twisting Honey's well-meant comment. "Maybe he's not up to intermediate-level workouts."

Dylan stared at her, deciding whether she'd give Lynsey the satisfaction of acknowledging her insult. Lynsey knew full well that Morello had tons of talent and had gone well in all the previous intermediate classes.

Ignoring her, Dylan stalked across the half-full class-room. The desks were set out in rows so students could work without being distracted. She glanced over to see who was monitoring them for the study period.

Everyone dreaded having Ms. Marshall, because she came ready and willing to distribute extra work if anyone finished her assignments early. Dylan breathed a sigh of relief when she saw Mrs. Hudson's red hair bent over a book at the front desk. The art teacher usually became so engrossed with sketching in her pad that she didn't notice what the girls were doing, as long as they kept quiet.

Dylan headed for her favorite desk. It was close to the window and had a fabulous view of the campus. This afternoon there was hardly anyone outside except for Mr. Lyttle, one of the grounds assistants. He was busy raking up grass clippings and stacking the bags in the wagon attached to the back of his riding mower. Dylan sat down and began to pull out her books. *I'm never going to be able to concentrate on studying,* she thought. The demise of the riding lesson was in the center of her brain, and it wasn't going anywhere anytime soon. Her round had been going so well that she couldn't figure out why her aunt had stopped her short.

Dylan wasn't the only one who was restless; none of the girls seemed able to settle into their homework if the paper shuffling, coughs, and sighs were anything to go by.

Dylan stared at the page in her geography book and realized she had read the same paragraph on irrigation three times. She leaned back and stretched her arms above her head. She frowned as she saw Patience pass a note to Razina and then nod her head in Dylan's direction.

What's up? Dylan wondered. *Something fun, please. It feels like I haven't laughed in forever.*

Razina spent a few seconds reading the note and then glanced up at Mrs. Hudson. The art teacher was hard at work with her charcoal pencil, so Razina held her arm out for Dylan to take the piece of paper. Dylan quickly leaned over her desk and grabbed the note. She smoothed out the paper and read: *All Adams seventh-grade girls are invited to a truth-or-dare game tonight at 11pm in Room Three. Be there, or be you know what!*

Dylan felt excitement shoot up her spine. She loved truth-or-dare! When they'd played it at camp last summer, she'd out-dared everyone by swimming across the lake and hanging their counselor's swim trunks from a tree on the other side. She was totally up for this. Folding up the note, she tossed it over her shoulder to Lani, who let out an exclamation that made everyone in the room look her way. Dylan glanced over her shoulder and saw Lani rubbing her forehead. Dylan raised her eyebrows and looked pointedly at the note teetering on the edge of Lani's desk. Lani snaked out her hand to catch the paper.

"Is everything okay, Lani?" Mrs. Hudson asked, looking up.

"Yes, Mrs. Hudson. I . . . I almost dropped my book," Lani said as she pushed the note up her sleeve, her brown eyes full of innocence.

Dylan grinned and turned back in her seat as Mrs. Hudson walked up their row, running her eyes over each of their books.

"Well, from what I can see, there's not a whole lot of work going on here," the teacher said, standing over Dylan's desk and looking down at the snowy white page of her notebook. "You had better get a move on unless you want to be eating dinner at your desks tonight."

Dylan picked up her pen and tried to look as if she was hard at work, but now her mind was filled with thoughts of the night ahead. How come she could devise a truth and a dare for every girl on the floor, but she couldn't focus enough to answer the first question on her geography handout? *Who cares?* she thought. *It's almost the weekend, and truth-or-dare is less than six hours away.*

Lights were out at ten and the girls had to lie in the dark for the next hour, until they were certain the housemothers were fast asleep. Dylan had set her cell phone to vibrate at ten fifty-five in case she snoozed, but everyone in her room was too excited to slumber. They took turns talking about life at home and what they'd done that summer, and when Dylan pressed the "off" button on her phone, she figured there wasn't a lot more truth about themselves that they could reveal for the game. Now it officially felt like they were roommates. Even Lynsey seemed to have let down her guard — Dylan was almost considering the possibility that the majority of Lynsey's wicked, mocking, egotistic attitude was an act. *No one is that conceited*, Dylan insisted to herself. But not even that semirevelation would alter Dylan's take-no-prisoners game plan for truth-or-dare.

She kicked off her covers and stood up, her heart racing with the knowledge that they were going against house rules.

"Ready?" Honey whispered, clicking on her flashlight and accidentally shining it straight in Dylan's eyes. "Oh, sorry."

Dylan pretended to faint, and Honey gave an explosive laugh.

"Shhh, you guys. You're gonna get us caught!" Lynsey hissed.

Dylan reached under her bed to get the plate of cupcakes she had commandeered from the student center. She slid her feet into her blue sheepskin slippers and padded to the door, holding it open for the others to slip out. Then, suppressing nervous laughter all the way, she followed Honey's flashlight down the hall.

The rest of the girls were already waiting inside Patience's room. A faint eerie light shone from a bedside lamp that had been put down on the floor, and there was a pile of food on a coffee table. Dylan put her slightly smooshed cupcakes down next to a bowl of almonds and dried cranberries, a small mountain of Hershey bars, corn chips and salsa, Chips Ahoy and Oreos, and two bags of Starburst.

"Go ahead and eat," Patience invited. Dylan's teeth almost hurt from looking at all that sugar, but she ripped open the pack of Chips Ahoy, took three, and passed it around.

"No, thanks," Lynsey shook her head. She pulled out a granola bar from the pocket of her lavender velour pajamas and peeled it open, looking virtuous. Dylan caught Lani's eye and shrugged.

"Let's start," Patience said, patting the space next to her on the bed for Lynsey and Honey to sit down. Alexandra, Malory, and Wei Lin were sitting cross-legged next to Razina on her bed. Lani was lying stretched out on the remaining bed, resting her chin on her hands. She pulled herself up to make room for Dylan.

"So," Lynsey said, leaning forward. "Who's going first?"

"I think Patience should, since it was her idea," said Alexandra, cleaning her glasses on the sleeve of her flannel robe.

"Does it have to be truth-or-dare?" Malory asked. "Can't we do something else, like tell ghost stories?"

"Ghost stories are so juvenile," Lynsey said scornfully.

"You got something against truth-or-dare, Malory? We'll all start thinking you have something to hide," Lani teased, stretching for an Oreo. "Did you bring the cupcakes, Dyl? There are only six. Do we split them or can I have a whole one?"

"Take a whole one," Patience urged. "You can have my half. Just don't leave crumbs. I don't want any bugs."

"I'll start," Lynsey said impatiently. "Once Dylan and Lani start talking about food, there'll be no stopping them." She looked across at Wei Lin. "Truth or dare?"

Wei Lin sat up, surprised to be the first up. "Truth," she said after some contemplation. She secured the tie on her silk polka-dot robe and leaned forward to hear her question.

"What's the most money you've ever spent on a pair of shoes?" Lynsey demanded.

"What kind of a question is that?" Lani protested.

"She chose truth," Lynsey reminded her.

"Five hundred dollars," Wei Lin admitted. "And they were secondhand."

"Who'd you buy them from? Elvis?" Honey blurted, her eyes wide.

"It was a charity bash — raising funds for orphaned children in Mexico. It's something my mom really believes in," Wei Lin began, not the least bit embarrassed. "Anyway, celebrities donate their shoes. And my mom bought a pair for me."

"No way!" Lynsey exclaimed, sounding horrified.

Dylan raised an eyebrow. She couldn't believe that

Lynsey would think five hundred dollars was a lot to spend on a pair of shoes — at least not judging by the labels in her dirty clothes hamper.

"How come my mom wasn't involved with that event?" Lynsey went on indignantly. "She's on the board of three major children's charities and she misses one with celebrity shoes?"

"Well, the auction was in L.A.," Wei Lin told her.

"Oh," Lynsey said, losing interest, like anything on the West Coast didn't figure in her social orbit.

"So whose shoes did you get?" Patience demanded.

"Drew Barrymore's, I think — or maybe Cameron Diaz?" Wei Lin frowned. "I can't remember now. But the shoes were totally fabulous! They were limited edition Manolo Blahniks, but the bad news is that they were way too big, so my mom donated them to another charity and promised to buy me my own pair." She looked across at Razina and smiled. "I think I'm off the hook, so — Razina, truth or dare?"

Razina hiccupped as she said, "Dare. No, truth!"

"Okay, then. Have you ever gone on a date?" Wei Lin asked. "An official date."

From the way Razina's high cheekbones colored, it was obvious that they were in store for some juicy gossip.

"Come on, Raz. Fess up," Patience whispered, suddenly sounding chummy.

Razina tipped her head to one side and bit her lower lip. "Is someone at the door?"

Everyone froze and stared at the door, expecting to see the handle turn at any moment. Dylan, who was closest, leaned down to see if she could see the shadow of feet under the door and soon realized they'd been tricked. "Razina," she whispered dramatically. "You don't get off the hook that easily."

"Okay, okay!" Razina held up her hands. "There's this guy named Marcus who's in ninth grade. I met him because his dad is an exporter my mom works with."

"So, where'd you meet him?" Lynsey asked eagerly, hugging her knees.

"In a warehouse — not the most romantic of settings, I know!" Razina rolled her eyes.

"Where did you go on your date?" Patience wanted to know.

"It wasn't exactly a date," Razina confessed. "He came to my mom's gallery in New York, and we went for a walk in Central Park and then for coffee after. But it was at the end of the summer and I haven't seen him since. I'm not even sure my parents would let me go on an official date."

"Have you called him since you got here?" Lani asked.

Razina smiled. "Not yet. But I e-mailed him a few times. And he's written back twice."

"No way!" Lynsey exclaimed. "What does he write?"

Razina's cheeks darkened. "No, that's enough, I'm done now. Your turn, Mal. Truth or dare?"

Malory took a deep breath. "Sorry, guys, but I'd rather sit this one out."

Dylan frowned. *What was it with Malory? Why did she have to be so private?*

"Do you have some deep dark secret you don't want to let us in on?" Lani voiced Dylan's thoughts. "If you do, you really should think about playing — confession's good for the soul and all that."

"No, really. I'm fine listening," Malory protested, her voice apologetic but determined.

"Well, if we all thought that, there'd be no game," Lynsey said dismissively. "You'll have to ask someone else, Raz."

Malory looked down at her hands, but not before Dylan had noticed the relief in her eyes. *What is the deal with her*? she wondered as Razina threw down the challenge to Lynsey.

"Dare," Lynsey said, the corners of her lips slowly curling.

Razina's dark eyes gleamed. "I dare you to sneak down to the foyer and bring back a leaf from one of the potted plants."

Dylan was glad someone finally chose something other than truth, but she thought the dare was a little lame.

Patience, however, was grimacing and shaking her head. "You are allowed to appeal against your dare," she said. "It's a bit risky leaving the floor."

Lynsey tossed her hair over her shoulder. "Give me some credit! I'll be back in two minutes. Time me if you like." She slipped off the bed and tiptoed across the room. She glanced back at the girls with a grin before slipping out the door.

The stunned silence in the room was broken by Honey. "She didn't even take the flashlight."

"If she falls down the stairs and breaks a leg, do you think she'll let me ride Bluegrass for the tryouts?" Lani suggested, making Dylan stifle a laugh.

"I don't think that's very funny," Patience said when Dylan and Lani had recovered. "Chestnut Hill needs Lynsey on the team."

Dylan rolled her eyes. It seemed that Patience had appointed herself president of Lynsey's fan club. Dylan realized that she had not seen much of Patience without Lynsey around. And in her in a deep-pink velour track suit, she looked like a brunette clone of Lynsey. Even though Patience was the only other Adams girl in Dylan's English class, the two really hadn't talked. Patience quiet during the lectures and usually left as soon as the bell rang.

By the time five minutes had passed and Lynsey still hadn't returned, the girls were all beginning to feel anxious. When the door opened a crack and a large, waxy leaf waved through the gap, Dylan felt a flood of relief.

Lynsey stepped inside the door and took a sweeping bow.

"What took you so long?" Patience worried. "My heart was pounding. Are you okay?"

Lynsey shrugged. "I thought I heard a noise, so I crawled up on the windowsill at the end of the hallway and hid behind the curtains."

"What was it?" asked Alexandra.

Lynsey shrugged. "Maybe nothing, but I waited a couple of minutes to make sure no one was there. That's it for me, then." She looked at Dylan. "Truth or dare?"

"Dare," Dylan said, raising her chin.

Lynsey smiled and carefully dropped the leaf in the wastepaper basket. "I dare you to take Morello around the last half of the course that Ms. Carmichael wouldn't let you finish earlier today."

The mood in the room changed like someone had flipped a switch. "Come on," Honey said. "That's hardly the same as stealing a leaf!"

Lynsey shrugged and looked at Dylan. "Of course, if you and Morello aren't up to it . . ."

Dylan took a breath and closed her eyes. She'd had enough of Lynsey making smart remarks about Morello. This was a direct challenge. Before common sense had the chance to weigh in, Dylan impulsively jumped to her feet. "You're on!"

CHAPTER NINE

"You're crazy! You can't really do that!" Malory exclaimed.

Dylan ignored her. "I just have to change into my jodhpurs. I'll meet you at the jumping ring in ten minutes." Her heart was pounding, but there was no way she was backing down now.

"No offense, but I don't think I'll come. This is taking things too far," Razina said with certainty.

Dylan shrugged. "That's fine. No one else should have to risk getting caught for my dare."

"This is insane! What about Morello?" Malory insisted. "Have you thought what it'll be like for him being dragged out of his stall and forced to jump in the middle of the night?" Her eyes were dark with anger.

Dylan felt her own temper flare. "I'll know if he's up for it!" she announced.

"Dylan, I'll come back to our room with you, but I won't go down to the ring," Honey said in a hushed voice. "Sorry if you think I'm bailing out on you."

"Like I said, it's cool," Dylan told her, forcing a smile. But the solemn expression on Honey's face rattled her. *At least there'll be less chance of getting caught if it's just Lynsey and me down there*, she thought, trying not to panic.

"I'm going back to my room," Malory said. She got up and went to the door, followed by Alexandra. Malory looked back at Lani. "Are you coming?"

"You've gotta be kidding, right? I haven't had this much fun since my cousin entered his first rodeo!" Lani grinned at Dylan. "I'll be waiting down there, ready to cheer you on."

"Just as long as you keep it quiet," Dylan told her, feeling a guilty pang of relief that she wasn't going to be on her own after all. She waited for Malory and Alexandra to leave and then headed back to her own room, where the adrenaline rush that had been quieting her fears soon disappeared.

❧

The moon was high and full, spilling light on the path to the stable yard. While Dylan was comforted by the fact that it was easy to see, she also realized that it would make it easy to be seen as well. As she neared the stable, she cast a nervous glance over her shoulder toward the dorm house. She had arranged to meet the others at the ring in ten minutes, which meant she didn't have much time to get Morello ready. Dylan cut off the path and jogged over the last stretch of lawn, relieved to see that her aunt's house, set deep in the trees at the far end of the yard, was in darkness.

She pulled back one of the barn doors and winced at the creaking hinges. It was a grinding, metallic sound — so distinct, she thought she'd recognize it anywhere. She hovered in the doorway, wondering if she should risk turning the lights on. She decided against it. The horses might think it was morning and start up a chorus of whinnies, anticipating their breakfast.

She hurried along the aisle, keeping the flashlight pointed down on the concrete floor. She went to the tack room first to fetch Morello's bridle and saddle, clenching the light between her neck and shoulder so she could use both hands.

Dylan then crossed to Morello's stall and pulled back the bolt. Focusing the flashlight beam on the ground, she found that the paint gelding was lying down with his front legs tucked underneath his chest. He blinked sleepily at Dylan and scrambled to his feet with a disoriented groan.

"Come on, sleepyhead," she said, unbuckling his sheet. "We're going to have some fun!"

🐎

Dylan couldn't believe how loud Morello's hooves sounded as they clattered out of the barn. Each step punctuated the silence of the night, reminding her that she was breaking an unlimited number of school rules.

She glanced at her watch and saw that she had taken a full fifteen minutes since leaving the dorm. Lani, Wei Lin, Lynsey, and Patience were all waiting by the arena gate, and Morello pricked his ears when he saw them. *Please don't call out to them*, Dylan thought frantically, covering his nose.

She halted him outside the gate and checked her girth before swinging onto his back. Instinctively, she gave him a pat.

"Go easy," Lani told her, sounding serious for once. "If you don't think it's safe to jump, then pull up." The moonlight made her face look ghostly as she stood back for Dylan to enter the arena.

Dylan squeezed the gelding closer to the jumps, giving him a chance to get a good sense of his surroundings. It didn't take long for her to realize that, even with the moon, she couldn't see clearly enough to jump Morello safely. "We need more light," she whispered, turning Morello back to face the group.

"You wouldn't be trying to back out on your dare, would you?" Lynsey said, her voice uncomfortably loud.

"Of course not!" Dylan snapped. "I don't want to risk hurting Morello."

"I think we should go get the forklift from the barn, drive it down here and shine the headlights on the jumps," Lani said.

Lynsey tossed her head. "If you want us all to get caught, why don't you just turn on the floodlights and use the loudspeaker to announce what Dylan's doing?"

"I was making a joke," Lani said defiantly.

"What if we just went back to the dorm to get more flashlights?" Patience suggested.

"You know, you guys, if we get away with this, it will be an absolute miracle," Wei Lin whispered, her eyes glinting like a cat's in the half-light.

"Well, if it's the only way she's going to do it . . ." Lynsey asserted. She was just short of accusing Dylan of fabricating unreasonable excuses to shirk her dare.

"We won't be long," Wei Lin promised over her shoulder as the girls hurried back toward the dorm, quickly vanishing into the shadows.

Dylan nudged Morello to walk around the ring so he wouldn't get antsy. Her teeth were chattering, but she had the suspicion that it was from her nerves rather than the damp autumn night. Still, she had only stopped long enough to pull her jods on, and her fitted pajama top was a thin layer against the chill. As she walked, she reconsidered the situation. She was insane to have agreed to this. Riding without a trainer and without permission was one thing — riding without light was suicidal.

She leaned forward and slipped her arms around Morello's warm neck. "I'm so sorry, boy," she murmured into his mane. "Please help me get us through this, and I promise I'll never do anything so stupid again."

Morello's ear flickered back and he snorted, his breath making clouds that faded into the black night.

When Dylan caught sight of three flashlights bobbing toward the arena, she straightened up and shortened her reins. Her heart was pounding so hard that the sound filled her ears, and she felt nauseous as she pushed Morello into a trot.

Lynsey, Patience, Lani, and Wei Lin stood by the fence and aimed their flashlights at the red-and-white parallel bars of the first jump. The beams illuminated the area surrounding the fence, giving Dylan added confidence. She could do this. She nudged Morello with her heel, and he eased into an even, lively canter. Dylan sat back and tried to settle in with his rhythm. As she turned Morello toward the fence, his ears pricked and he sprang forward. Morello didn't falter as he gathered himself and took the jump with an eager leap. Dylan's heart surged with love for the brave pony. He was so willing and generous, despite the odd circumstances. She knew Morello would show them all.

They landed smoothly, and Dylan was sure she heard Lani give a hushed cheer as she turned Morello toward the next jump, which was five strides away.

Suddenly, the lights all veered from the pony's path and the ring was absorbed by darkness. Dylan pulled hard on the reins as the jump disappeared before her. Morello skidded to a halt, and she waited for her eyes to adjust.

"Dylan Walsh! Get off that pony — immediately!"

Dylan forced some cereal into her mouth and tried to concentrate on chewing. As soon as breakfast was over, she was headed for Dr. Starling's office. Dylan was certain that a nine o'clock appointment on a Saturday wasn't the best way to formally meet your principal. The cafeteria was almost deserted since most of the other girls were enjoying the chance to sleep in. There was a selection of cereal and fruit for students who were up early for approved extracurricular activities. Somehow, Dylan knew midnight jumping courses were not on the list.

Both her aunt and Mrs. Herson had been furious. They had shown up at the arena at the same time. Once Ali had ordered Dylan off Morello, Mrs. Herson marched her and the others back to the dorm. She had had few words for Dylan, but she made it clear that she would be expected outside the principal's office at nine sharp.

Dylan had hardly slept all night.

She didn't notice Lynsey and Patience sitting down next to her until Lynsey bent her head close to Dylan's and whispered, "Thanks for not saying that I dared you to ride Morello."

Dylan looked up from her bowl. "Aren't you guys up kind of early for a Saturday?"

"Are you kidding? We couldn't let you be on your own after what happened last night," Lynsey said. "So, what did Mrs. Herson say? Do you have to meet with Dr. Starling?"

"Right after I've eaten this." Dylan nodded at her cereal.

"Are you going to tell her everything that happened last night?" Patience asked, drawing a circle on the table with her finger.

Dylan shrugged. "You mean about the game? I can't see the point in getting anyone else busted."

"Dylan, I feel really bad," Lynsey said, pressing her hands against her cheeks. "I didn't really think about what would happen if you took me up on that stupid dare. I never thought you'd do it."

"Well, I proved you wrong," Dylan said with little satisfaction. She knew Lynsey and Patience were there to convince her not to turn them in, and it would probably work. She wondered if she would get any leniency if she told the whole truth. "Besides, you didn't make me do it.

It was my decision. I rode Morello without permission, so I'm the one who should pay for it." Dylan knew it was true. She had no one to blame but herself. She was the one who couldn't stand up to Lynsey. She was the one who did not want to back down on a dare.

"I just hope you don't end up being expelled. We'd really miss you — wouldn't we?" Lynsey looked at Patience, who nodded.

Dylan shoved her bowl away, knowing she couldn't eat a bite more. Already, her stomach was churning with nerves. She forced herself to smile at her table companions. "Well, if my only punishment is cleaning the student center bathrooms for three weeks, I'll give you both some Lysol and assign you a stall," she said, standing up.

"Good luck," Lynsey and Patience called after her. But Dylan didn't look back. The inside of her mouth was totally dry and the churning in her gut felt like it was steadily expanding to the rest of her body. At that point, she would be willing to clean all the bathrooms on campus for the remainder of the year if she could somehow avoid getting expelled from Chestnut Hill.

⌬

Dylan waited in the seating area outside Dr. Starling's office, staring at the plaid of her uniform skirt. She decided that was far more comforting than looking at the portraits of past principals that were hanging on the walls, their eyes looking down on her in dismay.

And Mrs. Danby, the principal's assistant, was giving off judgmental vibes as well. She sat behind her desk, reading, but Dylan noted that she hadn't spoken a word to her except when she directed her to sit down and wait. Dylan wondered if the administrative staff always worked on Saturday mornings.

Folding her hands in her lap, she ran her eyes over the books on the oak shelves. It was a pretty impressive collection, with Shakespeare's complete works, Tolstoy's *War and Peace*, Tolkien's *The Hobbit*, and various poetry anthologies lining the top row. Before Dylan had the chance to scan other shelves or wonder who actually read these books, the door to Dr. Starling's room clicked open and Dylan's housemother came out. Dylan swallowed. She'd never have guessed that Mrs. Herson's brown eyes could look so expressionless, so cold.

"You can come in now," Mrs. Herson said.

Dylan trailed after her into a beautiful, wood-paneled room that was flooded with morning sunlight. The principal waved her hand for Dylan to enter. There were three chairs in front of Dr. Starling's desk; her aunt was sitting in one, but she didn't turn her head as Dylan stepped forward. Dylan hovered uncertainly, not knowing if she should sit or stay standing.

"Sit down, Dylan," Dr. Starling said.

Dylan sat on the edge of the empty chair in between Mrs. Herson and Ali. She felt more and more anxious as Dr. Starling closed a blue file on her desk and stood up to put it away in a cabinet. She wouldn't have bet in a million years that, only three weeks into the semester, she would have been sitting here in the principal's office. Dylan looked out of the huge windows, which were framed by long cream drapes. She wished with all her heart that she was outside, riding over the distant hills, miles away from all this trouble. Her eyes wandered to a beautiful framed charcoal sketch of a horse's head that hung over the mantelpiece just behind the desk. Dylan wondered if that was Dr. Starling's horse. Everyone knew that the principal was a dedicated horsewoman who took personal pride in the success of Chestnut Hill's program. Dr. Starling certainly wouldn't have ridden a horse over a course of fences in the middle of the night. Who would do that? Dylan felt she could no longer relate to the person who had made that steady string of bad decisions the night before. What had she been thinking?

The sound of the filing cabinet closing startled her, and she looked up nervously as the principal lowered herself into her high-backed chair. "I'm going to cut to the chase with you, Dylan," she said, picking up her pen and holding it at both ends. "We're all incredibly disappointed in your actions last night."

Dylan's chest felt hollow, as if she could hardly get a

breath. She bowed her head, feeling her cheeks burn with shame.

"It wasn't just that you broke school rules," Dr. Starling continued without raising her voice. "You broke something far more valuable." Dylan glanced up, concerned that something awful had happened to Morello after all. "You broke the bond of trust that is given to every girl at Chestnut Hill," Dr. Starling carried on, her gray eyes fixed on Dylan. "And once that trust is broken, it is my decision whether it can be granted a second time."

Dylan's heart began to race. *Well, that's it*, she thought frantically. *This is the moment when I get kicked out of boarding school for playing truth-or-dare*. What would her parents say? Considering how hard her aunt had been on her this semester, she wouldn't have been surprised if Ali had already called them with the stellar news.

"I've spoken with Ms. Carmichael and Mrs. Herson." Dr. Starling glanced at them both. "They have given you excellent references and neither can understand why you pulled that stunt last night or what might have made you think it was a good idea. Really, Dylan, jumping in the dark is not something an intelligent or rational student would do." She paused, and it was clear she was waiting for Dylan to offer an explanation — some proof that she was either intelligent or rational.

Dylan twisted her hands in her lap. This was about the worst she had ever felt, and there was no way she was going to put anyone else through this interrogation. Of course, it was tempting to admit that she hadn't dreamed up the insane scheme on her own, but she knew she had to take the full blame. "It was all my fault," she said. "I totally messed up, and all I can say is that I'm really sorry." This time she didn't look away from Dr. Starling's piercing gaze. This was her plea, short but sincere.

"You should know, Dylan, that Ms. Carmichael has spoken quite passionately in your defense. She explained that you spent quite some time riding Morello this summer and that you formed a real bond with him. She feels this is one of the reasons that you acted the way you did. She also feels you wouldn't have taken any of the other horses here and ridden them without permission, unsupervised, and at such an hour."

Dylan felt a surge of gratitude toward her aunt. She had not expected Ali to take her side, but what she had said was true.

"Nevertheless, this doesn't take away from the fact that what you did wasn't just breaking the rules, it was downright dangerous." Dr. Starling began tapping the desk with her pen. "I've checked your references from your old school and they describe you as a mature, conscientious student, and Mrs. Herson echoes that. And it's because of this that I've decided to give you one more chance to prove yourself."

Dylan sat expressionless and let the words sink in,

feeling a small seed of hope start to swell in her chest. Then, all at once, she thought she would yelp for joy.

But Dr. Starling was still looking at her seriously, and Dylan was determined to prove her dedication by giving the principal her full attention. "That said, I'm sure you understand that you still have to be punished for what you did last night. Nothing so drastic can go undisciplined. After discussing the situation with Ms. Carmichael and Mrs. Herson, I've decided that you should complete a week of afternoon and evening detentions." She paused and leaned forward, pressing her fingertips together. "And no riding for two weeks, starting today."

CHAPTER TEN

Dylan felt as if an electric shock had just jolted through her body. She stood up, her heart pounding. "No riding for two weeks? What about the tryouts?"

"Dylan, sit down!" Ali Carmichael said sharply, to remind her that she was in the principal's office and should show some respect.

"But the tryouts," Dylan protested. "Please! Getting onto the junior team is all I care about."

"Now, Dylan," Mrs. Herson warned. "Surely your commitment to Chestnut Hill goes beyond the riding team."

Dylan slumped back into her chair. *This is a total nightmare*, she thought. She stared at the blue carpet until it began to blur. *Except it is worse than anything my subconscious could create.* She wrapped her arms around her stomach, swallowing her feeling of nausea. She glanced up, and her eyes fell on the school motto mounted on a gold plaque on Dr. Starling's desk. *Veritas, Sapientia,*

Fides. It was Latin for Truth, Wisdom, Loyalty. She shook her head. *Yeah, right.* If she'd had a little more wisdom last night, then she would have chosen truth instead of dare, and she wouldn't be in this trouble now. And no matter what she had said to Lynsey earlier, Dylan didn't think the nature of her roommate's dare had shown much loyalty, either.

Ali Carmichael cleared her throat. "What you have to understand is that both you and Morello were very lucky not to have had a serious accident with that stunt you pulled last night. I asked you to stop jumping Morello in your lesson yesterday because he had already completed a class. You didn't seem to have trouble putting his needs first then. No one is impressed by a show-off. And I, personally, cannot tolerate one, especially when she endangers the safety of one of my horses."

Dylan's fingers tightened. It hadn't been like that at all! She bit down hard on her lip, knowing that if she talked back, her relatively tame punishment might be exchanged for a much more severe one. She concentrated instead on the thought that, even with the two-week ban, she would still have a short window of time to get ready for the tryouts.

🐾

Dylan left Dr. Starling's office feeling lost. She was longing to go down to the stables to give Morello a huge hug and make sure that he was okay after she'd dragged him out in the middle of the night. But she wasn't allowed to go to the stables while she was in detention. The idea of going a whole Saturday without being able to hang out on the yard was totally unthinkable. For once, Dylan wished her dorm weren't so tantalizingly close to the stables.

"Dylan!" Lynsey was peering around the corner of the first-floor hallway of Adams, waving her fingers.

Dylan made her way over. The way Lynsey was acting, she looked like she was trying out for a role in the latest Bond movie.

"What's with all the secrecy?" she asked.

"Come on, Dylan," Patience said. "What did Starling say? Are we all busted?"

"I told you I wasn't going to get anyone else in trouble," Dylan said scornfully. Then she looked at them questioningly. "I am kind of surprised that I'm the only one who has to go see her. I mean, I wasn't going to say anything, but Mrs. Herson knows I wasn't the only one down at the ring. . . . Granted, I was the only one cantering over verticals."

"Maybe we'll get called in later," Lynsey interrupted, taking Dylan's arm and pulling her across the foyer. "Come on, you have to tell us what happened. Everyone's waiting!"

🐎

Wei Lin and Razina abandoned their game of chess when Dylan and Lynsey walked into the sitting room. "Over here." Lani waved, pulling out her iPod earphones. She patted the sofa beside her.

Alexandra closed her book and put it down on the table. It was one of their assigned titles, *The Color Purple*. "How did it go?"

"It could have been worse, I guess," Dylan said, sitting next to Lani and tucking her feet up. "I didn't get expelled, at least."

"So, what did you get?" Lynsey asked, her voice loaded with sympathy as she sat down on the opposite sofa. Patience and Honey switched off MTV-2 on the plasma screen and came across to listen.

Dylan noticed that Malory wasn't around, but apart from that, it seemed everyone had hung around to see her. "I never thought last night would turn me into a celebrity!" she joked. "But I guess it's more like being on the cover of *National Enquirer* than *Vogue*."

"Come on, tell us what happened," Wei Lin said.

"I have a week of afternoon and evening detention," Dylan announced. "And I've been banned from riding for two weeks."

Lani gasped. "You must be freaking out!"

"Pretty much," Dylan admitted.

"Wow, that doesn't leave you much time. Tryouts are

the week after," Lynsey murmured. "Dylan, I'm sorry I gave you that stupid dare. I was originally going to make you eat three of those smashed cupcakes."

"Yeah, were you going to lace them with arsenic?" Lani asked drily, and Lynsey shot back a look of genuine hurt.

"What gets me is that nobody else has been busted. There were four of you who were out after curfew," Razina said, frowning.

Lynsey shrugged. "I guess Mrs. Herson thought we were out looking for Dylan."

Razina stared at her. "You think? Lani said you were essentially lighting the course. Sounds like conspiracy to me."

"Maybe they wanted to limit the number of Saturday appointments," Wei Lin suggested. "I'm not sure we're in the clear."

"Well, I'd like to know who snitched," Lani said, looking around. "It was a pretty lousy thing to do, whoever it was."

"What makes you so sure that someone told on her?" Patience demanded.

"Oh, come on! Like Hersie woke up in the middle of the night, decided to check Dylan's room. Then, when she wasn't there, woke up Ms. Carmichael and they knew to look in the jumping arena. If you believe that, I have to wonder how you passed the tests to get into this school," Lani said, her tone short and harsh. "It doesn't take much to figure it out."

"It was a dumb idea from the start. You're all lucky that nobody got hurt," said a new voice.

Dylan had been so caught up in what Lani was saying that she hadn't seen Malory come into the room.

She stared at her, and Malory met her gaze head-on. "I hope you realize how stupid it was trying to jump Morello in the middle of the night, now," she went on, refusing to drop her glare.

Dylan narrowed her eyes. Everyone in the room understood that it was stupid now. Why did Malory feel the need to point it out? Dylan had a sudden suspicion that the snitch was standing in front of her. "Was that what you said to Mrs. Herson? 'Dylan had this dumb idea to jump Morello in the middle of the night. Go and see for yourself!'"

"Dylan," Razina said in a cautionary tone.

"At least with Mrs. Herson finding out, Morello didn't get hurt, crashing into a fence that he couldn't even see," Malory said, crossing her arms.

"I can't believe you!" Dylan snapped, getting to her feet. "Do you always have to be right? From the start of semester, you've acted like you're better than the rest of us. You'd rather clean tack than watch movies, you sit out truth-or-dare. Does winning the Rockwell Award make you too good to be one of us?"

Malory's cheeks drained, and her blue eyes were bright with moisture. Without saying another word, she spun on her heel and walked out of the room, banging the door.

"Well." Lynsey broke the silence. "I'm glad you weren't expelled, Dylan. I don't know what we'd have done for entertainment without you around."

Later that evening, Dylan wandered down to the lake and pulled out her cell phone to call Nat. She gazed across the silvery water while the phone rang, watching the pale sunlight dance across the surface. Tiny dragon-flies flitted just above the water, disappearing when two swans left the sloping lawn to glide into the shallows.

With each unanswered ring, Dylan felt a deeper pang of rejection. She had already called her parents and tried to explain her side of the story. She didn't want them to find out that she was an irrational show-off from anyone else — particularly if that someone was Ali Carmichael. Not surprisingly, Dylan's dad was disappointed. Dylan was certain he had read in some psychology book that being "disappointed" with your child made much more of an impression than being angry, and he was right. It had been awful telling him, but, after Dylan had sput-tered out all the details, he seemed to understand the circumstances that had led to her "unacceptably impul-sive behavior," to use his exact words. Her mom, however, declared that she wanted Dylan to report all of the other girls who played truth-or-dare. It had taken both Dylan and her dad to convince Mrs. Walsh that it was in her daughter's best interest to refrain from telling Dr. Starling of the other students' involvement.

Dylan really needed to talk to someone who knew her well — someone who wasn't investing in her private school education. She could call one of her friends from home, but she had decided her best bet was to dial Nat. Just as she was about to hang up, Dylan heard a click.

"Hey, what's going on?" Nat asked.

"Um, not much," Dylan responded, knowing that any other Saturday she would be far too busy to call him. She'd either have gone into town with friends or be hanging out in the stable, but she was currently suspended from both activities.

"Huh." Nat sounded distracted. "Do you want me to believe that? Or do you want to talk about it?"

"Don't tell me you already know," Dylan said to her cousin. She plucked a blade of fresh-cut grass from the lawn and started to pull it apart along one of its seams.

"I could lie to you," he said dryly. "Would that help?"

"Nat! Do you have to be such a jerk?" Dylan heard an elongated sigh from the other end of the line. She hated when her cousin played coy.

"No, I guess not," he replied with another sigh. "Okay, I have to be honest with you, Dylan. I heard my mom's version of the story at three o'clock this morning. She was really worried, wondering if she would get fired. She said she knew she had been hard on you over the past weeks because she knows how good you are, and she wondered if you were trying to get back at her. She wouldn't normally call me about something like that, but she thought I might have some clue what was going on with you. I didn't. I couldn't think of a single thing that would make you do what you did."

Dylan was struck silent. Nat was the last person she had expected to give her a lecture. She had heard her parents talk about some of the things he had gotten into with his friends from Kentucky, but he obviously saw the situation with Dylan differently. He had been very protective of his mom since she and his dad had gotten divorced. Dylan guessed he couldn't see her dare as just another petty prank because he was so concerned about how it would affect his mom.

"Well, that's how I found out," Nat continued. "I guess it's only fair to hear your side, too."

Dylan hesitated, not certain she should unload anything else on her cousin. Still, she wanted him to know that it wasn't some master plan that she had engineered — and she certainly hadn't meant to get Ali in trouble. "It was so stupid," she began, being careful not to mention any names. "I have been frustrated with Aunt Ali, but that's not what it was about." She knew Nat wouldn't say anything to his mom, but she wanted to minimize the social damage. It was her tale to tell, and she did just that, recounting every sorry scene.

"Well," Nat said when Dylan finished, "that does sound stupid."

"Thanks a lot," Dylan replied, but she could tell that Nat's tone wasn't incriminating. He now sounded like he was in on the joke, willing to laugh at Dylan's predicament rather than judge her for it.

"I totally get how you were pulled in, though. An outright dare is hard to resist," Nat sympathized. "And now you're on detention duty for a week?"

"Yeah, and no riding until the week of tryouts."

"That bites. I'm sorry. Do you want to try to meet up next Saturday? You'll be stir crazy by then. Maybe we can see a movie to keep your mind off everything?"

"That would be great, Nat. Thanks." Dylan was relieved that he understood after all. Seeing him would be something to look forward to as she sat through the endless days of detention. After she hung up, she tossed a pebble into the lake, watching the ripples spreading out on top of the surface. She couldn't help but think of the night before, and how one bad decision had caused so many aftershocks. Deep down, she knew she was lucky to have gotten off with just a two-week ban. It could have been much, much worse. But, still, she couldn't wait for all this to be over and things to return to normal.

❧

B<small>Y</small> Wednesday, Dylan was all caught up in her classes. Sitting alone in a room left her little to do other than homework and reading. If it weren't for the staff monitor who checked in at random intervals, Dylan would have been IMing everyone in her address book, but she didn't want to get caught and get her sentence doubled. The worst part was that she was in Room Eleven of the liberal arts hall — the room that looked directly at the back of the stables. Dylan could see the length of the closest barn as well as the muck heap, but she couldn't catch a glimpse of the paddocks or the riding arena from any desk — and not for lack of trying.

The first half of the week had been even longer than she had anticipated. After her sitting-room reception on Saturday, not that many people had talked with her. Dylan didn't think that they were trying to ignore her. It was more like they didn't have anything to say — not even Honey and Lani. She had overheard several conversations about the courses Ali had set up for the intermediates, but the discussion had drawn to a quick close as soon as Dylan came near.

As for Malory, she was nowhere in sight. *She's probably busy shaking out every single saddle pad in the stable or picking lint off of Ali's hard hat*, Dylan thought. But even as she lingered on the thought, trying to get satisfaction from her momentary cruelty, Dylan felt a pang of disenchantment. She had really liked Malory at the start. Sure, the other girl had seemed closed off about her personal life, but she was still fun. Dylan pictured Malory crawling along the paddock ground, trying to tempt Nutmeg into letting her put the halter on. That day had felt so new, so full of possibilities. So how did Dylan find her way to Room Eleven and a permanent record?

All she could do was to check the syllabus of every class and do her best to get ahead. Then, as soon as she was able to get back in the saddle again, she could concentrate fully on the tryouts and not let coursework get in the way. That was her best chance, maybe her only one.

Dylan pressed her forehead against the van window. After a week of double detention, she felt like she had been in an isolation chamber! She was just relieved to be looking out the window and seeing something besides a manure pile. She'd be happy if she never set foot in Room Eleven again. *Still*, she thought, watching the cars on the opposite side of the road zip by, *at least Lynsey's been pretty cool through all this*. That's a huge improvement. She glanced down at the silky oyster-colored Versace T-shirt her roommate had loaned her for the trip into town. The term "T-shirt" hardly did this garment justice. It had gold embroidered detailing around the collar and cap sleeves and asymmetrical pleats down the front. Lynsey had insisted Dylan borrow something festive to celebrate her halfway mark to freedom — one more week and she'd have full riding privileges again. Dylan smoothed the supple fabric. The shirt was brand-new. Lynsey had cut the tags off before handing it over. All week it had felt as if Lynsey was trying to make up for giving Dylan the dare in the first place. She had even agreed to take carrots to Morello! Dylan was starting to think she'd gotten Lynsey all wrong. She was showing potential for being a good friend after all.

Lynsey's attitude adjustment was good news, but what made Dylan truly happy was Morello.

She smiled, remembering that morning. Before breakfast, she had raced down to the stable to see him, and he had greeted her with an exuberant whinny. It seemed his loyalties were still firmly with Dylan despite Lynsey's carrot offerings. Having to tell Morello that she still couldn't ride nearly broke her heart, but she was glad that she was no longer banned from the barn.

"Do you guys want to come bowling with us later?" Lynsey turned around in the seat she was sharing with Patience.

"Thanks, but I don't think we'll have time to do that and still catch a movie," Dylan replied. She glanced over at Honey and smiled. The school rule was that they could only go into town in groups of three or more, and Honey was part of Lynsey's crew. Dylan was relieved when Razina and Wei Lin had been game to hang out with her and meet up with Nat because they had wanted to catch a movie themselves.

"Okay." Lynsey shrugged. "If you change your mind, call my cell."

The van stopped outside Starbucks, at the far end of the sprawling outdoor mall. Before Dylan even stepped onto the sidewalk, the rich smell of coffee mixed with baked goods hit her, making her mouth water. *First stop, coffee and calories,* she thought, taking in another breath of autumn air. "Hey, can you guys handle a caffeine jolt?" she asked Wei Lin and Razina.

"Are you kidding? I can't remember the last time I had a decent latte." Razina laughed.

"It wouldn't happen to have been at a certain coffee shop in New York?" Dylan teased, remembering Razina's confession about her date at the end of the summer. She grinned at Wei Lin as Razina headed toward the shop, struggling to suppress a smile.

Inside, a long line snaked past the glass display counter toward the back of the café. "Why don't you two grab those seats while I get in line?" Wei Lin suggested.

"You don't mind?" Razina hesitated.

"Go!" Wei Lin flapped her hand.

Dylan quickly gave Wei Lin her order and rushed after Razina.

"You wanted a large green tea, right?" Dylan playfully asked Razina as soon as they were settled on their stools.

"What? Tea? No, I wanted a latte," Razina announced, making a move to storm Wei Lin in line. Dylan broke out in laughter. Razina was very confident and bordered on being too serious, so Dylan took special pleasure in teasing her. Razina's jaw dropped when she realized Dylan had tricked her again.

"Really," Dylan declared, "for someone so smart, you fall for a lot of stupid jokes."

"Thanks, Dylan," Razina said, tossing her braids so they fell evenly down her back. "For someone so smart, you pull a lot of dumb pranks."

While Dylan took Razina's jab as an offhand compliment, she also assumed the girl had been referring to the truth-or-dare debacle. It would be a long time before she lived that down.

All of a sudden, Razina's eyes widened with alarm as she looked over Dylan's shoulder. "Watch out!" she warned.

"You'll have to try harder than that," Dylan grinned, unwilling to fall for such an obvious trick. But a moment later, she wished she hadn't laughed off Razina's warning.

She suddenly felt a freezing sensation ooze through her T-shirt — correction, Lynsey's T-shirt. Dylan looked down, catching her breath in horror as she watched half-melted chocolate ice-cream drip down Lynsey's new Versace top.

"Oh, I'm so sorry!" the woman behind her said.

Dylan spun around to see a toddler waving an empty ice-cream cone in the air. A pair of blue eyes twinkled in a face that was almost completely covered in sticky chocolate. When the child realized her dessert was on the floor, she started to cry.

"Don't worry about it," Dylan said, trying to camouflage her frustration. She held up her hands in an attempt to stave off the woman, who looked as if she was about to attack Dylan with a tub of baby wipes. "These things happen, I guess." The words stuck in her throat as she pictured Lynsey's face when she returned her chocolate-stained top. She turned back to Razina, who was staring in horror at what had been a very stylish, very expensive shirt. "Any ideas on how to get ice cream out of Versace?"

"Sure. Put it in the trash and buy a new one on eBay," Razina said, dabbing at the huge dark stain with a napkin. "I don't think this is going to come out. Sorry."

"It's Lynsey's," Dylan told her. "I bet she's going to have a thing or two to say about it."

"When doesn't she?" Razina said, quitting her efforts and wiping her own hands with a napkin.

Dylan was surprised by Razina's comment. She had always thought that both Razina and Wei Lin liked Lynsey. They seemed to be two of the lucky few to have earned Lynsey's approval. "Actually she's been cool recently," Dylan pointed out charitably, realizing both Lynsey and Patience had been more supportive than anyone else that week.

"It's about time!" Razina's eyebrows shot up. "Lynsey's got enough nerve for our whole class. I'm surprised you're putting up with her at all."

"What?" Dylan felt confused. She looked over to see how Wei Lin was doing. She was still third in line. It looked like the guy at the counter was ordering for four tables.

"I don't think I'd be as forgiving if she'd gotten me a week of detentions and a riding ban," Razina said, pulling off her graphite-beaded cardigan and draping it over the back of her stool.

Dylan frowned. She hadn't counted on discussing conspiracy theories with Razina. "But that was Malory," she insisted.

"Really?" Razina looked doubtful. "I'm not so sure. Think about it. Lynsey was the one who gave you the dare in the first place. And I know Malory wasn't exactly encouraging you to take the bet, but she still doesn't seem like she'd rat you out. It's not her style."

Dylan stared out of the window at the crowded mall, not really seeing the shoppers as she turned Razina's words over in her head. "Malory as good as admitted that *she* did it," she protested.

"From where I was sitting, you told her she was a snitch and she didn't say she was or wasn't," Razina said quietly.

Dylan started shredding a paper napkin as her conscience began to nag at her. Razina was right about Malory not seeming the type to tattle.

Razina shrugged. "I could be wrong about it being Lynsey, but I'd bet my Gucci cocktail dress it wasn't Malory."

Dylan felt like her insides were going through a wringer. Could it have been Lynsey? She kept on trying to push the thought away, but each time she did, it came back stronger. And to think she'd actually been grateful for Lynsey's gestures that week. *Grateful! Hah!* Lynsey must have been rolling with laughter behind her back.

Dylan didn't like to feel gullible. Her fingers worked through the napkin until she had built a small mountain of shredded paper on the counter. "I just don't get why she'd do it," she said, trying to get a grip on the red-hot anger rising inside.

Razina shrugged. "I wondered that. I mean, I know the two of you haven't exactly been kindred spirits. . . ."

Dylan looked long and hard at Razina. She thought that Razina was the only person who would describe her relationship with Lynsey that way. Everyone knew they struggled to be civil. Dylan wasn't sure why. It just seemed like it was easier to exchange snarky insults than say nothing at all. Dylan glanced down and screwed the napkin shreds into a ball. But it wasn't just that she hadn't bonded with Lynsey. She wasn't best friends yet with anyone in her class, even though she liked them all. Almost all, she corrected herself.

"Maybe she figured if you got busted you wouldn't be allowed to try out for the team," Razina said, jumping down from her stool to help Wei Lin, who was making her way toward them balancing a tray full of steaming cups and pastries. "You could even take it as a kind of compliment, I guess, if she felt threatened. I can't explain it, but I'm suspicious. I wouldn't put it past her."

In the back of her mind, Dylan thought that Lynsey was far too secure in her riding abilities to try to pick off competitors, but Dylan was too frustrated to think straight. She might not have a plan, but she wasn't going to let Lynsey believe she had gotten the best of Dylan Walsh.

CHAPTER ELEVEN

Dylan was still fuming as she walked to the movie theater with Razina and Wei Lin. The more she thought about everything Razina had said, the more she suspected Lynsey was the one who had stabbed her in the back. *But if it was Lynsey, she didn't get what she really wanted — I'm still allowed to compete in the tryouts.*

At the theater, she scanned the crowd for Nat. Finally she saw him standing near a small group close to the entrance. His red hair made him easy to find. Dylan recognized one of the two boys with Nat. It was Caleb, the cute guy who had been checking out Malory at the symposium. She hurried forward, anxious to tell Nat everything Razina had said and get his take, but she stopped abruptly. Straight ahead was the one person Dylan least wanted to see.

"Oh, great," she muttered, her defenses going into

overdrive. She started to button up her green suede jacket. She wanted to at least try to clean the T-shirt before Lynsey saw it.

"What's up?" Wei Lin asked. "Isn't your cousin here?"

"He's over there." Dylan pointed to the bench underneath one of the coming-attraction posters. "But I need to make a call before I go into the movie."

"That's cool. We'll go get the tickets," Razina said.

"Great. Thanks, guys," Dylan said. She wondered if there was any way to get through to Nat and tell him she couldn't handle sitting through the movie if Lynsey was going to tag along.

"Oh, hi, Dylan," Lynsey called, spotting her before Dylan could get Nat's attention. Dylan could not believe her luck. There was a massive swarm of people in front of the theater. How had Lynsey noticed her? Dylan blamed her own red hair as she made her way through the crowd.

"I hope you don't mind us crashing, but we figured a movie sounded more fun than bowling," Lynsey explained, acting as the designated spokesperson for Patience and Honey as well.

Dylan wondered if her disappointment was obvious because, when Nat's eyes met hers, there seemed to be a hint of apology in them. "Dylan, this is Josh and Caleb." He introduced the two boys with him. Both had thick, short hair, but where Caleb's was dark, Josh's was a pale blond. "They heard I was planning to go to the movies today and begged me to let them tag along."

"What he really means is that he doesn't have any friends, so he paid us to look like we want to hang with him." Josh's green eyes crinkled at the corners. Dylan knew Saint Kit's had the same rule for a minimum of three students leaving campus when not accompanied by an adult.

"Hey, Dylan. You're not here on your own, are you?" Patience asked, stepping back to look for Dylan's off-campus companions.

"You know you'd get kicked out of school for sure if you got caught breaking rules a second time," Lynsey added. She smiled at Nat. "Dylan's on her best behavior at the moment."

"Really?" Nat raised his eyebrows at Dylan. "That sounds difficult for you."

"Well, you know me," Dylan told him, praying that he'd figure out what she was trying to do. "I took on this dumb dare to jump a pony at night, and I got caught. You know, misuse of school property and all."

"Whoa! Nat, does delinquency run in the family? We could do with a little more action at Saint Kit's," Caleb said, trying to ease the awkwardness after Dylan's confession.

Patience looked straight at the cute dark-haired boy. "I can't believe it's dull with you guys there."

Come on, Dylan thought. *Could Patience be any more obvious?*

"How'd you get busted?" Josh asked, feeding Dylan the perfect line.

"You know, I can't quite figure it out," she said. "I thought that our housemother had checked on us and seen our empty beds, but that doesn't really make any sense."

"What makes you say that?" Nat said helpfully.

"Because I wasn't the only one who went down to the ring. Lynsey and Patience were there, too," Dylan explained, looking her classmates in the eye. "There were five of us in all. Anyway, the weirdest thing was that it wasn't even our housemother who showed up first. It was the riding instructor," she continued with the boys' full attention, "and the other really weird thing was, before the instructor even got to the ring, before she could have seen who was riding, she yelled my name."

"Dude, you were set up!" Josh exclaimed. "That sucks."

"Sure sounds like it," Caleb agreed. "Do you know who turned you in?"

"She doesn't know," Lynsey blurted. "The instructor must have assumed it was Dylan because she was on the stable's only painted pony, which Dylan *loves* for some reason."

Just then, Honey clicked her cell phone closed and walked over to the group. "Sorry about that. Hey, Dylan," she said, smiling. But the atmosphere was crackling with negative vibes, and her smile quickly faded to a puzzled frown.

"That's a good point," Nat added, always wanting to consider all the possibilities. "A paint might show up in the dark."

"That sounds too convenient. I think that instructor knew exactly who was in the ring," Caleb offered.

"Well," Dylan said with a sigh, "I'm going to try not to think about it. It isn't something you'd expect one of your friends to do."

"Some friend," Josh said, his voice heavy with irony.

"Yeah, that's low. So, do you know who it was?" Caleb ran his hand through his thick dark hair, and Patience's eyes widened so far that Dylan thought the rest of her face would disappear.

"I have some ideas," Dylan replied, "but I don't want to be a snitch, too."

"I don't understand," Honey ventured. Dylan looked at Honey's uncertain expression and felt bad for bringing her into this.

"I agree. Who would want to get you in trouble?" Lynsey absentmindedly pushed her purse up on her shoulder. "Besides, you only have a week left and you'll be riding again. What's important is that you weren't expelled."

Dylan thought Lynsey's comment sounded defensive.

"That's true. I'll be back in the saddle just in time for tryouts," she confirmed. "I know how worried you were about my missing them."

Lynsey's cheeks went pink under her Bobbi Brown blush. "You know, I've seen this movie already, so I think we'll go bowling after all," she said, brushing an imaginary piece of dust off her velveteen jacket. "Come on," she said to Patience and Honey, not waiting for them as she stalked off.

Honey stared after Lynsey, looking completely baffled. Patience bit down on her lip, clearly reluctant to lose her chance to be with Caleb. She glared at Dylan, "What's the deal? Sometimes I wonder why Lynsey bothers being so nice to you."

She turned on her heel and hurried after her friend.

"Well, I guess I'll see you back at the van," Honey shrugged, turning to catch up with Lynsey and Patience, who were walking with their heads close together, deep in conversation.

Nat waited for Honey to get out of earshot and then looked at Dylan, his amber eyes dancing. "I don't remember telling her what movie we were going to see."

"Oh, that's too bad," Dylan dramatized. "I was so looking forward to spending more time with her."

☙

Dylan stared down at the hot plates. "I've died and gone to heaven," she murmured to Honey. On Sundays the girls had brunch instead of a separate breakfast and lunch, and Dylan hadn't been too thrilled to be losing one meal out of a day at first. But now she was a convert. Hash browns, grits, tomatoes, sausages, bacon, scrambled eggs with smoked salmon, cereal, toast, muffins, pancakes, fruit, yogurt. Dylan eyed them all. Her appetite, which had waned after her meeting with Dr. Starling, had returned. In fact, it seemed stronger than ever since she had trumped Lynsey at the mall in front of Nat and his friends.

When she finally finished piling up her plate, Dylan joined Honey and Lynsey at a table by the far windows. It looked out over a grassy slope that ran down to the library and art studios.

"You didn't need to bring breakfast for all three of us," Lynsey remarked, eyeing Dylan's tray. "We've already got ours."

Dylan stared back at Lynsey's tray in amazement. All she had was a bowl of cereal and a small plate of fruit. Dylan thought this was another strike against Lynsey. Who could trust someone who selected cereal and dried fruit when there was a full buffet?

"Prunes?" Dylan asked, trying not to grin.

"Dates," Lynsey snapped.

"So," Honey said, "are you going to see Morello today?"

"Of course," Dylan said enthusiastically. "Just as soon as I make my way through this. It's not often that I get a bigger breakfast than the horses! Anyway, I thought I'd smuggle Morello an apple. I've got to stay on his good side with the tryouts so soon. I'm only going to have a few practices before the big day." She looked at Lynsey, but her roommate did not respond with a tailor-made retort. She just stirred the leftover flakes of Special K around in her bowl.

Dylan scooped up a forkful of eggs. As far as she was concerned, she didn't need to hold any ill will against Lynsey. She felt she had let Lynsey know what she thought of her role in her detention, so they were on even ground again. Lynsey, however, seemed to be brewing a long-standing grudge.

Dylan saw Malory leave the cafeteria, and she swallowed her last mouthful of coffee before hurrying after her. They hadn't talked in over a week, and Dylan knew Malory probably wanted to keep it that way.

"Hey, Mal, wait up!" she called. She wasn't sure if Malory had heard her. Malory kept on walking down the hallway at the same even pace, and Dylan had to run to catch her.

"Mal!" she called out again as she grabbed her arm. "Didn't you hear me?"

Malory pulled her arm out of Dylan's grasp. "Yes. But I didn't think you'd say anything I wanted to hear."

Dylan flinched a little, but knew she deserved it. "Look, I just wanted to say I'm sorry for accusing you of calling Ali. I know it wasn't you."

Malory stared at her for a moment. "There's a surprise. So who was it?"

"I don't know for sure," Dylan admitted. "But I have a pretty good idea. Anyway, I shouldn't have blamed you."

Malory's face darkened. "You know, if you'd apologized before finding out it wasn't me, I'd have listened. But the only reason you're saying sorry is because you think you've found out that someone else turned you in. That doesn't matter to me. I just can't believe you thought that I would have done something like that. What did I ever to do you?"

Dylan's mouth dropped open. She couldn't think of a single thing to say, because she knew that Malory was absolutely right. They had disagreed over the whole Emily and Morello mess, but that felt like nothing now.

"You're just a typical Chestnut Hill girl, Dylan," Malory went on, her voice trembling. "Always thinking that you're better than everyone else, thinking you deserve to be an exception."

"Hey!" Dylan protested feebly.

"Truth hurts, huh?" Malory said before turning away. As she pushed past Dylan, she murmured, "And I thought you might be different."

Dylan stood still and watched Malory head down the hallway, too stunned to try and call her back. She realized the repercussions of truth-or-dare would not be over by the end of her ban. She might never earn back Malory's trust.

❧

"No, no, no! A violin should be played with feeling. You are dragging the bow across the strings as if you're waging a war!" Mr. Highland tapped his baton on Dylan's music stand. "Start again, and this time, think about the emotion in the music."

The emotion in the music? What about the emotion in me? Dylan thought. Usually she enjoyed her private violin lessons — her mother had forced her to pursue something "cultural" and had been ecstatic when Dylan had actually shown some skill. But today the clock hands seemed to be moving in slow motion. It was Monday, the first day she was allowed back in the saddle. As far as Dylan was concerned, every minute away from the stable was a minute wasted.

How could she concentrate on a Schubert waltz when her heart was racing to the *William Tell Overture*? She'd missed Morello like crazy right from the start, but she was now more anxious than ever to ride her best at the tryouts. She and Morello had something to prove — to Lynsey and everyone else. To misquote Mr. Highland, this wasn't just a feeling — it was war! She glanced at her watch for the hundredth time. Just another five minutes until she could grab a sandwich and head down to the yard.

🐎

"Ms. Carmichael," Dylan called to her aunt, who was crossing the yard carrying a grooming kit. "Would it be okay if I groom Morello for this afternoon's lesson?"

"What about your lunch?"

"I already had it," Dylan said, thinking of the half-eaten cheese sandwich that she'd tossed in the trash on the way down to the yard. "I'd just like to spend some extra time with Morello before riding him — you know, bond with him again?"

"I don't think there's much chance he's forgotten you!" Ali Carmichael smiled. "I think he's as keyed up for your return as you are. Go on," she said. "I'm pretty sure Kelly hasn't gotten the chance to groom him yet."

"Sounds good," Dylan said. "Thanks, Ms. Carmichael." Before her aunt could respond, she darted toward the barn. She couldn't wait to get a body brush in her hand and start working it over the paint's satiny coat. She might not have any best friends in her class, but at least she had Morello.

🐎

"Come on, Dylan!" Lani was waiting outside the barn on Colorado. She gave her the thumbs up as Dylan led Morello onto the yard. Dylan had been a little concerned that Lani might have turned against her. She had no idea whether Malory would have told her roommate about their latest argument. But Lani seemed as open and supportive as ever.

While being back in the yard felt like second nature, Dylan had to hop twice before she managed to swing herself up over Morello's back. "Argh." She made a face as the muscles in her thighs protested. "You'd think it was two months since I last did this, not just two weeks."

Lani leaned down to check Colorado's girth. "You're going to be sore tomorrow, that's for sure."

"Thanks for reminding me," Dylan said. "Are there any other words of encouragement you want to share before I head down to the arena?"

"Yeah, eat my dust!" Lani whooped, squeezing Colorado into a trot. His hooves clattered loudly as he passed Morello.

Dylan laughed as she felt Morello pull forward. "It's great to be back," she told the paint gelding, shortening her reins as he followed Colorado.

Down in the ring, Ali Carmichael already had the rest of the group working without their stirrups. "Drop your irons and fall in at the end of the line," she told Dylan and Lani. Dylan crossed her stirrups over Morello's neck, then waited for the group to ride by before joining them.

"Nice to have you back, Dylan," Honey called as she bounced past on Kingfisher. Even though she was one of the smallest seventh-graders, she had the long-legged gelding working really well, with his nose tucked in and his quarters under him. Dylan could tell his gait was a bit rough for a sitting trot, but Honey made it look easy. Dylan felt a warm glow at how good it felt to be back with the group, even if Lynsey and Malory trotted by without sparing her a glance.

She spent the warm-up session concentrating harder than she ever had before. She was determined to give herself every chance of turning in a great performance on Saturday. It was as if Morello was rooting for her. He didn't put a foot wrong, and Dylan felt a thrill as he bent around her leg on the corner with his neck arched at the canter.

"Excellent job, everyone," Ali Carmichael said. "Take your stirrups back and ride down to the other end of the arena. Except you, Malory."

Knowing they were done on the flat and moving on to fences, Dylan felt her stomach flip with a mixture of nerves and excitement. She leaned forward to pat Morello's warm neck as Malory cantered a circle around the course of jumps, admiring the quiet way she was able to get the very best out of Hardy. When he laid back his ears halfway through the course and tried to swerve back to the other horses, Malory already had her outside leg pressed against his side and her inside rein shortened to redirect him.

Hardy was a careful jumper who needed his rider to give him encouragement while still keeping him balanced, because he tended to use speed instead of power to get over the fences. Dylan noticed that Malory held him in check between every jump but still gave him plenty of impulsion with her legs and seat. She never let the chestnut cob feel he was jumping by himself for one second, and she made him look like a winner.

It struck Dylan that she never saw Malory so relaxed as when she was riding. *It's like she's more at home when she's with the horses*, Dylan thought. There was so much she admired about Malory. *But I blew it*, she figured ruefully as Malory approached the final combination. She couldn't think of anything to say that wouldn't sound like she was trying to suck up to Malory after their argument. Instead, she dropped her reins and clapped hard when the pair sailed over the final fence.

Malory shot her a startled glance as she cantered past, making way for Lynsey on Bluegrass. But Dylan noticed that her cheeks flushed pink when the rest of the group took up the applause.

Bluegrass went over each jump easily, and Lynsey stroked his neck just once with her immaculate white-gloved hand as they finished. Dylan noticed that even though they had a clear round, the applause wasn't as loud as it had been for Malory, and she wondered if anyone else suspected that Lynsey had told on her. Not that it made any difference, since Dylan was trying to move past that whole mess anyway.

As Bluegrass returned to the group, Dylan marveled at the pony's perfection. He didn't even pin his ears or bite at flies. Dylan smiled and flicked some of Morello's mane over his neck so it was lying on the right side. *Give me a real horse any day*, she thought, gathering her reins as her aunt nodded for her to ride next.

It was as if the two-week ban had never happened. Dylan felt that she and Morello were totally in sync as they took the first jump. When they thudded down on the other side, the gelding snatched at the bit, making it jangle. Dylan quickly gave and took with the reins to get his concentration back on the fences. "Good boy," she murmured, and he lowered his head and flickered back his ear to show he was listening to her.

She was almost convinced they were going to make a clear round as they approached the last fence, but she leaned forward a stride too soon and broke Morello's concentration. Morello rattled the last part of the combination with his back hooves, and Dylan looked around to see the pole bobble in its cup holders and then fall with a thud onto the sand. "Never mind, boy," she leaned forward to pull gently at one of Morello's ears. "That was wonderful!"

She grinned at Lani, who shouted, "Yay, Walsh!" Picking up on Dylan's high spirits, Morello snatched at the reins and gave a playful buck. Dylan had to trot two circles before she could persuade the gelding that they were done.

Bring on the tryouts, she thought, crossing her fingers. She and Morello were back on track, and she knew that, together, they had a shot at getting on the team.

CHAPTER TWELVE

❧

It was Friday, the day before the tryouts, and none of the seventh-grade intermediate riders had been able to concentrate during art class.

It had been that way all week for Dylan. Every hour felt like five, unless she was in the stable or actually riding. That time raced by, and she had to pray that she was making the most of it, practicing the very things that would come into play on Saturday. Dylan worried that she and Morello still struggled with combination jumps and had little experience with the timed rounds, which would be important if they managed to get into the deciding jump-off. But, first things first. For now, Dylan was supposed to be painting a tree.

Paintbrush in hand, she stood back from the giant wall mural, which was based on an aerial shot of Chestnut Hill. Each girl was responsible for painting her own square. Dylan looked over and smiled at Lani, who had the tip of her tongue sticking out of her mouth as she dabbed at a detail on the fields around the school campus.

"Um, Lani, since when do cows have bushy tails?"

Lani leaned closer to her picture and let out a dramatic groan. "I've just painted Colorado's tail on a cow! I've got horses on the brain. When was this picture taken, anyway?" she asked. "We don't have any cows on campus now, do we?"

Dylan was trying to come up with a good response, but Honey spoke first.

"Don't worry, it can be painted out. Maybe you should let it dry a little and then go over it with green."

Lani's shoulders drooped, but then the bell sounded and the room exploded with activity as the girls hurried to clean their brushes and pack away their supplies. All of the intermediate riders had planned to go down to the yard during recess. There were no riding classes so the horses save their energy for the demanding workouts of the next day, but the girls didn't care. They all wanted as much last-minute bonding time as possible.

"Quietly, please," Mr. Woolley said, walking around with a jar for the girls to put brushes in. As usual, his button-down shirt had almost as much paint on it as the mural. Even his loafers had dried multicolored blobs all over them. Dylan absentmindedly plunked her brush in the container and took off her smock.

"Are you going to grab a snack before we go down to

the stable?" Lani raised her voice over the noise of taps running.

"Yeah, as long as it's fast!" Dylan said, putting her paint tray on the drying rack. Then she grabbed her books and waved to Honey and Lani as she headed out the door.

🐾

Dylan headed across campus with her fingers crossed. Lynsey hadn't said a thing about the fact that she had not yet returned her shirt, and Dylan could only hope that was a good sign. Dylan had gone to the laundry room and requested specialist cleaning for the shirt, along with her best tan breeches for the tryouts. But when she pulled the T-shirt out of the netted bag, her heart sank. The chocolate ice cream had left a faint but obvious mark down the pale oyster silk.

Dylan tried to compose an acceptable excuse as she hurried across the lawn, dodging groups of girls trying to soak up the last of the afternoon's sun. As she ran up the steps that led to Adams, she swore she could smell the chocolate chip cookies that would be waiting for her. She contemplated taking the laundry back to her room, but the aroma was too tempting. *Well, I might as well get this over with,* she thought, anticipating a showdown with Lynsey.

The lounge was full of noise when Dylan pushed open the door. Her class had claimed their usual sofas by the window. Dylan dropped her laundry bag just inside the door and headed over to claim her share of the cookies.

"Hurry up. We're all ready to go down to the yard." Honey handed her a soda while Lani held out a plate of chocolate chip cookies and blondies.

Dylan offered a tentative smile, fully aware that Lynsey was right behind her. She headed over to her laundry bag and gingerly lifted the damaged garment.

"I had your top dry-cleaned," she said, handing it over. "I'm really sorry, but there was a stain that wouldn't come out."

"What stain?" Lynsey interrogated, grabbing the top and turning it over in her hands.

"I had a close encounter with a chocolate ice-cream cone," Dylan said apologetically. "I'll get you another one."

"Sure, the next time you're in Milan," Lynsey growled. She wadded up the T-shirt and threw it toward the wastepaper basket in the corner of the room.

"Oops, you missed," Lani said, breaking the stunned silence.

Lynsey ignored her. "I guess some people find it easy being careless with other people's property." She glanced knowingly at Patience, who was sitting alongside her.

Dylan's mouth dropped open. Was Lynsey trying to make a connection between her T-shirt and Dylan's riding Morello at night? "Well, we all know that I haven't been very careful recently. Like choosing who to trust, for a start. You practically forced me to borrow the shirt."

"I thought we were going down to the stables?" Malory stood up and put her drink down on the table. "Come on, Lynsey, it's just a T-shirt."

"It's not *just* a T-shirt," Lynsey retorted. "It's a Versace that my dad bought for me."

"What's the big deal about a label?" Malory asked back, picking her jacket off the floor. "Don't you have enough already? Can't you just have your dad call someone to get you a new one?"

Lynsey's jaw jutted out, and she put one hand on her hip. The room seemed to shift slightly as everyone took a breath to prepare for Lynsey's response. "What are you getting at, Malory?" It was more of an accusation than a question, and it sounded like Lynsey was just getting started. "Maybe I could ask my dad to call someone and order a new shirt, but you're one to talk. You're the one who used your connections to get the Rockwell Award. Everyone knows that's the only way you could have landed it."

Dylan wasn't sure what Lynsey was suggesting, but it seemed to have had an effect on Malory. All of the color had drained out of her cheeks. "And just what is that supposed to mean?"

"Come off it. You don't own a horse, and you don't

ride the decent show circuits. How else would you manage to win that grant?"

"That's what you think?" Malory spoke slowly.

"Yeah, I do," Lynsey snapped.

"Well, that's pretty funny," Malory said. "Because it just proves that you only think about yourself, your possessions, and the fact that you didn't get the precious Rockwell Award even though you're way more qualified. I wish you had gotten it, because then there is no way that I would be here right now." She looked around the room and took a breath.

Dylan thought she would turn around and leave, but she started talking again, staring at her hands.

"I have never felt so alone as I do here." Malory's voice faltered with each word. "And the funny thing is, I knew it would be like this. I had heard what Chestnut Hill girls were like, and I never wanted to be one."

Lynsey let out an exaggerated sigh, making Malory look up.

"I didn't get the scholarship because my dad bought it for me, if that's what you're all thinking," she hissed. "It's not like he'd be able to afford it, working at a shoe store."

"Your dad works at a *shoe store*!" Lynsey spoke the words like they were contaminated. "You've gotta be kidding me! There's no way they'd let anyone from a family like that into Chestnut Hill. How did you think you were going to fit in?"

"I didn't." Malory's eyes were bright and her voice shook, but she looked Lynsey straight in the eyes. "I knew I wouldn't, and I didn't even want to try. I'm only here because my dad made me come."

"Yeah, go tell that to someone who believes it." Lynsey rolled her eyes. "I know about girls like you. You'd give your last pair of Steve Madden mary janes to come to a place like this." She glanced down at her cherry-shimmer fingernails and shrugged. "Your dad does sell Steve Madden, doesn't he? Hmmmm, maybe not."

"I don't care what you believe!" Malory yelled. "My dad insisted this school was such a great opportunity." She glared at them and Dylan flinched. "I can't believe he was actually proud of me for getting the scholarship!"

"Why? Wasn't the local high school good enough for him?" Patience said.

"It suited us just fine . . ." Malory stopped.

"Until what? Why'd you come here?" Lynsey asked, raising an eyebrow.

"I came," Malory said flatly, "because my mother died. My dad thought I'd be better off here than at home. He was working all the time trying to pay the hospital bills. And the truth is, part of me did want to come here — for him. I wanted to be able to make him proud. He wanted me to have the chance to make something of myself."

She looked around, and Dylan felt herself drop her gaze in order to avoid the defiance burning in those blue eyes. "I wonder what he'd think if he could see me here now — with all of you," Malory finished quietly. Keeping her head high, she turned and walked out of the room.

There was a stunned silence in the room. Slowly, the girls looked around, trying to assess the damage. Lani was the first to speak. "Way to go, Lynsey."

"Don't blame her," Patience insisted. "It was Dylan who started the whole thing by ruining Lynsey's shirt."

"Did any of you guys know about her mom?" Alexandra asked in a hushed voice.

"How could we?" Wei Lin said in a guilt-ridden tone. "The girl hardly ever talked."

"It was news to me," Lynsey stated, glancing around the room. But Dylan noticed that none of the other girls would meet her eyes. Lynsey turned to Patience. "I'm going to see Blue — are you coming?"

The room fell silent as Lynsey and Patience gathered their things and left.

"Wow," Dylan breathed. Even the upperclassmen on the other side of the room were staring at them. "We sure know how to keep things exciting around here."

"Should we go after Malory?" Razina asked, her brown eyes troubled.

Lani looked thoughtful. "Maybe she needs some time on her own."

"Yeah," Alexandra agreed. "It couldn't have been easy having all her personal stuff hit the fan in front of everyone. I mean, she's always been a bit secretive, but I guess she had her reasons. I can't believe Lynsey would drag all that stuff out of her like that."

Honey broke off a piece of cookie with one hand. "I think everyone seems the same when they arrive at boarding school. We go through all the same day-to-day stuff together, but who knows what's going on under the surface?"

Razina nodded. "Totally. And it looks like Malory has had a lot more to deal with than the rest of us. It was probably just a matter of time before she'd need to confess it to someone."

"Yeah," Lani agreed. "But I'm guessing the last person she would have chosen was Lynsey."

Dylan didn't say anything. She was wondering if Malory had headed to the stables. That's where she would have gone if things had blown up like that. She was frustrated that she hadn't been able to be a friend to Malory. She had been suspicious of her secrecy, and, apparently, so had everyone else. And now that Malory needed a friend, there wasn't anyone who could comfort her.

🐎

When Malory didn't show up for dinner, Dylan became concerned. "I'm going to see if I can find her," she announced, pushing away her uneaten dinner. She got up from the table and headed for the door.

"Wait up!" Dylan looked over her shoulder and saw Lani and Honey hurrying to catch up with her.

"We'll come with you," Lani offered. "I can't eat, either, which is saying something when it's quesadillas. I really love Monterey Jack!" Dylan gave Lani a sideways glance as she pushed open the dining hall door.

"Where do you think she'll be?" Honey asked, out of breath.

Dylan shrugged. "The most obvious place is in the barn, with Hardy."

Honey glanced at her watch. "For all this time?"

"It's worth a shot, isn't it?" Dylan said. The longer Malory stayed away, the worse it made her feel. It hardly seemed possible that the whole thing started when Malory had tried to stick up for Dylan when she confessed about ruining the T-shirt. *I'm never wearing Versace again,* she vowed.

The girls walked down to the barn in the fading light without talking. It was almost seven o'clock, and although there were a few girls hurrying toward the athletic center, the rest of the campus was quiet.

As they entered the stable, Dylan strode ahead, almost running down the aisle to Hardy's stall. She was sure she'd find Malory curled up in the back corner. But when she peered over the door, only Hardy was there, pulling at his hay. He looked at Dylan with his ears pricked hopefully.

"Sorry, boy. I don't have anything for you," she apologized, showing her empty hands.

"Any luck?" Honey called.

"No." Dylan shook her head bleakly. "What do we do now?"

❧

"You don't really think she could have run away, do you? Maybe we should let Mrs. Herson know," Honey said as they walked back to Adams House after searching the rest of the campus.

"I think we should give her a while longer," Dylan said. The last thing she wanted was to get Malory in trouble. *This semester has been hard enough for her. She doesn't need to have a record for truancy, too.*

"How about we check the dorm rooms again before we decide what to do next?" Lani suggested.

"We could get the others to help. Eight of us covering the dorm has got to be better than three," Honey pointed out.

"That's a great idea," Dylan said. "She's got to be somewhere close by." But remembering the expression on Malory's face earlier, Dylan wouldn't have blamed her if she had gone as far as she could.

Lani led the way up to the room that she shared with

Malory and Alexandra. Honey squeezed Dylan's arm as Lani pushed open the door and stepped inside the room. Lani let out an exclamation. Dylan and Honey looked at one another in alarm and hurried into the room in time to hear Lani say, "Hey, where've you been hiding? We missed you at dinner tonight."

"I went for a walk, and I wasn't hungry so I decided to skip dinner." Malory was sitting cross-legged on her bed, polishing her riding boots.

She must have walked around the campus six times! Dylan thought, thinking how long she'd been gone. They hadn't seen her for hours, but Malory still looked the same — drained and disheartened.

"We thought you might have been down with Hardy," Lani told her, sitting beside Malory on her bed.

"We were really worried about you," Dylan added.

Malory gave a short, humorless laugh. "Sure you were."

Dylan felt her cheeks burn. "Mal," she started awkwardly.

"Look, we've all got a busy day tomorrow, and I'd really appreciate it if you would leave me alone so I can get some sleep," Malory said without looking up.

Dylan felt like she had a lot more to say to Malory. And even though she didn't know where to start, she didn't want to leave.

Honey tugged gently on her arm. "Come on," she said.

"Malory's right. We all need some sleep, and maybe things will look better in the morning."

But as Dylan followed Honey from the room, she had a gut feeling that, come the light of day, things wouldn't be any better at all.

CHAPTER THIRTEEN

Dylan's fingers fumbled as she tried to button up her riding shirt. She couldn't remember the last time she had been this nervous — not even before the state finals at the end of the summer. Honey and Lynsey had already left for the stable, but Dylan was running late. She hadn't been able to find her boots, completely forgetting that she had put them outside the door the night before.

Just as she finished tying her laces, Lani appeared at the threshold of the room.

"Oh, great!" Dylan exclaimed, "We can go down together."

But Lani just stood there with a shocked expression. "It's Malory," she burst out, her cheeks flushed. "She's packing. She's leaving Chestnut Hill!"

"What?" Dylan jumped off the bed and rushed for the door.

"I've tried everything to make her stay," Lani said as

they raced down the hallway. "I even promised to stop singing Celine Dion songs in the shower! But she's determined to leave. She says she has nothing to offer Chestnut Hill and it has nothing to offer her. I tried telling her that she's got more talent in her little finger than Lynsey has in her entire body and that her dad would want her to stay, but she just isn't listening."

"What makes you think I can stop her?" Dylan asked as they neared the room.

Lani stopped outside her room and shrugged. "Everyone else has already gone down for the tryouts. You were the only one here."

"Thanks," Dylan said.

"I'm just kidding. But I really don't know. You like to pick fights, right? Here's your chance. Just do your best, okay?"

Dylan nodded, although she didn't have a clue where to start. If anyone deserved to be at Chestnut Hill, it was Malory. She had proven that. "Go down to the stable," Dylan said to Lani. "There's no point in both of us being late for tryouts."

"Okay, if you're sure," Lani said, watching as Dylan stepped into the room.

Malory looked up from folding a pair of jeans. Two suitcases were open on the bed, both half full of clothes.

"You won't change my mind, so why don't you close the door on your way out?" she said bluntly, turning to place the jeans in one of the cases.

"Come on, Mal," Dylan began. "You know that no one wants you to leave." But she had to admit that her words didn't sound very convincing.

"Really?" Malory snapped, turning back around. "I bet when Lynsey finds out, she'll throw a party."

Dylan's lips twitched. "Maybe. But I bet it will be black-tie with a limited guest list."

Malory clearly wasn't in the mood for Dylan's sense of humor. "Look, you should leave. You'll miss the tryouts."

Dylan glanced at the clock on the wall and saw that they were both cutting it close. Her own tryout slot was in less than thirty minutes, and Malory's might even be before that. Her heart skipped a beat, but as she looked at Malory, she remembered how she had tricked Nutmeg that first day, crawling on the ground, and somehow Dylan knew she couldn't leave yet.

But the question was, how would she convince Malory to stay? After all, Dylan was part of the reason Malory wanted to go. Malory had been frustrated with her for valuing Morello's safety over Emily's. Then Dylan had wrongly accused Malory of turning her in to the administration. Dylan had done just what Malory expected of a Chestnut Hill girl — put her own interests first, no matter the cost. But now it was in Dylan's interest to change

Malory's mind. She wanted her to stay, and she wanted to know her better. And she really wanted Malory to teach her tricks like the one she used on Nutmeg.

"So this is it?" Dylan asked before she realized what she was saying. "You're going to take the easy way out? It's not really what I had expected from you."

"What?" Malory looked up from what she was doing, obviously thrown.

Dylan shrugged. "I didn't think you were a quitter. I thought you were stronger than that. But I guess even I can't be right all of the time."

Malory's mouth dropped open. "You've got a lot of nerve."

Dylan crossed her arms. "You know you don't really want to leave," she said.

"Oh, yes, I do."

"No, you don't," Dylan said with more conviction this time. "If you did, you wouldn't be carefully folding all of your clothes into your suitcases — you'd be stuffing them in. Anything to get out of here as fast as possible."

Malory's hands clenched into fists at her side. "First of all, Dylan Walsh, you don't know me. And secondly —"

Dylan raised her eyebrows.

"You don't know me," Malory snapped again, turning around to empty another drawer of clothes. She banged it shut with her foot.

"You know something, you're right," Dylan confessed.

"I don't know you. I had you down as the most together girl here. Sure, it bugged me the way you never opened up about anything and I didn't get why you always wanted to clean tack instead of hanging out —"

"Not that it's anything to you," Malory interrupted in a huff, "but I didn't play truth-or-dare because I didn't want to do anything that would make me lose the scholarship."

Dylan realized her argument had gotten off track. "I don't care about that now. It's fine if you don't want everyone knowing about your personal life."

"I think it's a little late for that." Malory dropped a pair of socks on the floor but didn't seem to notice. "Great, fine, whatever. If you're so big on privacy, why don't you just leave me alone?"

"Well, I could. But, as a last favor, I'll help you pack." Malory looked at Dylan but didn't say anything. "Because if you really think that you have nothing to give Chestnut Hill and Chestnut Hill has nothing to give you, then maybe you *should* leave." Dylan bent down to pick up the socks and tossed them into the case. "It's probably for the best. I mean, why should anyone rival the Lynsey Harrisons of the world? They know that talent doesn't really matter — it's all about how much money you pour into equitation classes. There's no way you have anything worthwhile to teach the classic Chestnut Hill girl. I know I have nothing to learn from you — not in life and especially not anything to do with horses. You're really just wasting

our time if you don't have any clothes we can borrow."
Dylan stopped, not knowing if she was getting any-
where. She had a bad feeling she was just proving
Malory's point.

Malory reached into her closet and grabbed a bunch
of shirts still on their hangers, but she looked back at
Dylan expectantly.

"Where do you want your riding stuff?" Dylan asked,
pulling out a dresser drawer.

"Anywhere," Malory said.

Dylan started pulling stuff from the drawer and putting
it in the closest suitcase. "You know, I'm glad you're going,"
she added. "Because now I don't have to feel bad about
accusing you of telling on me. I mean, we wouldn't have
been friends anyway, so no loss, right?" She bent down
and lifted up a pile of jodhpurs. "And, Malory, I have to
say that the real winners in this are the horses. I'm sure
Hardy will be glad to see you gone. He probably wants
to be ridden by someone who competes in all the top
shows. A real Chestnut Hill girl who thinks she can buy
ribbons. Someone like that would really get the best out
of him — might even make the competition team."

"Oh, we would have made the team," Malory declared.
Dylan recognized a defiant tone in her voice. "What are
you doing with my jodhpurs?" Malory asked suddenly.

"Packing them."

"Hand them over," Malory said, reaching out her hand. "We both know Hardy deserves to be on that team."

Dylan looked at Malory. Her eyes looked soft with tears but her jaw was determined. "Really? Are you sure?" Dylan asked.

"Don't ask me that. I might change my mind," Malory threatened. She tipped her head to the side and gave Dylan the first genuine smile she'd seen. "Okay, you convinced me, I do have something to offer Chestnut Hill. And maybe there are some things about this place that aren't so bad. I actually like some of the horses."

"Oh, stop your gushing and hurry up," Dylan said, throwing a pair of riding pants at Malory and rummaging through her luggage in search of a shirt and jacket. She felt something start to swell inside her, and she recognized it as hope. "Quick, put on your show clothes. There's no way we can miss tryouts now!"

🐎

Malory and Dylan ran across the lawn toward the indoor arena. The air was clear and crisp, but the sun was bold — an exquisite day for riding. Horses were tied along the outside wall of the barn, their tails swishing as they waited their turn. Everywhere Dylan looked, girls dressed in dark coats and pristine breeches were dashing around with sponges, buckets of water, and armfuls of clean, well-conditioned tack. Dylan could practically smell the saddle soap.

"There's Lani with Hardy!" she panted.

The moment Lani saw them, she slipped off the halter that had been buckled over Hardy's bridle and led him over. A cheer burst from the indoor arena as Joy Richards rode out. Her pony's flanks were flecked with foam and, instead of tying him up when she dismounted, she led him to the far end of the yard to walk him in circles so that he could cool down.

Like clockwork, Kathryn MacIntyre from Meyer was announced and she disappeared into the indoor arena on Snapdragon, a dapple-gray pony.

"Not a second to spare." Lani grinned at Malory. "I tacked him up in case you changed your mind."

"Well, I did," Malory smiled, tightening her chin strap.

"You'd better get on — you're next," Lani told her. She looked across at Dylan. "Morello's waiting for you in the barn, cooling off after his last round. I checked on him a few minutes ago."

"Thanks, Lani. We both owe you," Dylan said, holding Hardy's stirrup so Malory could mount.

Malory swung into the saddle and then glanced down at her. "If I don't see you again before you ride, good luck. Remember not to get ahead of him and you'll do great."

The girls looked up to see Kathryn ride back out of

the arena. She looked disappointed. "Watch out for the final combination," she called to Malory. "You just have to look at the top pole for it to fall off."

Malory glanced up from checking her girth and gave a nervous smile. She and Hardy hadn't even had time for a practice fence.

"You heard the girl. Ride it with your eyes closed and you'll be fine." Lani gave Hardy's quarters a gentle slap as Malory squeezed him forward.

"Good luck," Lani and Dylan called at the same time, watching Malory and Hardy disappear through the doors. Dylan felt all her hopes go with them until Lani snapped her fingers in front of Dylan's face.

"Okay, Dyl. Emily Page had the final fence down on her round with Morello," Lani told her. "In fact, she had the second and fifth fences down, too, so she's almost definitely out of it. Morello seemed kind of nervous with her."

Dylan nodded. "I'm going to go get him now. I'm up just one after Malory."

She jogged a few strides toward the barn and then paused. "Wait! How did you do?" With the distraction of getting Malory into the ring, she'd totally forgotten that Lani had ridden earlier.

"We scraped by with a clear," Lani told her with a smile. "I bribed Colorado with my mom's homemade apple pie. All that sugar really helps him focus."

"Congrats!" Dylan said, with a little clap.

"Thanks," Lani smiled. "Oh, and Honey got eight faults — she ran into some grief on the combination. Lynsey — surprise, surprise — went clear, and quite a few of the eighth-graders had clear rounds, too."

"So the competition's stiff," Dylan called over her shoulder as she set off again.

"Nothing you can't handle, Walsh," Lani's voice rang out after her.

Listening to her footsteps echo down the barn's central aisle, Dylan wasn't so sure. She'd had a surefire plan to make certain that Morello was ready for their round — a plan that had included several practice fences and some solid bonding time. Persuading Malory not to take off was the last thing she had expected, but Dylan didn't really care if it had blown her chances of winning a spot on the junior jumping team. Malory was staying, and that fact made Dylan feel as if she'd already won.

CHAPTER FOURTEEN

When she rode through the double doors to the indoor arena, Dylan gulped at the sea of faces lining the bleachers. She took a deep breath and tore her eyes away from the seating gallery. The only thing that mattered for the next minute and a half was the course of eight fences that she and Morello needed to jump clear if she wanted a chance of making the junior team. There was little consolation in the fact that Morello had already seen the course with Emily Page. Based on Lani's report of their faults, his earlier round could prove to be a psychological disadvantage. Dylan had to ride with enough confidence to overcome Morello's past missteps.

Dylan gave the gelding a quick scratch on the neck. "It's you and me this time, boy," she murmured. "We can do this."

His ears flicked back at the sound of her voice, and, from the bounce in his step, Dylan knew that he was just waiting for her to tell him what to do next. She pushed him into a steady canter and circled once before heading for the first fence. On her way past the door, she caught a glimpse of Malory standing in the gap.

Remember not to get ahead of him. Malory's advice echoed in her mind. Dylan knew Malory was right. It was all about rhythm. If she and Morello were together at every fence, they had a good shot. Dylan tried to see all of the fences through Morello's eyes, holding him in until the last moment on some, urging him forward on others. Morello responded each time, adjusting his pace just as she asked. Dylan knew he needed to have his hocks right under him to spring over the uprights but more speed to clear the spreads. When they approached the final combination, Dylan wasn't even sure how they had done. All her concentration had been in getting over one jump and then preparing Morello for the next. She hadn't even thought to listen for any falling poles.

Her heart began to pound uncomfortably at the sight of the final dreaded obstacle. It was a classic in-and-out, with two fences paced just a stride apart. But now Dylan saw that the two red-and-white jumps were placed incredibly close, which was why the second one kept falling. The takeoff was incredibly tight. Picking up on her hesitancy, Morello faltered in his stride.

"Sorry, boy. I'm with you all the way," she whispered.

Morello recovered quickly, and with his ears pricked

forward, he cleared the first fence, put in one short stride, and sailed over the second. Dylan sat quietly until they landed on the soft sand. She didn't look back at the jumps to see if any poles were lying on the ground. All she could hear was the thudding of Morello's hooves as she slowed him from a canter to a steady, bouncing trot.

It was only when the arena filled with the sound of clapping that she dared to believe that they had actually scored the clear round they needed.

"Nice work," Ali Carmichael announced as she joined Dylan just outside the arena. She spoke briskly, glancing down at her red clipboard. "I didn't see you earlier, so I'll give you the full rundown on the jump-off. You're going to have to ride against everyone who went clear. That's Lynsey, Lani, and Malory from your group, and Eleanor Dixon, Aster Sachs-Cohen, Olivia Buckley, Victoria Rasmussen, and Joy Richards," she said. "This round is timed. You're fifth in line, so you'll have a chance to develop strategy." Ali shrugged off her yard coat and slung it over her shoulder before looking her niece in the eye. "You rode Morello better than ever. Just make sure you do it a second time."

"I'll do my best," Dylan promised, slipping off Morello and loosening his girth. When she looked up, her aunt was already hurrying away, calling out the riding order to the other girls who had a clear first round. Most of their ponies were tied to rings along the barn wall so they could rest while still tacked up. Sarah and Kelly were busy filling buckets of water at the outdoor tap, preparing to sponge the ponies down later.

Dylan caught Malory's eye as her friend swung herself up onto Hardy. She was riding second, after Lynsey. "I'd wish you luck, but I don't think you need it."

Malory smiled. "Everyone can use a little luck, so thanks. I'll be pulling for you, too."

Dylan let Malory's words sink in and realized how much they meant to her. She wondered if it was really possible that they would become friends after all they'd been through. But her thoughts didn't linger there long; she needed to focus on her timed round. She just wanted to get back into the ring so Morello could prove how talented he was again.

With a clatter of hooves, Lynsey rode past on Bluegrass without even acknowledging Dylan. Her back was stiff, and Bluegrass tossed his head in protest over her tight hold on the reins. Dylan felt a jab of sympathy for her. Even though Lynsey had a top-class pedigree in competitions, none of that mattered today. Everyone had an equal chance, and it was obvious that the pressure was getting to her. *It must be difficult to have a reputation to live up to,* Dylan thought, watching her disappear into the arena.

Morello stamped his foot impatiently, and Dylan decided to walk him toward the paddocks to calm both of their nerves. She rested her arm over his neck and thought through the next course. The fences were in the same order, but they would be a few inches higher, which would affect the pacing. And she needed to figure out where she could shave off time. It seemed like only seconds before she heard the loudspeaker crackle to announce that Lynsey had pulled off another clear round in one minute, eighteen seconds. *As to be expected*, Dylan thought. Dylan led Morello to the end of the fence and turned around when the loudspeaker came to life again.

"Malory O'Neil on Hardy-Har-Har, zero faults, one minute and twenty seconds."

Dylan let out a whoop of celebration and quickened her pace back to the collecting area. She waved as soon as she saw Malory. "Congrats!"

"One minute twenty!" Malory sighed with relief. "One more second and I would have picked up a time fault. I know I was on the slow side, but Hardy is such a careful jumper that I worried about pushing him for more speed."

"You totally deserve a place on the team. I'm sure you'll make it," Dylan said warmly. "You, too, Hardy-Har-Har." The pony's show name made her smile, and she gave the stocky gelding a pat.

Malory laughed. "We're not on it yet. Everyone else might ride a faster round than me."

As if to prove her wrong, Victoria Rasmussen rode out with two time faults. "And I knocked down the last fence," she said, slipping off Soda, who looked much bigger than his 15.3 hands against her tiny frame. "They changed that last in-and-out, so it's now a really long stride between the two." Dylan smiled sympathetically at the petite blond as she led Soda away, and then thought about how the change to the combination affected her.

"Do you think I can cut the corner heading into the spread?" she asked.

Malory frowned. "Yes, but don't make it too tight. He'll need to take off a little early to clear the width."

Just then there was a groan from inside the arena. One of the favorites to make the team, Aster Sachs-Cohen, who was riding on her own pony, Mermaid, rode out with six faults. Dylan felt a tug of disappointment; Aster was in Adams, and it would have been good for the dorm if she'd made the team.

"I took the whole thing too fast," Dylan overheard her say to Eleanor Dixon. "You need to watch out for the wall — it might look like you can take off two strides away from the corner, but you're better off with a short three!" Aster bit her lip as she patted Mermaid's neck. "It wasn't your fault, girl," she said.

Dylan's turn came around much faster than she had anticipated. Malory had tied Hardy to a ring so she could watch Dylan from inside. They walked together until they reached the arena doors. "You can do it," Malory called.

"Go, Walsh!" Over on the opposite side of the arena, Dylan saw Honey, Razina, and others from their floor, waving.

Dylan's mouth was dry as she shortened her reins and sent Morello forward. She looked up at the digital clock on the wall. It was set to zero. She knew that the moment she crossed the starting line, the seconds would start racing against her.

As Morello crossed the starting line toward the first fence, the buzzer went off. Morello kept his pace to the easy vertical. The moment he landed, Dylan closed her legs around him, telling him he needed to go faster than before. With a snort, Morello extended his stride to the second fence of the line, which was at the top of the ring. When they reached the corner, Dylan closed her hands on the reins, knowing they needed to keep their rhythm through the turn. Morello flicked back his ear and brought his quarters under him before clearing the wall easily. Next was the spread, and, instead of allowing Morello three strides after the wall, Dylan turned him after two to save time. She saw almost immediately that it was a mistake. The distance was too much for Morello to cover in two strides. She half-halted to make room for a third, but he was still too close. Morello pitched himself forward, jumping almost on top of the fence.

Sure enough, Dylan heard his hooves hit the top bar, but she was right with him. When he landed, she sat back and gave him leg. Morello lengthened his stride to come out okay on the other end of the combination, but Dylan knew she couldn't afford to knock anything else down. She glanced at the clock and saw that her pace put her a whole second in front of Lynsey. *If I don't pick up any other faults, I might still have a chance of making the team.* She steadied Morello and concentrated on the final three jumps, remembering she'd need some speed to make it through the long in-and-out.

Morello opened up his canter and flew over the final combination, and Dylan's heart raced with adrenaline. Then she heard a groan from the bleachers. Dylan glanced over her shoulder and saw the top pole of the final fence lying on the ground. Her stomach dropped. Knocking down two poles gave her eight faults, which would surely take her out of the running. She couldn't believe it. They had taken all the fences together, but it wasn't enough.

"Never mind, boy." She swallowed hard as she rode out of the ring, feeling mad at herself for trying to shave off time between the wall and the spread.

When Dylan rode out into the sunshine, Malory was waiting. "Way to go!" she cried. "One minute, ten seconds. No time faults."

Dylan bit her lip. "I knocked down two poles. That puts me behind Aster Sachs-Cohen."

Malory shook her head. "No, you didn't. You only knocked down the last fence. He bumped that spread, but the rail didn't fall. So you only got four faults. Didn't you listen to the loudspeaker?"

Dylan slipped off Morello. "Well, I guess four faults are better than eight, but there are four more riders to go, and someone's bound to go clear. I mean, I don't think Eleanor Dixon knows what it's like to bring down a fence. And Lani is an absolute speed demon."

As if to prove her point, a few moments later Eleanor Dixon trotted out of the arena, calling out, "Clear, one minute nine," to Joy Richards, who was waiting to go on Buttercup. Joy gave her girth one last check and then disappeared through the entrance on the palomino. *So that's Eleanor, Mal, and Lynsey all ahead of me. And it will be a walk in the park for Joy Richards, who made the team last year as a seventh-grader. It looks like the reserve place is going to be fought out between Lani, Olivia, and me.* Dylan glanced across at the two girls, who were quietly walking their ponies around the far end of the yard. Lani had disappeared after Dylan rode her first round, and she seemed unusually subdued now. Dylan thought it best not to disturb her.

Dylan heard clapping come from the arena, and Joy trotted out. "Good work," Dylan called, trying to swallow her own disappointment. Joy gave her a tight smile before slipping down to the ground.

"Are you trying to rub it in?" Malory whispered, giving Dylan's arm a nudge.

"Huh?"

Malory tightened her grip on Hardy's reins as he stamped his foot. "She had eight faults. That was consolation applause. You really have to pay attention to the announcements!" Malory shook her head in disbelief. "So there are still two slots left."

"And Olivia and Lani still have to go," Dylan pointed out.

"Dylan Walsh! You are a lousy pessimist," Malory exclaimed.

"I'll have you know I'm never pessimistic," Dylan said as Olivia trotted past on Shamrock. "I am, however, always realistic."

"Do you have an answer for everything?" Malory asked.

"Yes," Dylan assured her. "It's a gift." Despite her jittery stomach, she smiled.

Malory rolled her eyes, but Dylan was feeling grateful for her company. Malory now knew that she was guaranteed a spot on the team, and, instead of celebrating, she was willing to wait it out until they knew Dylan's fate as well.

For the next few moments they stood in silence, stroking Morello and Hardy's noses as they waited for Olivia to finish. When she clattered out onto the yard on the bright bay mare, the loudspeaker announced, "Clear round, one minute nineteen." Dylan's heart began to pound.

She's in. It's down to Lani and me. She couldn't believe her luck. Why did it have to be Lani, of all people?

At that moment, Dylan saw Lani ride by, looking straight ahead with a determined expression.

"Good luck," Dylan and Malory called. Of course Dylan wanted Lani to ride her best, but she couldn't help hoping that her best wasn't less than four faults. Malory grinned, as if she knew exactly how torn Dylan was feeling.

"I can't take this," Dylan said after a moment. "Will you hold Morello for me so I can go watch?"

"Sure," Malory agreed with a self-assured smirk. "I'll tighten up his girth as well — just in case you need to be riding back into the arena in a few minutes for a formal celebration."

As Dylan hurried to the entrance, she crossed her fingers, but she knew it was a long shot. When it came to racing the clock, Lani was the most amazing rider Dylan had ever seen. *Granted, her equitation leaves something to be desired,* Dylan thought, but Dylan knew that sitting up straight and keeping your heels down didn't matter here. It was all about speed and faults, and Lani had speed down. Even though Dylan had watched her carefully at every practice, she still couldn't figure out how Lani managed to shave as many seconds off the clock as she did. She made Colorado look like he'd been trained for barrel racing. *She's gutsy, that's all there is to it.*

Dylan peered through the entrance and saw Lani racing

between the wall and the spread, with Colorado going great guns. As far as she could tell, there were no fences down. Dylan glanced at the clock. Fifty seconds! If Lani kept up this pace, she was going to finish at about one minute five. Lani landed clear of the spread and raced around the corner, looking over her shoulder at the next fences. Dylan worried that Colorado's stride was starting to look sloppy. *Tighten up,* she thought just as the pony seemed to slip. Dylan gasped as the pony struggled to keep his feet.

Lani sat back, letting Colorado regain his footing, but she slowed the pace considerably when she pointed him at the fence. Colorado was clearly shaken and tipped the top pole. Dylan held her breath. The pole bounced but stayed in place. Lani turned the pony for the final combination and asked him for more speed so he could clear the distance, but Colorado had lost his nerve. He swerved right around the jump.

Dylan's fingers tightened. *Come on, Colorado!* She was no longer thinking of her own place on the team but simply wanted her friend to finish the course. It had been such an amazing start! Lani took Colorado almost to the top of the ring before driving him strongly at the jump again. This time the gelding jumped. He was crooked, but he came through the in-and-out cleanly. Lani leaned forward and gave Colorado a generous pat before slowing him to a trot.

"Lani Hernandez on Colorado," the announcer said. "One minute, twenty-six seconds. Six time faults."

Applause filled the arena, acknowledging how well Lani had salvaged her round. But Dylan stood motionless, realizing she had made the team. The extra circle Lani had taken to redirect Colorado had cost her valuable time, and Dylan ended up with fewer faults.

"Get a move on, Walsh. You've got a ribbon with your name on it," Lani said, slipping her feet out of her stirrups. She was grinning broadly, genuinely pleased that one of them had made it.

Dylan didn't know what to say. Lani gave Colorado a good-bye pat as Sarah took his reins. "Have fun!" Lani said, rushing into the bleachers.

And then Malory shouted, her voice filled with excitement. "Dylan! Come on!"

Dylan ran over to Morello and, before putting her foot in the stirrup, she gave him a big hug. "You did it," she told him as she swung into the saddle, feeling as if her heart was going to explode with joy.

"Here." Malory steadied Hardy alongside Dylan and brushed a smudge of sawdust off her black coat. "We can't have you letting down the team. This is our grand entrance!"

"The team!" Dylan put her hands in the air, feeling triumphant, and Morello threw up his head at the sudden commotion.

"Trying out for cheerleading next?" Lynsey inquired as she rode past with Eleanor Dixon.

Dylan rolled her eyes behind Lynsey's back. "There's going to be no living with her now," she commented.

"Like there was before?" Malory smiled as they waited for Olivia Buckley to pass them, so they were all in order of how they had placed. Fourth up was Malory, who held her head high as she rode through the double doors to a storm of applause. Finally, Dylan followed. Coming fifth had earned her a place as the reserve rider for the team — and right now she couldn't be more thrilled if she'd come in first.

Ali Carmichael, Aiden Phillips, and Roger Musgrave were waiting for them in the center of the arena, holding rosettes for the ponies and Chestnut Hill junior jumping team crests for the girls' riding jackets. The sound of cheers echoed around the arena. Dylan looked over and saw all the Adams girls sitting together. Lani let out a piercing whistle and stood up, clapping her hands over her head. "Way to go, Adams!" she shouted, and the rest of the Adams girls cheered even louder. Honey stood up and blew a congratulatory kiss.

Dylan had to steady Morello so that Ali Carmichael could pin the pink rosette on his bridle. "Great job, both of you," she said.

Dylan looked down at the crest her aunt was holding. The fabric badge displayed the same emblem as on the gates at the school entrance: a chestnut tree with leaf-laden branches and spreading roots and a horse's head.

"You did it the hard way, but you did it," Ali added, her eyes shining with warmth. "I'm really proud of you, Dylan."

The huge lump in Dylan's throat seemed to prevent her from finding the right words, so she just grinned.

At last the riding coaches stood back so that Eleanor Dixon could lead the team around the arena in a lap of honor.

Over the loudspeaker, Mr. Musgrave announced, "Three cheers for this season's junior jumping team!"

As they cantered up the far side of the ring, Dylan had to hold Morello back. With each stride, he threatened to overtake Hardy. She knew exactly how the paint gelding was feeling. If it was up to her, she would be standing in her stirrups, racing ahead of them all, waving her crest in the air for everyone to see. Somehow, she managed to restrain herself and savor the moment.

Malory glanced back and met her eye, and Dylan could tell she was feeling just the same — and to think they had almost missed their chance.

When she came to the double doors, Eleanor Dixon led the other riders out onto the yard. It was still midday, and Dylan shielded her eyes as they adjusted to the sun. She didn't even realize that Lynsey had held back Bluegrass until he and Morello were walking side by side.

"Now that we're going to be spending even more time together, I thought you'd like to know something," Lynsey said, her eyes still focused on the path ahead.

Dylan frowned, distracted by the red rosette clipped to Bluegrass's bridle. "And what would that be?"

"I know you've somehow got it into your head that I was the one who called Ms. Carmichael on you," Lynsey admitted, "but, as usual, you're completely off the mark."

"Just leave it, Lynsey," Dylan said, not wanting anything to spoil the afternoon. "It doesn't really matter now."

Lynsey shrugged. "Do you really think I would need to sabotage your getting on the team? I mean, Blue was a sure thing from day one. Think about it."

Before Lynsey had even finished, Bluegrass pulled ahead, and Dylan was left with her thoughts. *So what if it wasn't Lynsey?* she wondered. *Would someone else have wanted to keep me out of the tryouts? Did I really get it all wrong again?*

Why did Lynsey have to tell her this now? Dylan pulled Morello to a stop and dismounted, absentmindedly running up her stirrups. She clicked to Morello to walk forward, playing with his mane as her mind lingered on the possibilities.

"What do you think, boy?" she asked. Morello's eyes were half-closed and he gave a light snort. "I fully agree," Dylan responded with a smile. She convinced herself it really didn't matter — not today. Besides, she now had a much better sense of things, and she knew which girls she hoped would become her closest friends. She'd go with her gut and hope for the best.

Dylan was drawn from her thoughts by the sight of Lani and Honey tearing across the yard. "Dylan! Malory!" they yelled between gasps for breath.

Malory halted Hardy and waited with Dylan and Morello as Lani and Honey ran the rest of the way.

"You guys were brilliant!" Honey said, reaching up to give Morello a pat.

"They certainly were," Lani exclaimed, putting her hand on her chest with a dramatic flair. "You make us proud to be your roommates."

"Oh, Lani, you were so close to making it, too," Malory said with a hint of apology in her voice as they all headed toward the barn.

Lani shrugged. "You know, the better riders won, and all that."

Dylan wasn't sure she could have been as laid-back about not making the team, but she admired Lani's easygoing approach to everything.

"Besides," Lani added. "I don't think I could take any more of Lynsey Harrison than I absolutely have to."

Dylan and Malory exchanged knowing glances. Dylan noticed that Honey didn't say anything, and she assumed it was out of loyalty to their other roommate. And no one brought up Malory's near-departure. It felt like the distant past, and Dylan hoped it stayed that way. "Well, I have to admit, three Adams girls on the Chestnut Hill jumping team can't be bad," Dylan offered.

"And maybe even more next year," Malory added.

"That's right. We're taking over!" Lani announced.

"For now, how about we get the horses put away so we can go to the celebration buffet," Honey suggested.

"It's a plan," Lani said as she headed for the tack room with Hardy's saddle.

"I'm in," Malory confirmed before kissing Hardy on the forehead.

Dylan gave Morello a long pat. "Sounds perfect," she agreed. And, looking around at her new friends, Dylan realized that was just the right word. *Perfect*.

Look for the next Chestnut Hill title:

MAKING STRIDES

Mallory wanted to cheer along with everyone else after Dylan's solid finish, but it was her turn to jump. She scooped up the reins, trying not to think about the hundreds of eyes trained on her. *Please, please let me go clear,* she begged. It was her first official course after making the competition team, and she didn't want to let the other riders down. Even more, she wanted avoid being the target of Lynsey Harrison's petty taunts.

Hardy snatched at the reins as they cantered toward the red-and-white poles. "Steady," Malory whispered, holding her legs against him to maintain his bouncy stride but keeping a firm rein so that he wouldn't rush and flatten over the fence. Three yards away, she pushed her hands forward and let him take a fast, powerful stride before the jump. *Go, boy!* she thought as Hardy launched into the air.

The next two fences flashed past, and then they were cantering toward the parallel bars. Hardy listened to Malory right until he took off, forming a beautiful rounded arc over the fence. Malory felt a thrill of delight as she turned him to face the upright. *All of our practice has really paid off!* She relaxed a little as she judged the distance to their takeoff.

The next thing Malory knew, Hardy's nose was in the air and they were going too fast on the approach. When Hardy took the jump, he lost the graceful outline he had had over the previous fence. His forelegs knocked against the top pole, making it bounce in its holders. *Please stay up*, Malory prayed, not daring to look back and risk losing Hardy's focus again. The crowd groaned as the pole thudded onto the sand, and Malory felt her stomach drop with disappointment. She bit her lip and put a hundred and ten percent concentration into getting over the remaining jumps.

When Hardy landed clear over the final fence, the crowd burst into applause that was just as loud as for Dylan and Lynsey's rounds, but that didn't make Malory feel any better. She cantered back to the group, staring down at Hardy's mane. As far as she was concerned, she'd let the entire team down. It was not the ride the audience would have expected of the prestigious Rockwell Grant recipient.

"Good job," Eleanor mouthed.

Malory gave a half smile.

"That was great," Dylan whispered when Malory halted alongside her.

Malory watched Olivia fly around the course on Shamrock. The dark grey mare pricked her ears as they raced toward the wall. "I feel like such an idiot for losing my concentration before the upright," she muttered.

"I think you're being too hard on yourself," Dylan replied. "I have no doubt that everyone in this arena thinks you did really well."

Malory couldn't help shooting a glance at Lynsey. As

always, her round on Bluegrass had been flawless, and she would no doubt remind Malory of that fact.

✎

Malory led Hardy into his stall, still feeling mad at herself for the dropped pole. Every other member of the team had gone clear. She listened to the running commentary Dylan was giving Morello in the next box stall. "You're going to get a treat tonight, boy. In fact, I might snag some apples from the dinner buffet. Or some carrot cake."

Malory rubbed Hardy's nose. *I hope Diane Rockwell wasn't here,* she thought, slipping the bridle over his ears. She didn't want to think that her scholarship might be in jeopardy if she didn't start turning in tight, clear rounds. Suddenly Hardy lifted his head and looked past her. The sound of lively, chatting voices came down the aisle and two tall young women looked over the door.

"You're Malory O'Neil, right?" said one of them. Her shining blond hair was cut into neat bangs that swept stylishly over her forehead, and her green eyes were bright and friendly as she smiled at Malory.

"That's me," Malory said, her brain whirring as she tried to place the alumni, who somehow looked familiar.

"I'm Rachel and this is Sienna," the girl explained, placing a hand on the shoulder of her companion. *Lynsey's sisters!* With a jolt, Malory realized why they looked so familiar; they had the same sleek blond hair and high cheekbones, although Lynsey's eyes were a smoky blue, not green.

"We just wanted to congratulate you on your round," Rachel told her warmly. "You were great. I've never seen Hardy jump like that. He's been here since before I came to Chestnut Hill, and he was always so stubborn. But he looked like a champion out there, and I know he is a tricky pony to figure out."

Malory blinked. *Are you guys really related to Lynsey?* she wanted to ask. There was no way her classmate would have given her an ounce of credit for her riding today. "Thanks," she said, feeling her cheeks turn pink. "I just wish we'd gone clear! Hardy jumped his heart out, but I lost my concentration before that one fence."

"No worries," grinned Sienna. "It's still early in the year. I didn't ride here — I was on the tennis and field hockey teams — but even I can tell that it takes real talent to get this pony to look as good as he did. You two are quite the team. He'd jump mountains for you."

Malory was a little overwhelmed. It was clear that the sisters were going out of their way to be supportive of her. She was trying to think of a gracious reply when she saw Lynsey walking down the aisle.

"Well, I'll be around to see Lynsey at some of the shows," Rachel said. "I'll be on the lookout for you, Malory. I think you and Hardy could have quite a year."

Lynsey's eyes seemed to smolder, and all Malory could do was give Rachel and Sienna a tentative smile. She had a feeling that receiving compliments from the older Harrison sisters was not the best way to make nice with Lynsey.

Rebecca Goldstein receives rave reviews for
The Mind-Body Problem

"An absorbing and entertaining novel, penetrating and poignant."
—*Sunday New York Times*

"A terrific novel . . . The first 50 pages or so are so clever and funny that I had to put the book down and go to the fridge to cool off. 'I'm often asked what it's like to be married to a genius' is the first line, and the novel proceeds to explore the answer to that question."
—*New York Times Book Review*

"Goldstein is intelligent and perceptive, bawdy and witty—an articulate writer of great talent. Will keep you turning pages to find out how it all turns out."
—*Los Angeles Times Book Review*

"A confectionery of delight, laced with equal parts of wit, humor, and philosophical argument. Goldstein succeeds brilliantly in smuggling into her novel short courses on everything from the history of mathematics to the trouble with Talmudic logic."
—*MS.* magazine

"A remarkably good novel, full of good writing, wry observations and shrewd characterizations."
—*Minnesota Daily*

"Perhaps the best American Jewish novel to be published in years . . . Vibrant humor and sophistication give *The Mind-Body Problem* a unique dimension."
—*Hadassah Magazine*

"One of the most intelligent and funny pieces of fiction to surface this year. Goldstein's ability to translate complex philosophical or mathematical problems to such basics as friendship and sexual desire leaves the reader giddy with inspiration. . . . One of the most original laugh riots to successfully disguise itself as literature."
—*Kansas City Star*

"Brilliantly humorous, slyly witty—shades of Fran Leibowitz."
—*South Bend Tribune*

"An especially fine book that blends intelligence and feeling, intellect and sexuality."   —*New Jersey Monthly*

"A funny, thought-provoking novel . . . fictional characters so intelligent you learn from them and so believable you argue with them."   —*The Charlotte Observer*

"A stimulating and provocative novel . . . deserves close and contemplative reading for the utmost enjoyment."
          —*The Chattanooga Times*

"A considerable performance: witty, compassionate, and full of fascinating divagations."   —*The London Observer*

"Strong writing, a story of an original group of misfits collected to entertain in a sophisticated way."
          —*The Indianapolis Star*

"As wise as it is funny . . . deserves an honored place amid 'The Groves of Academe' (McCarthy), 'The War Between the Tates' (Lurie), and 'The Professor of Desire' (Roth), each of which has revealed the pain behind the ivy of our most sacrosanct preserves."
          —*The San Diego Union*

PENGUIN BOOKS

THE MIND-BODY PROBLEM

Rebecca Goldstein attended Barnard College and Princeton University, where she earned a Ph.D. in philosophy. She returned to Barnard, where she taught for ten years. She is the author of *Strange Attractors*, *The Dark Sister* (both available from Penguin), and *The Late-Summer Passion of a Woman of Mind*. Her latest work of fiction, *Mazel*, is also available from Penguin.

REBECCA GOLDSTEIN

The
MIND-BODY
Problem:
A Novel

PENGUIN BOOKS

PENGUIN BOOKS
Published by the Penguin Group
Penguin Books USA Inc., 375 Hudson Street, New York,
New York 10014, U.S.A.
Penguin Books Ltd, 27 Wrights Lane, London W8 5TZ, England
Penguin Books Australia Ltd, Ringwood, Victoria, Australia
Penguin Books Canada Ltd, 10 Alcorn Avenue, Toronto,
Ontario, Canada M4V 3B2
Penguin Books (N.Z.) Ltd, 182–190 Wairau Road,
Auckland 10, New Zealand

Penguin Books Ltd, Registered Offices: Harmondsworth,
Middlesex, England

First published in the United States of America by
Random House, Inc., 1983
Published in Penguin Books 1993

9 10

Although this novel is set in Princeton, New Jersey, the characters appearing in it are fictional, composites drawn from several individuals and from imagination. No reference to any living person is intended or should be inferred.

Grateful acknowledgment is made to Houghton Mifflin Company for permission to reprint an excerpt from "The Poet of Ignorance," by Anne Sexton from *The Awful Rowing Towards God*, copyright © 1975 by Loring Conant, Jr., Executor of the Estate of Anne Sexton. Reprinted by permission of Houghton Mifflin Company.

THE LIBRARY OF CONGRESS HAS CATALOGUED THE HARDCOVER AS FOLLOWS:
Goldstein, Rebecca, 1950–
The mind-body problem.
I. Title.
PS3557.0398M56 1983 813´.54 83-3268
ISBN 0-394-52474-8 (hc.)
ISBN 0 14 01.7245 9 (pbk.)

Printed in the United States of America

In memory of my father
BEZALEL NEWBERGER

CONTENTS

1 · THE QUESTION | 3

2 · THE COURTSHIP | 9

3 · THE FAMILY | 53

4 · THE HONEYMOON | 81

5 · REALITY | 125

6 · MORE REALITY | 163

7 · OTHER BODIES, OTHER MINDS | 199

8 · SOLUTIONS AND DISSOLUTIONS | 257

THE MIND-BODY PROBLEM

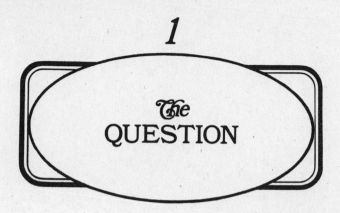

The QUESTION

The atmosphere surrounding this problem is terrible. Dense clouds of language lie about the crucial point. It is almost impossible to get through to it.

—LUDWIG WITTGENSTEIN,
NOTES FOR LECTURES ON
PRIVATE EXPERIENCE
FROM *THE PHILOSOPHICAL
REVIEW* (1968)

I'm often asked what it's like to be married to a genius. The question used to please me—as an affirmation of my place, of my counting for something (if only through marriage) in the only world that counted for anything. But even back then, at the beginning of my marriage (three years by the external calendar, more than half my life by my internal one), I was uncertain how to answer. "Wife of the genius" does not in itself define a distinct personality. The description, and my own fluid nature, left me the burden of choice. And I found it hard to choose. I could never even decide how I should arrange my face when I answered. Should I radiate the faintly dazed glow of one who stands within sweating distance of the raging fires of creativity? Or should my features exhibit the sharp practicality capable of managing the mundane affairs of an intellectual demigod? I could never decide, and usually ended up trying to look both dazed and practical, to look a logical contradiction, which is, I suppose, to look a fool. And that, of course, is the very, very last thing I have ever wanted to look.

As you see, the question was never an easy one for me. But these days! These days it's become a test of my strength. (I fear this remark borders on the melodramatic. My present state is perhaps conducive to such excesses. I must take care. The melodramatic pose, especially when directed toward one's own life, is another of the many ways of playing the fool.)

What do they want to hear from the wife of the genius? "Living with Noam is an intellectual adventure, a cerebral challenge . . ."? This morning was a typical challenge. I was drinking my coffee in the kitchen when Noam burst into the room, his face dissolved in anger.

"Renee, where's my pen? My God, I can't find my pen. What did you do with it?"

"Noam, I didn't touch your pen. Wait, I'll get you mine."

"I don't want yours, I want mine." His voice had climbed up into the whining range: "You know I can't stand losing my pen," then slid back down into the register of decision: "Listen, I've got to find it. Would you please help me instead of smugly sitting there?"

"Think back, Noam, when did you have it last?"

"I don't know. You think I can be bothered remembering trivialities like that?" Unstated premise, implied by the focused glare: that's one of the purposes of the wife. "I don't know. I know I was using it last night."

"Do you think that was the last time?"

"I *think* so. God, I don't know. I think so, yes."

"Okay, good. We'll proceed on that hypothesis. Now, where were you using it last night?"

"My study. I was at my desk."

"And you looked all over your desk?"

"Yes."

"Are you sure? Did you look carefully?" My question was informed by experience.

"For Godssakes yes! I wouldn't have said the pen was lost if I hadn't thoroughly searched. That's what it *means* for the pen to be lost! Now would you stop driving me crazy and help me!"

"Noam, I'm trying. Calm down or we won't get anywhere. Now, you must have taken it away from the desk. Did you get up for any reason while you were writing?"

"No. Listen, Renee, you must have taken it. We ought to be cross-examining *you*. You're always taking my things."

"No, Noam, believe me. I'd remember if I had. I know how important your pen is to you. Did the phone ring while you were writing?"

"I don't know. In any case, I didn't answer it."

"Did you get up to get something to eat?"

"Hmmmm, let me think. I can't remember. Renee, how can you ask me to remember a trivial thing like that?"

"What time were you writing?"

"About eleven, twelve, I don't know."

"Well, did you eat late last night?"

"Yes! God yes! I had some ice cream!"

Hearts pounding, we ran to the refrigerator and flung open the freezer door. There, sitting absurdly between a can of orange juice and the rum-raisin Häagen-Dazs, gleamed a very cold black-and-silver Papermate.

Again and again they ask me, the other faculty wives, the worshiping graduate students, the lesser professors: What is it like to live with him, to live with a genius like Noam? If it were only the truth they were after, and not legends of greatness, I think I would know how to answer them. I believe I could describe life with Noam Himmel, that blazing star who first burst upon the mathematical heavens in 1950 at the age of twelve with his brilliant seminal paper, "On the Properties of Supernatural Numbers."

I lay my answer, my life, before you.

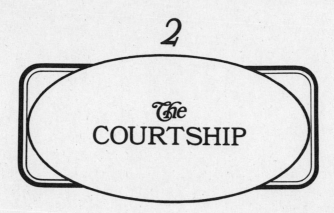

2

The COURTSHIP

Princeton is a wonderful little spot, a quaint and ceremonious village of puny demigods on stilts. . . . Here the people who compose what is called "society" enjoy even less freedom than their counterparts in Europe. Yet they seem unaware of this restriction, since their way of life tends to inhibit personality development from childhood.

—ALBERT EINSTEIN,
IN A LETTER TO QUEEN
ELISABETH OF BELGIUM

I met Noam Himmel soon after his triumphant arrival in Princeton. The sense of conquest was more on the part of the welcoming community, for once Himmel let it be known that he had tired of Cambridge and wanted to come back to the States, every prestigious mathematics department in the country had courted him. Princeton had had to promise him much. Besides rather a lot of money (in academic terms) and very light teaching duties, he was told that he might pick up and go on leave to another university whenever the spirit moved him. By accepting Princeton he wouldn't have to give up his other suitors entirely.

Noam Himmel was then thirty-eight, and had already been famous for twenty-six years, ever since the first startling publication presenting the supernaturals, the "Himmel numbers"—a new category of mathematical existence, to be counted amongst the naturals and integers, the rationals and irrationals, the reals and imaginaries and surreals and surds, the cardinals and ordinals, transcendentals and transfinites. The supernaturals were well named by their discoverer, for they are numbers so big that they are used for collections too large to form sets. How can there *be* such numbers? And yet there are. Himmel had proved them, these numbers that realize—in their immensity and enigma, their inaccessibility to reason too simplistic— all the suggestions of their name. If the work of the great Georg Cantor in the late nineteenth century had led mathematics up past the finite realm into the sublime heights of the transfinites, then the work of the twelve-year-old from Manhattan had led even beyond— to the transinfinites.

But Harvard had refused to accept the boy until he finished high school. (Some among the faculty had groused about prodigies who often burn themselves out early.) He had entered Harvard at sixteen, and four years later was teaching there. He had never bothered to get a Ph.D., and nobody had bothered to ask him to. And he hadn't burned himself out early. The twenty-six years had produced many mathematically important results, though none perhaps to equal the dazzling supernaturals.

My own position in the world of Princeton was incomparably inferior. I was a graduate student in philosophy, and not a highly successful one at that. My first year there had been disastrous, and my second, just beginning, gave every indication of being worse. In short, I was floundering, and thus quite prepared to follow the venerably old feminine tradition of being saved by marriage. And, given the nature of my distress, no one could better play the part of my rescuing hero than the great Noam Himmel. For the man had an extravagance of what I was so agonizingly feeling the lack of: objective proof of one's own intellectual merit.

My Barnard undergraduate experience had not prepared me for Princeton, not on any level. Even the physical presence of the place confounded my views of How Things Ought To Be. This affluent suburban town, so distressingly similar to the Westchester community in which I had grown up, this was a seat of serious scholarship? And its outrageously suburban-looking inhabitants were serious thinkers?

Princeton is an anomaly among college towns, I suppose because it really is not a college town. What it is is an old-wealth exurb with a pedigree reaching back to colonial times, *further* distinguished by the presence of a prestigious university laid out in the grand English manner: all massive gray stone and ivy-muffled red brick, archways and courtyards, sweeping lawns and ancient trees. There is none of the student-faculty grubbiness of an Ithaca or Cambridge, Mass. The town's tone, rather, is established middle age shading off into contented dotage, with no compromise made in the direction of student youth. The shops lining old Nassau Street, the main drag and the Western border of the campus, are stocked with Waterford and Wedgwood, Lenox and fine linens. Instead of the university's population imposing its character on the town, the school has absorbed the affluent attributes of its setting. Undergraduates are abnormally groomed and tailored here, looking the pampered parts of the children and grandchildren of privilege that they largely are.

My eyes were used to the gloom of Columbia's Broadway campus and were having trouble focusing amidst Princeton's brilliance. And not just my eyes were in need of readjustment. My views on The Life of the Mind had been modeled on the people I had known at

Columbia: urban intellectuals, unkempt, graceless, morose creatures who walked around with eyes downcast, muttering to themselves. Those were the sorts of bodies—neglected, misshapen, decaying—that serious minds belonged in. But here were these first-rate thinkers who worried about their backyards and backhands, who discussed Buber and black holes over barbecues. The genteel goyishness of the place overwhelmed me. There were Jews at Princeton, of course, but nobody *seemed* Jewish. At Columbia even the non-Jews had seemed Jewish.

The need to create this new category of being, the gentile suburban intellectual, threw me into a state of cognitive dissonance. The past few years I had gotten used to thinking of myself as an intellectual. I had assumed that certain properties of mind and body were entailed by this description and had designed myself accordingly. It's hard to discover you've constructed yourself on false premises.

But the dissonance reverberated in far deeper regions of my being. Not just my views of the intellectual were being challenged, but, more personally and painfully, my view of my own intellectual worth. I suffered badly the emergence from the dark womb-warmth of Barnard into the bright, brisk air of the Princeton philosophy department, where vagueness was not tolerated and people conversed fluently in the language of counterexamples. Every time I hazarded a statement someone would hurl a counterexample at it, or else accuse me of meaninglessness or metaphysical tendencies. I couldn't get anything past them.

I am not in the habit of dismissing any criticisms of myself, and am in general always willing seriously to consider any denunciation. Perhaps it was true, I therefore found myself thinking, that all the questions that interested me were really pseudo-questions, mere phantoms of my mental night. I couldn't deny that I suffered from metaphysical tendencies, though I hadn't realized until then that they constituted an affliction. In my pre-Princetonian backwardness I would have said that Reality is the subject matter of philosophy, but the very word, I now learned, was philosophically taboo for its suggestion of metaphysical tendencies.

The field had made the "linguistic turn" and I . . . had not. The questions were now all of language. Instead of wrestling with the large, messy questions that have occupied previous centuries of ethicists, for example, one should examine the rules that govern words like "good" and "ought." My very first seminar, given by a prominent visitor from England whose field, they told me, was metaphysics, was on adverbs. The metaphysics of adverbs? From Reality to . . . adverbs?

It appeared I was to spend the rest of my philosophical life thinking about language. For language is humanly manufactured and thus, presumably, thoroughly intelligible. The questions it posed might be difficult but were not, in principle, unanswerable. No more inexhaustible Reality to contend with and make us feel our human limitations. No more dark, inaccessible regions lying beyond the reach of reason's phallic thrusts. Reality was but a creature formed from one of the intellect's own ribs, from language. We could take care of her, fill her up and leave her spent.

The philosophical mind has long craved a limited universe. The pre-Socratic Pythagoreans, in their table of opposites, listed "limited" on the side occupied by "order," "light," "good," and "male." But only the last generation or two of philosophers have managed to show how very limited reality really is, extending no farther than our powers of expression. What a relief. What a blessed relief. No more bogeymen jumping out of dark corners shouting, "It can't be known! You'll never understand it!" These epistemological horrors used to be waiting at every philosophical turn. Now the nursery lamp of linguistic analysis has been turned on, dispelling all those scary shadows. There is the bright, cheery world of the nursery, small and familiar, with no sense of the unknown creeping in.

Einstein found most Princetonians rather green when compared with their ripened counterparts in the European hothouse: "Their way of life tends to inhibit personality development from childhood." Perhaps. It's possible to view the place as a kind of quality day-care center. That's not really my view, but then I'm not so old and wise as Einstein was in Princeton. It has struck me, however, that I know a surprising number of people who have never gotten beyond the "magic years," beyond the child's belief in his own supernatural powers. And a disproportionately large percentage of these are members of the philosophy department. Philosophy used to be thought of as the academic subject requiring the most maturity: it was all old men tripping on their white beards. But that was before they discovered the magic word, "meaningless." A phrase like "the meaning of life" is guaranteed to crack them up, producing the hilarity of preschoolers at bathroom words. They know how to make all such problems disappear. The meaning of life? Sentences have meanings, the conditions and nature of which they can elaborate in the greatest detail. Pondering about "the meaning of it all" is silly baby talk. Abracadabra.

It was confusing that philosophy had become the most antiphilosophical of all academic fields, not only refusing to consider any of the mysteries of existence (which is a position I can understand) but adamantly denying that there *are* any (which is a position I cannot understand). All metaphysical questions are meaningless, and anything that exceeds our comprehension can't *be*. Mystery is as impermissible as the logical contradiction, a sign that something is amiss in the reasoning. There is a kind of *reductio ad arcanum* form of argument employed by philosophers throughout the Analytic Philosophy Belt, from Oxford to Princeton and Harvard to the mispronounced Berkeley (named after the Irish idealist philosopher Bishop Berkeley, whose name is pronounced Barkeley). It's an analogue to the ancient *reductio ad absurdum*, the indisputable method of proving propositions true by showing their negations to lead to absurdities. Only with the *reductio ad arcanum* one proves that certain kinds of things can't exist by showing that their existence would present us with one or more nontrivial questions. Some, for example, have employed this method to argue away consciousness. For *its* existence would present us with the notoriously impenetrable mind-body problem.

"Reality doesn't accommodate itself to the size and shape of the human mind," I protested at one point in a philosophical discussion soon after my arrival, when I still felt entitled to voice philosophical opinions. Everyone stopped talking and stared at me. Finally, mercifully, someone spoke.

"That's a metaphysical statement" came the deadpan reply.

There could not, in that context, have been a worse insult.

Obviously I had little idea of what the philosophical enterprise was about, as I chokingly confessed to my assigned adviser, Professor

Herbert Pfiffel. Professor Pfiffel shook his great mane of yellowing white hair in solemn agreement, an act at once of sympathy and dismissal. For he was a kind man, but one whose philosophical life had been single-mindedly devoted to the opposition of people like me, the incurably metaphysical. He was one of the last living members of the famed Vienna Circle of logical positivists, the group that can be credited above all others with having discovered the powers of the word "meaningless." ("Metaphysicians are musicians without musical talent," said Rudolf Carnap, one of its founders.)

"Vell, my dear Miss Feuer, vat do you propose now to do?" Professor Pfiffel asked.

What indeed? I had come to believe in my philosophical ability and had been planning my life on the assumption of its existence. At college, once I made up my mind to work, nothing but praise and success had come my way. These had entered my bloodstream, never causing much of a high, but I needed them like a drug. Withdrawal was excruciating. My faultily constructed self crumbled. I thought, therefore I was. If I was not a thinker, what was I?

SOMETIME AROUND APRIL of my first year I stopped doing any work and occupied myself instead with seducing various graduate students who lived, like me, at the Graduate College. (This is the great cathedral dorm for unmarried graduate students that was built when Woodrow Wilson, who had wanted to model Princeton after Oxford, the Platonic Form of all universities, had been president of the university.) The world outside the campus gates surrendered itself to the senses, and so did I. If I couldn't find any affirmation of my worth in the mind, I would seek it in the body. There are other faculties of the person besides those of the *res cogitans*. I recalled and cherished once again my feminine powers, which had been lying dormant during the past years of serious intellectual occupation. As it had been in college with my cerebral efforts, which had brought immediate and abundant results, so it was now with my exertions in seduction. (Why am I repeatedly set up for the fall?)

Among my conquests was Peter Hill Devon, an epicene musicologist with exquisite taste and a pallid beauty advantageously displayed against the Princeton background. I had been aware of him ever since my arrival in autumn—the season of decaying beauty, Peter's season, in which he had made a perfect picture, striding across the lushly dying landscape in his genteely crumpled brown tweed jacket and brown cashmere scarf. He was blond and blue-eyed, but not in that banal, open-faced manner common to the Wasp species. His face was shut tight, the intrigue most acute around his eyes, which were large but appeared larger still because of the charcoal smudginess surrounding them. The whole image suggested prep gone slightly seedy, for me an unknown raised to a higher power of mystery. There had certainly been nothing like Peter walking Columbia's Broadway campus. And so, in the spring, when my body reasserted its existence, it immediately turned to Peter.

Student that I was, I had much to learn from this lover, and he assumed the role of pedagogue on the subject of Beautiful Things, his single interest. One couldn't rightly call Beauty his passion, for he had not been put together to be enthusiastic; but the finer things did cause the slight ripples in the general flow of his insouciance. We ate in his room from antique china plates with rims of deep blue and raised gold, and the wines in which he instructed me were sipped from heavy goblets with blood-red stems, while we sat opposite one another on his Dagestan prayer rug. We stared at one another, across that blue expanse of intricate pattern, from backgrounds so estranged as to endow the other with the flattering appearance of exoticism. For my part, the stories he told me of his world—of the upper reaches of Wasp society into which he had been born, and the underside of life to which he had been borne by the variety of his sexual interests —were as remote as fairy tales. He enjoyed, in his perversity, regaling me with anti-Semitic remarks of friends and relatives, which I, in my perversity, mildly enjoyed hearing. (Not that I believed all. The unadorned truth presented no special appeal to Peter's aesthetic sensibility.) Even he once said, with unwonted tenderness, as he lay beside me on the prayer rug in a quiet interlude after making love:

"You really could pass for Christian, you know." He was turned toward me, his golden head propped up on one open palm, while with the other he lightly traced my profile. I remained silent, smiling.

"And your name, too," he continued. "Feuer. It's not tellingly

Jewish. It could simply be German. You really could pass yourself off quite easily as a scion of German Protestant stock."

I laughed. Imagine *wanting* to pass yourself off as a scion of German Protestant stock. "Are you offering me suggestions or compliments?"

He laughed, too, giving my nose—which, like my name, wasn't giving away any secrets of lineage—an affectionate punch.

"Just wondering how to present you to the family."

Jack Gottlieb, another of my lovers at that time, was refreshingly familiar and straightforward, in contrast to Peter. He had gone to Columbia, though we hadn't met there, and when he first took me to his room at the Graduate College, and I saw his Sam Steinberg painting, I was overcome with a nostalgia that surged into desire. (Sam Steinberg has been, since 1931, Columbia's cherished artist, commuting from the Bronx apartment he shares with his sister, selling his pictures and candy bars in front of Ferris Booth Hall. "You don't want that picture. Maybe you want a Milky Way instead?")

Jack too was a first-year graduate student, but in math, with two impossible parents on Long Island mourning the fact that he hadn't gone to medical school. ("They kept hoping I'd outgrow the math.") He was very nervous about treading the sacred Princetonian ground, for the math and philosophy departments were rated the university's best, and tops in the country. Graduate admissions standards were correspondingly high—only eight to twelve were admitted each year by the two departments. Those who made it were exquisitely conscious of their acceptance into the circle of the elect, though some, like Jack and me, worried whether their own particular election was merited. Much anguish resulted from these musings. Everyone arriving had been the best at his or her college, unused to competing with equals. In many minds (mine included) "not the best" was synonymous with "worthless." I'm happy to report, for I actually liked Jack, that he persevered and overcame. His dissertation was an elegant solution to a difficult problem in analysis, and he's now got a peach of a job at Cornell.

Leonard Heiss was the last of that season's amorous crop, a man of letters who *never* removed his pipe. He was a precocious lad, with

18

a young mind already running to pomposity, as his body was running to fat. An interesting fact about Leonard that I gradually discovered was his not much liking women. (I reasoned he must be either homosexual or sadistic—and I always try to think the best of people.) He has me to thank for his eventual enlightenment. He went on to have an affair with Peter Devon, an unpardonable lapse in the latter's fastidiousness. Even I must ask myself, with some distaste, how I could have gone through the movements of love with someone I so little liked. But then I hardly acknowledged the actions as my own. I dissociated myself from them, and from the body so acting. *I* remained untouched and unpenetrated, a bloodless virgin in spirit through all my promiscuity. While I fancied myself a D. H. Lawrence woman, physical pleasure was quite irrelevant to me. What I was after was the feeling that I existed, that I mattered, if only to Peter, who inhabited the world of Protestant privilege in which, despite my profile, I felt my immigrancy; to Leonard, in his world of cocksure scholarship, in which I stood naked and ashamed; or to Jack, who connected me to the familiar and therefore dear world I had left behind. If these men desired me, then surely I counted for something in their worlds. Once again I felt little high, only need.

Things really deteriorated over the summer. The other philosophy graduate students seemed to take no notice of the change of season. Perhaps they weren't even aware of it, down in the climate-controlled depths of Firestone Library, in their minuscule carrels three flights below ground level. They and the mosquitoes thrived through the humidity of June, July, and August. (The university had originally been moved from Elizabeth because of the mosquito problem *there*. If only they had been able to think beyond New Jersey.) That humidity dissolved the last particles of my moral will. All faith grows faint in New Jersey in August. Even making love seemed hardly worth the effort. The embarrassing squashing sound that two damp bodies sometimes emit when they come together; having to peel one's wet body away from the other's: these details alone would have been sufficient to turn me away from the body—which is simply too . . . corporeal in the heat—had there been anything else to turn to. But the pleasures of the mind were gone.

The fall, when it came at last, cheered and revived me. Like all people in academia, I count my years the way the Bible does, from September to September. (Like schoolchildren, too—just one of the many ways in which the life of an academic is continuous with his childhood.) The new year gave me hopes of a fresh start, only slightly diminished when I ran into my adviser, who shook his great yellow-white mane in amazement that I was still around, and proffered no advice.

I went to the first few meetings of almost all the graduate philosophy seminars being given that fall; but my new hopes vaporized in their thin, analytic atmosphere. I'd sit at the large seminar table, trying but unable to keep my mind there. Incorrigible mind. It would drift off and become engaged in vivid fantasies—involving the seminar participants, for example, in arrangements devised by the Marquis de Sade—and then drift back down into the heat of the seminar discussion, in which my peers were devising complicated counterexamples for shooting each other down. A great wave of self-hate would rise up and threaten to knock me over. What was wrong with me? I didn't belong here. I didn't belong anywhere. I'd close my eyes and see myself doing myself some kind of violence, usually shooting a revolver into my head or slashing my wrists and throat. Not a good sign, I decided, and stopped attending seminars. I went back to my seductions in a more deadly earnest.

The teeth dream had returned, almost nightly. The dreamer feels her teeth loosening, tries desperately to hold them in, but tooth after precious tooth drops down into her cupped and trembling palm. The apple into which she has just bitten carries away dozens. I had had the dream so often before that even my dreaming self suspected I might be dreaming, but argued nightly that *this* time (because, for instance, the gums themselves were now loosening) it was no dream. (Do only dreaming philosophers try to determine whether they're dreaming—a habit begun by my namesake, René Descartes?) For those of you who have never dreamt the teeth dream, let me tell you, it's terrifying, much more unnerving than even real dental problems would be. Clearly, *gnädige Damen und Herren,* we are dealing here with the chitter-chatter of the unconscious. But what is it trying to say? Freud's interpretation is that (what else?) this is a castration dream: "The dream-work represents castration by baldness, haircut-

ting, the loss of teeth, and beheading." (And the apple? The apple!)
Here as elsewhere, however, the Doktor's thinking seems too nar-
rowly phallic. The loss of a penis is but one of the countless forms
of human powerlessness. We thrust not only with our penises. Perhaps the castrated member is itself but a symbol?

ONE MONDAY in October, Jack Gottlieb invited me to a party
given in honor of the famous Noam Himmel. I was of course anxious
to see the (aging) *Wunderkind,* and grateful to Jack for the invitation. I was familiar with many of the stories about the mathematician; he is rather an important figure in philosophy as well, because
of the work in logic he had done some years before, to which there
is yet another tale attached. Himmel had once told a colleague that
the problem with logic is its traditional connection (due to the accident of Aristotle, the first logician and one of the greatest of philosophers) with departments of philosophy rather than math. A decent
mathematician, Himmel claimed, could revolutionize the poky field
were he to think about it for a few days. The other mathematician
challenged Himmel to do so, and he did—producing a spare and
elegant solution to an outstanding problem in modern logic that
yielded a cornucopia of consequences.

   This was but one of the tales that contributed to the Himmel
legend. Like others I possessed a whole stock of Himmel stories, half
devoted to his genius, the remainder to his adorable ineptness in
dealing with the mundane world: Himmel taking the plane to Budapest while his colleagues were waiting to pick him up in Bucharest;
Himmel wandering around Cambridge in his pajamas; Himmel
hauled into a Berlin police station after innocently asking for directions. Eccentric personalities like Himmel provide fertile ground for
apocrypha (did Einstein really give daily help in sums to a little
schoolgirl, and did a local bus driver really snap, as Einstein fumbled
around for his fare, "Bad at arithmetic"?). But in Noam's case a
rather amazing number of these crazy tales actually turned out to be
true. It was a favorite activity at math and philosophy parties to swap
these stories—not only about Noam Himmel, of course, but about
all our greats (with a preference for those who were still living). And

the spirit informing the taletelling was love—hero-love. For when the superiority differential becomes large enough, we stop envying and start adoring.

Everyone loves a hero. What we differ on is the question of who the heroes are, because we differ over what matters. And who matters is a function of what matters. Here in Princeton what matters is intelligence, the people who matter are the intelligent, and the people who matter the most, the heroes, are the geniuses.

We Princetonians live together on the mattering map as well. But now I have lapsed into my private language, constructed around a private image of a vast and floating map composed of untouching territories. Philosophers may prove the nonexistence of mental images; yet I don't think a week goes by that this one doesn't flash momentarily before me, called forth by someone's saying something revelatory of his location in my private picture. A good deal of my thinking happens to go on in images (from which certain people have inferred that I do not think), so that verbalization presents problems of translation. I'm faced right now with a problem of translating all that this particular vision means to me.

People occupy the mattering map, though they don't happen to be present in my mental picture of it. The map in fact is a projection of its inhabitants' perceptions. A person's location on it is determined by what matters to him, matters overwhelmingly, the kind of mattering that produces his perceptions of people, of himself and others: of who are the nobodies and who the somebodies, who the deprived and who the gifted, who the better-never-to-have-been-born and who the heroes. One and the same person can appear differently when viewed from different positions, making interterritorial communication sometimes difficult. And then some of us do an awful lot of moving around from region to region.

At times I picture the separate regions as differently shaded, ranging from the palest of gray to true black, depending on how many and various are the perceptions they contain. Take the territory where what matters above all is music. It's a rather pale gray. Those who live here have heroes, of course, but they lack really general standards by which to judge people. Those who worship Mozart and Bach don't, as a rule, revile the tone-deaf. Gourmets, on the other hand, occupy a slightly deeper gray area, for they know not only whom to look up to—great cooks—but whom to look down on—consumers of frozen dinners, floury sauces, iceberg lettuce. People to whom clothes matter seem to live in a still deeper shade of gray where the heroes are the *couturiers*, or those who are clothed by them, and the *shlumps*, attired in indifference or bad taste, are dismissed out of hand. Since we are just about always presented to one another as dressed, those who see us through our clothes see much.

Then there are those regions (and we're getting into deeper gray now) where what matters is not a person's relationship with some external thing, such as food or clothes or music, but rather some intrinsic quality of his or her own: beauty or physical fitness. Or intelligence. Since we can discard these attributes even less easily than our clothes, we can always be strictly categorized according to the perceptions emanating from these areas: of who matters (the beautiful, the athletic, and the intelligent, respectively) and who doesn't (the ugly, the flabby and the dumb). Contempt for the unfit is stronger, I think, than disdain for the plain. Perhaps because of the passivity of beauty? But no, intelligence is every bit as passive, a gift either granted or denied. And yet the scorn felt for the unintelligent is an almost moral outrage. Never mind that the dull can't help themselves, that they would, granted the sense to do so, have chosen to be otherwise. Their very existence is felt as a moral affront by those of us who dwell where the genius is hero. The color of our zone is only just discernably lighter than the true black of those who perceive people according to their acceptance of some moral or religious or political code.

And so at those parties, when we sat around sharing stories of our heroes, of those now gone, like Einstein, or those still with us, like Himmel, we would get high on love, on love for our idols and love for each other. For in loving our great men and women we unite ourselves not only with human excellence, but also with one another. Those who share my heroes are, in the deepest sense, *of my own kind.*

"I should so much like to do something to hold together our colleagues in the various 'Fatherlands,' " Einstein wrote to the physicist Ehrenfest in the stormy days of 1915. "Is not that small group of scholars and intellectuals the only 'Fatherland' which is worthy of serious concern to people like ourselves?"

And now Noam Himmel had come, like Albert Einstein before him, to Princeton; and those to whom this mattered the most were celebrating. This party was but the first, given by the chairman of the victorious math department, Adam Loft. His house was a large Tudor on a block of large Tudors, all of them owned by the university and rented out to faculty. This particular one had been gutted and redone in very modern style, all white and light and angles, so that its interior was nothing like what one would expect from the outside. Tonight the house was packed with slightly hysterically hilarious mathematicians and their consorts. Himmel himself I picked out immediately, before he was pointed out by the flushed and bright-eyed Jack. (All the graduate students were flushed and bright-eyed that night.) Himmel was surrounded by eight or nine admirers, and everyone else kept glancing his way, like iron chips indicating the position of a magnet. His looks lifted my spirit, for they were of the type I knew best: shaggy and Semitic. His black hair was long and straggly, his beard rabbinically full, his clothes without apparent style or age. His incipiently paunchy body had almost certainly never jogged or chased a tennis ball, unlike the bodies of most of Princeton's population. Nevertheless, he was on the whole remarkably boyish-looking. It was hard to believe that this was the man who had worked out the supernaturals three years before I was born.

I could tell even at a distance that his face was unusually animated as he spoke, which he seemed to be doing constantly. As I came closer, I saw that the basically familiar features had an interesting variation: the eyes were a very clear blue. The voice, when I had worked my way into its range, which was wide, also seemed familiar: loud and unaffected, with lovely subdued hints of New York in the small rise at the end of the sentences. But as I listened more I heard that here too was a variation. The rate of speech was eccentric. For the most part Himmel spoke very quickly, sentences spilling out, as if impatient with the amount of labial effort required for the articulation of thought. Then occasionally his speech slowed down to such a rate as to leave one wondering, in between the drawled clauses, whether he was going to speak again or was rather waiting for a reply. It was the speech pattern of someone who was allowed, by an ever indulgent audience, to speak at the rate at which he thought, the eccentricity of one who could always be assured that his listeners awaited every uttered word.

As I had been majoring in seduction and minoring in parties for the last months, I could, after a little observation, detect the difference in the flavor of this one.

"Having your husband at a party is like adding anchovies to a salad," my friend Ava, who loves to speak in edible metaphors, once told me. "I love anchovies, but you can't taste anything else."

Sometime in the course of the evening I was introduced to him. I was but one in a surrounding circle, yet his eyes rested on me for a flatteringly long few seconds.

It was months before I saw him again. Over the winter I wrote a few papers, so I wasn't kicked out of the department. "But you're marginal, very marginal," the director of graduate studies had warned. I had enjoyed those papers. The old love of philosophy had returned. The process of thinking about philosophy always reminds me of fireworks. One question is shot up and bursts into a splendorous many. Answers? Forget answers. The spectacle is all in the questions.

But the moment I stepped out of the isolation into which I always retreat when I'm really working, and began to talk with other members of my department, all the doubts returned. Doubts not about the objects of thought, but about the thinking subject, me. I was overwhelmed again with the sense that I didn't know what philosophy was all about. One of my fellow graduate students suggested that my problem lay in my religious background; I had transplanted the attitude of Awe Before the Unknown to philosophy, where it definitely didn't belong. This analysis was provoked by my commenting that a certain question seemed very deep to me.

"Nothing is deep," he had drawled back reprovingly.

It was an unusually cold winter that year, with many days of clear blue skies and trees glistening with the frozen moisture. My relationships too became glazed over with ice. None of the men I was sleeping with touched me. Only one human contact, very slow in starting and developing, radiated any warmth. This was with a

woman, Sarah Slater, who attended the Plato seminar I had begun but given up along with the others. Sarah's field is history of philosophy, as opposed to philosophy proper. She was almost finished with her dissertation on Locke's theory of identity, but she was still attending as many seminars as she could. At first she infuriated me. She seemed the closest thing to a disembodied spirit this side of the veil. Her face is a Puritan's, quite literally. Her ancestors on both sides go back to colonial New England, where one was burned as a witch. (I can easily imagine a believing age burning my friend on similar grounds.) Physically she's composed of lines and angles and planes: a tall, rigidly held body, long, straight brown hair, long, straight eyebrows stretching perpendicular to the straight outlines of her face. There isn't a compromising curve to be found in Sarah. This external severity made the discovery of the softness and humor within all the sweeter.

But I made the discovery only slowly. I would watch Sarah as I sat in the Plato seminar, her face pale and expressionless, making subtle points about the Greek in her colorless voice. (In college she had written a little Greek grammar book that is still used.) I would watch her and feel rage. "My God, she's a virgin," I would think with fury. I don't know why I was so angered by the thought. I remember the words "She doesn't have the right" going through my mind. The right to what? To purity, I suppose, though it's characteristic of our relationship that after all the years of intimacy I still have no idea whether this initial assumption of mine was or is correct. The physical fact is of no consequence. For what I discovered, as we saw more and more of each other through the late winter and early spring, was that one could tell anything to that puritanical face and have it exposed to intelligence and wit, but never moral disapproval. She shut nothing and no one out.

Sarah and I often shared our meals together in the formal dining hall at the Graduate College, where the university came closest to approximating the Oxford ideal. The immense cathedral-like room has stained-glass windows and wooden gargoyles carved along the beams. (I seem to recall one grinning creature with a toothbrush, being somehow connected with a gift from Procter & Gamble, but the image is so surreal that I suspect it has been gleaned from a dream.) Meals were served promptly, preceded by a Latin grace from the master at high table. I would remind myself that I was separated from Barnard's grubby Barnard-Hewitt-Reid cafeteria not by the Atlantic but by nothing more than most of northeastern New Jersey. We were required to don black robes at meals, yet another Oxford affectation, this one abandoned soon after I left, since the students had taken to shredding the full sleeves into long kinky fringes.

Yet I had loved the sight of Sarah in her robes, in which the rest of us looked so absurd, for her external form had come into its own amidst the severity of those folds. The two of us spent much of our time laughing about philosophy and philosophers, although for Sarah this meant laughing about her life. Always when she left me it was to return to her carrel to work.

IT WAS MARCH when I saw Himmel again. I had just boarded the dinky, the two-car train that shuttles between Princeton and Princeton Junction to meet the trains going north to New York and south to Philadelphia, when I saw a figure loping down the hill toward us. That's what "galumphing" means, I thought, as I watched it approach: hair, tie, jacket, papers all flowing. I was surprised that something could move at once so awkwardly and so quickly. As the localized commotion got nearer, I saw it was Noam Himmel running to catch the train. Wouldn't it be exciting if he were to sit with me, I thought, and then dreaded that he might. How would I ever keep up a conversation with him?

He galumphed onto the train a second before it started. A girl and a boy holding hands glanced up at him, and then the boy whispered something to the girl and they both laughed. I was infuriated on Himmel's behalf. It was outrageous that these nitwits (in comparison, surely) should share a superior laugh at the expense of a genius. Like the prisoners in Plato's cave, I thought, laughing because the sun-dazzled philosopher can't see in their darkness. He spotted me immediately and came toward me. God help me, I thought, feeling stupid and inadequate, dreading the exposure to the bright light of his understanding. Many of the stories about Himmel were devoted to his intolerance of stupidity.

"Renee Feuer, isn't it? Graduate student, philosophy?"

Remarkable memory. But then what else should I have expected? He was looking very pleased as he sat down next to me. And then I remembered, with that small surprise I always feel when I consider myself from the outside, that what *he* was seeing was a delicate-featured young woman with long legs and waist-length honey hair. From that point of view I was acceptable. At least for the moment, I thought, until I start speaking.

"New York?" he asked.

"Yes, of course. You?"

"I'm giving a talk at NYU. You?"

"Oh, I'm just going in for my weekly fix of the city."

He simply smiled at that. I assumed it was a smile of comprehension.

"You're a New Yorker, aren't you?" I asked.

"Well, I grew up in Manhattan, but I've lived there only very occasionally during the past twenty-two years. New York's proximity to Princeton was one of the deciding factors in my coming here."

Common ground. *Terra sancta.* I feel an immediate closeness to anyone who loves New York or hates Los Angeles. Either condition is sufficient, but I've found that satisfaction of the one usually entails satisfaction of the other.

"I would never have lasted out this year in Princeton if I couldn't get into New York and breathe," I said.

"Oh, don't you like Princeton?"

"I find it difficult to breathe in an atmosphere in which one's intelligence is always being assessed. But of course you wouldn't know about that."

"What do you mean?" The blue eyes, which were so unexpected in that face, had a very powerful stare. Noam is a man who insists on eye contact. I was already finding this somewhat disconcerting and kept gazing slightly ahead of him. He, in response, kept moving his head forward to meet my gaze squarely. At this rate he'll be off his seat before the Junction, I thought.

"I don't suppose you ever feel stupid."

"On the contrary, I very often feel stupid. I often have the experi-

28

ence of not being able to understand what everyone else seems to. Somebody will say something and I'll think, Now what the hell does that mean? That doesn't make any sense. And then someone else will answer and his response is as incomprehensible as the first one's statement. And back and forth they go, intelligible to one another, unintelligible to me. Obviously there must be some meaning there if they're understanding one another. And usually the things being discussed aren't even supposed to be deep." He laughed. His laugh was higher pitched than his speaking voice. "It's curious, but the things I find obvious other people find difficult. They're amazed that I can see them so easily, and it sometimes takes me a tremendously long time to get others to see what I saw instantaneously. But then fairly average people will have intuitions on a whole range of topics that I can't get a hold on at all."

"Maybe you're simply not interested in those topics."

"I'm not. However, it's impossible to tell which is a function of which. Am I uninterested because I'm dense or dense because I'm uninterested?" He laughed in a way that showed this question too didn't overwhelmingly concern him.

"Is it lonely to have one's mind work differently from most people's?"

The blue eyes widened: "Lonely? It's damned lucky. A lucky thing for me that it's been decided the things I can see are the important ones, so I turn out smart instead of stupid. Oh, I think maybe when I was very young I was lonely for a while. There weren't too many other kids interested in playing around with numbers all the time. But I discovered early on that I liked ideas much better than people, and that was the end of my loneliness. For one thing, ideas are consistent. And you can control them better than people." He smiled. "Hell, to be honest I've just always found them more interesting. Logical relations are transparent and lovely. Human relations, from what I can tell, always seem pretty muddy."

"I suppose you're right that human relations are rarely very pretty," I said hesitantly. "But there are reasons besides the aesthetic for valuing them, aren't there?"

He leaned toward me as I spoke. He seemed to want to suck all the contents from my comments, as if they mattered that deeply to him. There could be no greater reassurance for me, short of the declaration: "You are brilliant. Speak."

"I'm not talking about valuing them," he answered. "That's a psychological or perhaps an ethical question. I'm talking about thinking about them. One can think they're good things to have even if one doesn't think they're interesting to contemplate. I've just never found anything much to engage the mind there. Of course that might just be my particular brand of stupidity again." He grinned.

"What *about* the ethical questions? Do you think they're interesting?"

"Well, when you talk about ethics you change the subject. It's no longer human relations that are your objects, but rights and obligations. And those are, I would say, important topics. But for myself, I don't derive much pleasure from thinking about them. The properties of rights and obligations are not what I would call theoretically pleasing. They don't form lovely patterns." He smiled. "Of course, perhaps I ought to think about them anyway. That's yet another ethical question, whether we have an ethical obligation to consider ethical questions, including this very one. However, since I haven't considered the question, I don't know that we do have such an obligation and thus feel no obligation to consider this question. If you follow." He grinned.

Self-referring propositions, as I was to learn, are a favorite source of humor for Noam, and he loves constructing them.

I ought to mention that in the course of our conversation we had arrived at the Junction, had crossed the tracks and boarded the New York–bound train. Himmel had never stopped speaking, had paid no attention to the details of descending, crossing, and ascending, of finding new seats. I wondered how he managed when alone.

"I seem to remember a poem by someone, Edna St. Vincent Millay, I think, beginning, 'Euclid alone has looked on Beauty bare.' I can't remember the rest."

"Yes?" He smiled. "Well, surely others beside Euclid have had the privilege. Euclidean geometry isn't even the prettiest of the geometries. But Beauty bare. That's good. I like that. So many people have no sensibility whatsoever for mathematical beauty, are even arrogantly skeptical of its existence. But of course beauty is what math is all about, the most pure and perfect beauty."

"You're really an aesthetician," I said. Or a strange breed of hedonist, I thought.

"Yes? Perhaps. Perhaps all mathematicans are. I've never thought about it before. You see," he grinned. "At least I'm consistent. I don't find people in general very interesting to think about, so I don't find myself in particular an arresting object of thought. A lot of people seem to assent to the universal proposition but decline instantiation when it comes to themselves."

By now I was feeling quite comfortable holding his high-intensity gaze, and we both laughed into each other's eyes. It was a happy moment.

"Oh dear." I smiled. "We seem, you and I, only to talk about boring things."

"That's true." He smiled back. "I wonder why I'm enjoying it so much. I wonder why I'm wondering when I can discuss these mind-deadening issues with you again."

We made a date to meet for dinner the following evening.

The next evening, as I walked up Witherspoon Street toward La-hiere's, the restaurant I had suggested since Himmel was apparently unaware of the existence of any such establishments, I saw him coming up Nassau Street from the direction of Fine Hall, the mathematics building. He was walking very quickly, everything still flowing, including the pile of papers he was carrying under his arm—a figure which, even in a town like Princeton, attracted stares. He of course was oblivious to the attention, lost in his own head. As I watched him cross Nassau Street against the light, I thought surely God must love mathematical geniuses.

His brow was, I saw as he got nearer, deeply furrowed and his lips were moving slightly. He didn't notice me until he was right alongside and I put my hand gently on his shoulder to halt his full pace.

"Oh." He looked at me, blank for a moment, then focused that full beam of his in on me: "How are you? how are you? how are you?" Leaning toward me he searched my face for I knew not what.

"Just fine, just fine, just fine." I laughed.

"You know, it occurred to me that I never asked you what kind of philosophy you do."

"Oh, I guess right now I'm doing philosophy of body."

31

"Philosophy of body? I've heard of philosophy of mind, but not of body. Tell me about it."

He hadn't understood my comment as the joke I had meant it to be. I was embarrassed at having put forth a joke that didn't even succeed in making its presence felt, and tried to recoup.

"Well, if there's a philosophy of mind, why shouldn't there be a philosophy of body? After all, the main question in philosophy of mind is the mind-body problem. Why assume only the mind makes the relationship between them problematic? Why assume only mind needs analysis? Why prejudge the issue by approaching it only from the point of view of a philosophy of mind?" And I worried that I couldn't think on my feet.

"I see what you're saying. There really isn't any such established area in philosophy. What you're saying is, you're working on the mind-body problem and you believe it's body rather than, or perhaps as well as, mind that is problematic."

"Very problematic. Fraught with difficulties," I drawled in my most pedantic manner.

This conversation took place out on the sidewalk in front of La-hiere's. Himmel had made no move to go in, had become completely absorbed in our conversation out there, leaning toward me, concentrating on my comments. I realized that if we were going to eat at all I'd better take some initiative, so I moved toward the door.

I asked him, as we were being seated inside, whether he was interested in philosophy.

"Oh yes, very, though I've never had the time to read as much as I'd like. I've mostly read in those areas that are contiguous with math, you know, foundations of math, philosophy of logic. I've read a little Quine. I find his views baffling."

Noam then launched into a critical discussion of the views of Quine and Putnam, two Harvard philosophers, that logic is empirical and that it perhaps ought to be revised to overcome the paradoxes posed by quantum mechanics. Noam thought these ideas the height, or depth, of absurdity: "not worth considering, except that they have had, incredibly, some influence, especially among the physicists.

"Some of the most idiotic statements I've been forced to listen to have come from physicists talking about math and logic. It's hard to

32

find one—especially among the younger set, whose minds have all been warped by quantum mechanics—who has sensible views. I have a feeling that they don't even know what they're saying, that they're just mouthing words. That's the most charitable interpretation I can give to their babble. Otherwise I'd just have to conclude that they're imbeciles. Is it anything but imbecile to believe that a truth like the law of noncontradiction is empirical? That the only grounds for its truth lie in the nature of experience? Of course, a lot of these characters don't even know how to make the elementary distinction between the psychological grounds for our *belief* that some fact is true and the actual grounds for its truth. All knowledge turns out to be trivially empirical then, although I wonder if they even realize this. Anyway, it seems this confusion is partly responsible for their imbecile views. Their arrogance seems to be another factor. Everything's empirical, it's all up to them." He was shaking his head and smiling, rather meanly. "They're going to get out their little measuring sticks and meters, and tell us which of the many logics is the empirically true one. As if it really were in the realm of possibility to adopt a new logic, a quantum logic. What's the realm of possibility supposed to *mean* if that's possible? You know, it's rather funny. Previous ages believed that only God is mysterious and powerful enough to transcend logic. God is the only being for whom it's all right to predicate contradiction. Now it's electrons. Irrationality hasn't been wiped out by the physical sciences, it's just been rechanneled."

Noam went on to a less polemical, more detailed analysis of this view he despised, showing how its proponents contradicted themselves, using the very logic they would abandon in the argument for its abandonment.

"Of course"—he laughed—"the charge of self-contradiction may not bother them. They can respond by just giving up the law of noncontradiction."

Noam's "little knowledge" of these philosophers sounded more coherent than anything I'd heard in the countless discussions of them in 1879 Hall, Princeton's philosophy building. And the topic came alive as Noam discussed it. The beauty of his conversation has always been the simplicity with which he discusses the most complex of subjects. Often, as I listened in the early days, there would come into my mind the image of a soggy piece of cloth, crumpled and beginning to mildew, being shaken out with one powerful *thwack*—Noam's intellect—and hung up flat in the sunshine.

His obliviousness to external details was contagious, and when the waiter came to take our orders neither one of us had yet opened the menu.

"I'll have the soft-shelled crabs," I told the waiter, having sampled them on previous occasions. "They're good here," I said to Noam, who was looking pitifully at bay. This transition from extreme intellectual confidence to just as extreme practical helplessness was the sharpest I had ever witnessed. One minute ago this pathetic specimen had been magisterially denouncing the views of the most influential American philosopher as contemptible. It's quite clear where the borders of his turf are drawn, I thought, feelings of protectiveness oozing up in me.

"Good. I'll have them, too." Noam looked as if he had solved a major problem.

"I bet I'll enjoy them more than you." I told him as the waiter left, emboldened to the point of flirtatiousness by the display of Himmel's awkwardness.

"Oh, why is that?"

"Because I was brought up an Orthodox Jew. For me they're seasoned with sin."

"I'm afraid I don't understand."

"They're *trayf*, unkosher."

"Crabs? I thought only pig products were unkosher."

Noam, it turned out, was amazingly ignorant of things Jewish for someone who had grown up in New York (a more relevant fact than his being Jewish). He, in turn, was amazed by my account of my upbringing, particularly the girls' yeshiva I had very hastily been enrolled in when non-Jewish boys from my public school began telephoning for dates. I had gone to public school only because my parents couldn't afford to send both my brother and me to the expensive day school, Hillel Academy, serving Westchester's conservative and (less populous) Orthodox communities. My brother, being male, got priority. And sending me to a yeshiva in the dangerous city had been out of the question. But not quite as out of the question as those boys calling nightly on the phone. So I was soon commuting to the Lower East Side, to one of the more right-wing of the all-girl schools. The teachers here checked our hemlines for modesty every morning, and the principal came into our biology class at the start of our lesson on evolution, informing us that although they were required to teach this for the New York State regents' exam, it was all unproved *apikorsus*, or heresy, and we shouldn't believe any of it. But, as my mother often wails, "It was too late. You were already an *apikoros.*"

And so I was. The word is derived from the same source as the noun and adjective "epicurean"—from the Greek philosopher Epicurus, who taught that pleasure is the good and "the root of all good is the pleasure of the stomach; even wisdom and culture must be referred to this." Hence our "epicurean," although in practice the philosopher found that the pain of stomachaches outweighed the pleasures of indulgence and so kept to a diet of bread and water, with a little preserved cheese on feast days. "I am filled with pleasure of the body when I live on bread and water, and I spit on luxurious pleasures, not for their own sake but because of the inconveniences that follow them." Epicurus was really no epicurean. But he was an *apikoros*, even about his own Hellenistic religion. "We, and not the gods, are masters of our fate." Definitely an *apikoros*, this Epicurus. Dante found his followers in hell. *Apikoros* was a much used word in my high school, and it wasn't too difficult to be labeled one.

"We weren't supposed to go to college."

"Why not?" Noam asked. "What were you supposed to do?"

"Get married, of course. And be fruitful and multiply, God's very words to Abraham."

Noam was dumbfounded. "It's a world I never knew existed. I pretty much took it for granted that Jews are generally enlightened. It sounds like a description of the Middle Ages."

"Oh, much older than that. How about the Babylonian captivity?"

"And you didn't swallow any of it. What about your siblings? Do you have any?"

"My brother swallowed what they fed him and hollered for more. My parents had wanted him to go to college, but he wouldn't. He sits and learns."

"He what?"

"Sits and learns. That's the expression for studying Talmud. You have heard of the Talmud?" He nodded. "That's what he does, at a yeshiva in Lakewood, New Jersey. His wife supports him. It's a very accepted, even respected *modus vivendi.*"

"And here you are studying philosophy at Princeton, having been suckled on all this irrationality. It's amazing. You're an amazing woman."

His words kindled my ever ready vanity, but I also felt that pinch of uneasiness I always get when people put rationality on one side and religion on the other. Not that I haven't been known to think in exactly those terms, especially when I'm in the company of my religious relatives. But people remote from religion, whether they were born there or struggled there, tend to simplify the other side. (It goes without saying that the religious do likewise.) I'm amused when people talk of the "religious mentality" or the "religious personality," and always think of my father, my mother, my brother and my sister-in-law, all of whose religious personalities had little in common apart from their being Jewish.

"Oh, I wouldn't say that I don't take any of it seriously, at least on a very primitive level. Sometimes, especially on insomniac nights, I start worrying that there may be a God, and worse, that he may be Jewish."

"So?"

"So, if there is and He is, I'm in a lot of trouble. You too, by the way." I bit down hard on a forkful of crab to give my statement emphasis.

Noam shook his head. "I just can't connect to any of this. It's a world I can't make any sense of."

"Unfortunately, I can. I can make sense out of both worlds: Lakewood, New Jersey, and Princeton, New Jersey. So I can't feel really comfortable in either."

Noam just shook his head and shrugged.

"Is it really so alien to you?" I asked him. "Aren't your parents at all traditional, or your grandparents?"

"My parents are both dead. They both hated religion—opiate of the people and all that. I never knew my grandparents."

"And you hate religion?"

"It doesn't arouse the passion in me it did in my parents, but then I've never had to deal with it. It just seems juvenile, a child's conception of reality. I'm always a little surprised when I find reasonably intelligent people who haven't outgrown it." Again he shrugged.

"Have you ever read *Moses and Monotheism?*" I asked.

"No, what's that?"

"Freud," I answered, again surprised. Noam and I would always amaze one another by what we didn't know. Of course, my shock was always the greater, since I expected so much more; nothing less, in those days especially, than omniscience.

"Oh, him." Noam's smile was nasty. "What's he say? Religion is an incestuous desire for the father?"

"You're not too far off target. It's a neurotic fixation on the repressed tribal memory of the murder of the primeval father."

"Don't bother to explain."

Noam finally gave his food some attention as our first silence fell upon us. I was regretting having brought Freud up. It occurred to me that perhaps this entire subject of religion was utterly boring to Noam and that I hadn't noticed the signs because of my own neurotic religious fixation, tribal or otherwise. But *he* continued the discussion:

"You know, come to think of it, my parents did name me after my paternal grandfather, who was killed in a pogrom in Russia. That's a piece of Jewish tradition, isn't it?"

"Getting killed in pogroms?"

"Cute." Noam laughed. "But what about it?"

"Yes, you're right. In fact, if Jews name after a person at all, it's someone who's dead."

"Why is that?"

"I'm not quite sure. To honor the dead, I guess, to keep their memory alive. It's taken very seriously. I've known people who actually had a child because there was a name they wanted to pass on." (This has always seemed to me an extraordinarily insufficient reason for creating a person. A *person*, for Godsakes. But then the awesomeness of this act of responsibility so impresses me that I don't know if I'll ever come up with a reason I can judge sufficient.) "Wait a minute. I remember once hearing of a superstition that in passing on the names you passed on the souls. That would explain why you shouldn't name after the living, too."

"What?" Noam said very loudly, leaning across the table, his beard grazing my broccoli.

"Well, you know, there was a lot of superstition in the old country."

"But tell me about this, about passing on the souls. I'd never heard that Jews believed anything like that."

"I'm afraid I don't know very much about it. It's not the sort of thing one studies in yeshiva. Jewish thinkers for the most part devote themselves to the interpretation of the law, not to metaphysical questions. It's very different in that regard from Catholicism."

"Is there a belief in transmigration of souls?" he asked impatiently. He was obviously excited, rocking back and forth in his chair. Funny, I thought, he looks like he's *shuckling,* making the rhythmic motions of Orthodox Jews in prayer. Could this too be genetic, another tribal inheritance? Let his *payess* (sideburns) grow, stick a yarmulke on his head, he'd be the perfect picture of a yeshiva *bocher.*

"I don't think so," I answered. "Not officially. Just like heaven and hell aren't official. But there might have been some such belief among the people. And for all I know, that might be the source of the naming tradition."

"Interesting." The self-absorbed *shuckling* was attracting glances and, again, those infuriatingly superior shared smiles. He asked me some more questions, none of which I could answer. It was his turn to be surprised by my ignorance. How could someone of my background have failed to apprise herself of the facts on the subject?

"It's just not the kind of thing one studies in yeshiva," I repeated defensively.

Suddenly Noam (I was now thinking of him as Noam rather than Himmel) looked at his watch, which was fastened at one chink of its band with a paper clip. (Much of Noam's life is held together by paper clips.)

"Oh my God! I'm terribly late! This is really awful. I've got to run." And he pushed back his chair, almost toppling it, and ga-lumphed out. Everybody in the vicinity but me was very pleased by the performance. I hadn't even given him the copy of the Millay poem I had xeroxed in Firestone Library. I paid the check and left.

He called me the next day, having gotten my phone number from the philosophy department. I was touched by these efforts, which I (rightly) suspected were preternatural.

"I'm sorry for rushing off like that yesterday. I had promised to speak at Fitzer's graduate seminar and I was terribly late. I realized after that I had left you with the check." He invited me to a party for the following evening, given by Professor Fitzer.

The party was pretty dreadful. (How much more dread would it have inspired had I realized how many similar parties awaited me.) Fitzer's small brick house was near Lake Carnegie, not far from the Harrison Avenue bridge. It was a modest, strictly Euclidean affair, rectangular from the outside and divided up inside into a few rectangles and squares. The majority of the house seemed to be on the subterranean level, in a paneled den that seemed to enjoy a larger area than the frame of the house would allow, extending out perhaps beneath the small square front garden. The party took place in the den, which was furnished entirely in Lucite, perhaps to minimize the furniture's interfering with the geometry.

After the initial fluttering around Noam, the men, all mathematicians, settled down to talk shop while the women spoke among themselves of children, grandchildren, travel and gardening. It was a party of the senior faculty—in fact, it seemed, the senior of the seniors, the departments' gray eminences. The women were all soft-spoken and sweet, cherishing, quite clearly, the appearance of unflappable exteriors. I tried to modulate my voice accordingly. There was nothing to be done about my obvious raw youth. I was gratified, though, by the women's discreet inquisitiveness about my relationship with Noam. They asked subtle, indirect questions, to which I gave subtle, indirect answers.

There was one amusing little outburst from (of course) the men. Noam and this fellow, Raoul, the only other non-gray mathematician there, had a disagreement over the terms "obvious" and "trivial." Raoul had said that something was obvious.

"No, it's not," said Noam. "It may be trivial, but it's not obvious."

"Obvious, trivial, what's the difference?"

"A great difference. A theorem is obvious if it's easy to see, to grasp. A theorem is trivial if the logical relations leading to it are relatively direct. Generally, theorems that are trivial are obvious. If the logical relations leading to it are straight, it's easy to get to. And conversely. Thus the sloppy conflation of the terms." He glanced darkly at Raoul. "But the meanings are different, as are the extensions. Sometimes the logical relations are direct but not so accessible. You know the old joke about the professor who says that something is trivial and is questioned on this by a student and goes out and works for an hour and comes back and says, 'I was right. It is trivial'?" He paused for the laughter to stop. "Well, he concluded, "you couldn't substitute 'obvious' for 'trivial' in that joke."

"But of course there's another sense of 'trivial,' " someone said. "Insignificant, undeep."

"Yes, of course," Noam said. "That's a secondary sense." This secondary sense is a great favorite of Noam's. Events, ideas, people —oh, definitely people—are classified as trivial or nontrivial. It's his way of distinguishing between what and who matters and what and who doesn't.

"Your explication seems vague to me," the persistent Raoul objected. "A theorem is obvious if it's easy for *whom* to see?"

"For God and Himmel," someone said.

Noam laughed. "Make that Himmel and God."

"I'm sorry, that wasn't really an evening together, was it?" Noam said as we walked back to the Graduate College in soft silk air smelling of spring. Can't he even take my hand? I was thinking. "Unfortunately, I have a dinner party tomorrow night. But why don't we have dinner on Friday? This time I'll pay, I promise. It will have to be quite late, though. I won't be free until after nine."

We had our late dinner that Friday night, and a long lunch on Saturday, lunch on Sunday, and dinner again on Wednesday. Through all this Noam's vivid gaze and conversation were the only things that held me. I hadn't had such a chaste romantic relationship with a man since high school. (I was fairly certain it was romantic.)

I began to realize, as I had on the sidewalk outside Lahiere's, that I would have to take the initiative if we were going to do more than eat and talk.

That Thursday was a glorious, blooming day. When we met for lunch, I suggested that we just buy some strawberries at Davidson's and a bottle of Beaujolais at Nassau Liquors and go have them over on the other side of Lake Carnegie.

"I'll show you where the wild asparagus grow."

And I did.

There's been so much serious discussion devoted to the profound question of the vaginal vs. the clitoral orgasm. Why doesn't anyone speak about the mental orgasm? It's what's going on in your head that can make the difference, not which and how many of your nerve endings are being rubbed. Judged on the quantitative neurological scale, our lovemaking wasn't memorable. It's other details I remember:

Noam downed more than his share of the wine, according to his characteristic style of mechanically finishing off whatever he's given, saving himself from having to deliberate over what and how much to eat. I watched him in pleased (get 'em drunk) astonishment as he gulped the wine down like a bottle of Coca-Cola.

He lay back, positioning his face in the shade of my body, looking up at me. He was quiet for once. Was it the wine or the sight of me with the sun pouring down on my head? I had a very sharp impression —now transformed into an equally vivid memory—of how I must have appeared to him, lit up against the brilliant blue sky.

"Like sunlight made tangible," he said, tentatively touching my hair.

Our first kiss was hebetically clumsy, for I took him by surprise. I took him by surprise a good part of the way. At each early stage of our very linear progress from first kiss to final gasp he searched my face, all his features asking: "You don't mean to . . . ? I couldn't possibly . . . could I?" and then expressing their pleasure at the answer they found in my look. This catechism of facial expressions only once broke out into speech:

"Could we be arrested?" he asked before entering me.

And I remember too the intensity of my pleasure, which wasn't at

41

all physical, as he shuddered within me while inside my head sang the triumphant thought: I am making love to this man . . . to Noam Himmel . . . the genius.

NOAM AND I saw each other nearly every day after that. Often we'd go driving on the country roads that radiate out from Princeton. I always took the wheel. It was my car, for Noam had none—in fact, his license had expired three years after he had gotten it. And anyway I love to drive, and am rather vain about how well I do it: fast and smooth, with consummate skill. (I would really like nothing better than to climax this narrative with a car chase: me at the wheel, burning up the tires on Ivy Lane, Faculty Road, fleeing from or after God knows what. But such, alas, is not the nature of my story.) Some of my moments of deepest self-satisfaction have been brought on by the perfection of my parallel parking. No one can get into tighter spaces with greater ease. (How appealing I find the suggestiveness of language. I don't envy Noam the precision of mathematics in the least.) And there is a metaphysical kick to be gotten out of controlling a car, out of the expansion of one's spatial boundaries that driving involves. One's consciousness almost seems to move beyond the epidermal limits as one maneuvers in space, the body image subtly diffusing itself outward.

Actually, I do recall one occasion when Noam took the wheel. I think it was because I had drunk too much wine at lunch. I discovered then that Noam's rate of thinking set the pace not only for his rates of talking and walking, but for his rate of driving as well. We decelerated from seventy miles an hour to twenty in a matter of sentences, and then, Noam having thought through the point, raced up to eighty. It was my one experience of car sickness, and afterwards I always drove. Noam was quite content to sit back and be chauffeured, as he is content to sit back and let others take care of all of life's practicalities.

And there have always been people only too happy to do so. There was a long chain of surrogate mothers and fathers (but especially mothers) in all the university towns along the way, extending back to the first, the natural mother, who had devoted herself to the cause of his genius almost from his infancy, when it had emerged quite spectacularly. He learned to count early; numbers were among his first words. Before long he was proving some numerical truths algebraically, having discovered this way of thinking on his own. In those early years he recapitulated some of the early history of mathematics, producing, for example, a proof of the Pythagorean theorem.

So Mother Himmel had certainly had a worthwhile cause. The father I picture as having been somewhat alienated by his son's genius and his wife's rapturous devotion to it. But I don't really know. Such details are supplied through the faculty of my imagination. Noam has always had very little to say about the elder Himmels—even back then in the days of our courtship, when, in the first flush of his attraction to me, he found himself a passably interesting object of thought and was willing to talk about himself. Almost all my special acquaintance with his history, knowledge apart from the commonly shared legends, derives from those few months before our marriage. He was willing then to consider almost any of the personal questions I put to him, although he often could not provide the answers. He had noticed so little.

"What was she like, your mother?" We were driving back toward Princeton in the dusk.

"Oh, I don't know. A fairly ordinary kind of woman." He considered several moments. "She was a very good mother."

Both his parents had died when Noam was in his late twenties, within two years of each other, the mother from a brain tumor, the father from a stroke.

"Do you have any pictures?"

"No. I once had a picture of her, when she was in college, I think. It got lost during one of my moves."

I could understand that. I could well imagine the chaos that must have accompanied Noam's change of domicile.

"Was she very smart?" Was she smarter than I, I was thinking. Does Noam long for a woman who can approximate the brilliance of his devoted mother? "Where did she go to college?"

"She was reasonably intelligent." He looked uncomfortable. The question hadn't pleased him. Why? "She went to City College. My father, too. I think they met there. I vaguely remember something about their having met on some campus march. They were both interested in politics."

"Marxist?" I recalled Noam's use of the expression "opiate of the people" in connection with their views on religion.

"Yes, I suppose. I never paid too much attention."

His father had been a pharmacist. I induced Noam, not too long after this conversation, to take me to see the ancestral drugstore, on the corner of Broadway and 89th Street. (The family had lived around the corner on Riverside Drive.) It's still a serious specimen of the kind, given over more to pharmacopoeia than to beauty aids. But a concession to frivolity has been made since the Himmel days, in the form of a long counter stretching along one side wall, cluttered with cosmetics and perfumes. Noam told me that in his family's day a soda fountain had stood there, where he had spent most of his after-school hours playing with numbers. The supernaturals had been pursued and apprehended there. "They ought to have a plaque," I said, staring at the trifling display. "In Europe there would be a plaque. We should tell the owners. Imagine how good it would be for business." But the look of the woman behind the cash register, produced by an abundant application of the goods on the offending counter, didn't encourage the belief that she would be overly moved by the history of the store. We bought some Tums—for old times' sake and for Noam, who suffers from chronic stomach problems— and left.

"Can't you remember anything specific about them?" I asked him once. "They must have been unusual to have had a son like you."

"Why? Why must they have been unusual?" He seemed to be getting angry.

"Because you're so unusual. You must have gotten it from somewhere."

"Not from them." His tone was decidedly short. "I assure you, they were extraordinarily ordinary. No, no, not ordinary, not average. They were certainly a good deal smarter than the deplorable average. But they were well within the range of normal. There certainly was nothing unusual about their mathematical abilities. I could never get either of them to really understand the supernaturals."

Had the young Noam felt contempt for his intelligent but unexceptionable parents? To use the terminology of Plato's "one royal lie": the progenitors had been made of silver, the son of gold. Was this anger I was now encountering the guilt the boy had repressed for knowing that he was made of a different stuff? Whatever the reason, the look on Noam's face didn't encourage my pursuing the question of inheritance further.

But when he spoke again, after a brooding silence I hadn't dared to break, it was of his mother.

"You know, it's funny. I've been trying to picture her, my mother. I suppose I haven't in some time. And I can only see her crying."

"Did she cry a lot?" I was intrigued. This was the closest Noam had come to revealing an emotional underside.

"I can't say I recall her crying much. In fact, I remember her as being quite a cheerful sort of person. She used to sing a lot of light opera around the house, when she was vacuuming and cooking." He closed his eyes. "But I keep seeing her sitting at our kitchen table, crying. And it's a much younger version of herself."

"Younger than what?"

"Well, than when I was a man, when she died."

"Perhaps she cried a lot when you were a boy. Perhaps you were a very nasty little boy."

"Oh no, I was quite good, I think. I don't remember her ever having gotten angry at me." From which you infer there was never anything at which to get angry? A very sloppy deduction for one of the world's greatest logicians.

"Maybe it was the miscarriages," he said suddenly.

"What miscarriages? How many?" He was an only child.

"Oh, I don't know. I vaguely remember that she had quite a few. Someone mentioned them to me when I was much older. Perhaps my father. Apparently she took them very hard." He smiled slightly. "She thought probably all the babies would have been mathematically gifted, that either she or my father was carrying something in their genes."

"A genius-gene."

"Yes," he said. "A genius-gene."

I tried but failed to extract more details of this woman, who suddenly emerged real and rather tragic, sitting at her Formica kitchen table, weeping for her dead geniuses.

In general I didn't have to work to get Noam to speak. He usually did most of the talking, and on his chosen subjects. Every time I put forth an idea he'd regard it with his intense concentration, asking me whether I had meant thesis one, two or three by my remark. Very little that I had to say merited such consideration, so I learned to say little. Besides, it was a joy to listen to him, speaking on the most complicated of topics in the simplest of terms. I sometimes pictured his mind as a perfectly tempered knife, moving with awesome speed, paring away the fatty irrelevancies and unimportant gristle, carving up questions at their precise joints. It was exciting for both of us when I'd understand his point, follow the proof. He liked teaching me math, and he is a wonderful teacher. (All my loves have loved teaching me. I'm such a smart little girl.) There was one trivially practical hurdle. Noam finds it almost impossible to talk to someone without that adhesive eye contact, and I find it almost impossible to drive without watching the road. At times Noam, quite unconsciously, would stick his head right over the steering wheel in an effort to catch my gaze. (He's done this when I'm cooking, too, placing his head right over the pot. Once the results were so serious that he had to be brought to the university infirmary.) At this point I'd pull off the road onto the shoulder, where we could talk, or rather Noam could talk and I listen.

The day he spoke to me about the supernatural numbers I had to pull off the road. We were driving along Canal Road in Griggstown, a few miles north of Princeton, a lovely shaded way that runs alongside the old Raritan Canal. I parked right beside the water, which was covered with delicate pale green algae-lace. We left the car and walked to a little white wooden bridge straddling the canal, beside an ancient stone house, still occupied. We sat there on the bridge, and Noam talked to me of his creations.

Actually, Noam regards them not as creations but as discoveries. He holds, as so many great mathematicians have, the Platonist point of view. For him mathematical truths are descriptions of a suprasensible reality, an objective reality that exists independent of our perceptions of it. The moons of Jupiter were circling in their orbits before Galileo put the telescope to his eye, Noam said once, and mathematical truths are there for the mathematicans to see. (*How* see? Through what faculty? Spinoza said the eyes of the mind are proofs, but Noam regards proofs more in the way of spectacles, bringing the visions of intuition into sharper focus.) Anyway, whether they are creations or not, Noam loves the supernaturals.

"I've probably discovered just as important and interesting things since them, but they were my first. When I was very young, before I was two—I know because it was one of my mother's stock stories —I used to count my way up into the millions. I was so excited by there being all those numbers, an unending supply. I can still remember it, it's my earliest memory." (Mine is of getting burned by someone's cigarette.) "I wanted to hit a number no one else ever had, to be the first to get to it." He laughed. "And then, you know, with the supernaturals I really did it. A whole new realm, beyond any of the others." His voice was uncharacteristically soft. "Numbers so big. A beautiful vast infinity of them, waiting there in the great solemn silence, waiting there for me."

We were quiet for a while. I was thinking about the unlikely places in which one can stumble on poetry. I can't report what Noam was thinking, for I haven't the novelist's privileged access to other minds.

Finally I asked him, "Did you name them the supernaturals?"

"Yes, of course. And I worked out most of the important theorems about them."

"There at the soda fountain?"

"There at the soda fountain. They're mine, or at least about as much mine as a piece of mathematical reality can be. They're often called "the Himmel numbers," but I dislike the human presumption of that. It's okay to name theorems after mortals; after all theorems are only our descriptions, they are our creations. But the objects themselves are a different story entirely."

THERE WERE ONLY TWO topics on which I felt I had something enlightening to say to Noam. The first was human behavior. Noam confessed to bewilderment about the motivations of most people

47

most of the time, and he listened in those days with interest to my attempts to characterize individuals and interpret their actions. We tended to like and dislike the same personal qualities, sharing an overriding horror of what we dubbed the "peacocks," a rather common Princeton species (though more plentiful in some disciplines than others), always strutting and posturing and looking around to verify the impression they make on others. Noam hated peacocking when he saw it, but I was better at detecting it.

The other topic on which Noam listened to me as if to a superior was art. Noam has a passion for music, particularly Mozart. He's perfected his whistling to the point, he claims, of obviating any need to learn an instrument. He used to perform quite often for me, whistling entire sonatas and symphonies. Sometimes he would stick to the score, his precise memory of which was truly astounding; other times he would indulge himself in his own variations.

But he has no interest in visual aesthetics, in art or nature itself. Whenever I'd point out some natural scene, he'd glance and nod and continue talking. One afternoon we walked together through the university's McCormick Museum. Noam displayed the same aesthetic apathy, barely glancing at the pictures, while he recounted for me the story of how non-Euclidean geometry had accidentally been discovered through attempts to prove the parallels postulate (that parallel lines never meet) through the indirect method of proof, that is, by taking its negation together with the other Euclidean postulates and deriving a contradiction. But instead of a contradiction several mathematicians had independently derived consistent non-Euclidean geometries. This was a revolutionary event, overturning fundamental conceptions of math and confuting the prevailing Kantian view of space.

"Listen, Noam," I finally said as we stood before a large Pearlstein nude, "this is fascinating, but I can't concentrate on what you're saying and the pictures at the same time."

"Then let's leave." When we were once again outside, he said, "I'm sorry, Renee. I have no appreciation for art, no feel for it at all."

"It's hard for me to understand, Noam. How can you not appreciate art? You love music so much."

"But the two are so different. There's no logical development in art the way there is in music. A picture is just there, static, all given at once. Oh, some things are very pretty, you know, sunsets and flowers—you are extraordinarily pretty—and pictures of pretty things are pretty, too. And I can appreciate the technical facility involved in executing a work of art. I'm really quite awed by people who can do that. I can't draw anything, not a simple face. I have no sense of what to put in and what to leave out. But that's about as far as my critical evaluation extends. I don't know what you're supposed to be looking for in a picture, what's supposed to hold your attention."

"Don't you see, Noam?" I was pretty amazed by his lacking intuitions I considered elementary. "The world isn't simply given to us as it is. It's given to us from within the points of view we each occupy, points of view that condition the way the world looks to us. In certain respects the appearances are probably alike for all of us, just because of the way things objectively are and the way the mind works. But then there are the interpersonal differences. One's special attributes color and shape the world one ends up seeing. The interesting thing about art is you're being presented with another's point of view, looking out at the world from his perspective, seeing the dreaminess of Renoir's world, the clarity of Vermeer's, the solemnity of Rembrandt's, the starkness of Wyeth's."

"That's an interesting way of approaching it, though you're not going to get another's viewpoint as a bare uninterpreted given any more than you get anything else as a bare uninterpreted given. Your perception of his perception is going to be conditioned by your own outlook. But anyway, that's an interesting way of looking at art."

"It's not an interesting way of looking at art. It *is* art." Noam's apathetic ignorance encouraged this outburst of pomposity. It was a rare treat for me to play the authority, even if it did involve a little dishonesty. For I had little confidence in my simplistic pronouncement, am skeptical, in fact, of any statements pretending to say what art is. (How, asked Wittgenstein, can one define "games"? Is there any property all games must share in order to be games? Or are games linked rather in a network of similarities, akin to family resemblance, where some family members have the same nose, some the same walk, some the same temperament?) What I was stating was only my own preoccupation (and not only in matters artistic) with the subtle, pervasive contributions of subjectivity and the different worlds we each occupy as a result.

"Well," Noam answered, smiling at me, "I'll have to take your word for it. If that's art, I can see why it's never interested me at all. I'm just not interested in the qualities of appearances, mine or anybody else's. It's the reality out there, not as it appears from within any point of view, but as it *is* from no point of view at all, that interests me."

But if Noam wasn't particularly interested in the world-as-it-is-for-Himmel, I was. The fact that my account of our courtship is primarily intellectual is no accident. The great attraction for me, of course, was Noam's mind, and the pleasure I had in contemplating the rigor and purity of its executions. And to think that now I was included in the contents of that inestimable consciousness, that the faculties that had apprehended the supernaturals and other *himmlische* marvels should now be preoccupied with thoughts of me. For they were, you know, quite raptly focused on me. Here was a man who had never had to make any effort outside his superhuman exertions in the mathematical sphere. Even the five or six love affairs of his past seemed, from the little he had to tell me (again, he wasn't unwilling to give me details—he simply didn't have them), to have never come about through his own initiative. He was quite content to let himself be seduced (were they all genius-groupies? I wondered), though the idea would probably never have occurred to him on his own.

But that spring he did exert himself in nonmathematical matters, in the matter of me. He wanted me. I would like to make clear what that meant to me, a person of dubious substantiality. Often it had seemed to me that my existence was as ephemeral as the objects in Berkeley's metaphysics; that, like them, my *esse* is *percipi*, my being a function of others' perception. I am thought of, therefore I am. And now I was the object of an adoring attention, not just in *any* mind, but one superior to almost all others. Would I ever again require statements testifying to my existence and worth?

Toward the end of June, Noam had to go to a conference in Vancouver for two weeks. He called me every night, and we held long transcontinental conversations. The evening he returned we ate dinner in my room in the Graduate College. Before he had quite finished his chocolate mousse Noam got up very suddenly, knocking his chair backwards. He stood there in confusion for several seconds, staring down at the chair as if trying to place it. Then he rushed over to me and threw his arms around me, rather awkwardly, as I was still holding a spoonful of mousse.

"I love you, Renee, I love you. Marry me. Please marry me."

Noam Himmel that spring was a thirty-eight-year-old boy drunk on love for the first time. You might say that our relationship soured as he sobered.

3

The
FAMILY

Thus suddenly an object has appeared which has stolen
the world from me. Everything is in place; everything still
exists for me; but everything is traversed by an invisible
flight and congealed in the direction of a new object. The
appearance of the Other in the world corresponds therefore
to a congealed sliding of the whole universe.

—JEAN PAUL SARTRE,
BEING AND NOTHINGNESS

*O*ne hour after Noam's proposal and my immediate and euphoric acceptance, I was standing out on the golf course in front of the Graduate College searching the darkened skies for three stars. Let me explain.

The minute Noam proposed to me I wanted to tell my mother. That was about the second or third thought that flashed through my triumphant head. (Can thoughts go faster than the speed of light? I wonder.) Not that my mother and I are that close. Quite the contrary. But I very much wanted to tell someone the news, someone who would consider it momentous. And my mother, who had greeted each announcement of my educational plans with "Nu, Renee, is this going to help you find a husband?" so that the consequence of all my academic honors, Phi Beta Kappa, *summa cum laude,* scholarships, fellowships, prizes, was only a deepening sense of guilty failure; my mother, who had always taught me that a woman is who she marries, that "There's more than one hole a man has to fill in a woman": my mother was such a person. Noam had proposed to me on a Saturday evening. My mother would not answer the phone until three stars were visible, indicating that the skies had truly darkened and Shabbos was over. That night in June, Shabbos wasn't over until after nine.

"Gute voch," she answered the phone. The Yiddish phrase means "good week."

"Hi, Mom, it's me."

"Renee! *Gevalt!* Is something wrong? What's the matter?"

"No, Mom, what makes you say that?"

"Well, here you are calling a minute after *Havdalah,* so anxious." (*Havdalah* is a ceremony that uses wine, a candle and sweet-smelling spices to bid farewell to the Sabbath. The word literally means division—the division of the Sabbath from the rest of the week, of the sanctified from the secular.) "Of course, maybe you didn't know it was a minute after *Havdalah.* Maybe you didn't even know that today was Shabbos?"

"Sure, Mom, I knew. I just came in from counting the stars."

"Renee darling, you're keeping Shabbos?"

"No, Mom, I just knew it would be futile to try and call you too early."

"Nu, so at least you still remember a little something. If you still remember, there's hope."

"Listen, Mom, I have something to tell you."

"I'm listening."

"I'm getting married."

A gasp. Then: *"Oy gevalt!"* Then the question: "Is he Jewish?" Sadistically, I paused several seconds before answering her. "Yes, Mom. He's Jewish."

Total silence. I couldn't even detect any breathing.

"Mom, are you still there?"

"Yes, of course, Renee, I'm here. When isn't your mother here? I'm just a little speechless with surprise. A daughter calls me up out of the blue, I don't know *how* long it's been, and tells me she's getting married. I don't even know she's going with someone. How *should* I know? So I'm surprised."

"Aren't you happy? Isn't this what you always wanted?"

"Yes, of course I'm happy. Of course this is what I always wanted."

But she didn't sound all that happy. All that anxiety over whether and whom I would marry should, one might have thought, have made this moment one of great jubilation. A giant hosanna ought to be swelling out of the phone. I had pictured my mother—a little woman, barely five feet tall, dark and very thin, for she can't eat when she's worried, which means she averages maybe one good meal a week— bursting out into *Hallel,* the song of praise to God, in which He is called by every good name in the Hebrew vocabulary. How had I failed her this time? What maternal expectations was I once again in the process of thwarting?

And then I understood, saw it as I had never seen it before. My mother's whole life is devoted to worry. In the last few years she had been consumed in despair about two things: Would my brother's wife, Tzippy, who had been trying to have a child for two years, never succeed? And would her prodigal daughter, Renee, remain forever single (I was, after all, an overripe and bruised twenty-two), or worse, marry a *goy?* These were big, satisfying worries, requiring constant attention.

Then a few weeks ago she had learned that Tzippy was pregnant, and now I was calling to tell her that I'm marrying. A Jew yet. No wonder she sounded wounded. We children had callously deprived her life of its substance and meaning. She was holding the telephone receiver and staring down into the existential abyss.

"Of course I'm happy," she repeated weakly. "Overjoyed. Tell me, what is the young man like? What does he do? Don't tell me he's also a philosopher." Do tell me, do tell me, her voice was begging.

"He's a mathematican."

"A mathematician? From numbers he makes a living?" Her voice gathered some strength.

"Yes, Mom. He's famous. He's one of the greatest living mathematicians. He's a genius. He was written up in *Life* magazine." This is true. When Harvard had offered Noam an appointment at age twenty, *Life* had done a story on "the youngest American professor."

"Really? A famous genius? *Life* magazine? This is really something then. This is real *yiches.*" (*Yiches* is prestige.) "You should be very proud, Renee, that such a man should love you. Of course, I know you're not just any girl. Who should know if not me? This is why God gave you such good brains, so that you could make such a man like this love you. I only wish your father were alive today to hear such news."

So did I. God, how I wished it. He would have been genuinely delighted. Everything that he was was genuine. My father. How to describe him in an age whose face is set in a knowing Freudian smirk? Can anyone accept without interpretation a daughter's love for her male parent? But almost everyone, at least everyone who had the slightest bit of good in him at all, had loved my father. Why should I be excluded just because of my incriminating relationship with him? These words, "I loved Reuven Feuer," in anybody's mouth but mine, reflect well on the speaker, revealing a susceptibility to the power of goodness. Why in my mouth alone must they be interpreted in terms of infantile sexuality? A faithful description of my father would contain adjectives like "saintly" and "heroic." How can I protect such a description from analysis?

My father had been a cantor, a *chazzen,* a sweet singer of Israel, as it says in Hebrew on his tombstone. His pure, sweet song was like a picture of his soul. Snatches of *chazzanes* would escape from him all day long, pieces of the internal singing that must have been almost constant with him. He had loved his work in all its aspects: chanting the prayers on behalf of the community, comforting the sick and the sad, instructing the boys in preparation for their bar mitzvahs. His teaching powers were legendary. He was sent all the unteachable boys from around Westchester County—the retarded, the disturbed, the hyperactive. Each yielded to his softness and managed to be bar mitzvahed.

From the external point of view, however, the details of my father's position were pretty dismal. He was scandalously underpaid. In fact, the cantor who was hired after my father's death was given more than twice the salary for doing less. Life in that wealthy community had been hard for us. (I wasn't just the lone Jewish kid in my class. I was also the only poor one.) And there was more, far more, than the mere economic hardships of my father's job. But I won't dwell on the dirty details. My father never did. He soared above it all, leaving my mother and me below to feel the humiliation.

My father's lack of ambition was an acid eating at my mother's life: "I can't understand your father. That such a man, with such a head, such an education, should be content to be a little *chazzen*, to put up with what he puts up with in that community. You should see when we go to the *chazzanes* conventions what kind of people are there. Such plain uneducated *pruste Yiddin.*" (Roughly: vulgar Jews.) "Your father stands out among them like a stallion among the swine, you should excuse the expression. But he's content."

The last line was always delivered in a profoundly accusatory tone. (I think it was while listening to my mother complaining about my father that the image of the mattering map first occurred to me. I know it's been a feature of the internal landscape for a long time.) And there's no denying that the man was supremely content, all in all the happiest person I've known. And he maintained his sweet outlook through his final terrible illness. One of the more illustrious members of his congregation said to me, as we watched my father limping in great pain up to his place on the *bimah* shortly before his death, "There's not a man I envy more."

He was born in Borstav, a little *shtetl* in Galicia, where his father was rabbi and his mother the town beauty. (Around Easter, pogrom time in Poland, she would have to go into hiding. Being the rabbi's wife, and beautiful besides, she was prime rape material.) My father's two brothers loved to tell the story of how the Cossacks would come thundering into town and scoop my father, a little boy with long banana-curl *payess* tucked behind his ears, up onto their horses, and have him sing in his sweet boy's soprano. They roared with laughter at the incomprehensible Yiddish songs—some of which poked fun at the drinking and other habits of the *goyim*. The kid was sweet, but he had a sense of humor.

One of my uncles, Sol, the oldest, left for America and slaved in New York several years until he could bring the rest of the family over. Only one sister remained behind, Raizel, who was also a great beauty, with the delicate-featured blondness of my grandmother. (My father too was fair, with high pronounced cheekbones—very good-looking in his gentle manner, although I suppose you'll find this description also suspect.) A very rich man from a neighboring village had seen Raizel at the marketplace and sent the *shadchen*—the professional matchmaker—over to my grandfather's house. The *shadchen* had laughed when he heard the dowry Raizel's family could offer. "We'll forget the dowry for now." So she was the only one left behind. The family tried to get her out when the Nazis came, but it was impossible. She died at Auschwitz with her rich husband and five children.

My father had been a student of German literature. He had gotten his master's degree from City University and was studying for his doctoral exams. But one of the very minor casualties of the news from Europe was his love of German culture. He didn't even like speaking the language after that. He fell back on his fine tenor to support his family.

Sometimes my father would tell me about his coming to America in that detached, amused way in which he spoke about himself. The older brother, already Americanized, had wanted my father, who was ten, and his brother, who was eight, to go to public school, to learn English faster. The school was primarily Irish and Italian.

"When I walked into the classroom, with my *payess* down to my shoulders, you should have seen how they looked at me. If looks could kill, I wouldn't be here laughing now."

The teacher put him next to the only other Jewish boy, thinking they would understand one another.

"He spoke as much Yiddish as I spoke English. I glanced at him, such a puny little thing. He wasn't going to be any help at protecting me from those hoodlums."

Sure enough, as soon as school was over that day, they all gathered round to take turns punching him.

"When I arrived home, my father took one look at me and said: 'We're putting him into a yeshiva.' "

The following Sunday my father and his younger brother went to a neighborhood park. This brother, Izzy, was as tough as my father wasn't. (He now lives in Houston and is supposed to be quite rich.)

"There were two games going on, baseball and soccer. Since we were from Europe, of course we went to watch the soccer. And who should also be watching but the hoodlums from the public school. They saw me and wanted to repeat the fun. Let's run, I said to Izzy. Let's fight, said Izzy. When they saw he wanted to fight they all fell on him, and he was happily swinging away when I noticed suddenly that one of them had taken out a knife. I was a *chazzen*-to-be, and we *chazzonim* have our own defenses. I hit a high G. Believe me, it was the note of my life. People started running toward us and the bullies ran away."

It was a rare treat when my father spoke about himself. There were so many things I had always wanted to know about him. I wondered if he had struggled to arrive at his moral level or had been born there. I spent a lot of time puzzling over the question of which—the struggle or lack of it—would make him the better man. Many ethicists, following Kant, opt for the struggle: those who are naturally good aren't really good. Yet the striving after moral perfection requires a concern for one's self: one has to want one's self to be good. And it seemed that even this sort of self-interest was incompatible with the nature of my father's pure goodness. This paradox was, and still is, very confusing to me. But on the few occasions when I overcame my shyness and tried to ask him about himself, he didn't get the point of my questions. (Though, natural teacher that he was, he rarely did fail to understand another's perplexity.) It wasn't simply that he didn't think of himself as good. He didn't think of himself at all.

I always worried about my father. When I was a child, I would run upstairs to my bedroom window when he left the house. I would strain to keep him in my sight, trying to watch over him. I knew that goodness suffered in a bad world. Yet he managed to get down the street unharmed. Only at the very end, in the last year and a half of his life, did he suffer terribly, when the cancer spread into the bones of his legs. It was as if they were fractured, the doctor told us, urging us to try and get him to keep off them. But my father was determined to continue working as long as he could, doing what he loved: comforting the sick, teaching his boys, praying for the community. The six-block walk to the synagogue took him forty-five minutes on Shabbos, when it's forbidden to ride. He would go not just for the morning prayers, but for the evening service as well, back and forth, four times, leaning heavily on his cane. Finally the disease invaded his liver, and he had to go into the hospital. He had one more bar mitzvah to prepare, a difficult case. He died immediately after, having assisted his last boy through the token acceptance of manhood.

We heard so many stories the week we sat *shivah*, observing the rituals of mourning. People now felt that they could tell what my father had done for them, the secret acts of charity, the advice that had averted the disaster, saved the marriage, brought the child back home. His was a life built out of quiet words and gentle acts. "The *shtickele chazzen*" I had heard members of my mother's family call him: the little (in a sense implying insignificant) cantor. But the *shtickele chazzen* was a hero, although, like all heroes, you had to be standing in the right place on the mattering map to perceive the dimensions of his greatness.

My father had deserved to have at least one child like him, but all he had was my brother and me. Avram is three years my junior, and, though born in Westchester, he has all the mannerisms of the *shtetl*. Dressed in black suit and hat (the standard uniform of the ultra-Orthodox), the fringed white tassels of his *tzitzith* trailing behind him (all Orthodox males are required to wear these tasseled undergarments beneath their shirts, but people like my brother let it all hang out), he might just have stepped off the boat. He even talks with a Yiddish accent, waving his hands about in the wild gesticulations of Talmudic discourse. Though he used to speak perfect English and play baseball, he now makes the grammatical errors of an Eastern

European immigrant, and is round-shouldered from the hours spent hunched over a Gemara. (The Gemara, written in Babylonia, is the commentary on the Mishnah, which is the compilation of the laws and sayings of the rabbis—part of the oral tradition until written down. The Mishnah and Gemara together compose the Talmud, the primary study material for those who "sit and learn.") Although, like our father, he's passionately religious, the passion—and the religion—are entirely different. His is all anger and hate. Every other word out of his mouth is "pagan." The *goyim* are pagans. The irreligious Jews are pagans. I, of course, am a pagan.

"You're a heretic, a pagan, wallowing in pagan *shmutz.*" *Shmutz* is filth. I noticed that his ears still get red when he gets emotional. "You're a *shiksa,* an idol worshiper."

Of the last charge, at least, I felt innocent. "Avram, I'm not an idol worshiper."

"You are."

"I'm not."

"Are."

"Not." It was nice to see we could still fall easily into the dialogues of our childhood. "I don't worship anything."

"You worship nothing?"

"Yes, I suppose."

"Nothing!" he concluded in triumph. "You worship nothing! That's your god, your idol! Nothingness!"

I urged him to take a course in formal logic so he could see the fallacy of his reasoning, but he just continued to gloat, his ears now red with glee over his sophistical victory. He probably keeps a score-card: Religion: ——, Philosophy: ——. And he never perceives himself as losing the argument.

Avram, favoring my mother's side of the family, is dark and . . . well, puny. I must admit that my father and his people weren't very big, either. My long legs were among the items in my adolescent catalogue of guilt-provoking personal attributes. I felt like such an overdeveloped Amazon, towering over my mother and brother, involuntarily displaying my physical superiority. Although my interior is unmistakably Jewish, I have an exterior that would have inspired a poster for Hitler Youth. My mother often remarked, throughout my childhood and adolescence, that she couldn't think where I had gotten my looks from. I remember once, when I was about fourteen, she said that, and I was pierced by the terrible thought that perhaps I was a corporeal throwback to some brutally Jew-hating gentile who had long ago raped one of my forebears.

When my brother was eighteen he asked his *rebbe*, who is something like his guru, to find him a wife. The *rebbe* appeared with Tzipporah, a sweet-faced girl of seventeen, who taught first grade at the yeshiva in the Boro Park section of Brooklyn from which she had recently graduated. None of the teachers there had attended college. They were mostly graduates of the school, who taught until they got married and pregnant, returning after the birth to support their husband's "sitting." (The word "yeshiva" comes from the Hebrew for "sitting.")

In my habit of endlessly comparing the various worlds I've occupied, I've given much thought to the variety of forms that women's oppression takes. While liberated specimens among her goyish counterparts struggle against the myth of helplessness and the tradition of dependence, the Orthodox *ayshes chayul* (woman of worth) is traditionally the sole support of her (very large) family. (Contraception is strictly forbidden.) *Her* liberation wouldn't require her being freed from a dollhouse or lifted off a pedestal. As her lucky husband can, if he chooses, sing to her from the prayer book on Friday nights, before he sits down to the Shabbos meal she has prepared for him:

> She is like the merchant ships—
> She brings her food from afar.
> She rises while it is yet night,
> And gives food to her household . . .
> She considers a field and buys it;
> With her earnings she plants a vineyard.
> She girds herself with strength
> And braces her arms for work.
> She finds that her trade is profitable;
> Her lamp goes not out at night . . .
> Her husband is known at the gates,
> As he sits among the elders of the land.

The roles are reversed, but only along one dimension. Hers is still the indisputably inferior position in those matters that matter in this society: the spiritual and intellectual, which are one and the same. (It's no accident that Spinoza, *apikoros* though he was, identified the state of human blessedness with the "intellectual love of God," which is a noetic state, approaching total knowledge, knowing what is truly what.) For Jews learning is the highest spiritual activity, but one from which women are barred. And what, I once asked my mother, does Judaism offer its females in the way of spiritual experiences? At the top of her list was going to *mikvah*, the ritual bath that's a monthly requirement for married Orthodox women. (For the men: Talmud and logic, while the women try to clean up their bloody messes.) In a world where personal merit is measured in the number of pages of the Talmud one has mastered, power doesn't rest in bringing home the kosher beef fry. Ask the *ayshes chayul.*

Avram and Tzippy met once, approved one another, met again, and got married. Tzippy looked terribly pale being led to her wedding canopy, her lips moving in prayer. When she reached my brother's side, they glanced quickly at each other. After the ceremony the women took Tzippy into a little room and cut her long, thick brown hair, replacing it with a *sheitel*, or wig. She had a wonderful time, though, at the dinner celebration afterwards. Men and women sat on separate sides of the *mechitzah*, the physical boundary placed between men and women, in this case a six-foot-high white fence covered with fake greenery. In between the endless courses there was wild Chasidic dancing on both sides. A little band of two clarinets and an accordion played the songs of the Eastern European *shtetl.* The men did the kazatska and cartwheels, making up with exuberance what they lacked in grace. The women danced with more restraint, in complicated circular patterns. There was a bullfight, one of the girls, fingers held up as horns, charging into the napkin flourished by another. Tzippy danced in the center of the women, her partners constantly changing: her mother and mother-in-law, her grandmother and four sisters, the many sweet-faced friends. I too got to dance with the bride. The friends brought out a jump rope, and Tzippy and they played. The men lifted Avram on a chair, the women held up little Tzippy, and they danced around with the two of them. At one point each took hold of a corner of a handkerchief over the *mechitzah* and laughed shyly into each other's face as they were held aloft. I watched them and was filled with disgust at my own life, which, in the glow of their purity, seemed dirty and sordid. I often think of Tzippy as she was that night, a little child-bride with the absurdly mature wig, giggling with her friends, dancing shyly with her new in-laws, jumping rope.

Poor little Tzippy. Six months after her wedding, in her tenth week of pregnancy, she had a miscarriage. Another followed four months later, again in her tenth week. And after that she had been unable to conceive. On one of the rare occasions when I went to visit them in their little two-room Lakewood apartment, right off Yeshiva Plaza, Tzippy brought me into the tiny dark bedroom and closed the door.

"I have to talk to someone. I know why I'm having all this *tsuris*. I got angry at your brother soon after our wedding and I said terrible things to him."

"Oh?" It was not without pleasure that I imagined my righteous brother being called down a bit by little Tzippy. "What was it all about?"

"A great big nothing." She blushed the deep pink of the bed-spreads. Sex, I thought. That's why she thinks she's getting this particular punishment. "Stupid, really, my fault completely. But the things I said! They were terrible. I've never spoken to anyone that way, and to my own husband I spoke like that! This must be why I'm being punished, why I'm a barren woman."

"Oh, Tzippy, of course it isn't." I put my arms around her shoulders. I was startled to feel how slight they were, like a child's. But then she was a child, this barren woman. She was crying without noise.

"What else could it be? I've searched my memory over and over. I can't think what else I've done."

"Why think it's because you've done anything? Why think it's a punishment at all?"

"What else?" She pulled back out of my arms to look into my face with surprise. *"Der Aybishder"*—the Everlasting—"wouldn't be doing this for no reason. But one thing I haven't been able to figure out. Your brother suffers because I'm barren. Why should he be made to suffer for my *averah?*" (An *averah* is a sin.) "It must be because I'm his responsibility. He's responsible for my *averah.* That's what's so hard. My poor Avram."

And now sweet Tzippy was pregnant. She had called me the day she found out, laughing and crying. We waited until she was past the critical tenth week, and out of the first trimester altogether, before telling my mother. We wanted to spare my mother the worry. Which brings me back to my mother. And her worry.

All mothers worry. Jewish mothers worry more. But my mother can find something to worry about in anything. No topic is innocent. In some way, direct or Talmudically indirect, some danger to her family might be lurking. "It's her way of loving. Try to understand," my father would tell me when I'd come complaining about something I'd been forbidden to join my friends in doing: going to the beach (the undertow); tennis (sunstroke); hiking in the woods (sex maniacs). Her worrying is, like all the best thinking, vigorous but subtle. Every possibility is followed through and analyzed. And she is knowledge-able, too, admirably informed on current events: local, state, national, international—for all could adversely affect her family. She watches the news on television from four in the afternoon until eight in the evening, and then again from ten until twelve. If the phone rings at eight I know who is calling, to tell me to get rid of my house plants (a four-year-old has died from nibbling on a castor oil plant), not to answer the door (a man-and-son team has raped three women in northern New Jersey), not to make any plans to visit Seattle (a geologist has predicted that Mt. Rainier could go off sometime in the next twenty-five years). She reads the New York *Times,* the New York *Post,* the *Daily News,* the local Westchester paper, and a certain tabloid expression of Jewish paranoia published in Brooklyn (typical headline: COPS SECRETLY ARMING BROOKLYN BLACKS TO RISE AGAINST JEWS). I am always getting clippings in the mail.

My mother has probably worried about my virginity since the moment the doctor announced I was a girl (and after she had prayed for nine months for the blessing of a male firstborn). Our relation-ship, which was never very good, changed drastically for the worse when I hit puberty at around eleven. I looked old for my age, and it was a couple of years before my psyche caught up with my body. My mother, no dualist, held me responsible for the overdevelopment.

"Stop it," she would hiss as we walked down the street to do the shopping.

"Stop what, Mommy?"

"Stop walking like that. Don't you see everyone is staring at you? You're embarrassing me."

She was embarrassed? Was everyone really looking and laughing at me? What was I doing wrong? I tried to concentrate on my gait. It seemed to me that I was walking as I always had . . .

"Stop it," she hissed in our kitchen, having lured me out of our living room where we were entertaining guests.

"Stop what, Mommy?"

"The way you're sitting. It's disgusting. Don't you see the way the Levine's son is gaping at you, the dirty boy? But then you have to expect that from boys. They'll get what they can, a look or more. It's *your* fault. I'm ashamed of you."

She was ashamed? If only I could figure out what I was doing wrong. What had happened to me? There used to be no problems with my walking and sitting . . .

"But, Mommy, I can't help it. I'm not trying to do anything wrong."

We were walking home together from Saturday morning services, my father and Avram ahead, my mother and I behind. She was berating me for the attention she accused me of having attracted in *shul.*

"Bobby Grossman, Frank Nassman, Eli Gherkoff, they all couldn't take their eyes off you. And I saw them laughing together. What am I going to do with you?" Her voice sounded desperate.

Laughing together, about *me?* Those big high school boys? And *she* was desperate? Hot throbbing waves of humiliation swept up from my feet to my head.

"Mommy, tell me what I'm doing wrong. Tell me what I should be like."

"What you should be like? You should be a modest, clean Jewish girl who doesn't attract any dirty thoughts. You should be like Ruth Kornblit and Frances Spitzer, refined and *edel.* "

If you tried to guess the meaning of the word *edel* from the two girls my mother held up as examples, you might arrive at the conclusion that it means pathetically homely. (It doesn't. It means modest and refined.) Ruth had greasy, stringy hair and skin covered by pimples in various stages of development. Frances's face, poor thing, was three-fourths occupied by nose. Both held their shoulders rolled forward, although it was clear neither had anything to hide. But certainly my mother didn't mean I should be ugly or have bad posture. It was their souls she was talking about.

"You don't see any boys staring at Ruth and Frances, do you?" she demanded. I knew she was wishing that I wasn't her daughter, that she was the mother of *edel* Ruth or Frances.

As I got older she worried that the worst was soon to happen, or, God forbid! already had, but she didn't give up. She got more subtle, but persevered, collecting stories of the misfortunes that befell girls who had no morals. Having morals means not having "anything to do" with anyone but one's husband, and not until he is one's husband. I remember mentioning to her once that I was taking a course in moral philosophy at Barnard. She had looked at me queerly. How could there be a whole course on *that?* It was a mistake to mention the class to her; it became her primary obsession for the duration of the semester. Obviously the professor was saying a whole lot more than that a girl should have morals. Whatever he was saying, it couldn't be good.

"I'm only afraid, Renee, that with all your so-called intellectualizing, you're only going to end up rationalizing doing things you shouldn't even think about."

If her normative ethics consists of this one simple proposition, "Girls should have morals," her metaethical theory is somewhat more complex. It's a mixture of intuitionist absolutism ("What do you *mean* what makes it wrong? It's wrong. Anyone can see it's wrong") and utilitarianism ("Men, they squeeze the orange and then they throw it away").

But really the attempt to compress my mother's views into a consistent theory doesn't do justice to her style of thinking. She has a Quinean attitude toward logic: logic is disposable. In fact, she's done Quine one better and has already disposed of it. It's no good demonstrating the logical inconsistency of something she's said. Her response is always to say, irritably or indulgently, depending on her feeling about me at the time, "Oh, there you go with your philosophy again." She seems to think my concern with consistency is like a dressmaker's interest in fabric or a beautician's in hair: a result of my narrow professional concerns.

During my four years at Barnard her life had been full. What wasn't there to worry about with a daughter living alone in New York City? ("Mom, I don't live alone. I live in a dorm with hundreds of other girls." "And how many live in your room?") She could rattle off crime statistics like a police spokeswoman or a politician trying to get elected with a stop-crime campaign. (Subway crime was her specialty.) I thought she'd be overjoyed to learn that I was moving out of the jungle and into the pastureland of Princeton. A few days later I got a clipping in the mail: ANTI-SEMITIC INCIDENTS ON THE RISE: NEW JERSEY LEADS THE NATION.

But the night I stood out there on the golf course counting the stars, I couldn't wait to speak to her. This would be one conversation we would move through together, hearts and minds as one. I was deflated when I finally hung up the phone. I still wanted that exultant conversation I had imagined and decided to call my friend Ava Schwartz in New York.

Ava had been three years ahead of me at Barnard, where she had come from the Bronx High School of Science. She had decided when she was eleven to become a physicist. ("I happened to ask someone what physicists do and was lucky enough to be given a pretty good answer: they study matter and energy, space and time. I decided right then that was for me.") I suppose I owe you a physical description of some sort, although it's hard for me to see that so familiar face objectively. She's fairly regular-featured, with jowls perhaps a bit too full. She's a big woman, large-boned, not fat, very strong. (She has yet to confront a twist-off cap she couldn't handle.) In college she used to wear a kind of round, monkish haircut, the straight bangs ending just above the eyes. It's the eyes—enormously large and warm and expressive, brown with flecks of gold—that lift the face up above plainness. I think they're the most beautiful eyes I've ever seen.

We had met my first month at Barnard, and it was she who helped me make the leap out of Babylonia.

"I don't know if I ought to tamper with you. You're a find, a perfectly preserved specimen of an ancient civilization. I ought to donate you to the archaeology department."

I was surprised. Compared to the other girls at my high school, I had been daringly liberated. Ava laughed for several minutes when I told her that. She worked hard with me, knocking me over the head with her earthiness, and went so far as to devote a large part of one evening to trying to get me to say "fuck."

We had been sitting in the West End Bar drinking beer and I was telling her a story about something I had heard on the subway. The punch line contained the word "fuck." I hadn't known I wouldn't be able to say it. I had never tried before. We were already silly with beer, and my attempts to get out the single syllable had reduced us both to hysterics.

"Look, say 'truck.'

"Truck."

"Muck."

"Muck."

"Suck."

I regarded her with mock reproach.

"My God, Renee, what a mind you have. Suck a lollipop, suck your thumb. There are other things in the world to suck, you know."

"Okay, suck," I managed to gasp between beery giggles.

"Okay, we're almost there. Now, fuck. Come on, ffff."

"Fffff."

"Fffffuck. You can do it, kid, I know you can. Ffffuck."

"Fffffff."

"That's right, fffffuck. Come on, do it for the other daughters of Israel. Fuck."

"Fffff."

"For your mother, Renee, do it for your mother. Fuck."

"Fffff."

"Fuck."

"Fffffffudge!"

We collapsed into our beers. "Fudge it" became one of our favorite curses.

"Look, Ava," I finally was able to say. "It's the slippery slope of sin. First you'll have me saying it, then you'll have me doing it."

"Let's hope so. But let's take one step at a time."

Ava took maternal pride in any vulgarities I could handle, in word and deed, during my four years at Barnard. Yet she never really did like the men I chose. Noam was the first she warmed to. Hillel, my first, she couldn't stand.

"A yarmulke," she had wailed. "A whole university stocked with beautiful blond gentiles. From the Midwest we've got them, even. And your first choice is a yarmulke from Brooklyn? A Hillel Schoenfeld?"

"I like Jewish men."

"It's just conditioning. You're conditioned to think of non-Jewish men as *trayf.*"

"They're all *trayf.* This isn't a question of keeping kosher. It's a question of taste. I don't even like blonds. I like them dark and Semitic."

"Well, you got it. Hillel Schoenfeld is definitely dark and Semitic. Did he have to be Orthodox, too? He's as screwed up as you. Probably more, since he's a man. You know what's going to happen, don't you?"

"I hope so." I gave what I intended as a lascivious smile.

"Yeah. And then you're both going to wallow in your dark and Semitic guilt. Go running back to your Gemaras to hide. The best thing for Hillel would be a nymphomaniac Irish girl, and the best thing for you would be someone like Paul."

Paul was Ava's current boyfriend—or perhaps "lay" would be the more precise terminology. She didn't take her men very seriously. Whereas *I* have to make heroes out of my lovers, need to be lying under an *Übermensch*, Ava seems to enjoy looking down on her men, which, given the men she prefers, is an almost unavoidable position to assume. I don't know if my friend is specifically attracted to idiocy or whether the qualities she likes just aren't compatible with much intelligence. In any case, her boyfriends were generally a pretty primitive lot, what she used to call "elementary particles." There were the protons with a large positive charge, the positrons with a small positive charge, the neutrons (neutral), electrons (negative), and peons. Ava never expected too much of them out of bed.

71

Which is why she and I started laughing at the mention of Paul in this context, since the very night before he himself had tried to convince me that the very thing I needed was a Paul. He was one of the freshman mistakes of the admissions office at Columbia College (Ava had a knack for sniffing them out—they could have used her in admissions). Paul was a disciple of Wilhelm Reich, the psychiatrist and madman, charlatan or hounded genius (depending on your point of view) who thought he had discovered "orgone energy"—the life force, which is released during orgasms, can cure cancer, and is yet one more instance of Einstein's $e = mc^2$. In fact, Reich wrote to Einstein in 1940, identifying himself as having been Freud's assistant at the Polytechnic in Vienna, and reporting his discovery of a "specifically biologically effective energy which behaves in many respects differently to all that is known about electromagnetic energy." He added that it could be "used in the fight against the Fascist pestilence," which was a lure that was impossible for Einstein to resist. Probably anyone else would have been warned off by the letter, which also stated that the monumental finding hadn't been reported to the Academy of Physics because of "extremely bad experience." So Reich pilgrimed to Princeton, together with a little accumulator, to demonstrate his phenomenon to Einstein, who found a rather commonplace explanation for it. ("What else do you do?" he asked.) Einstein's explanation was of course rejected by Reich, who continued to nudge poor Albert for years and privately published the exchanges between them in *The Einstein Affair.*

There was a little enclave of Reichians at Columbia who took the hounded-genius point of view, and Ava's Paul was among them. Three sentences into any conversation with him, and he was telling me about, and staring at, my "pelvic armor," which was restricting the flow of my orgone energy. But he hadn't offered to remove the armor himself until the night before this conversation with Ava.

Many such offers were coming my way. I was the object of much male attention and wasn't exactly comfortable with it. I had just come from an all-girl yeshiva. I wasn't even used to the company of males, aside from my rabbi teachers, father and brother. My new circle of friends, Ava's friends, didn't always make me feel comfortable either. I could of course have chosen to associate with Barnard's coterie of Orthodox Jewish women, who pretty much stick together, keeping behind the invisible *mechitzah* that separates them from the alien environment. (And they're not the only ones.) Only that's not what I had come to Barnard for, for more of the same, and I wasn't getting more of the same with Ava and her friends. But it was hard for me sometimes. I envied the other girls their easy, familiar ways, the way they casually touched men, for example. Where I had just come from there were only two intersexual relationships recognized: potential marriage partner and actual marriage partner.

Hillel Schoenfeld was a graduate student in physics over at Columbia, and he was the teaching assistant for the course in classical mechanics I was taking. (I had begun college with the intention of majoring in physics, thinking that was where the most fundamental questions are asked. That's how my friendship with Ava began—she was thrilled to find another Barnard physics major.) And to me, then, Hillel was the most desirable male imaginable. To a certain extent he was what any Orthodox Jewish Barnard woman wants: Jewish, brilliant, kind, handsome. However: his faith was wavering, and that of course is what made him attractive to me. Ava's talk about *trayf* and kosher wasn't really off target. Hillel wasn't *trayf,* not like the Pauls, who were just unthinkable to me. Hillel was certified kosher. He just wasn't *glatt.*

It's true that Hillel had been wearing a yarmulke (knitted by a previous girlfriend; it's something Orthodox girlfriends do.) But a few weeks after we started seeing each other, off it came. If he was going to sleep with me (and we discussed little else), he would have to give up all elements of belief. He just couldn't tolerate inconsistency.

Still, we took a while to take the big step, months of agonizing, delicious, sex-obsessed temporizing and messing around. After some hesitation I described to Hillel the very strange thing that had been happening to me, a gradual buildup of sensation that would end in a towering peak. He had looked at me incredulously.

"That's an orgasm. You've just described an orgasm." I honestly hadn't known. "That's hard to believe. I thought it could only happen to a woman during intercourse."

Our lack of knowledge was no obstacle to pleasure. Quite the contrary, I think. In truth, I wouldn't want anything about that time changed. Rather, I feel sorry for people brought up with no sense of boundaries (all the better for crossing), for whom the sexual terrain appears as unmarked and open as it perhaps really is. Can they ever share such experiences as Hillel and I shared? The sense that what we were doing was momentous, the exhilaration of breaking through miles and miles of fences: a man can't listen to a woman singing; a male above the age of six and a female above the age of three can't be alone together in a room with the door closed. There are a hundred and one such prohibitions, all of them designed to keep one from penetrating to . . . *this very spot.* A group of us were once drinking at the West End when the conversation turned to Alex Comfort's *The Joy of Sex.* Hillel said that he and I were using the *Kitzur Shulchan Aruch (The Code of Jewish Law)* instead: "We're systematically doing everything it says you shouldn't." (Though, truth to tell, this system wouldn't take one very far into kinkiness. It wasn't SM or bondage the author was concerned with, but rather making love by the light of a candle or by daylight, or holding any conversation during or immediately before "except in matters directly needed for the copulation.")

My relationship with Hillel lasted through the end of my sophomore year. I ended it. Of all the men I've known, I wish I had been, could now be, in love with Hillel. For one thing, and this is no small matter I've since learned, we always understood each other's jokes, perhaps because we both knew what it was to make fun of the *Kitzur Shulchan Aruch* by day and to lie in bed in the dead of night in the stomach-churning anguish of repentance. And in human terms Hillel was the best of them all. But it's never been such factors that determine my (or maybe anyone's) desires. The truth is, my attraction to him flagged, despite my desire to desire him.

Perhaps I still idolize him. And of course there's still a haze of guilt: Do I think he's the best because he's the one I hurt the most? I have to remind myself of his failings, his tendency to ignore my wants in typical Orthodox Jewish male fashion. We did what *he* wanted. And I'm not just talking about deciding on which movie to see. When he decided to move back to a modified form of Orthodoxy, he took for granted that I'd make the move with him. I did. I even went to *mikvah* once, at his urging. For he claimed there really isn't any

Talmudic prohibition against premarital sex, but rather the law is against having relations with an "unclean" woman—one who hasn't purified herself in the *mikvah* of her menstrual blood. Of course, there *is* a law against single women, who have no intention of getting married, going to *mikvah*. But that, urged Hillel, was a more minor interdict than the one we would otherwise be violating. He, as you can see, had a solid Talmudic background.

It was also assumed that we'd get married as soon as he got his doctorate. I didn't tell him (so how was he to know?) how little I wanted to get married, how it had seemed to me that I had just begun to live, and that our relationship, which had been part of that beginning, seemed now to have become the end. Not a word. I couldn't bring myself to stand up to the parental authority he had acquired over me. (He was horrified that I smoked; I quit. He told me which courses to take; I took them and brought him my A's. I made him proud, much prouder than my parents had ever been over the school doings of a girl. My mother, in fact, had always hidden my report cards so that poor Avram wouldn't have to see how much better than him his sister had done.) I also felt—this will give you some idea what an anachronism I was—that I had no choice but to marry Hillel, that I had given myself, in the form of my body, to him.

I came very close to marrying him. I can easily picture the life, in some "modern Orthodox" community—Teaneck, New Jersey, or Silver Spring, Maryland. I'd have children by now; the oldest would be starting the local Hebrew day school. Our friends would be other "modern Orthodox" couples whom we would visit and have over on Shabbos, the highlight of our social life. The men would talk to the men, the women to the women. I can see it very clearly. But my counterfactual vision blurs on the matter of whether I'm happier there than here. (I'm fairly confident that my counterpart there thinks she'd be happier here, in Princeton, married to a genius.)

It was a close, possible world that split off from the actual quite incidentally: My professor in symbolic logic began to make some nonsymbolic gestures, coming out finally with a proposition that went beyond the elementary calculus. Hillel's stature in my eyes diminished sufficiently to allow me to take the step away. What was the parental authority of a former teaching assistant compared to that of a current full professor? I joke, but it was a painful break. I had assumed that somehow or other Hillel would remain a part of my life. (Had I known otherwise, would I ever have dared to break off? Dear René, most noble and knowing namesake, surely you erred when you claimed that one knows one's own mind immediately and incorrigibly.) But Hillel told me, in the angry scene that continued to play in my head for months, that the only way he could get over me was to have nothing more to do with me. (I've heard echoes of this since and have reconciled myself to being viewed in terms that sound medical, as something to be gotten over, worked out of the system, like a stomach virus. My former loves never remain my friends. I don't know why, but I know it doesn't speak well for me.) A few weeks later I learned that he was making *aliyah,* moving to Israel. Everyone said I had driven him to it. Oh well, we all do whatever we can for the Zionist state. (Hillel, my love, I'm sorry.)

My professor, Isaac Besdin, and I proceeded to deduce the entailed conclusion in his office on a bleak wintry afternoon. I happened to be suffering from a bad head cold that day, and sex in those circumstances proved interestingly suggestive, with subtle associations drifting just beneath the surface of consciousness. As a consequence, nasal congestion has since carried with it the faint whiff of lubricity.

But the affair that followed brought little joy. I was but a part of Isaac's miserable midlife crisis, the symptom known as the infatuation with the younger woman. He was forty-six years old and coming around to the realization that his life had led to this: to the cold, resentful wife; to the son and daughter pursuing their adolescent rebellion with the same uninspired conformity to the norm as their father was demonstrating in his response to his own life change; and, most painfully, to the unbrilliant career. The conclusion was waiting to be drawn, even if he shrank from its final acknowledgment. The promise of his youth would not be fulfilled, the spark had never caught, the moment for it was over. There would be no fire, and now even the feeble glow of hope was giving out.

His was a misery so large and insatiable that it swallowed me whole (and then he complained that he hadn't tasted much of anything). I was paying the price, without knowing it, of having loved a father too well. But if ever a father had been worth the price, it was mine.

This unwholesome relationship (even *I* could see that) ended when the real father, the perfect father, whom none of these father-lovers could ever approximate, passed away. The grief that ensued, together with the misery of this last liaison, sent me hurdling back toward the life of the mind. (You begin to see a pattern? Mind, body. Body, mind. Memoirs of a dangling woman.) Issues of love and death had turned my mind to philosophy. I switched my major and two years of purity followed, two years of intense intellectual introversion, rewarded upon graduation with every kind of academic honor, including a commitment from a leading journal to publish my senior paper and generous fellowships from every prestigious graduate philosophy department in the country. (None of which really convinced me that I wasn't still a dope, briefly enjoying a lucky spell.)

If my father-substitutes have generally left me wanting (their model being so Platonically ideal), I have been abundantly blessed with a mother-replacement. When Ava graduated (the only physics major Barnard had produced in years), she crossed Broadway to Columbia and continued on for her doctorate. I had her with me until my own graduation.

Ava was given a terrible time on the other side of the street. Her adviser, a Big Name, always referred to as "The Shmuck" in our conversations, was milking her for ideas. He was burnt out, a has-been who knew a good thing when he saw it. He had already gotten seven publications out of Ava under his own name and he wasn't about to let her go. He refused to read what she had written of her dissertation until she finished yet another paper for him. When she had, he demanded yet another.

"I'm going to rot away here. I won't be the first. This place reeks from corpses. I can't expose him because I need his recommendation to get a job when I get out. *If* I get out. I'm at his mercy."

At last she decided it was rot or riot. She typed up a letter of resignation to the chairman of the department, telling him her reasons for leaving. She gave a copy to The Shmuck and said that unless he had her dissertation read and back to her with comments within a week, the letter was going out.

"I finally realized I had nothing to lose. He was never going to let me go."

It worked, and now Ava was almost finished.

Ava is wonderful, witty, and wise, but she was the wrong person to call on the night of Noam's proposal. She's suspicious of marriage in general, and her suspicions about mine in particular grew as she listened to me talk about Noam.

"The problem with you, Renee," she finally said, "is that you think the male sexual organ is the brain."

But she did give me wonderful news. She had applied to the Institute for Advanced Study in Princeton for a postdoctoral fellowship.

"It's always been a secret dream of mine," she said. "That place is holy to me, the haunt of gods. Only let's not count on it. I may not be ready yet for the ascent up Mount Olympus."

As it turned out, she was. Two weeks later she called me with the news of her acceptance. Ava and I together again! She would be like a fresh breeze from the Bronx blowing through the stale air of Princeton.

MY MOTHER called me early the next morning, with some of the old fight back in her voice. She was first of all anxious to meet Noam, a meeting I dreaded, but it would have to be. Beyond that, though, she had bigger worries.

"Renee," she began, "do you and your young man plan to get married by a rabbi? Will you have a kosher wedding?"

I am a very spiteful daughter. What did that skinny little Jewish woman ever do to earn such spite? (I could write a book.)

"Okay, Mom. We'll have a Jewish wedding. For you."

"Oh . . . how nice." It came out small and hopeless. I had vinced the invincible.

Noam did not at all like the idea of being married by a rabbi. Religion had never touched his person (he had even been circumcised by a doctor), and in his scheme of things there wasn't that much difference between going to a rabbi to get married and to a voodoo master to have a spell cast. He began to make increasingly vigorous noises of protest, and I don't know where it all would have ended if my mother hadn't put a stop to it.

My mother is an extremely ambitious woman. You give her a bean, she wants to make a whole cholent. I was being so amenable about a rabbi that she figured she could slip some other things past me as well. "I'm glad to see love has mellowed you, Renee." First she called to ask if she could make a little party after the ceremony, invite some of the relatives to the house. Fine, I said. This really fueled the fires of her ambition. The next morning she called early.

"Renee darling, I want to speak to you about something very serious, very solemn. I know you're not a religious woman, but I hope you'll give what I'm about to say the consideration it deserves. A good marriage, Renee, is a spiritual marriage. Are you listening?"

"I'm listening," I answered, wondering what she was getting at.

"A spiritual marriage requires preparation. You have to purify the spirit, *cleanse*" (she came down very hard on the word) "the spirit." Suddenly I knew what she was talking about.

"Mother, are you asking me to go to *mikvah?*"

"Well, Renee, I think—"

But I didn't give her a chance to finish her thought. "Mom, I've had it. You're never satisfied. I give you a son-in-law, a Jewish genius son-in-law, you want a rabbi to marry us. I give you your rabbi, you want a party. I give you a party, you want me to go bobbing around naked in holy waters. I've had it. No *mikvah*, no party, no rabbi. Be happy you're getting a son-in-law and an honest daughter."

In the end, we were married by a justice of the peace in Trenton.

4

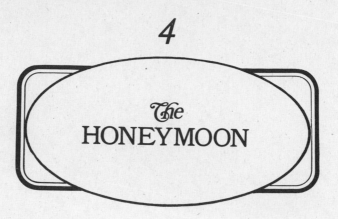

The HONEYMOON

What is the soul? We know nothing about it. If this pretended soul was of another essence from that of the body, their union would be impossible.

—BARON D'HOLBACH,
IMMORTALITY: AN ABSURD
SUPPOSITION

I do not want to die—no. I neither want to die nor do I want to want to die; I want to live for ever and ever, I want this "I" to live—this poor "I" that I am and that I feel myself to be here and now, and therefore the problem of the duration of my soul, of my own soul, tortures me.

—UNAMUNO,
THE TRAGIC SENSE OF LIFE

*I*nvitations to Noam are always pouring in from around the world. Any mathematical gathering is distinguished by the Himmel presence. The summer of our marriage Noam accepted invitations to lecture at the University of Rome and to attend a conference at Esztergom, Hungary. We planned to take the train from Italy to Hungary, stopping over for a few days in Vienna. Had we been disposed to use such a word, we might have called the trip our "honeymoon."

A few days before we left I received my mother's bon voyage in the mail, a little pile of news clippings, the dateline of each underlined in red, shadowing our itinerary: *Rome:* "Leftist Terror Heightens: Random Pedestrians Shot in Knees"; *Vienna:* "Neo-Nazis Celebrate Hitler Birthday"; *Moscow:* "Harassment of Jewish Intellectuals Intensifies": (But, Mom, Moscow is in Russia. We're going to Hungary." "It's all the same. It's all controlled by Russia. I beg you, on my knees I beg you, don't venture behind the Iron Curtain. Rome and Vienna are bad enough." "I really can't understand what you're worried about. What exactly do you anticipate?" "I'm afraid to think. You could be kidnaped, made slaves in Siberia, be committed to a mental institution for the rest of your life. Didn't you read what I sent you?" "But, Mom, those are Russian citizens that are being harassed. We're American. Noam's been invited. They want contact with Western scholars." "American, Russian, Hungarian. Anti-Semites don't make such fine distinctions. Jews are Jews.")

Our Alitalia flight left Kennedy at eleven at night. It was my first trip abroad and I was too excited to sleep. Noam worked all night on the lectures he was to give in Rome, pacing the aisles of the 747, muttering to himself. Occasionally, when he passed my seat, he'd lean over and absent-mindedly kiss the top of my head. The stewardesses kept giving me funny looks, but I didn't give a damn. I dismissed them. Since childhood I had been prey to the Look of the Other. Does he like me? Does she approve of me? A look on the face of *anybody* interpreted as a smirk or a sign of dislike would sear me, make me dizzy with pain. But now I was Mrs. Noam Himmel, on a different plane entirely, and I finally had the power to dismiss. "I am flying at last," I thought all night long.

When we arrived at the airport it was three on a steamy afternoon for the Romans, eight in the morning for us. After my night of flying high I felt weak and disoriented, and decided I didn't like foreign travel. But as we straggled out of customs—where the officials listened to Noam's garbled answers with cold stares and glanced at each other with raised eyebrows while Noam frantically went through his pockets, searching for his passport (we found it rolled up in the sweater he had used as a pillow during the last few hours of the trip) —we were met by a smiling delegation of three from the mathematics department of the university. Again I was enveloped in the sweet sense of our importance. I now belonged to an international society. I could travel from country to country with my husband and be swathed in the same interest and regard that surrounded us in Princeton. I had married intellectual royalty.

One of the three, Enrico Trotti, turned out to be the chairman of the math department, and it was his little red Fiat into which we all piled, our luggage tied to the roof. The four men immediately became absorbed in shop talk. Noam was sitting in the back with me (a mistake I never repeated), and Enrico, who was driving, kept turning around to talk with him, gesturing with both hands all the while.

"Perhaps you ought to sit up front," I whispered to Noam, but he ignored me.

So that shabby secret of my inner life is out. But then how could you begin to know what it's like to be me (and that is the end of all this scribbling: to give you myself as I am to myself, the *en soi,* the *être intime* of me) without knowing that at heart I'm a physical coward? I have inherited or learned, I don't know which, my mother's despised habit of imagining the worst. At each risk the mind leaps ahead to visions of possible disaster. And it shivers, it cringes, it longs to stay put. Coward. What chances I have taken in an attempt to erase the inglorious self-characterization. But each leap, each climb, each dive, has always been preceded by a ghastly inner picture of the slip, the plunge, the brain-splattered rocks below. I am my mother's daughter. Beneath the external swagger the phenomenological reality is fear.

I was the only one in that car whose attention was riveted in terror on the road, a horror film of counterfactuals reeling through me: if Enrico had taken two seconds longer turning back his head . . . if the distance between us and that truck had been one centimeter less . . . Noam, oblivious to it all, was far more courageous than I.

But we made it to our destination, a large apartment on the banks of the Tiber, not far from the Vatican. The apartment belonged to Enrico's mother, who summered on the island of Sardinia and made it available to us for our three weeks in Rome. We were whisked by an open elevator, with elaborate grillwork, up the five flights to the apartment—eight or nine rooms filled with large, dusty antiques. Enrico pointed the way to the bedroom, where Noam and I fell into an immense baroque fourposter and a long dreamless sleep. We were awakened several hours later by a festive troop of six mathematicians and their consorts, who arrived to take us out to dinner. We lingered at the restaurant, amidst an air of celebration, well past midnight. "Himmel, *l'enfant terrible*" was repeatedly toasted.

The next morning Enrico arrived about nine in the morning to escort Noam to the university. He gave me a ticket for the bus, good for the week, and a map of Rome. I hadn't realized until then that I would be left to amuse myself.

Noam didn't arrive home that day until after six. I had come back to the apartment at about two, after visiting the Vatican, and had sat waiting. I hadn't been told he'd be gone all day.

"I thought we'd be here together. I thought we'd see things together."

"I'm sorry you thought that. I assumed you understood. I was invited here to work. They *are* paying me, you know. They're all anxious to talk to me. I have only three weeks here." Three weeks, I was thinking, would be a very long time.

"But I don't like going around by myself. It's no fun."

"Well, I'm very sorry. Do I really have to apologize to you? I didn't have to bring you along to Europe at all." Clearly, "honeymoon" was not the right term for our trip. "All you have to do all day long is amuse yourself while I work. And *I* have to apologize? It isn't fun. You sound like a child."

I felt like a child. I had discovered that day that I didn't like knocking about alone in a country where I couldn't understand what the drivers yelled out at me as they passed, couldn't understand the labels on things in the stores, couldn't understand anybody's directions to anywhere. A child is precisely what I felt like, walking with uncertainty through the unintelligible.

Rome is so beautiful, I knew I ought to be rejoicing in its offerings. I thought of Freud, dreaming (quite literally), year after year, of visiting the Eternal City. What kind of soul had I, to walk coldly through such splendor? Why wasn't I charmed by the novelties of a foreign country, as tourists are supposed to be, instead of discomfited by them? It was true: I didn't like foreign travel. And that was like admitting to a dislike of art or music. It indicates a lack in one's soul.

I had walked over to the Vatican that day because it was only a few blocks away and hadn't required my braving a bus. I never did use the passes Enrico brought me each week. If I couldn't walk to it, I didn't see it. The next day I crossed the Tiber and wandered around, inspecting the incredibly beautiful things in the shop windows, never venturing inside. I sat for a while on the Spanish Steps and then made my way dutifully over to the Trevi Fountain, the Pantheon, and Piazza Navona.

At the piazza I finally rested, body and soul. Nobody sitting at the outrageously priced cafés and restaurants was speaking Italian. They were all as foreign as I, and I felt at home. I sat there the rest of the day, sampling drinks and admiring the Fountain of the Four Rivers, the spectacular work by Bernini, representing the four major rivers of the seventeenth-century world: the Danube, the Nile, the Ganges, and the Río de la Plata of the Americas, all of it topped by the papal arms and a dove with an olive branch, indicating the position of the Pope as custodian of the world under God. I became a real connoisseur of this statue.

Every morning I had to force myself to leave the apartment, so dark and protected, its walls lined with books. I stared longingly at the few English titles scattered among them. No, I'd tell myself sternly, you will not sit in an apartment in Rome reading William James' *Varieties of Religious Experience*. Get out there and have some experiences for yourself, religious or otherwise. And I'd push myself out into the relentless noise and glare.

I would have liked, at least, to be able to walk these foreign streets inconspicuously; the Roman men would not allow it. Their demonstrativeness surpassed anything I'd encountered (with the possible exception perhaps of the time I almost caused a riot walking down the Upper West Side's Broadway in a pair of yellow shorts on an airless August afternoon). Here in Rome men would walk beside me for blocks, declaiming. One jumped out of his car and fell before me on his knees. I didn't enjoy any of it. I felt embarrassed and exposed, and was thrown back into the agonizing uncertainty of my early adolescence, when male attention had been undesired and undecipherable. Now here, years of experience later, I once again didn't know what to make of it. In New York I could fit my response to the tone and content of the comments, staring stonily ahead, shrugging my shoulders and smiling, or yelling something back. But here I had no idea what the street protocol is, much less what they were saying. Should I look offended or smile graciously? If only I were with a friend, I wished again and again. If only Ava, brave and wise, were with me now. Ava's purple-stained lips would know how to suck the pleasures from this place. Ava's strenuous tongue would burst Rome's grape. Trying to escape the eyes of the men, aware of (and hating) the involuntary wiggle of my ass, I'd hurry back to the sheltered island of Piazza Navona, where I could order in English, fall into conversations with elderly Irish nuns and wandering tribes of American students, or read.

I had brought two books along from Princeton, Quine's *Word and Object* (I still cherished hopes of a philosophical career) and Eliot's *Middlemarch*. I made slow progress through Quine and rewarded myself generously with rapturous reading from Eliot. Her book is, on one level, about marriage, and in that respect blended well with my own preoccupations. This was particularly true of the central story, setting forth the fortunes of the hapless Dorothea, who had also spent her "honeymoon" in Rome left largely to herself, while her scholarly husband, the fiftyish Mr. Casaubon, toiled away at his research in the Vatican library. Dorothea's Italian sufferings, her "oppression by the weight of unintelligible Rome," were keener than mine. It was here that she got her first whiff of the fetor of marital disillusionment, from which she turned her delicate middle-class English nose. She was altogether too righteous to engage my full sympathy, despite the parallels in our stories, which went further than Rome. For she too had married with the hope of being lifted up above herself by her husband's genius: "Since I can do no good because a woman/Reach constantly at something that is near it," Eliot had quoted from *The Maid's Tragedy*. Only poor Dorothea had made an unfortunate mistake. *Her* husband turned out to be no genius. The appearance of brilliance had slowly faded, bringing into focus the rather pathetic figure beneath. The marriage finally ends in a Pietà of sorts, Dorothea tending the moribund Casaubon, nursing her failed father-figure (instead of a child). It's a good thing, it occurred to me, that such errors as Dorothea's don't happen in math, where a proof is a proof whether of a theorem or of genius. (Casaubon was an historian of religion, his futile research on a *Key to All Mythologies*.) I, at the very least, had the real thing.

Eliot gives us a picture of the inside of a marriage but without divulging any sexual details. Her Victorian readers were meant to infer the hidden reality from such facts as Dorothea's pathetic pallor and the desolate loneliness of that wedding trip. But I am no George Eliot (my misfortune) and you are probably not content to infer (your misfortune). And so I must take you back with me, from the piazza to the apartment, into Signora Trotti's oversize antique bed.

I had had thoughts, early on, of educating Noam in the bedroom, of teaching him the detours and the backways off the main straight road. But he was an unwilling student, when not altogether truant. It was not even possible to speak with him on the subject. He showed such distaste—not for the act itself, but for all reference to it. It was as if one ran the risk of glorifying sex beyond its station by admitting it as a topic of discourse. My few pedagogical attempts left me feeling shamed, and Noam obviously, though silently, furious. Had he responded, it might have been to say that certain things are not spoken of. They are simply done, without words or thought. The body takes over for a while, and when it is finished the mind can resume its activity, giving no indication of having noticed what the other half was up to—like the separated brain hemispheres of a patient with a severed corpus callosum. A sentence begun before desire would plunge him down (no doubt that's the direction) into his body, would be completed when the desire was spent. The prolonged "hmmmm" beginning the second half of the sentence was the only spoken acknowledgment of an interruption. These are perhaps the most interesting and telling details of our early conjugal relations, the sentences that bracketed the unspeakable action—which in itself was swift and to the point.

The young wife was frustrated, you diagnose, using the term as demanded by the context. Not so fast. Don't be misled by the appearance of the obvious. (That is the sum of my wisdom.) Of course I was frustrated, but in attaining precisely *what?* Bodily pleasure had never been the goal that propelled me along. Appearances to the contrary, I was every bit as unsexual as Noam, more so really, since *my* body—in which I was lodged like an ice cube in a furnace —never took over. And always there were dreams of purity, of a body spare and a mind chaste, the waking dreams of sleepless nights.

What tied me to my body was not so much its desires as the desires it aroused in others—the more (both desire and others), the better. Through it (my matter, so to speak) I mattered to others, and thus mattered. Through it I had mattered to Noam, who himself mattered so much, at least from where I stood. But it occurred to me in Rome, where Noam's sexual aloofness seemed to increase, that his interest in me was inconsistent with his general indifference to people, himself included, or so he had claimed. "At least I'm consistent," he had told me on the dinky. "I don't find people in general very interesting to think about, so I don't find myself in particular an arresting object of thought. A lot of people seem to assent to the universal proposition but decline instantiation when it comes to themselves." For how long could Noam—Noam *Himmel*—be expected to suffer a logical inconsistency? This thought terrified me, perhaps as no other ever had. For from it followed, with a certainty almost mathematical, the unrelieved bleakness of my future. Being rational, I therefore dismissed it as best I could. But it lurked in the background of my lonely Roman musings and occasionally would erupt into the words: He has no right. No right to what? I questioned myself nervously. To have married, came the ready answer.

And *I?* Had *I* the right to marry? Other disturbing thoughts pushed themselves forward: One should not marry to save oneself.

Anyone in need of saving has no business marrying. Matrimony is not the cement for a cracked self, but is more like someone leaning on the self's point of least resistance. But these thoughts too were hurriedly pushed away for the frightening consequences they entailed.

The days I spent by myself; at night we were entertained by Noam's colleagues. He would return home between six and seven, and then we and some of the mathematicians and their wives would go to a restaurant or to one of their homes.

"It's almost like we're having *shayva broches,*" I said to Noam as we walked back from a restaurant late at night.

"Which you will no doubt proceed to explain," Noam answered, preparing his face to be amused; for I only dredged up my religious past for purposes of entertainment.

"It's a week of festivities following a wedding. The object is to divert the newlyweds from thinking about sex." I paused, trying to goad Noam into asking the obvious question. But attempts to force Noam's thinking are always futile. He ignores the obvious, or perhaps rather has his own ideas of what *is* obvious. He remained silent, his face still set for amusement. "Because after the wedding night's activities, which no doubt caused the heretofore virgin bride to bleed and thus become unclean, the couple aren't allowed to touch each other."

"For how long?"

"She has to count five unclean days and seven clean days, and then she goes to *mikvah* and is purified."

"And the same thing every month, I assume."

"Right."

Noam smiled while raising his eyebrows and shaking his head, a response that had already become part of an established pattern between us.

The Italian mathematicians were a charming, jolly lot. We'd stay out late each night, laughing and drinking, getting up from the table well past midnight, often to go and find an all-night ice cream shop. It was possible to forget in their midst, among their joking and light airy flirtations, that they were mathematicians. Did Enrico, with his black hair shot through with silver and his large, mocking black eyes, with his obvious pleasure in laughter, wine, and women, really spend his daylight hours doing pure mathematics?

"Yes, he's really quite good," Noam told me when I asked. "Very decent, solid intuitions. He'll never do the best, but he'll be one of the first to appreciate it."

And every morning, at a solemnly early hour, Enrico would arrive at our apartment to accompany Noam to the university. No one expects Noam to make his own way on foreign buses, I thought once in anger. But that was ridiculous. Of course no one expects such things of Noam. Noam is Noam—Noam Himmel. Everyone makes allowances. His excuse is his genius. The genius's wife has no such excuse.

I was looking forward to leaving Rome for Vienna, where we would be traveling incognito. Noam hadn't informed any of the Viennese mathematicians that he was passing through. There, at least, he would be a tourist with me.

The train ride from Rome to Vienna is fourteen hours. For the first four hours Noam worked. (Four hours of creative work a day is the limit for a mathematician, Noam always says.) I had thought perhaps we ought to get off at Florence and spend a few hours there. Noam had never been there, either. And disgracefully as I had fulfilled the requirements of tourism in Rome, I hadn't given up completely, which I felt I would be doing if we didn't bother to get off at Florence. But Noam was deep in work when we arrived.

"Get off if you like," he said without looking up from the pad on which he was writing. "I'll meet you in Vienna."

I had little faith in our meeting in Vienna and didn't relish the thought of wandering alone through Florence. So I stayed put, sitting opposite Noam and alternating my observation between the country-side and him.

He was rapidly filling up yellow sheets of blue-lined paper. When the spirit is upon him, the pen flies. If there's no proper paper handy, he'll use napkins, toilet paper, tablecloths, his shirt cuffs. I learned early on in our relationship always to travel with a yellow blue-lined pad, his chosen medium.

Noam in action, in the grip of mathematical intuition, is an awesome sight, like some natural wonder, expending vast amounts of energy. Sometimes the intense outer activity lies in his rapid writing, as was the case now—page after page in his large scribble. If he gets to the end of the pad, he reaches out blindly for whatever is available. His desk blotter at home is an inky mass of symbols, a record of past instances of paper deprivation.

More dramatic even than the writing is the pacing that sometimes accompanies the thinking. I've often watched him at home: hands clasped behind him or gesturing slightly before him, eyes downcast, he moves wonderfully fast across the room. Oblivious as he is at such times to his surroundings, I used to watch for his crashing into walls. But he never does. Just before hitting, he executes a neat little pirouette and continues on his way.

Then sometimes he'll halt quite suddenly and stand there motionless, his REMming eyes now off the floor and on God knows what. I'm entirely free to observe, with little danger of interrupting. Once, for example, I walked into his study at home, this time with the intent of interrupting, for he was wanted on the phone. He was writing at his desk. I stood there within a foot of him, waiting for him to look up. For several minutes I watched and waited, as the symbols appeared on the yellow pages. He never looked up, never knew I was there. Awed, I finally left the room.

These physical manifestations—the pacing, the writing—must themselves consume much energy. But they are nothing but the visible smoke escaping from the great conflagration within, from Noam's intensely concentrated mental activity. Any of you who have ever put in a really good day's worth of mental labor know of what I speak. As there's no suffering like mental suffering, or so they say, so there's no exhaustion like mental exhaustion. And mathematics is probably the most exacting and demanding of all mental activities. No wonder mathematicians are known to burn themselves out relatively young.

There was a rapid turnover for a while in our second-class compartment. An American serviceman and his discontented-looking young wife had gotten on with us in Rome. They were soon going back to the States, the serviceman told me, after having spent two years in Italy. He and I spoke (while the wife stared gloomily out the window) about the wine produced in the Chianti region, which we were riding through. When we reached Florence, they got off to have a last look at the great brass doors of the Battistero S. Giovanni. An enormously fat Italian woman took the serviceman's place on the seat next to Noam, with a fat baby, pacifier stuck in its mouth, under one arm and a big straw basket under the other. She took a huge salami out of the basket, a huger breast out of her blouse, chewed the salami and nursed the baby. Noam, within inches of this agreeably stereotypical sight, never looked up. The greedy consumption of mother and child activated my own enzymes and I went off to the dining car. When I got back, the compartment had cleared out and Noam had put his pad away.

"Hi." He smiled up at me. "How have you been?"

"Just fine. You?"

"Good, good. Come sit down here next to me." He took my hand and beamed into my eyes. "You know, Renee, I wish I could share my work with you. It's been the one sustaining happiness in my life, at least until I met you, and I wish I could share it with you."

These words touched me deeply.

"Yes, I wish you could, too. Try to describe it to me. What's it like, what does it feel like when you're creating?"

"I wish I *could* describe it to you, could capture it in words. But I never could, not even if I had the verbal facility I lack. I wish I were able to describe the beauty and excitement when it's working, when I'm seeing it."

"Like the past few hours?"

"Like the past few hours. It's not always like that, of course. Sometimes I wander round and round in circles, going over the same ground, getting lost, sometimes for hours, or days, or even weeks. It was like that with the H-function theorem"—Noam's latest publication. "But I know that if I immerse myself in it long enough, things will clarify, simplify. I can count on that. When it happens, it happens fast. Boom ba boom ba boom! One thing after the other, taking the breath away. And then, you know, I feel like I'm walking out in some remote corner of space, where no mortal's ever been, all alone with something beautiful."

And I had been peeved about not getting off at Florence while Noam was off in Plato's heaven. I must remember, I told myself fervently, that Noam is not always where his body is.

"All the pleasure's in those moments," Noam continued. "Writing up the results, publishing them, that's all a chore, a bow to the profession."

He sat up and thought a few moments while I watched him and waited, enchanted by these glimpses into the private side of his genius.

"Once," he spoke again, "when I was in Switzerland some friends there took me up in some very high cable cars, climbing up a mountain, that had been built for a James Bond movie. *Diamonds Are Forever*, I think it was called. Anyway, there was a restaurant on top and the view was supposed to be sublime. When we got up there, it was a great disappointment because the clouds were obscuring everything. But then suddenly there was a rent in the clouds and there were the Jungfrau and two other peaks towering right in front of us." He smiled deep into my eyes, in that way he has. "That's what it's like, or the closest approximation to it I can come up with. I've never tried to describe it before. It never was important to describe it."

"It must be a tremendous feeling of power."

"Yes." He sat up very straight. "You understand that. It is a tremendous feeling of power. I suppose any creative act makes one feel powerful, but in math the power seems absolute. It's not art, it's not fiction, one isn't making up stories. It's truth. The scientist discovers truth, too, but his has to conform to physical reality. His creative freedom is severely limited. In the end it's the gross material world that has the last say. Just because a description is the most beautiful, that doesn't mean it's the one nature chooses to realize."

He searched my face, trying to see if I understood. I nodded, wanting him to continue.

"Take geometry, for example. The physicist has to get out his measuring rods to determine which geometry is physical geometry, actually describes physical space, and it's not necessarily the prettiest. But the mathematician's power is absolute. We have an infinity of geometries, each mathematically real, and we can use the standards of beauty in deducing them. The only limits we have to conform to are the limits of logic, and even God can't violate logic."

"Truth and beauty, beauty and truth," I murmured.

94

"Yes, exactly. The truth of science, the beauty of art. Math exceeds all."

Noam had been speaking very quickly. Now he slowed.

"Physicists like to think they're dealing with reality. Some of them are quite arrogant about it and talk as if they were the only ones with a finger in the belly of the real. They think mathematicians are just playing games, making up our own rules and playing our own games. But with all their physical theories the possibility still exists that space and time are simply Kant's categories of apperception, or that physical objects are nothing but ideas in the mind of God. Who can say for sure? Their physical theories can't rule these possibilities out. But in math things are exactly the way they seem. There's no room, no *logical* room, for deception. I don't have to consider the possibility that maybe seven isn't really a prime, that my mind conditions seven to appear a prime. One doesn't—can't—make the distinction between mathematical appearance and reality, as one can—must—make the distinction between physical appearance and reality. The mathematician can penetrate the essence of his objects in a way the physicist never could, no matter how powerful his theory. We're the ones with our fists deep in the guts of reality."

"You're like a god."

"Some are gods. Archimedes, Newton, Gauss, they were gods."

"A minor deity, then?"

"No, not that either. Euclid, Descartes, Fermat, Euler, Lagrange, Riemann, Cantor, Poincaré, Hilbert, and Gödel—they're the minor deities."

"A demigod, then, the offspring of a god and mortal?"

"Okay." He laughed. "Maybe I'm a demigod in the pantheon of math."

Did I ever love Noam? It's a question I've considered continuously these past months. Did I ever love anything beyond his position in that special world, the only world that's ever mattered to me? Did I ever, even back then, focus on the person who occupied that position? I know I never considered the person behind the genius— if there was such a person. Noam's personal identity was, at least for me, entirely absorbed by his genius. All the properties he had were defined in relation to his genius. But that would be okay, wouldn't it? If one can love someone for the curve of her nose or thigh, the charm of his laugh or his manner of smoking, why can't one love someone for his genius?

Yes, I understood when Noam spoke of the power of his work. I had always thought of intelligence as power, the supreme power. Understanding is not the means of mastery, but the end itself (see Spinoza). This belief, pushed through the dark channels of the libido, emerged as the determinant of my sexual preferences. I am only attracted to men who I believe to be more intelligent than I am. A detected mistake in logic considerably cools my desire. They can be shorter, they can be weaker, they can be poorer, they can be meaner, but they must be smarter. For the smart are the masters in my mattering region. And if you gain power over them, then through the transitivity of power you too are powerful.

And how is it given to a woman to dominate but through sex? Through sex a woman gains control over a man's body that he himself lacks; she can move him in ways he cannot move himself. And she invades and takes over his consciousness, reducing it to a sense of its own embodiment (see Sartre). Sex is essentially the same game for men and for women, but for women, most of whom are otherwise powerless, it assumes a life-filling significance. *La femme fatale, la belle dame sans merci*, is an otherwise impotent person who has perfected her one strength to an unusual degree.

I have always loved in terms of power. Does this mean I've never loved? Does one love only if one loves for the right reasons? Are there right reasons? I don't know. But if I ever loved Noam, I loved him that evening, on a train riding into Vienna, as he talked of his power, and feeling his, I felt my own. *Since I can do no good because a woman/Reach constantly at something that is near it.*

WHEN I WOKE the next morning in our hotel room in the center of Vienna, Noam was gone. I was shocked, for Noam usually sleeps until someone wakes him (and then stays awake until told to go to bed). I went down to breakfast, hoping to find him there, though I was doubtful. Noam rarely seeks food on his own. He'll go hungry until told to eat (and then eat until told to stop). I don't know if he simply ignores, doesn't know how to interpret, or somehow lacks basic somatic sensations. But, as you might expect, his body, in particular his stomach, has suffered the consequences. We never make a move without Maalox.

As I expected, Noam wasn't to be found in the café attached to the hotel. I felt annoyed, and then, as the next few hours passed, increasingly worried. Something must have happened to him. I began to imagine all sorts of unlikely scenarios: Noam hopelessly lost, with no memory of the name of our hotel; Noam once again carted off by German police after innocently asking for directions; Noam hit by a car, his precious brains splattered on the pavement like Pierre Curie's. You're just like your mother, I told myself, but the stream of disastrous possibilities kept flowing on.

Around noon Noam burst into our room, which I had been too nervous to leave after breakfast. He was in a state of high excitement.

"Renee, I've made the most marvelous discovery! Renee, I've been here before!"

"What are you talking about, Noam? I thought you said you'd never been to Vienna."

"Not in this life, Renee, not in this life. Not in the life of Noam Himmel. But *I*"—he pounded his chest with his fist—"I've been here."

"What?" I sat down on the edge of the bed and stared at my husband. "What?"

"Look, Renee, I've been walking all over this city. I *know* this city. This persona, this Noam Himmel, has never been here, but *I*"— again he was pounding his chest—"I've been here. I know the entire layout of the city, the names of the streets—though there have been changes since I was here last—where the parks are, everything. I made my way directly to the Schönbrunn. I didn't make a false turn. I might have done it hundreds of times. I probably *did* do it hundreds of times. I've finally located the space." He sat down on a chair and smiled. "Now all I have to do is find the time."

"You've done what? You have to do what?" If I applied the Cartesian test for whether or not I was dreaming, viz. the *coherence* of my perceptions, I'd have to conclude that I was.

"I know where I lived. I just have to discover when it was."

"Noam, you're saying that you've lived before." A memory-image flashed before me: Noam in Lahiere's, *shuckling* fervently at the suggestion that the Jewish naming tradition is connected with a belief in the transmigration of souls.

"Yes, of course, Renee. And now I know where."

"But, Noam, if you do have knowledge of the city, it's probably because you read about it once or saw it in a movie or something. Something you've forgotten. There has to be some other explanation."

"Don't be an idiot. My knowledge of this city is that of an inhabitant. There's only one explanation. Don't be close-minded. I've always known that I lived before, that this particular persona wasn't my first. All of us probably have. I don't see any reason why I should be special. I've known since I was a child."

This is Noam, I told myself, Noam Himmel, the genius, your husband. He was standing there in front of me, talking as he had so often, loudly and rapidly, intensity streaming from his eyes. This is the way he had spoken to me of his brilliant discoveries—the way he had spoken to his colleagues, who always listened reverentially. I just had to take what he said seriously. Who was I not to? But my *God!*

"Noam, I can't believe what you're saying! I can't believe that you of all people are saying it! You're the one who's always ranting and raving against the lunatic irrationality of religion."

"I don't see what one thing has to do with the other, nor do I rant and rave. This isn't a religious belief. Look, Renee, I'll explain the principles of rationality to you. Rationality consists in accepting what the evidence points to, in figuring out what that is, and then accepting it, the inference to the best—in this case the only—explanation. It's irrational to believe the world is a certain way, when its being so is not supported by the facts, just because you'd like the world to be that way. That means it's also irrational to refuse to believe the world is a certain way, when the evidence supports that it is, just because you don't want it that way. People who pride themselves on their hard-nosed scientific outlooks are terrified of having the world exceed their comprehension. They refuse to recognize any phenomenon that doesn't fit into their simplistic physicalistic framework."

"But what evidence is there for reincarnation?"

"You see! You people don't even bother to examine the evidence! That's really the height of rationality, closing your eyes to the facts if you can't understand them. We can't understand consciousness, either, not in physical terms. Are you people going to deny that you think? Well, maybe *you* people don't." He laughed nastily. "The evidence for reincarnation is overwhelming. Haven't you ever heard of Stevenson, Dr. Ian Stevenson? His *Twenty Cases Suggestive of Reincarnation* is a classic in the field. He's certainly much more cautious and scientific than many of the physicists I know, with their mumble-jumble about giving up logic. He was the chairman of the department of neurology and psychiatry at the University of Virginia School of Medicine. He became interested in reincarnation because he realized that neither heredity nor environmental influences could entirely account for personality; for example, certain phobias some of his patients had. He's traveled all over the world, amassing a wealth of material supporting reincarnation. Children knowing facts about some person who died before their birth, facts they couldn't possibly have access to through natural means. Verifiable facts. And cases of xenoglossy."

"What's that?"

"People, often quite uneducated, knowing some foreign language they've never been taught, sometimes in an archaic form that a scholar must identify. Sometimes these people just recite, as if by rote, and sometimes, in the case of responsive xenoglossy, which is rare, they can actually converse. If you're truly interested in evidence, open-mindedly interested, I can assure you it exists. But you don't want it. You people need your blinders, you members of the so-called scientific community. You couldn't take a step without your blinders. You'd get lost if you had a view of the vast sweeping panorama."

I was mildly taken aback at being cast as a representative of the scientific community. (Professor Pfiffel would have been more surprised.) But this was drowned in the greater shock. The two attitudes were still battling within me, whether to regard Noam seriously or as a lunatic. It was really unthinkable, come to think of it, that I should be debating this question at all. Up until some ten or twenty minutes before, I had regarded my husband as the most reasoning of humans, a very paragon of rationality against which to measure all others. He had always been so cautiously critical, utterly unwilling to accept any claim until it was shown to meet his stringent criteria for justification. He had almost driven me crazy at times with his analyzing, often applied to matters I considered fairly obvious, and his endless questioning: What precisely do you mean by this? Why do you believe that's true? Perhaps Noam is like the anal compulsive who keeps a secret messy drawer in which to indulge in the wicked delights of disorder, I thought. Maybe this is the back drawer of Noam's mind, where he can indulge in the forbidden pleasures of uncritical thinking. Or maybe he's just crazy. For the first time that know-nothing truism of the vulgar crossed my mind: all geniuses are crazy. Good God.

Noam was pacing about the room like a caged tiger, thinking hard.

"How did you know when you were a kid?"

"Wait a minute." The pacing continued for several minutes while I watched him. Finally he came to rest in front of me. "Now, what did you ask me?"

"I asked you how you knew when you were a kid that you had lived before."

"Because I saw things so easily. Mathematical truths, I mean. I just knew things. Before I'd see why, before I'd have any inkling of the proofs, I'd know the results. I knew exactly what to look for."

"You're a genius, Noam, a mathematical genius."

"No, Renee. It's very hard to describe, but I knew these things because I was remembering them. That was very clear to me. The phenomenology of remembering is quite recognizable. You don't in general have any trouble distinguishing when you're remembering from when you're not, do you? And then, of course, there was the question of my parents. It baffled me how they could be so different from me until I figured out the answer." His face briefly assumed the uncomfortable expression it always has when the topic of his parents comes up. "Now, of course, it's different. I've gone beyond the mathematical memories of my former knowledge. I did that long ago, with the supernaturals. I've made progress in this life."

"Plato said that all learning is recollection," I said slowly. "That our souls knew everything before birth." And, I remembered, it was precisely mathematical knowledge he had used in his argument, getting an uneducated slave boy to deduce certain geometrical truths. (The hidden premise of his argument was: all things that we know, we've been taught. If we know something, but weren't taught it in this life, the learning must have taken place in another life.)

"Yes, I know. I read a lot of Plato when I was a kid. I think in this matter, as in so many others, Plato was very nearly on target. Except I don't think we knew everything before." The sentences were spilling out. "We make progress from life to life. That's what gives the entire series meaning. But Plato was very nearly right. He was right about the independent existence of the soul and its survival of the body. And he was right about the obscuring influences of the body. Matter muddles. When we become attached at birth to a corporeal existent, our memories and knowledge are largely canceled. Almost the entire contents of consciousness is emptied. It probably has to be that way. Most people would probably feel that their precious individualities were undermined if they knew they'd existed before. They'd be jealous of that former existence. But the uniqueness of the self is inviolate. It's always the same self, just a different life."

I couldn't resist directing a typical question of Noam's back at him: "How do you *know* all this?"

"It's the only thing that makes sense, given the facts. I figured it all out when I was a kid."

Then maybe it's time to rethink the issue, I thought but didn't say. (I was getting into the marital habit of thinking but not saying.) Instead I asked:

"What do you think the self is? If it's not a body, but can change bodies, and it's not a collection of memories, but disposes of these from life to life, then what is it?"

"That's a very good question, Renee, very penetrating. I've given it some thought, although I'm by no means confident of the answer. I think the identity of the self consists primarily in its moral and intellectual attributes, interpreted as dispositions, potentialities. Not the actual actions and beliefs that are the results partly of these dispositions and partly of external factors, the situation in which the self finds itself. And certainly not any of the properties of the body. Bodies are disposable."

"Our moral and intellectual attributes? That's it? What keeps them together?"

"What keeps material attributes together? I don't see why the one question is more difficult than the other. It's just that you physically see bodies, or at least instantaneous stages of bodies, so you people don't realize there's any problem there." I rather resented that, for it seemed to me I had quite a keen sense of the mystery of bodies. "There is some kind of attractive force. I don't really know. But unlike you people I don't expel things from the universe just because I can't explain them."

You people? Since when was I the thick-skulled positivist? I was supposed to be a misty-minded metaphysician. Noam had quickly assigned me the role of the empiricist enemy, the positivist skeptic. He was, quite obviously, aggressively defensive about his supernatural beliefs. (Had *these* been behind his naming his numbers the "supernaturals"?) And really it was no wonder, for they would have met with little assent, and probably much amusement, in the world in which Noam moved. Come to think of it, I was surprised that this particular Himmel eccentricity hadn't yet been immortalized in legend. Did people know? What an attention-grabber its revelation would be at a party in Princeton—although now, of course, I was barred from such action through the duties of matrimony. One must stand by one's husband, *mishagoss*—craziness—and all.

"But why are you special? Why do you remember your former life?"

"I don't. I don't know who I was. All I had, at least until I arrived in Vienna, was the mathematical memories. I think that the mathematical knowledge was simply too forceful, that the mathematical intuitions really constitute the essence of my person, and so they came bursting through the mortal bounds. Obviously I was a mathematician, a Viennese mathematician. But, as I told you, Stevenson has found plenty of people who have real memories of their former lives, memories that have been independently verified. Look, I don't know, I don't pretend to understand. One possible explanation is that only certain people become reincarnated, that it's a restricted phenomenon. But then why them? It's simpler, and therefore preferable, to assume that reincarnation is the norm and that there is a general amnesiatic effect. My own amnesia about my former life supports this. But there do seem to be exceptions. For some reason the mnemonic block breaks down. Maybe the memories are always there, buried very far down, the way my memories of Vienna were. But, you see, they can be brought up, they can be retrieved!"

He made the motion with his hands—outstretched fingers pushing away air—that means he wants conversation to stop and went back to his rapid pacing. I sat on the bed and considered the question of immortality.

I had never taken the possibility seriously. We are our bodies, we die with our bodies. That had been my metaphysical position. And anyway, the prospect of survival had never much appealed to me on an emotional level. I don't much relish the thought of everlasting consciousness. At very black moments I could always comfort myself with the ever present possibility of self-annihilation. But there's no escape if we're immortal.

And then consider the tedium of eternal life. There's a play by Karel Čapek, made into an opera by Janáček, about a woman named Elina Makropulos, alias Emilia Marty, alias Ellian MacGregor, alias several other names with initials EM, who suffers from immortality. Her father, who had been court physician to a sixteenth-century emperor, tried out his elixir of life on her. EM is frozen at age forty-two, though at the time of the play she's been around three hundred and forty-two years and has had it. No circumstance can tempt her, no creature engage her. The world has become as frozen and static as her own age. "In the end it is the same, singing and silence." She does finally manage to die, having refused to take the elixir again. A young woman, fighting the protests of the old men, destroys the formula.

No, I can't say the prospect of ceaseless survival much appeals to me. Better never to have been born at all. But how many, asks the old Jewish joke, are so lucky? Not one in ten thousand. I do, however, find myself hoping quite often and inconsistently (given my metaphysical position) that my father has managed to survive his death, that he has simply parted company with his body and is still around. Not necessarily around me, though I'd more than welcome his presence (you have an open invitation, Dad), but just *some*where. I don't like to think of a world emptied of him. And, of course, the kind of life-hopping existence that Noam was describing wouldn't suffer from the tedium of EM's indefinitely extended life. But would that reincarnated person really be my father, that same person? Is a bare ganglion of intellectual and moral attributes, stripped of all memories, not to speak of the body, sufficient to ensure personal identity?

I looked over at Noam, who was still pacing madly around the hotel room. Suddenly he stopped and then started toward the door.

"I'm going out again."

"Wait! I'm coming, too."

I spent the next few days trying to keep up with Noam, clinging to his arm, clop, clop, clopping beside him in my Italian high-heeled sandals (my one Roman purchase) as he rushed around the streets of Vienna trying to fix the temporal location of his former life. The Ring encircling the Innere Stadt was quite familiar to him, he said, so he had been around after Franz Joseph mapped it out in the 1860s. But he stared at the Staatsoper in disbelief. What had happened to the opera house? The old one, we learned, had been destroyed in bombardments in 1945. He looked at me in blazing triumph.

"It's as I expected. My other life probably ended around 1938, the year Noam Himmel was born. But I need more architectural evidence."

Actually, I wasn't all that impressed with Noam's knowledge of Vienna. His confident predictions as to what we would find on the next block, around the corner, in the courtyard, were usually wrong. Amazingly, this never dimmed his confidence. He would simply shrug and rush on. The few times he was right he regarded me triumphantly, his expression demanding: How could you ever have doubted? But I remained skeptical. After several hours of circling round and round the Innere Stadt, I too had a kind of blurred knowledge of it and was making (unspoken) predictions at about the same rate of success as Noam.

During the course of our searching Noam managed to relate many tales of the supernatural, complete with names (first, middle, and last), dates, and all the sundry details his capacious memory contained. (It was the first time, I think, that he had allowed himself to talk on the subject to anyone other than his all-accepting mother.) He told me about the "strikingly similar" experiences reported by those who had died and were then resuscitated: their viewing their bodies from outside, their being able to relate what was being done to them, which doctors had wanted to give up, who was crying in the corridor. After some initial confusion most found their separation from their body very pleasurable (especially if their experience included their moving on to another realm, where they were greeted by dead friends and relatives and reviewed their lives with a warm and loving being of light); and they returned to the corporeal state only reluctantly and with no residual fear of death.

But much dearer to Noam's heart were the cases suggestive of reincarnation. He must have told me at least twenty such tales. The eeriest and, I thought, most impressive came from a British psychiatrist, Dr. Arthur Guirdham, who was treating an otherwise normal and intelligent woman for the nightmares she had suffered since a child, one of which was a very vivid experience of being burned at the stake. As a schoolgirl she used to write down her dreams, as well as other things that occurred to her that she couldn't understand, including some verses in what turned out to be medieval French. Dr. Guirdham sent an account to a Professor Père Nellie at the University of Toulouse, who responded that the doctor had sent him an astonishingly accurate description of the Cathars, a group of Puritan-like believers who had lived in Toulouse in the thirteenth century. Some of the details she reported—what color robes the Cathar priests wore, for example—were at variance with accepted scholarly views but were eventually verified when the records of the inquisitors who had persecuted the sect were translated. Many of the names of the historically insignificant people the woman had described were also found in these records.

"Now give me," Noam demanded, his eyes flashing, "an alternative explanation."

Noam is a man of remarkable energy, and his excitement only added to his reserves. He rushed about Vienna, often simultaneously lecturing me on the rationality of the supernatural, and never felt the need to pause for breath. But occasionally, ever the voice of carnal weakness, I would beg for nourishment or rest, and we'd settle down briefly at an outdoor café, where I sampled the inspiring pastries while Noam pondered his identity.

"I can't think of any prominent Viennese mathematicians of the right date. Jacobi, Weierstrass, Kronecker, Kummer, and Dedekind were all Germans. So were Riemann and Cantor, though I'm not in their class anyway. And it's sacrilegious to even mention Gauss—who was German also—in this context. And the university here doesn't have any special feel to me. You'd think it would. Schrödinger was Viennese, but the dates are wrong. He died too late. And anyway, I'm absolutely certain I couldn't have been a mathematical *physicist*" (Noam dislikes physicists as a group; we all have our little prejudices) "or any kind of applied mathematician" (one who seeks mathematical answers with a view toward their application in physics or engineering). "I must have been a *pure* mathematician" (pursuing mathematical matters for their own intrinsic interest).

"How do you know you weren't a butcher?" I asked, risking (and earning) Noam's contemptuous stare. I was feeling cynical. My initial dismay had given way to alternating moods of cynicism, boredom, and, occasionally, receptiveness. The cynicism was acutest when Noam said anything about having thought all this out when he was a kid. He certainly does take himself seriously, I couldn't help thinking. His disinclination to think *about* himself—to think himself as object—shouldn't be mistaken for humility. What he does think, he thinks with the utmost confidence, even if it was thought as a child. I was prepared to take seriously any view arrived at by the mature man; but my reverence didn't extend indefinitely back along his lifeline.

But I was more receptive—approached almost to a suspension of disbelief—when Noam spoke from the viewpoint not of the juvenile, but of (you guessed it) the genius. Of course he sees more, sees higher, wider, and deeper, than we others do. That's what it *means* to be a genius. Do we others have the *right* to cynicism? Perhaps the unorthodoxy of his view redounds to the discredit of the orthodox. That's the attitude Noam took:

"Most people's experience is limited to sensory input, and their capacities for conceiving are limited to the categories appropriate for organizing this input. No wonder so much is inconceivable for them.

They wouldn't even be able to get a grasp on such concepts as the hypercube in fourth-dimensional space, or infinities differing from one another by orders of magnitude, or even the square root of minus one. What are they going to say—that such mathematical facts are inconceivable? For *them* they are. One has to let go of one's sensory imagination, soar way beyond the physically conceivable. The physical limits aren't the conceivable limits."

And another time:

"From where I stand and what I can see from there—and I'm speaking only as a mathematician now—bodies and their space occupy only a rather insignificant stratum of reality. So it doesn't surprise me at all that we—or at any rate our minds—turn out not to be bodies. That's the way it really *ought* to be, that the thinking part of us, the part that can grasp the nonsensible, the purely intelligible, should itself be nonphysical."

From where I stand and what I can see from there . . . These words penetrated through to me. How could I—standing where I did—presume to judge? Remember, I told myself, the prisoners of darkness in Plato's allegory of the cave, judging the truth-seer by their own severely limited view of things: "If such a one," the philosopher, "should go down again and take his old place, would he not get his eyes full of darkness, thus suddenly coming out of the sunlight? Now if he should be required to contend with these perpetual prisoners in evaluating these shadows while his vision was still dim and before his eyes were accustomed to the dark . . . would he not provoke laughter, and would it not be said of him that he had returned from his journey aloft with his eyes ruined and that it was not worthwhile even to attempt the ascent?"

That's Plato I'm quoting, not Noam; but Noam shares Plato's view of the sense-oriented masses and has said similar things of his own.

"You prefer that other world, don't you?" I asked him at one point in Vienna. "You think it's superior."

"Superior? I don't know. It's certainly more beautiful."

"D. H. Lawrence said that all things that are beautiful have to do with the body, that the notion of incorporeal beauty is incoherent."

"That's rot. Arrogant rot. It's like the blind denying the existence and beauty of colors."

My husband sounded so much like Plato at times, I was tempted to suggest that before he was the Viennese mathematician perhaps he had been the Greek philosopher.

It was late in the afternoon on our third day of pounding the cobblestones when we saw a middle-aged man in Chassidic garb. Noam wordlessly followed him down Fleischmarkt, turning left on Judengasse, then right on Hoher Markt. We were in a little medieval square; JUDENPLATZ, the sign said, and in the center was a small chamber orchestra playing "Eine kleine Nachtmusik." Noam moved as in a trance to take a seat. I kept glancing at him throughout the all-Mozart concert. His expression never changed, which is unusual when he listens to music.

Dusk was falling by the time the musicians packed away their instruments. At last Noam spoke to me.

"I think this is it. I think this is where I lived."

"Judenplatz? Do you know what that means? Jews' Place." Noam's knowledge of German, as of French, is exceedingly slight.

"I *know*, Renee," he said coldly.

We walked slowly around the square. It appeared to be a garment district. In one corner was a building that housed some Israeli and Jewish religious organizations. We circled the square again and again, maybe fifteen or twenty times. Finally I said:

"Noam, I'm hungry. Can we eat?"

There was a little restaurant next to the corner building housing the Jewish groups. We sat down at one of the tables outside on the sidewalk.

"Is this restaurant kosher?" I asked the waiter out of curiosity.

"No, I'm sorry," he said apologetically.

"Oh, it's all right. I was just wondering."

"Our proprietess is Jewish," he said hopefully.

The waiter was apparently unwilling to accept my assurance that my question had been motivated by pure curiosity, and when he came back with our fruit soup he told me he had asked the proprietess and had learned we could attain kosher food at the Weihburg restaurant on Seilerstätte. I thanked him for his trouble. Noam asked me what we had been talking about. I was afraid of his reaction at learning that the waiter had mistaken us for observant Jews, but Noam simply nodded at my explanation and went on eating.

In the middle of the schnitzel the proprietess herself came out to talk to us. I explained to her that I had only been curious about the restaurant, about whether there were any kosher restaurants in Vienna.

"Only one now. We have only twelve thousand Jews left in all of Austria, eleven thousand of them in Vienna."

I noticed that the inside of her arm was stamped with the blue numbers of a concentration camp. "Were you born here?" I asked.

"Oh yes, I am Viennese. I was born right here on Judenplatz, that house." She pointed across the street.

"And you still live right here?"

"No, no, but not far. I lived in America for a few years after the war, in New York's Washington Heights." She spoke the name with pride. "But I am Viennese." She smiled and shrugged. "In spite of it all. In spite of the fact that I can look out onto this square and remember when it flowed with blood. I am Viennese," she repeated with her shrug.

"Doesn't he speak any German?" she asked a little later on, tilting her head toward Noam, who, having finished his schnitzel, was staring off into space. I felt the derogatory slight of her tilt and smile with the already familiar explosion of outrage I had first experienced on the dinky. I always had to contain myself, as I contained myself now, from saying irrelevantly that my husband is a genius. "Why don't you pin a little sign onto his clothes?" Ava said to me when I told her this. " 'Please excuse the appearance of stupidity. I am a mathematical genius.' "

"How iz your *Speise?*" the proprietess said to him slowly, smiling proudly at her linguistic fluency. Noam turned and looked at her. He stared at her without saying anything until the grin faded from her plump face and she shrugged and turned back to me. After a few more sentences, she left us and went back inside.

"You know what this means?" Noam asked.

"What what means?"

"I was probably Jewish. In my former life I was most likely Jewish. I find that extraordinary, don't you?"

"I don't know."

"Think of it. Think of the improbability of two consecutive Jewish lives. It can't be coincidental. Do you understand?"

"No.

"It means that my Jewishness is essential to my identity." (So I guess he wasn't Plato. Maybe he was Philo.) "I find that extraordinary." (*This* he finds extraordinary.) "One's membership in a religious or racial class seems so incidental. You see, Renee, these things just are not a priori." (I certainly wouldn't dispute that.) He didn't speak for several more minutes, then:

"Well, all I have to do is find a Jewish Viennese mathematician who died in 1938. The more complete the description, the easier the task. But, you know, maybe I wasn't a professional mathematician, though I've always assumed it. Maybe I was a Jewish tailor or a Talmudic student with innate mathematical ability." Or a kosher butcher. "I really can't take anything for granted. Wait a minute! 1938! I was born in 1938! That's the year the Nazis invaded Austria! It all fits! I was a Viennese Jew killed by the Nazis. Maybe I was very young, a child, killed before the flowering of my mathematical talent. That would explain my anonymity. Renee, I think that's it. Many of the cases of reincarnation concern the death of a child." His eyes shone vividly blue. "It has the ring of truth to it."

The next morning Noam woke in a happy mood, whistling "Ride of the Valkyries" as he dressed.

"I've really been somewhat absurd," he told me over our rolls and coffee in the hotel's café. "I shouldn't be overly concerned with the identity of one particular individual, even if that individual is me. It's the general facts that are important. Before I only had a heuristic grasp of the truth. Now I have proof."

WE WERE expected in Hungary the next day and discussed how to spend our last day in Vienna. We were both anxious to visit the Figarohaus, the museum devoted to Mozart in the house where he had lived the brief good years of his life. After leaving the museum we walked the short distance to the building where Mozart had ended up, working on his *Requiem* and dying a pauper at the age of thirty-five. The block was gloomy, preserving through the years the depth of the fall—a fall at least when viewed from one perspective. In terms of the music there had been no decline. He had died with his powers still raging. I said something of the sort to Noam, and he answered:

"Do you think that's a tragedy?"

"Well yes, of course, for him and for us. Don't you?"

"I suppose. Certainly for us. We have some similar stories in the history of mathematics, particularly the one about Galois. He was killed at the age of twenty in some sort of political duel. The night before, as legend has it, he feverishly wrote down page after page of ideas, mostly just in outline form, jotting down in the margin, 'I have not time,' working until dawn, when he was shot."

"My God. Were they very important ideas?"

"I don't know what he wrote that night. Legend says it was the foundations of group theory, but that's too romantic to be credible. But he really was the founder of group theory. He developed the whole concept of groups. He had started out considering the question that was the fundamental problem in the theory of equations at the time: namely, under what conditions is an equation solvable? And in trying to answer this he developed methods that went way beyond the theory of equations, although I don't know if he himself knew that."

"But think what he would have done."

"Perhaps." Noam stared straight ahead for several moments, then continued: "Perhaps not. Perhaps his greatest work had all been done before the morning of the duel. Then he would have lived out a different kind of tragedy."

I found this so perverse a reaction to the story of Galois that I wondered whether Noam himself was worried about outliving his powers, or that his greatest work had been done when he was a child of twelve. But I would never have dared to ask him such questions. So instead I quipped:

"That's one of the compensations for being mediocre. One doesn't have to worry about *becoming* mediocre," and we both smiled.

Noam also insisted on visiting the Schubert Museum, the Haydn Museum and the Beethoven Museum. I suggested the Sigmund Freud Museum. Noam was livid.

"Absolutely not! I'm not going to waste my last day in Vienna paying homage to that charlatan with scientific pretensions."

I forebore pointing out to Noam that I had wasted three days in Vienna chasing after Noam chasing after himself. He would, I feared, respond that my presence had been neither requested nor desired. Instead I asked him why he thought so little of Freud.

"Freud! Don't tell me you take that stuff seriously."

I mumbled something about Freud's having been the Galileo of the mind.

"The Galileo of the mind!" Noam exploded. "Is that what you people think?" (Among whom was I being classed now? It couldn't be the positivists anymore. Nonmathematicians? Humanists? Idiots?) "The Galileo of the mind," he repeated contemptuously. "What rubbish. You really surprise me." (It was his turn to be surprised.) "I can't tell you how enraged I feel when I read or hear people coupling Freud's name with Einstein's as the geniuses of the century. Coupling Freud with Einstein! How can anyone compare the achievements of the two? Anyone dumb enough to do that wouldn't have the brains to understand what he was comparing Freud to in the first place. It's not that I have such respect for the empirical sciences, but to call psychoanalysis a scientific theory is absurdly high praise. Freud's ideas are completely ridiculous, unverified and unverifiable nonsense. The whole thing's got a built-in mechanism for discounting all counterevidence. I read some of Fraud's—sorry, Freudian slip —so-called case studies when I was in high school. The Rat Man, The Wolf Man, Dora. Hysterical, all right. Not the patients, the doctor. He makes up some story that might be true, but then again probably isn't. If the patient accepts it, it's verified. What a genius. But if the patient rejects it, that's just because he's still repressing the truth.

"I remember at the crucial point he gives poor Dora his analysis, which she vehemently rejects. She's in love with her father, of course." Noam was laughing now. "The very force with which she denies it, shows how true it is. And had she accepted it, that also would have shown how true it is. Everything confirms his theory, so nothing does. In *The Interpretation of Dreams* he comes out with the lawlike statement that all dreams are wish fulfillments. What about dreams that don't seem to be wish fulfillments? *They're* motivated by the wish to falsify Freud's law that all dreams are wish fulfillments. I ask you: is that a scientific theory? It's a pseudo-theory, the fantasy of a sloppy and, I think, rather sick mind. The emphasis on sex is ludicrous. I'm quite confident that sex plays a very trivial role in my psyche." (I was, too.) "It's ridiculous to devote so much thought to it. It's a bodily sensation, very pleasurable to have, but what's there to *think* about? What's there to hold the mind? People give it too much thought anyway, but Freud gave this mindless preoccupation intellectual respectability. Sex is a subject for little minds that can't get a grasp on the truly interesting things."

I felt profoundly rebuked, as Noam, I'm sure, intended me to. For I, as I had made the mistake of revealing in Rome, am one of the little minds that thinks about sex. Noam's silent Roman fury had finally found its words in this attack on Freud. The intellectual disdain was genuine; but the anger with which it was spoken was for me, I felt, for my having revealed myself among the contemptible masses who find sex interesting.

But isn't it? I glanced up at Noam, who was furiously scowling down into his *Schlag,* and decided to keep the discussion of the matter to myself.

Is sex really uninteresting? It *seems* so interesting. If sex isn't provocative, what the hell is? That special dimension of excitement attaches itself even to sexual thinking, to sexual discourse. But then Noam would say that our finding something interesting doesn't show that it actually is. In fact, if ever an evolutionary explanation offered itself, it does so here. A species concerned with the processes of procreation is going to get the edge on survival. And so we evolved sex-obsessed, biologically determined to find intercourse fascinating.

But sex in itself? The noumenal phenomenon? How would it look from the point of view of extraspecies intelligence? The reproductive act, accompanied (at best) with pleasurable sensations associated with certain regions of the body. These sensational accompaniments also have obvious survival value: the better it feels, the more we do it. But just how interesting can sensations—even the Big One—be? There just isn't enough conceptual complexity to allow for much analysis.

And sexual desire is merely the desire for these sensations, and no more exciting to think about then they are. Isn't it?

Of course, there is the other view of sex, the view that elevates sex to the status of ultimate truth, the truth that tells us the truth about ourselves, the fundamental fact about our conduct and existence, the secret dark meaning pervading our thoughts, our actions, and our dreams. What of *that?*

That, I could imagine Noam replying, would be evidence not for the nontriviality of sex, but rather for the triviality of us. If our essential truth is sexual, we're just not very interesting.

But how, I asked my mind's Noam, could a simple appetite such as you've described be categorized in terms of such distinctions as obscenity, perversity, and sin? There must be some complexity involved to admit such qualifications as these.

So what? answered he. So we impose these categories on sex. It's just part of our biologically determined obsession and the delusions thus produced. Think of what the Jews do to the simple appetite for food.

But, Noam, I persisted (it's significant, I suppose, that I should have taken to discussing sex with "Noam" in this fashion), haven't you left a rather important element out of your analysis? Haven't you failed to consider that the object of sexual desire is not a sensation . . . but a person? If you overlook that, then all sex is a kind of masturbation, rather an awkward kind at that, when you do it with someone else. Only that's all wrong. Masturbation isn't even sex, not really. It's the form of sex without the content; even when attaining the sensations (often more successfully than in the real thing), it's still missing the point. Because the point lies, somehow or other, in the other person, in the reciprocal desiring. No, no, Noam, you are wrong. Sex is a personal relation, and that's what makes it so deep and complex and interesting. It's not a logical relation. It's not as transparently lovely as logical relations. But it's still damn interesting.

This was my first real rebellion, unvoiced and unmanifested, but still deep and complete, against the supremacy of Noam's thinking. An image floated briefly before me. I tried to call it back and identify it, and finally succeeded. It's an image that's occurred to me frequently since: of the odd little sketch by Leonardo da Vinci that

Freud discusses in his study of the artist, *Leonardo da Vinci and a Memory of His Childhood.* (I was grateful that Noam hadn't read that one. His outrage, particularly at Freud's theory that genius is sublimated libido, would have been uncontrollable.) It shows a man copulating with a female whose face isn't drawn, *his* face turned away with a slight grimace from the act in which his body is engaged. One would never guess from the man's expression that he was at the moment in intimate union with another person. (Leonardo is also quoted there as having said: "The act of procreation and everything that has any relation to it is so disgusting that human beings would soon die out if it were not a traditional custom and if there were no pretty faces and sensuous dispositions." Freud, deductively leaping with an abandon that would not have excited Noam's admiration, suggests an unresolved Oedipal complex and latent homosexuality.)

Noam and I did not visit the house at Berggasse 19. We compromised instead on the Schönbrunn and Belvedere palaces.

WHEN WE ARRIVED at the chaotic Budapest train station, we were at a loss. We didn't know whether anyone from the conference was coming to meet us, and since, as Noam now bethought himself to mention, he had never met any of the Hungarian organizers, he wouldn't recognize them anyway. Would we ever make our own way to Esztergom, wherever that was?

"Why didn't you think of this before?" As I said this, I turned to Noam and noticed a man parading up and down the side of the tracks with a large sign on his chest printed (in red) with the word HIMMEL. We were not forgotten.

The young man was a mathematician from the Bolyai Institute, which was organizing the international conference. (Bolyai, Noam told me, was one of the five independent discoverers of non-Euclidean geometry.) Our brief ride through Budapest was enchanting. The beautiful city was nothing like the somber gray socialist presence I had anticipated. It's really two cities, Gabor, our driver, told us, divided by the Danube, which approximates more closely to its sung description here than in Vienna. Buda is primarily residential, and Pest, where we had arrived on the train, is more commercial.

We drove past the Parliament on the banks of the Danube (looking like Westminster upon the Thames), then crossed the wide river to Buda and continued out of the city.

Esztergom was a forty-minute drive from Budapest. It's a very pretty, hilly little village on the shores of the Danube, the view of which is dominated by the large bishopric built on a hill in the center of town. But for the few days we were there what dominated the town was the presence of the mathematical luminaries who had gathered from around the world. For the first time I saw Noam with people whom he regarded as on his level. There was one in particular, the Russian Nicolai Maralov, for whom Noam felt a respect bordering on reverence. It was a unique experience to see Noam speaking deferentially to someone.

There was an ordering of mathematical talent at the conference. First were the *Kohanim*, the high priests, descendents of Aaron—about seven or eight mathematicians who conversed directly with God. Then came the tribe of Levis, very special but not allowed entry into the Holy of Holies. And last came the congregation of Israelites, awaiting word from those on high, but still a nation apart, chosen by God.

The mathematical hierarchy was duplicated in the groupings of the spouses. My first morning there, I was invited by the wives of the *Kohanim* to join them at breakfast, thus confirming, had confirmation been needed, Noam's position in the mathematical world. I met Olga Maralov, wife of Nicolai and a linguist; Marta Künig, wife of Hermann Künig and a museum curator in Munich; and Barbara Stern, the wife of Eric Stern of Harvard, who, at twenty-six, was the youngest member of the inner sanctum.

"I'm afraid," Barbara said, "that about completes my humble description. Wife of Eric, mother of Karen, Jonathan, and David, sometime poet, lousy housewife."

She was a large, pleasant-faced woman who gave the overall impression of sloppiness, though all the individual parts appeared presentable enough. Perhaps the impression had its source in her movements. But whereas the other two women's smiles of ostensible welcome left me out in the cold, Barbara's was the kind one couldn't help returning in full.

The rest of the *Kohanim* had either not brought their wives or were wifeless. At breakfast the dining room (outside, under the lindens) was almost completely given over to women, for most of the mathematicians had finished long before and gone off to the first lecture. Nina Trotti, Enrico's dark, chic wife, toward whom I had been heading, was sitting at another table with, I eventually discovered, the women of the Levis.

Olga and Marta were both in their late forties and very good friends, so I naturally turned throughout the conference to Barbara, who is warm, natural, and very talkative. She was visibly delighted to have the select circle enlarged by one. For it could be expected that we would meet at international conference after conference.

"We were terribly surprised when Noam showed up with you," she said as soon as I had sat down. "No, not terribly. Happily. Eric had just seen him in Vancouver in early June, I think it was, and he never said anything about being married."

"That's because we weren't married yet. In fact, Noam proposed to me the night he returned from Vancouver."

"You mean you just got married?"

"Yes, a little over a month ago."

"A month!" Marta, given to exclaiming, exclaimed. "Then this is your honeymoon!"

"Well yes, I suppose." A honeymoon with precious little honey and plenty of stings.

"And I bet you'll be seeing very little of your new husband," Barbara said. "At least in Esztergom. Well, I suppose that's good. Honeymoons shouldn't create any illusions. That's what makes their ending so awful. Noam was very wise to show you immediately what it's like to consort with a mathematician." They all laughed.

"I'm so happy for Noam," Barbara said to me at one point. "He really needs someone to take care of him. I've always wondered how in the world he managed. Every time he's stayed with us I've just wished I could keep him on, adopt him or something. But I guess he's more practical than he appears. Eric could never have survived all those years on his own." (They had married when Eric, also a prodigy, was nineteen and Barbara was twenty-three.) "He would have gone floating off if there hadn't been me and the kids to weigh him down.

Of course, sometimes I worry that the weight may be a little too much. Three kids add up to an awful lot of distractions. Sometimes when they're all yelling for his attention or one of them is having problems, I worry that I've set math back hundreds of years because of my irresistible maternal urge."

I was interested in watching Barbara with her Eric, a boyishly shy man, amazingly (and obliviously) handsome. Barbara revered and babied him. But there were few opportunities to observe them together, for the mathematicians were consumed from morning to night in mathematics. I would catch glimpses now and then of Noam walking the narrow hilly streets between lectures, never alone and quite often with a large group of talking men. But here, unlike in Rome, I had the company of the other nonmathematician wives (and two husbands). The organizers had not forgotten us and had arranged for various trips: around Esztergom; to the neighboring villages to view the remains of the numerous invaders who had passed through; on a boat down the Danube.

At night the mathematicians would rejoin us, and we'd gather in the dining room after dinner to play charades. I only watched (I have a horror of making a spectacle of myself), but Noam, who never gives a thought to such considerations, threw himself into the game with great enthusiasm and was very good. At one point he had to act out *Saturday Night Fever* (the Americans were counting on the Russians never having heard of the movie) and he began by madly wiggling his hips, a sight I'll never forget. But the Russians were the undisputed charade champions, triumphant and unbeatable. They must play a lot. The first night they challenged everyone else, chanting, "The Russians against the world." The next night it was the communists against the capitalists; the night after, the "imperialists" (Russians and Americans) against the Europeans. There was something wonderful, I thought, about their laughter at the differences that loom so large in the other world. As far as they were concerned, they all lived within the same borders, the only borders that mattered. They were all mathematicians.

Barbara and I decided to make a trip together into Budapest. The Künigs had their car with them, having driven from Munich, and Barbara asked Marta if we could borrow it for a day. So Saturday afternoon, the day before the conference ended, we drove the Mercedes along the Danube into Budapest.

"Barbara," I said as I pushed down hard on the accelerator, "I have to get myself one of these little toys."

"Try to get Noam to turn a fraction of his attention to the stock market. You'd probably be rich before the next semester was over." She laughed. "I've been trying with Eric for years."

"Fat chance. Unless there's some mathematical beauty to be found in the fluctuations of Wall Street."

Barbara was very excited on the trip in, for she was going to try to track down some relatives in Budapest.

"I've tried each time we're here." She and Eric had been in Hungary twice before. It seemed there wasn't a European country they hadn't visited in the seven years since they'd been married. "But this time I have what I think is their address. They're the only family left in Europe. My grandmother came to the States alone when she was something like fifteen. She had eight brothers and sisters. She managed to send for one, but they sent the wrong one. Grandmother never forgave Great-aunt Sophie for being the one to survive. The rest were all killed during the second world war, except for one brother and his two sons. This brother and one of his sons were walking back to their home after being liberated from Auschwitz and some Hungarian peasants shot them on the road only a few miles from their village."

"God, how awful! To have survived all that and then be shot."

"Yes. I've been hearing these stories all my life. Anyway, the address, which I have right here"—she patted her pocket—"is, I hope, the address of the other son's son."

The conference organizers had given us a map marked with the address, so we had little trouble finding it. It was in an old building in the center of Pest, the bottom floor taken up with stores.

"It's supposed to be on the fifth floor," Barbara said, looking up doubtfully.

"I'll wait down here for you."

She returned after five minutes, jubilant. "It's them, all right. They're not home. I met a neighbor, who luckily spoke German. She said they'd be home from work around five o'clock. There's my cousin, who's an engineer, his wife, a teacher, and their three-year-old boy, she told me."

We decided to go sightseeing until five. We drove around the beautiful streets of Buda, wondering who lived in its palatial homes now. My imagination rioted with scenes (greatly influenced by *Dr. Zhivago*) of aristocrats fleeing, once haughty women with beautiful children clinging to them. We also visited the old Buda castle, now a museum, and the new Hilton. Finally it was almost five and we drove back to Pest.

"Good luck," I said as Barbara stepped out.

"Thanks. We'll meet here at six-thirty."

I decided to drive around for a while, stopping if anything caught my eye. The traffic in Pest was very bad, and I decided to return to beautiful Buda. But before I reached the bridge crossing the Danube, I noticed out of the corner of my eye a large stone building that I thought was decorated with Stars of David. (Things like that still leap out at me.) I circled back, and sure enough there were Jewish stars worked into the stones.

I parked and got out. It was obviously a very large synagogue. The main doors were locked, but there was a side door open. I went through and climbed two flights of stairs, finding myself at the top in a long, narrow room that housed a Jewish museum. There was a rich profusion of old silver and gold religious articles crowded on long tables: ornate Torah decorations, kiddush cups for blessing the wine on the Sabbath and holidays, menorahs for lighting the candles on Chanukah, and spice-boxes for *Havdalah*, the ceremony bidding farewell to the Sabbath. Another table was heaped with old holy books. A wall was lined with pictures of Hungarian synagogues, the majority now destroyed. This synagogue, I learned, is the second largest in Europe.

At the end of the long room was a smaller one, devoted entirely to the destruction of the Hungarian Jews under the Nazis. There were framed copies of the various edicts issued against the Jews, a map showing exterminated communities, and the most simple and eloquent statement of the horror: a faded pair of the black and white striped inmate's uniform and a pile of tattered boots.

The main part of the synagogue was closed, but I went out back into a large courtyard, now a cemetery for Nazi victims. I wandered around, searching for some information beyond the blankness of the names, yielded by an occasional "Doctor" or "Professor." Against a long wall were small metal plaques with more names, a memorial bulb burning beside each.

I left the courtyard and walked the surrounding streets. Many of the buildings were engraved with Stars of David or Hebrew letters. This had obviously been the center of Budapest Jewry. During our three days of pacing Vienna, Noam had told me something of the history of the Austro-Hungarian empire. His knowledge is quirkily detailed, full of odd stories, names, and dates. He always overwhelms me with his factual knowledge (and sometimes with his ignorance) of the most unexpected topics. If something about a subject attracts his attention, he sucks up every detail and remembers it forever. For some reason, at some point in the past, the Catholic Hapsburg dynasty had attracted his notice.

Maria Theresa, in the eighteenth century, had been warm and motherly, but, alas for the Jews, very pious. The Jews had been expelled. Franz Joseph, on the other hand, the last of the Hapsburg rulers, had been stern and soldierly, but had a Jewish mistress, and the Jews had prospered under him. The Hungarian Jews, in fact, became the wealthiest of the European Jewish communities. Now I was seeing the marks of this former prosperity chiseled into the stones.

On Dub *utca* I came to a very large iron gate and peered inside to a long dark courtyard surrounded by great gray buildings. On a far flight of stairs I saw two girls supporting between them a crippled dwarf. I followed them up and found myself in what appeared to be a restaurant of sorts. The dwarf was leaning near the door (the two girls having deposited him and left).

"*Salut,*" he said to me.

"*Salut.* Is this a restaurant?" I asked him in German.

"A welfare kitchen. Everyone is free to eat." He bowed slightly. "I am Janos Seifert, electrical engineer." He barely came up to my waist. His head, topped with a black beret, seemed freakishly large on his twisted shriveled body, but the face looking up into mine had an expression of almost aristocratic refinement and intelligence. It was jolting.

"Are you German?" he asked.

"No, no, American. I am Renee Himmel."

"An American," he said in beautiful English. "How do you do." He bowed again, then turned to a woman sitting at a table right behind us. The left side of her face was all crumpled up, as if it had collapsed inwards, and the right side slanted toward the left as if partially sucked in by the implosion. "Helena, this young lady is an American. Her name is Renee Himmel." He spoke in German. "Helena does not understand English," he explained to me.

Helena smiled at me with half her face. "Won't you please join us for dinner?"

"I'm very sorry. I would like to, but I have to meet a friend at six-thirty."

"Well, we have a little time," Janos said. "At least share a cup of coffee with us. Would you mind, my dear young lady, helping me over to the table."

When he had succeeded in getting himself seated, and had ordered a cup of the sickly sweet Hungarian coffee for me, he spoke again.

"Now, tell us please how you come to be in Budapest."

I explained to them about the conference at Esztergom, all the while wondering about them. (They were not, it turned out, related.) Both were stamped with blue numbers. I could imagine the blow that had destroyed Helena's face, but what had been done to Janos' body to produce such total deformity? He would have been a boy then.

"And you?" Janos asked. "What is your profession?" The assumption that I too would have a profession was universal in Hungary.

"I study philosophy."

"Ah, philosophy. The queen of the sciences. I am most impressed. But, you know, this is Providence. You are just the one I need. Can you tell me please the name of the French bishop who said that reality exists in the individual sensorium?"

"French bishop? I'm afraid I don't know. You don't mean Bishop Berkeley, do you?"

"No, no, Berkeley was British. This was a French bishop."

"I'm terribly sorry. I don't know."

"Oh no, don't concern yourself." He waved his shrunken, crumpled hand with an aristocratic gesture. "It will come to me. I only wanted to save myself a little time."

"Speaking of time," I said, "I really must go or my friend will be kept waiting. She's been trying to locate some relatives." I explained as I stood up. "It's been a pleasure." It had been, though also disorienting. We whole-bodied persons make assumptions.

"Ah well, we must be philosophical and graciously permit you to go. The pleasure was ours, my dear young lady, a short pleasure, but sweet.

"Auf Wiedersehen," I said.

"Auf Wiedersehen." He looked at me questioningly and then said with a smile, *"A guten* Shabbos."

A guten Shabbos. It was Shabbos. I had been sitting at a table with people who had been enclosed in a different space, with people for whom it was Shabbos. I had, unknowingly, been sharing a Shabbos meal.

I walked slowly down the stairs and across the darkening courtyard. There were some elderly men at the other end of the yard, entering a doorway inscribed with Hebrew letters. They're probably going to evening prayers, I thought, to *Maarev.* As I passed by, I saw that one of them looked a little like my father: the delicate face structure, high, pronounced cheekbones, and gentle expression. I watched him disappear into the building and felt stabbed through with longing. I wanted to watch him *davening Maarev,* but I thought of Barbara waiting for me.

"It's Shabbos." The longing in me—for my father and his world —had risen to my eyes and was blurring my vision. And then suddenly I was back inside it, inside Shabbos. The world had that different feel, that closed-off, restful, floating calm. I was back inside its space, enfolded in its distances, feeling the enforced but real sense of serenity, bounded round by prohibitions. The appearances of things were softened, muted, subtly but thoroughly transformed.

I walked slowly out of the courtyard and back to Dohemy *utca,* where the car was parked. I tried the doors of the great synagogue again, but they were still locked. As I got into my car, the noise and hard outlines of the world reasserted themselves. I had broken through the cobweb borders, had stepped outside of Shabbos, was on the far side again of *Havdalah,* the separation between the sanctified and secular.

I drove back to meet Barbara. She was waiting outside the building where her relatives lived, and she looked close to tears.

"Barbara, I'm sorry I'm late. What's wrong?"

"Oh, Renee, it was such a disaster. They didn't speak any English or German or French, my only languages. They only spoke Hungarian and Russian. We couldn't communicate at all."

"It's a reflection of the political realities. The older people speak German; the younger ones, Russian."

"Yes, I really should have thought of it. But I just felt that if I could track them down, we'd find some way to communicate. I didn't think about being separated from them by anything so mundane as language."

"So what happened?"

"Nothing. It was awful. We just stared at one another. They seemed to understand I was a relative. I think the neighbor had mentioned it to them before she went out. They pointed to her door. And they acted very friendly. They seemed to know I wasn't just someone off the streets. I kept mentioning the name of my grandmother, but it didn't seem to mean anything to them. We just stood there staring at one another, smiling and shrugging. It was embarrassing. I left after about ten minutes, still smiling and shrugging."

We drove back to Esztergom in near silence, both of us brooding over the worlds out of which we had been shut, the pasts from which we were cut off. There's no going back, I kept thinking. You've made your choice, and now that life is dead to you. It was a world almost as inaccessible to me as that former existence Noam thought he had glimpsed in Vienna was now to him.

5

REALITY

We have no reason to seek for some criterion of personal identity that is distinct from
the identity of our bodies as persisting physical objects. We find our intelligence or our
will working and expressing themselves in action, at a particular place and a particular
time, and just these movements, or this voluntary stillness are unmistakably mine, if
they are my actions, animated by my inten-
tions. . . . I can only be said to have lost a
sense of my own identity if I have lost all
sense of where I am and what I am doing.

—STUART HAMPSHIRE,
THOUGHT AND ACTION

We returned to New Jersey in the middle of a heat wave. As we stepped out of the terminal at the airport, a steamy wave of air hit us smack in the face, knocking the breath out of us. Noam, usually so oblivious to his physical environment, stopped in midsentence:

"Hell, how are we going to breathe in this noxious stuff? This place isn't fit for human habitation."

My car was parked at the airport. I had to use a tissue to get the key into the burning ignition and then to hold the steering wheel. I'm usually paranoid about speeding on the well-patrolled turnpike, but right then I needed the sense of liberation that speeding gives me. Doing eighty blurred without softening the depressing scenery to our right and left, the factories eliminating their poisons into the already sick air.

New Jersey in August.

We left the turnpike at Exit 9. New Brunswick, a dying city, was never a pretty sight, and now it lay gasping in the heavy air. Its black inhabitants were sitting out on stoops and curbs, wordless, hopeless. We followed Route 27 out of the urban decline and into rural despair. Forlorn little houses stared out from behind their tangle of withered weeds, a sad, tired landscape in yellow and brown, parched and panting.

But when we reached the outskirts of Princeton—the northern shore of the large lake built with Carnegie money, where Einstein had done his sailing—everything changed. Stately homes looked serenely out over high, clipped hedges, and lush green lawns sparkled under whirling sprinklers. Even Dutch elm blight had been halted at Princeton's borders. Unperspiring women with tennis tans pedaled their bikes slowly through town, under the deep shade of ancient elms. The fertility of rationality. I had never before been so struck with the isolation of this world, our world. It floats like a glittering island of privilege in the vast dull Jersey sea.

And now it belonged to me. Nobody could question my right now to occupy this space. I was *there*, and not just anywhere. "You're marginal, very marginal," I remembered the graduate director telling me. Not anymore, not Mrs. Noam Himmel. (Gladly, gladly I took the name as my own.) I was at the glorious center, with all my world converging toward me in my new identity. I didn't have to try and hack it with my own questionable intellectual equipment. Any hacking I did (because I did plan to try—I planned on everything as I rode triumphantly into town) would be blissfully supererogatory. By the time we reached Princeton proper I was buoyant, floating high over the oppressive atmosphere.

We stopped off at Davidson's to pick up some provisions. As we walked together down the frozen food aisle, I heard someone calling Noam. It was Mel Bright, a mathematician I had met at several parties. He was with a man I didn't know.

"Hi, Noam, Renee. When did you get back?"

"Just now. We just got into town."

"Well then, welcome back. Welcome back to the heat. Don't think you've picked a particularly bad time to return. It's been like this all summer."

"Yes," the other man said. "We've been simmering in our own juices all season. I'm Ted Berliner, computer sciences." He reached out to shake Noam's hand.

"Oh, I'm sorry," Mel said. "I didn't realize you two hadn't met before. And this is Noam's new wife, Renee. Are you going by Feuer or Himmel?"

"Himmel."

"Ah, an old-fashioned girl." Ted shook my hand and then turned back to Noam. "Yes, I've of course been anxious to meet you ever since I heard you were coming. Say, why don't you two come over to our house for dinner tonight? It's a shame to have to start cooking as soon as you get back, and Liz, my wife, would be thrilled to meet you."

Stocked with a few groceries, we drove back to the house on Faculty Road in which Noam had been living and into which I had moved a few days after we decided to get married. The house belonged to a professor emeritus of economics, who would be returning at the end of September after a year in England.

"You'd better go over to the housing office first thing tomorrow,"

Noam said as we walked into the airless house. "See what they can get for us."

But that evening at the Berliners', when I mentioned our housing problem, Ted said to Noam:

"You really ought to buy a house, you know. It doesn't make sense for you to be paying out rent money when you could be investing it in real estate. And then there are the tax advantages."

"A house," Noam said. "I've never really considered it. It would be a burden, tie me down."

"But even if you sold after a year or two, you'd get your money back —probably even make a few thousand, the way real estate has been going up around here. Unless you have some better way of investing your money."

"Hmmmm. I'll have to think about it."

By the next morning the problem had been analyzed, the solution determined.

"Renee, I want you to find us a house."

"You're kidding." I was floored. I had lived either with my parents or in dorm rooms my whole life. An apartment of my own was somewhat daunting. But a house? I wasn't ready for that. It was too adult, too middle-aged. It belonged to the world of parents, and I wanted no part of it. Noam, however, was really sold on the idea.

"Don't be such a child. It's time to grow up."

"You want me to do it all by myself?"

"Well, I certainly don't have any time for it."

"But how do I do it? I don't know how to go about it." I heard and detested the whine in my voice.

"What do you mean? All you have to do is buy a newspaper, read the ads, and call up if something sounds promising. It shouldn't be beyond you. Everybody else seems to manage."

So after Noam left for Fine Hall I studied a copy of *Town Topics*. All the homes sounded very grand, much too much, with sunken rooms, cathedral ceilings, and swimming pools. And I had forgotten to ask Noam how much we could afford to spend. I tried calling him all through the day but kept missing him.

When he came home that evening, he asked me if I had made any progress:

"You know we don't have all that much time."

"Well, I read the ads in *Town Topics*. But I don't know how much we can afford to spend. Things seem very expensive."

"Give me the paper." Noam studied the ads and then paced around awhile. "Look, why don't you see a few houses and get an idea of what can be gotten for how much. Let's not waste time discussing this thing in a factual vacuum."

So the next morning I called up one of the brokers advertising a house that sounded relatively modest. Adele Nitkin, million-dollar realty agent, drove up to our house to pick me up. She was an elegant figure, tall and slim, and dressed in pale shades of taupe with matching makeup. I was impressed. But the image of elegance was shattered the minute she opened her mouth. Actually the voice came (loudly) out of the nose.

"Mrs. Himmel?" she asked icily, inspecting my jeans and sandals.

"You're from New York, aren't you?" I said as we drove over to the house in her pale yellow Coupe de Ville.

"Why, yes. How did you know?" I thought I detected dislike beneath the ice and wondered what I had done. Was it simply my clothes? I hadn't realized one is supposed to dress for real estate.

"What part of New York?" I asked in innocence, hoping to reach common ground with a fellow New Yorker.

"Oh, uptown."

"Really? I went to school uptown. Barnard. Did you live on the Upper West Side?"

"No."

"East Side?"

"No."

I tried farther uptown: "Washington Heights?"

"The Bronx," she said shortly. There was no mistaking the dislike now. Why am I *here?* I thought. She turned to me with a tight smile.

"You're just going to love this house. I know. It's a dream."

I hated the house. It looked like the kind of house they make television commercials in, a house in which to strive for shinier shines, whiter whites, fewer cavities. I could never live in such a house.

Adele sailed through, opening closets, switching on lights. She was enamored of the word "humongous." The living room was humongous, as were the bathrooms, the closets, and the yard. I asked her the price and was numbed by the answer. Up until then I had purchased in terms of tens, twenties, an occasional fifty. Even my darling Volvo, my biggest purchase, had cost only six hundred used. Now I was being asked to think in terms of hundreds of thousands.

"Is that in your price range?" The nasal icicle pierced through my reflections.

"I'm not exactly sure what our price range is. This is my first day looking. I'm going to have to discuss it with my husband."

"Yes, I can see you're new at the game. You haven't asked any of the right questions." She tittered, a tinkle of little ice cubes. "But at least give me an idea of the kind of house you like. Do you like this one?"

"I don't really think it's for me. I don't know. I guess it's a nice enough house"—I didn't want to insult her taste—"but it doesn't appeal to me at all."

"No? Why not? What do you want in a house?"

It was a question I had never considered, probably placing me, in Adele's scheme of things, at the far limits of eccentricity. "I'm not sure. This one feels alien, I don't know, cold. It's just not my world."

"I understand. You want warmth. You want charm and character. Am I right or am I right?"

Warmth, charm, and character sounded good, at least as properties of people. I wasn't quite sure how it came out translated into architecture, but could warmth, charm, and character be bad?

"Yes, I think you're right."

"You see? I know. I know the kind of house for you. Maybe an older house. That's where you usually find your character. Don't worry, I'm going to take care of you. I didn't actually think you'd like this one. Too sterile and nonindividualistic. You're an individualist."

She had apparently plummeted the depths of my person in the twenty minutes she had known me. I couldn't wait to get away from her. But life was not to be so kind.

During the next weeks Adele called me every few days with a house to show, with a humongous fireplace or family room or yard. Some of them were quite lovely, but I couldn't imagine how we could afford them, although *maybe* we could. I still hadn't been able to pin Noam down on that subject. Anyway I couldn't picture myself living comfortably in the midst of such grandeur. Then there was the other type of house, similar to, in fact indistinguishable from, the first house I had seen—happy-houses that depressed the hell out of me. I certainly couldn't imagine myself and Noam living in *them*.

For two weeks I did nothing but see and think houses. I was getting more and more depressed about the whole thing, and the prominent presence of Adele in my life didn't help. She always intimated that she and I were soulmates, of the same kind; that of all her many clients I was somehow special. I suppose that's how one gets to be a million-dollar agent. Only it was pretty obvious that we were not in the least of the same kind (and I began to fear that perhaps the difference was to her credit.) In fact, it was pretty obvious that she didn't care for me at all. And I'm always very hurt when people don't care for me, even if I can't stand their guts. On my part it wasn't just objective dislike of Adele; it was more self-referential. She made me doubt myself, my view of what—and therefore who—matters. She was coming from a distant mattering zone, and the self-assurance of her judgments made me suspect the validity of my own. She made me feel like a child, inadequate to the serious business of adulthood. Certain things (first and foremost, Property) were supposed to matter to grownups. I had better get *with* it.

I pondered the ethics of calling another agent. It wasn't exactly clear to me (little of all this was, and yet Noam presumed it was my affair), but from what Adele said it seemed she was my exclusive agent. She kept repeating that she could show me houses listed with other agencies, that if I saw anything that interested me I was to tell her about it. It seemed I had bonded myself to this realty tyrant with that first accursed phone call. I wanted to discuss the matter with Noam, but he grew impatient each time I mentioned it. I remembered Barbara Stern's worry about keeping Eric free from distractions, under which she included her three children. I too did not want to set math back hundreds of years.

Adele Nitkin invaded and took over my nightmares, dressed at one moment in coordinated shades of purple, makeup in plum, and the next in icy blue clothes and makeup. I wanted her out—out of my nightmares and out of my life. But how? If I could just find a house, that would be the end of it. My fingers itched to sign a contract.

Finally one morning I went in desperation down to the university housing office and was given a list of available apartments. The first one I looked at, a duplex in a stucco row on Prospect Avenue, owned by the university, was wonderful—a dark and woody place in which it would be possible to sit and daydream at high noon, unvisited by guilt's dark demons. This was the element, I now realized, missing from all of Adele's offerings. I could never have felt equal to those houses.

But this apartment, though classy, was comfortable. It would never challenge my right of occupation. On the first floor was a kitchen, a dining room, and a long, lovely living room. The kitchen had a back door leading out to a small garden (daffodils in the spring, I fantasized, roses through the summer, mums in the fall). The glorious living room had exposed oak beams, a red brick fireplace, and floor-to-ceiling bookcases stained in the same dark tone as the wooden floors laid throughout. (All very Oxford, I imagined. Leave it to Princeton.) A weighty oaken staircase led upstairs. Here there were three straight-forward bedrooms (we could convert two into studies) and a big white bathroom with an oversize tub on legs, which would have launched Adele into schemes of modernization but which I adored.

Apartments, unlike houses, were something I could judge, and this was the most wonderful one I had ever seen. In fact, I felt quite confident that it had charm, warmth, and character. It was, I felt, the right kind of home for a gifted man and his devoted wife, for it was just comfortable enough not to distract with either the deprivation or the superfluity of material goods.

When I spoke to Noam about it that night he was surprisingly agreeable, having lost interest in the housing project.

"Fine. If you like it, go ahead. As long as we have someplace to live."

Exit, and not very gracefully, Adele.

Some friends told us about a place that rents furniture to university people, and within two weeks we were all settled in (as I was once again settled into my view of the world). I'd buy furniture slowly, I told myself; to date, I have not purchased a stick. But anyway, Noam was pleased and told me our first night in our own (rented) bed in our own (rented) place that I had done a good job, quite sweeping me away on a crest of self-satisfaction.

It had been a narrow escape. I hadn't realized at the time the dangers with which I was flirting, the precarious nature of the world of property ownership we had almost entered: that world of intimate, complicated, aggravating relationships with painters, plumbers, carpenters, gardeners, and electricians. Much of the conversation at dinner parties was devoted to the intricacies of these relationships, the degree of sensitivity they required. And though they were always amusing tales, told with the lightness and gaiety suitable to the occasion, I could glimpse the soul suffering that lay behind, and always felt correspondingly grateful for a situation that allowed us to go running with any household woe—from a clogged toilet to a mouse in the pantry—to the kind and efficient people at the university housing office. Even *if* the Adele Nitkins are right (a question I could now happily forget), and people like Noam and me *are* inadequate to the business of adulthood, here, in the nourishing womb of the university, we need never feel it.

Thus Noam and I settled down to our housekeeping. Or rather I settled down to keeping, Noam to being kept. It was assumed, of course, that Noam would be under no petty domestic obligations. None of that liberated fifty-fifty stuff for us. My shoulders would bear, and bear gracefully, gratefully, all the sundry and tedious details of the house. Plenty of women before me, *without* the benefits of matrimony, had done no less—or not much less, anyway. There had always been some colleague's wife only too happy to mother Noam, to do his laundry and sew on his buttons, and thereby do her bit for the history of mathematics. But—and this will not be the last of the dirty confessions about my married life—I did not assume these burdens joyfully. I was of two minds. When I thought of Noam as The Genius, then of course I was only too happy to wait on him hand and foot, to pick up the dirty socks he thought nothing of kicking off in the middle of the living room, or jump up from the dinner table when he announced he wanted a glass of water. But then, in the course of our day-to-day living, I would sometimes just think of him as my husband Noam; and then I would feel the resentment curdle.

This resentment had historical associations. It had been suffered throughout my childhood, when, as the girl in the family, I was expected to help wait on The Men—a class which included that little twerp, my brother. "Hurry up, dish it out. You'll keep The *Men* waiting." God forbid! The women—even guests—always got the last and the worst, the dried and the burnt. God forbid The Men shouldn't be satisfied. Any shmuck with a shmuck was a power before us. I couldn't believe it when I first heard that in some segments of society women are actually served first. (This order of dishing out carries over, of course, to bigger goodies than portions of roast chicken. Education, for instance. I could never have gone to Barnard without arguing and a full scholarship. My mother still mourns it as a terrible mistake.) I had been brought up to believe it is God's way for women to wait on men. And yet still I would mutter as my brother ran off after dinner to play baseball, while I scrounged around under the table picking up his filthy crumbs.

So, you see, the assumed division of labor in my marriage smacked too much of an aspect of traditional Judaism I had hated and had hoped to leave behind. (And yet I accepted with delirium the name Mrs. Noam Himmel.) I didn't go to Noam with a list of his and her chores. Mostly I just continued my childhood habit of muttering under the table.

Occasionally, when things got to what I considered a ludicrous point, I'd say something. For example, at dinner soon after our return Noam asked me repeatedly to get him something or other: a sharper knife, another glass of water (he consumes great quantities of the stuff), another napkin (his was all greasy). Finally I allowed myself to show a little annoyance. The man had a great brain, of course. But he also had legs.

"Why can't you get yourself a napkin? I've been fetching for you all night."

"*I* don't know where they are."

"Well, *I* could tell you. Don't you think you should know where things are? This is your house, too."

"I don't see any need for me to know. You know."

I soon gave up on such arguments. They only ended in my feeling petty.

All in all, though, it felt good for us to be back in Princeton, where we were accorded celebrity status. We became, especially in the first months following our return, the most sought-after of guests. For the first time in my life I was faced with decisions as to which invitations to accept. (Noam wanted no more than one party a week.) But the real pleasure of the return lay in the opportunity to view Noam once again in his natural setting. Here his outline, which in Europe had occasionally shifted disconcertingly, firmly readjusted itself. He could be difficult, but he was unquestionably the great man I had married.

September came. The air thinned, the undergraduates returned, and classes began. Noam and his colleagues reluctantly resumed the yoke of teaching and grumbled over the numerous distractions from research that the students presented. It's amusing how outsiders think *teaching* is the job of professors and ignorantly exclaim over how few hours academics have to work. Just last week Noam's gastroenterologist (we've discovered an ulcer) asked him how many hours a week he has to teach and then laughed smugly.

"Three hours? That's all you guys have to work a week?" (Noam's teaching load is much lighter than the average—one of the lures Princeton had used to attract him.) "And with summers off? Boy, you people are really overworked." And he was the man treating Noam for an ulcer. Noam didn't—never does—bother to correct the man's faulty inference from three hours of teaching to three hours of work. What does he care what such people think?

But grumble though it might over the start of the academic year, the university world became more positive and purposeful. Here was a new year, a fresh morning in which to forget the terrifying nightmare shared by the town's collective unconscious: that the research won't pan out, or worse, that it won't matter a hoot if it does; that one's lifework is just so much mental onanism in the night. September brought the light of day, chased the nightmare away. No, no, it *is* important work, it *does* matter.

MY OLD FRIEND Ava Schwartz drove down from New York in a U-Haul truck the third week in September, with all her belongings. The Institute for Advanced Study provides neat furnished apartments with fireplaces for visiting members, set in motel-like buildings that wind along Einstein and von Neumann drives. (Einstein you of course know; von Neumann, perhaps not. He was one of this century's most important mathematicians, best known, perhaps, for his theory of games, which has so influenced economics. He was appointed to the Institute in 1933 and remained there until his death in 1957. All permanent members of the Institute, I think, choose to stay until they die.) Fuld Hall itself, the main administrative and academic building, looks like a grandish Howard Johnson's: a red brick Georgian building with a white cupola on top. (Had this architectural style motivated the remark of J. Robert Oppenheimer, the physicist who became the Institute's second director, that the place is "an intellectual hotel, dedicated to the preservation of the good things men live by"?)

Ava, who had lived with rats and roaches in her fifth-floor walk-up on Amsterdam, around the corner from Columbia, was thrilled with the ethereality (beats reality) of her new environment. It took the two of us about six hours to unload and sort out her stuff, mainly books. When we finished, we collapsed with a bottle of wine onto the modern blue couch and stared out the large picture window—across Olden Lane to the expansive green lawn, and beyond that to Fuld Hall. If ever a building stared wisely back, Fuld Hall did. In another setting the rather squat edifice would not have been prepossessing. But here, atop a slight incline, with the great lawn before it and the circular drive leading up to it—it dominated. Ava turned to me with a beatific smile:

"Oh, I'm a happy woman, a happy woman. Here I am sitting with my best friend looking out a window at Fuld Hall in my own glorious apartment on Einstein Drive. Einstein Drive," she sighed, "the sheer beauty of it." (Ava worships Einstein: "He wasn't just a genius. He was a *mensh.*") "I've got two whole years. Two years to work on my own stuff for the first time in my life. There's nobody over me. Free at last, free at last, thank God Almighty I'm free at last."

My friend's euphoria wasn't just a matter of what she was escaping from, the captivity of The Shmuck; it was also what she was escaping to. The Institute for Advanced Study has a special place in our region of the mattering map, whose terrain I am concerned to lay out for you. For how can I give you my life without describing my zone?

If Princeton is one of the sacred spots, then the Institute is Princeton's holy of holies. It was created in 1930, when Abraham Flexner, a reformer in education, persuaded two New Jersey department store heirs, Louis Bamberger and his sister Mrs. Fuld, to charter a new type of institution dedicated to the "usefulness of useless knowledge." (You see why the place means so much to us.) Here the "permanent members," chosen with infinite care, and the promising young "temporary members," would be free to pursue their ideas, unencumbered by teaching responsibilities. The Institute is composed of administration and faculty. The bothersome remainder of almost all other seats of scholarship, the students, has been mercifully eliminated.

In 1932 Flexner announced that the first two appointed members would be Oswald Veblen, the leading mathematician at Princeton, and Albert Einstein, the most famous scientist in the world, on the run from Nazism. Hitler ranks only after Bamberger and Fuld, someone once said, in terms of helping the Institute become what it is, as scholar after scholar fled Göttingen for Princeton.

The Institute was established from its inception as the incomparable gathering place of genius, the Mount Olympus of pure thought. Each of the permanent members must be judged by the faculty at large as godlike. (Gödel, the only contemporary on Noam's roll call of mathematical minor deities, and another legendary figure, was a permanent member until his very recent tragic death. Having convinced himself of an attempt to poison him, he refused to eat and eventually died of starvation. He published papers totaling less than seventy-five pages in his life, but every field he touched was thereby revolutionized. Our world is eagerly awaiting the posthumous publication of his works, which are rumored to contain an a priori proof of God's existence—a situation which has prompted me to flirt with the idea of a symbolism-heavy play entitled *Waiting for Gödel.*) This requirement of divinity has produced problems from the beginning.

At first Flexner thought to restrict the faculty to mathematicians. Mathematics, "the severest of disciplines," he called it, enjoys a great advantage when one demands only the best: mathematicians can unanimously agree on the identity of their leading peers. Just as the results in math are objectively certain, so too are judgments of the significance of the results, the degree of their importance, beauty and depth; and so too, therefore, are the evaluations of just how good the mathematicians themselves are. Arguments over the ordering do not exist, as they so destructively do in other fields. Mathematicians are also quite inexpensive to maintain, Flexner observed, requiring only "a few men, a few rooms, books, blackboards, chalk, paper, and pencils."

But Flexner and his successors eventually decided to expand and diversify the Olympian population. Flexner wanted some humanists, economists, and political theorists; Oppenheimer wanted more physicists. But the existing population, the mathematicians, fought the attempts of the would-be émigrés. They fought not out of the selfish desire to keep it all for themselves (these are *pure* mathematicians, remember) but rather out of their understanding of the nature of their Institute and the requirements it entailed. Were these others indeed gods? Where was the certainty: in the results they produced or the evaluations of them? The people in these other fields couldn't even agree among themselves. Why should they be taken seriously?

The Institute finally succeeded in establishing, in addition to the School of Mathematics, a School of Natural Sciences, composed primarily of physicists with interests sufficiently theoretical to require no labs, and a mongrel School of History (which even includes some historians of philosophy). But bitter controversy broke out anew when the current director, Carl Kaysen, an economist who had, from the point of view of the mathematicians, dubious credentials to begin with, decided to establish a School of Social Sciences. He had gotten his first appointment, a sociologist with credentials about as unchallengeable as a social scientist can hope to attain, past the puritanical mathematicians; but they balked at his second appointment, another sociologist, who, like the first, worked on the sociology of religion. The fight got ugly (although not personal, you understand), spilling over into the pages of the New York *Times* and even into an article in *The Atlantic Monthly* entitled "Shoot-Out on Mt. Olympus." Said one particularly pure mathematician: "Many of us started reading the worthless works of the candidate. I've seen poor candidates before, but I've never had the feeling of so utterly wasting my time." Soon the mathematicians were boycotting the cafeteria, which had been a pet project of Kaysen's. They were joined by some historians (whose motives I rather suspect—were they trying to appropriate some of the appearance of certainty from their allies?). The physicists for the most part sided with Kaysen, arguing that the standards for each discipline are intrinsically different, that the certainty of pure mathematics can't be expected anywhere else.

I tell you all this to give you an idea of how things look from within this region of the map, the sort of issue that intensely matters. A similar antagonism exists within my own field, between the so-called analytic or linguistic philosophers, who aim, at any price, to purify philosophy of all vagueness and uncertainty, and those who will tolerate (and even revel in) obscurity, accepting the uncertainty that comes with grappling with the foamy stuff. (Kant: "For long before men began to inquire into nature methodically, they consulted abstract reason . . . So metaphysics floated to the surface, like foam, which dissolved the moment it was scooped off. But immediately there appeared a new supply on the surface, to be ever eagerly gathered up by some; while others, instead of seeking in the depths the cause of the phenomenon, thought they showed their wisdom by ridiculing the idle labor of their neighbors.")

My husband, by the way, as purest of the pure, was in complete agreement with the mathematicians at the Institute. In fact, he a priori dismisses the work of sociologists, "pseudo-scientists all."

Ava came for dinner the night after moving in. It was the first time she and Noam were to meet, and I was very nervous. They both have such strong personalities, and I was afraid they might explode on contact. And, as I've mentioned before, Noam holds an uncharitable view of physicists as a group.

My worst fears were realized as dinner progressed. Ava had been speaking of Einstein's years at the Institute (which became popularly known as the Einstein Institute), the last twenty-five years of his life.

"It was tragic. His life as a physicist was essentially over. He didn't produce anything worthwhile, just kept toiling away at that unified field theory, a supreme exercise in futility. He was completely alienated from the mainstream of physics because of his refusal to accept quantum mechanics, even though the theory was the consequence of his own earlier work. He just refused to accept that reality didn't conform to his own philosophical presuppositions, that the most basic laws of matter are fundamentally statistical. He couldn't buy the indeterminacy of nature: 'God doesn't play dice with the world.' "

Ava shook her head. "Even the strongest minds have their weaknesses, and in the end he was destroyed by his."

"Einstein was absolutely right," Noam said.

"What?" Ava almost choked on her wine.

"Quantum theory is absurd. It produces paradoxes."

"It works. It gives us predictions that are confirmed."

"Hah." Noam turned to me and said contemptuously, "You see what I mean about physicists? That's a typical physicist's response. It works. They don't give a damn about reality. They're a bunch of tinkering engineers for the most part. Einstein was different, of course, and for that he's criticized."

"The fact that a theory works is pretty good evidence for its being true," Ava said. "That's the test in science."

"A theory with illogical consequences is not true, can't be true. If anything counts against a theory, it's that."

"What makes logic so absolute? Physical facts come first. Logic has to conform to them."

That remark raised the temperature of the atmosphere way beyond Noam's kindling point. He exploded.

"I'll tell you the consequences of quantum mechanics. Physicists' minds have been destroyed by it. They work with an illogical theory and they forget how to think." He turned away at last and addressed Ava. "You people don't know how to think anymore. Throw out logic, will you? How the hell are you fools going to deduce the physical facts, how are you going to deduce *anything*, without logic?"

Ava smiled calmly. "Look, it's just like with Euclidean geometry." "Everybody took it for granted that it was necessarily true until they discovered other geometries. Then they found that not only isn't Euclidean geometry necessarily true, it isn't even empirically true. It isn't the geometry of our space. It's the same thing with logic. We have to discover which is the empirical logic."

"Oh, you're going to lecture me on geometry. You physicists don't understand physics anymore. Don't presume to explain mathematics to a mathematician."

The nastiness of Noam's tone blew me over to Ava's side. Throughout the evening I silently sided with first one and then the other, depending on who I thought was being given the harder time.

"The analogy between logic and geometry is completely far-fetched," Noam said. "There aren't any alternative logics to choose from. What you get in so-called deviant logics are distortions of language. The logical laws aren't changed."

"I think the analogy with geometry isn't at all far-fetched. The lesson there was perfectly general. What determines truth is the brute facts of the physical world. The world is the way it is and it's all we've got. And if we want to know what it's like, we've got to *look* at it. There aren't any a priori necessarily true facts."

"Well, that's very interesting news to me, because I spend my whole life a priori discovering necessary truths."

"Uh huh. You only think they're necessary. Just like everybody used to think about geometry. The appearance of necessity isn't reliable. It ain't necessarily so. Nothing is."

"I'm afraid you don't understand the first thing about it."

"So explain it to me. Where do these necessary truths come from? I understand where physical truths come from, from physical reality. But where the hell do your necessary truths come from? Plato's heaven? *In den schönen Regionen, wo die reinen Formen wohnen?*"

Where had she picked up that one? She laughed snidely, and I swung back to Noam's side.

"You're thinking of it all wrong," Noam answered. "Logic doesn't derive from the way the world is. It determines the way the world has to be."

"And what determines logic?" Ava asked.

"That's a stupid question." Noam's tone was matter-of-fact and calm, but I cringed at the words. "Nothing, of course. Or logic itself."

"So logic is the Absolute, the Unmoved Mover, the First Cause."

"If you like."

"I don't understand such mysticism."

Noam laughed. "Well, if I'm a mystic, you're a farmer."

"A farmer?" Ava wrinkled her brow in perplexity and then grinned. "Oh, I see. You mean I get my hands dirty in the grubby real world."

"In the grubby *physical* world," Noam rejoined. "Which by no means exhausts reality."

With this remark they were off again, Noam accusing Ava of absurdity, Ava accusing Noam of obscurity.

"You Platonists all suffer from Plato's weakness. As soon as you get to the heart of the matter, you lapse into metaphor. Can't you say anything clearly? It's misticism, spelled with an *i.* "

"I prefer a vague but vaguely true view to one that is clear and clearly false."

Ava left at two in the morning.

"Nice girl," Noam said. "Terrible views, but then what can you expect? I like her, though."

And Ava called the next morning to tell me how much she had enjoyed the evening and how much she liked Noam: "He's great. The real goods. A genuine article. I can't tell you how relieved I am."

So was I. It's always the same when they're together. It took me a while to get used to it. The first few times when Noam called some statement of Ava's idiotic, her view nonsense, I suffered on my friend's behalf. Until I noticed that the insults didn't bother her in the least. Both of them have the same impersonal attitude toward ideas, whether their own or others'. It's the validity that matters, not the person incidentally attached. When I tried to apologize once to Ava, after an evening when I thought Noam had been particularly abusive, she laughed.

"It's not a personal insult, Renee. Don't you understand that? It's the view he's calling stupid, not me. And, you know, this time he was right. Sometimes I argue things with a force greater than I believe them with. You know, just to try them out, see how far you can push them. I think Noam understands that. Anyway, you don't have to worry about *my* feelings, sweetie. The only thing I feel toward Noam is grateful that he takes me seriously enough to call me dumb."

I felt, for the billionth time, overwhelmed with admiration for Ava. This was the kind of woman Noam ought to have married. *I* could never shrug it off when Noam called something I said stupid. Blind terror seized me. I had, from the beginning, feared that he'd penetrate to my essential confusion, that he'd make the simple deduction from stupid statements to stupid thinking, and from thinking stupid to being stupid. In short, to my secret: My intelligence, like my beauty, has always been overpraised, misperceived. The conjunction favors both conjuncts. I am beautiful for a brainy woman, brainy for a beautiful woman, but objectively speaking, neither beautiful nor brainy. My very presentation is an illusion, a deception practiced on others even with no help from me. The phenomenal self appears phenomenal, but the uneasy noumenal self knows. Beneath the external swagger, the phenomenological reality is fear.

Why did it matter so much, you wonder, whether I was brilliant or not? You have to remember where I stand, and how things look from in here. (Most of us manage to situate ourselves in that region of the mattering map where one's own self comes out mattering. Sick is the soul that can't quite manage to bring this off.) Here intelligence is the issue that draws the boundaries, provides the distinctions that make the difference: who are the somebodies and who the nobodies; who the cherished and who the despised; who the heroes and who the misfits.

These words of mine recall for me the dirgelike chant repeated throughout the Jewish period of repentance that falls in the autumn, beginning with Rosh Hashanah, the Jewish New Year, proceeding through the Ten Days of Repentance, and closing with Yom Kippur, the Day of Atonement, the holiest day of the Jewish year:

"On Rosh Hashanah their destiny is inscribed, and on Yom Kippur it is sealed, how many shall pass away and how many shall be brought into existence; who shall live and who shall die; who shall come to a timely end, and who to an untimely end; who shall perish by fire and who by water; who by sword and who by beast; who by hunger and who by thirst; who by earthquake and who by plague; who by strangling and who by stoning; who shall be at ease and who shall wander about; who shall have comfort and who shall be tormented; who shall become poor and who shall become rich; who shall be lowered and who shall be raised."

This first part is sung by the cantor. But at this point the whole congregation breaks out into a great rousing shout:

"But repentance, prayer, and charity cancel the stern decree!"

I would like to find some new words to end my own dirgelike chant: a great rousing shout that could inspire the same hope the other once did. For failing that, there is no salvation from the agony of suspecting I can't measure up.

And how long could Noam be hoodwinked? My reticence with him was the product of fear. Each statement potentially exposed me. Just let his infatuation wear off a bit more (it was already showing thin), he'd see me for what I am, or what I feared I might be, awaiting final confirmation from others. I'd managed to fool some, but they were ipso facto fools, just as those who judged me harshly were wise. I had captured the prize: the love of the genius. The trick was to keep it.

Ava has no fears like these. She's terrifically smart, knows it, and hardly gives the fact a thought. It's taken for granted, like the color of her eyes. She has confidence in her views, but I've never seen anyone give them up less painfully on good evidence. (Noam, for example, has persuaded her to change her mind about logic. They had been arguing the issue for months, Ava giving no indication of moving. And then, after one of Noam's little speeches attacking her view, she said: "You know, you're right.")

Unlike most people, Ava's behavior when with Noam isn't unlike her behavior at any other time. My friend Sarah Slater, on the other hand, with whom I became so thick my first year at Princeton, undergoes a radical decomposition when exposed to my husband. The first time he turned his high beam on one of her statements, she squirmed like some pitiful little creature pinned down on a biologist's slide. After that she hardly ever spoke in his presence. Even when he was somewhere in the house, I noticed, her already soft voice would fade still more. It was painful for me to watch that great expanse of intelligence and humor shrink inward to a vanishing point in fear of my husband. I asked Noam a few times if he couldn't try to be particularly friendly and encouraging to her, to try to coax her out of her shell.

"I think I'm friendly to her. I don't know what you mean."

"If she says something, don't pounce."

"I don't think I've ever pounced on her. I don't remember her ever saying anything for me to pounce on. I don't remember her ever saying anything at all."

"That's because she's afraid of you. It's such a shame that you can't see what she's really like, what a great person she is. She just shrivels up when you're around."

"Afraid of me? Well, I certainly haven't done anything to cause her fear. You can't blame me for her irrationality."

"Maybe it is irrational, and I'm not blaming you. I just wish we could do something about it."

"What do you want me to do? Agree with everything she says, should she ever say anything?" (This, you understand, was not a genuine suggestion. To feign agreement with a view not his own would be a violation of his deepest ethical instincts. He was trying to point out the absurdity of my request.)

"It's that way you have of dissecting every comment. Couldn't you be a little less critical with her?"

"Look, Renee, you can't ask me to stop being me. If one of your friends doesn't like me, okay, she doesn't like me."

Sarah had undergone a happy change of status. The previous spring she had come on the job market and had had spectacular success, made all the more impressive considering the current glut of Ph.D.s. In the great boom of the late fifties and early sixties, graduate departments, particularly at state universities, had expanded and conferred degrees in great abundance. But then the funds, from both government and private foundations, had dried up, and departments had shrunk, resulting in diminished need. Suddenly there was a large superfluity of Ph.D.s, compounded by demographic changes. And, of course, the uncooperative tenured faculty has refused to retire or expire at the necessary rate. The result has been a severe depression, in both the economic and psychological senses, in the academic community.

A field like philosophy, considered an impractical and therefore dispensable luxury, is especially hard hit. Some colleges have even eliminated the department altogether, or (sub)merged it into linguistics or comparative literature. At the annual meetings of the American Philosophical Association, the hunting ground for philosophical employment, there have been in recent years about eighty applicants for every one of the jobs coming up. Many of those on the breadlines are there for the second or third time, having come to the terminus of their non-tenure track job, or having been turned down for tenure.

As difficult as it has become to get those first jobs, it's become even more challenging to hold on to them. It's much more practical for a university to refuse tenure, and the salary increase that goes with it, and instead hire a freshly minted Ph.D.

What adds to the bitterness is that so few of the judging older faculty could themselves pass the standards they impose on their juniors. The majority of them were tenured in the good old days, when tenure was more or less automatic, when the whole tenure system was meant to protect faculty from unfair dismissal on political or other grounds. But the economics of university life have changed and tenure has become the exception on most campuses. One state university has been automatically turning down all young faculty who haven't managed to publish a book in their first six years of teaching. Recently they turned down a candidate who had written a book, and a well-received one. Unfortunately, judged they, he had written the book only to get tenure.

It's depressing but also impressive to consider these very bright people struggling after these insecure positions with salaries less than the average blue-collar worker's (the result of the laws of supply and demand and the absence of strong unions), when any one of them could, for example, take a short course in real estate and soon be driving around in a pale yellow Coupe de Ville, should he or she so desire. But then again, should one be impressed? It's not as if they're selfless. They're all reaching for prizes, too, even if not the cruder sort that one can ride around in or display in one's home. They, too, are motivated by the will to matter, which expresses itself in conformity to *their* mattering zone. So why should one be impressed, objectively speaking? Only if this is the zone that truly matters—not just mine, but God's very own.

My friend Sarah had sailed through the academic slump, getting interviews wherever she applied (the interview alone is, when so many are applying, a juicy plum) and receiving in the end five job offers, one from Princeton itself. But nothing could ever make her feel good about herself. There's always some way to interpret the evidence so that it doesn't reflect well on her.

"It's just because I'm a woman. Departments all need their token woman."

"That's ridiculous. There were plenty of other women hunting there. No one did as well as you. And beside, most departments already have their token woman."

"Well, I was the only woman this year from Princeton. And there was only one woman from Harvard. She, by the way, did very well, too. And that's not true about most departments already having their woman. Three of the five that offered me jobs don't have any." Whatever else one might think of affirmative action, its effect on people like Sarah has not been healthy.

Sarah is wonderful so long as she's looking outside herself, but she's dark and brooding Salem when she turns her gaze inward. Instead of rejoicing over her triumphs, she spent the next weeks agonizing over her decision. The thought of joining Princeton's faculty terrified her, but so did the thought of moving to a new and unknown academic setting. In the end inertia, as she put it, won out, and she accepted Princeton's offer. I, of course, was overjoyed. I had tried to be unbiased, but somehow had always managed to be very impressed with the virtues of Princeton when discussing the choices with her.

It was probably the wrong decision, and I've always regretted my part in it. It's difficult enough to come to regard one's former professors as colleagues, but in Sarah's case her shaky ego made it almost impossible to jump the Great Divide. I didn't get to see her all that much once the decision was made, especially after the semester got under way. She was constantly working, feverishly trying to build up a dam against the great sea of her self-perceived inadequacy. Her soft voice acquired a new quiver. She found her graduate seminar particularly terrifying.

"It was kind of fun to catch up the professor when I was a student, but the awfulness of being on the other side! I can't think with all those gun-happy sharpshooters aiming straight at my head, just waiting for a false move."

It was a night in late October, and I was visiting Sarah in the little monk's cell of an apartment, in the attic of a private house a few blocks from campus, that she had moved into when a student. The stairs leading to it were outside, in back of the house, and became treacherous when they iced over in winter. But this separate mode of access gave a fitting sense of isolation to the little set of rooms floating above. One never felt they were attached to a substantial house below. They were a world unto themselves, stark and pure. One walked into a smallish room, meant to be a living room, where Sarah had placed a mattress on the floor where she slept the four hours a night she allotted herself. A long, right-angled hallway led to a small but windowed kitchen on the left and the larger, lighter room where Sarah lived on the right. Here the furniture was a large desk she had built into the wall under the attic-slant of the ceiling, and orange-crate bookcases neatly crammed with books and papers. The desk functioned as a table, when one was required, and was large enough so that a place could always be found for one's plate without disturbing the work. There was a wooden folding chair before the desk, and Sarah could produce three more, if necessary, from a closet. I was sitting on one now across the desk from her.

Watching her as she talked to me of her trials, I thought again how surprising it was that this Puritan's face should belong to a dear friend, should be a face to which I could tell everything. She passed from relating the miseries of her teaching to the agonies of her research. One after another of her interpretations of Locke's notion of substance had collapsed. Her voice was flat with despair. How wrong we all are about her, I thought while I listened. Everyone thinks of her as without passion and blood. But it's all there, all tied up with her work. Or is it? For the hundredth time, at least, I found myself wondering about the inner Sarah, curious about whether all her passion is intellectual. I felt free to tell but not ask her anything. There is a fragility in her that I'm in fear of shattering.

But though Sarah's inner life was, and probably will remain forever, a mystery to all but Sarah, surely the facts of her outer existence were settled. When I thought of my own life in ten years, I really didn't know what to picture. Would I be in academia or out in the real world? A mother? I wasn't even absolutely confident I'd be married. But with Sarah the picture was all completed, the outlines all filled in. Did Sarah see it that way?

"Can you picture yourself in ten years?" I broke into Sarah's narrative suddenly. "I'm sorry for interrupting, but I was wondering if you think you'll be then exactly as you are now."

Sarah thought for a few seconds and then smiled. "Realistically,

I suppose I'll be then exactly as I am now. But very deep down, below the realistic level, I think in Cinderella terms."

"Cinderella terms?"

"You know, Cinderella, wicked step-relatives, fairy godmother, Prince Charming. Deep down I believe—no, it's too deep down to be called belief. It's just reflexive. Deep down I reflex that because I'm such a good, hard-working girl, someday, on the night of the ball, the great transformation will take place."

I tried to recall the details of the Cinderella story: the abused, overworked girl living among cruel step-relatives; the invitation from the castle to the great ball, given by the King and Queen (was it for the express purpose of finding the most beautiful girl in the kingdom for their son? I couldn't remember); the ugly stepsisters primping themselves, ordering poor, unwashed, sooty Cinderella around. And then, after their departure, appears the Fairy Godmother, that incarnation of all our desperate childhood hopes about our parents, who some of us continue to seek in friends and lovers and others throughout our lives. And the perfect mother has perfect power, possessed of a magic wand and the precisely right words. A pumpkin is transformed into a golden carriage, white mice into white horses, lizards into liveried footmen, and Cinderella's sad rags into the most beautiful dress ever seen. On her small (that's important) feet gleam little glass (glass?) slippers. "Be back by midnight," F.G. warns. Did she herself impose this condition or was it dictated from without? In any case, Cinderella departs for the castle and the glory that awaits her there. Everybody stares as she walks in. Even the musicians stop playing a moment to gape at the vision. Who is she, they all wonder, including the step-relatives, who have never seen the beauty beneath the cinders. And then she's whirling around the room in the arms of the smitten Prince, until her fast exit at midnight, the Prince in hot pursuit.

My recollection of the story was accompanied—dimly, at the back of my mind—by the kind of sarcastic annotations so easy to append to such a tale. The story contained all the elements of the feminine mystique, culminating in the final outrage: the girl's passive salvation by means of the handsome male, thanks to her beauty (and small feet). Was any tale more explicit?

And of course I believed in it, too, and, more importantly, believed I was living it. *I* had been forlorn among cruel insensitive step-relatives (the Princeton philosophers), abused and unappreciated; *I* had been saved by the unconquerable superhuman hero, chosen from all the others and swept away. The wonder was that Sarah believed in it. Had none of us escaped?

"It's a lovely story." I smiled across the desk at my friend, who was smiling back at me, the intelligence lighting up the planes and angles of her face.

"The loveliest," she answered.

I discovered that my own status at the Princeton philosophy department had changed as well as Sarah's. When I ran into Professor Pfiffel, my adviser, he greeted me quite cordially.

"Ah, Mrs. Himmel. I was delighted to hear of your marriage. My deepest congratulations."

His great yellow-white mane nodded in satisfaction at the happy conclusion of the case of the advisee with the unfortunate metaphysical bent. He obviously assumed, from the way he went on and spoke, that I had withdrawn from the department. This was the first time he showed any pleasure with me, and I didn't have the heart to tell him I hadn't sensibly withdrawn my sadly unanalytic person but had merely given it a leave of absence. I had told the department chairman, who also addressed me respectfully as Mrs. Himmel, that I wanted to take the year off to work on the problem on which I planned eventually to write my dissertation, the mind-body problem.

I never had told Noam that I was only making a poor joke out there in front of Lahiere's. And I suppose it wasn't only a joke. I've always been obsessed with the mind-body problem. During those periods when I think of myself as a philosopher and those periods when I don't, I never can get away from that problem that Schopenhauer called, quite wonderfully, the *Weltknoten*, the world-knot. That's exactly what it is, bringing together in one inextricable clump strands that weave in and out of the entire fabric of reality, entangling each of us (certainly me).

And I'm in good company here. The mind-body problem was the obsession of most philosophers before this century's crop discovered that it is, like all metaphysical questions, either meaningless or trivial. But I'll never be convinced of that. It's the essential problem of metaphysics, about both the world out there and the world in here. In fact, the dichotomy between the two worlds—the outer public place of bodies and the inner private one of minds—is exactly what it's all about. Are both these realms real, and if so how do they fit together? Can one of them be absorbed into the other? The answer a philosopher gives determines the entire shape of his metaphysics. Idealists reduce in the direction of mind, materialists in the direction of body, and dualists heroically assert the separate and equal reality of both. One after another of the great philosophical systems have attempted to untie the world-knot, pulling out some threads but leaving others impossibly entangled. What is the world? What am I? This is the mind-body problem.

There is reality, or the world, consisting of all the things that are. Scientists are in the business of describing reality, as metaphysicians hope to be. Common sense, too, has its ontological commitments.

To describe reality one must say what things exist and what they are like. What is the common-sense view (one has to begin somewhere, and where else but with common sense)? Certainly that material bodies exist, their most important feature being their objective existence: they exist "out there," independent of our observation of them. This typewriter doesn't pop in and out of existence as I look at and away from it. (If it does, it's not a material body.) It and its properties persist. And it and its properties are public. All of us can, in principle, know about the typewriter, both through observation (as we know its shape) and through science (as we know it is composed of atoms).

But in speaking of observation and knowledge we commit ourselves to beings who observe and know, to things with experiences, to conscious entities. And their inclusion is also a central part of the common-sense ontology. In fact, that there exists at the moment at least one such thing, namely, myself, seems an ontological truth impossible to deny (unlike all others). I can never falsely believe that I exist. The condition of this fact's being believed at all is sufficient to ensure its truth, as Descartes observed in his Second Meditation. (In his *Discourse on Method* he put the insight more crudely: "I think, therefore I am"—a phrase as catchy as it has been misunder-stood.)

But the unavoidable inclusion of this category of thing, the con-scious, in our ontological tally means we can no longer confine our-selves, in describing reality, to the facts "out there." Now there are also facts about the "in-here" of each of these conscious things, facts about what reality is like, at each moment of their conscious life, *for* them. To describe reality we must describe the things that exist, and a description of conscious entities includes a description of their inner worlds. And the interior decorating of a human being, even when it includes a consciousness of the world out there, will be lush with particulars not to be found out there, some of them determined by such givens of the moment as her sensations, moods, and memories, others by less transient features (such as where she stands on the mattering map).

In fact, if we believe the story science tells about what's out there, if we believe that what's out there is bundles of mathematically describable particles behaving mathematically in mathematical, rela-tivistic space-time, then very few particulars of the in-here are to be found out there. The out-there appears more and more remote, as the in-here gains in prominence.

The ways the world appears to those things for which there are appearances are facts about the appeared-to's. And since a descrip-tion of reality must include a description of all things that are, these facts too must be included. In this way the description grows by many orders of magnitude. Reality's complete description includes ac-counts of all the myriad inner worlds.

But more important than this quantitative increase is the qualita-tive uniqueness of these facts—the interiority, the privacy of them. And the question is: Can such facts as these be about material bodies? Material bodies exist in the objective and public out-there. Are they capable of inner lives? Does a rich and vastly complicated interiority, an *être intime*, gape open in the essential guts of some of them? For Godssakes, am *I*, who carries an entire world within me, a *body*?

I here give you the problem in its pure form. Unlike so many others dredged up out of the deeps in the course of the history of philosophy, this one is, I think, capable of engaging us all, *once* it is understood. For it concerns not only the nature of the world, but also the nature of that object which matters to each of us as no other does: one's self. What *is* it? And if this question seems still too abstract to engage, consider another, its logical bedfellow: Can you survive the death of your body? Not *will* you, but is survival even within the realm of metaphysical possibility? Not if you *are* your body. And if you are not, then what follows? Not the fact of survival. For it may be that even if you are not your body, you are so causally dependent on it—each one of your states preceded, because caused, by a bodily one—that you couldn't exist without it. If this were the case, we would find one-to-one correlations between the mental and the physical. Those who think too hastily and therefore miss seeing this (and every) philosophical problem, might think such linkages between the mental and physical dissolve the mind-body problem by showing that the mind is nothing but the body. But of course nothing of the sort is shown. For such correlations are perfectly compatible with—in fact, entailed by—the dualism between mind and body as Descartes presented it.

Descartes first posed the question: What am I? And he answered that he is most certainly not a body, but rather a separate entity, a mind, the subject of his consciousness. What makes Descartes Descartes, he argued, is the qualities of his consciousness; and what makes his body that particular body is the qualities of its extension. Two distinct sets of qualities, determining two distinct entities, although, quite obviously, intimately connected:

"I am not lodged in my body merely as a pilot in a ship, but so intimately conjoined, and as it were intermingled with it, that with it I form a unitary whole. Were not this the case, I should not sense pain when my body is hurt, being, as I should be then, merely a thinking thing; but should apprehend the wound in a purely cognitive manner, just as a sailor apprehends by sight any damage to his ship."

Descartes happened to have made things needlessly difficult for himself (and consequently too easy for the hasty to dismiss him) by ascribing two quite incompatible properties to the mind that he was: it's not located in space, and yet it interacts, in the region of the pineal gland, no less, with the spatially located body. By "located in space" he means situated in the out-there occupied by bodies. But if bodies are out there, while minds are not, how do they manage to interact, especially in the region of the pineal gland? But then why say that conscious subjects are not out there? Their experiences are not, their teeming inner worlds are not. But can't the subjects whose inner worlds these are be located in the same out-there as material bodies? Clearly, I am. I am right here, within four walls, in front of a typewriter, to the left of the window. In fact, I am precisely where my body is. Sufficient to show that I *am* my body, you point out, since two distinct things can't occupy the same space at the same time. Insufficient, the Cartesian retorts. Two *material bodies* can't occupy the same space at the same time.

Descartes presented the problem; not all philosophers have agreed he gave us the answer. His very own rationalist children, Spinoza and Leibniz, set about trying to mend the Cartesian rupture of reality into the two halves of objectivity and subjectivity. Spinoza absorbed all the world into the objectivity of that substance which can be viewed alternatively as God or nature *(Deus sive Natura)*. Both minds and bodies get sucked in and dissolved in the reality of the one objectively existing substance. Leibniz went in the other direction. Descartes, he said, leads us "into the vestibule of philosophy," and Spinoza "would have been right were it not for the monads." Spinoza's philosophy asks us to deny the reality of that inner world which is for each of us the world we know best, and to negate the existence of that subject of experience which each of us knows he is. Subjectivity is not to be denied. Much easier to deny objectivity, which is what Leibniz did. Reality consists exclusively of monads, an infinity of them, each of which is something like a mind, though not all achieve the full self-consciousness and distinct perceptions of those monads which we are. But all monads are like us in having successive points of view of the world. The world, in consisting of monads, consists of nothing but an infinity of inner worlds. There isn't exactly perception as we normally think of it, since, for reasons too complicated to get into here, the monad's points of view are determined from within, each representation following from the preceding according to the internal laws of the monad. The monad doesn't interact with anything outside itself; the appearance of interaction is but appearance. Monads are, says Leibniz in one of the more whimsical statements of seventeenth-century rationalism, "without windows." Whimsical, but terrifying too. At least, I've been terrified on those occasions when I've suspected that we may indeed fit Leibniz's description: that interaction between us is only apparent, that we are each of us a closed world, without windows.

Spinoza's approach to the problem is so unique that one can only tautologically categorize it as "Spinozistic." Almost all other philosophers can be accommodated by the following categories: the materialists, who assert that everything that exists is a body; the idealists, who claim that nothing that exists is a body, but is rather mind or something like it; and the dualists, who, like Descartes, say that some things are bodies and some things are not.

But there are categories within the categories. Take materialists. Some have inferred from the identity of people with their bodies the fundamental mystery of matter. "I know very much less than you do about matter," wrote Bertrand Russell. "All that I know about matter is what I can infer by means of certain abstract postulates about the purely logical attributes of its space-time distribution. Prima facie, these tell me nothing whatever about its other characteristics." The public view of bodies we get through observation and science can never penetrate into the interiority of which some of them are capable, we know, because we know the interiority of which we are capable. And then there are materialists who make no such inference, who believe there are no secrets from the public view. Any facts there are to be known about those bodies which are people can, at least in principle, be known through observation and science.

The hatred of mystery and worship of science characteristic of Anglo-American philosophers of this century has dictated that this last is the position almost all of them take. And, of course, they arrive at it through linguistic analysis. The world-knot, they maintain, can be unraveled by studying how certain phrases function in the language. Logical behaviorism is a favored answer: all states of the inner world are simply defined to be states of, or dispositions to, behavior. Abracadabra. With this trick one not only dispels the mystery of the mind-body problem; one gets rid of the annoying inaccessibility of the inner Other. One need never wonder. That moaning and thrashing about, for example, just *is* the orgasm.

My pre-Noam intuitions had put me with the materialists who assert the mystery of bodies. The view I grabbed for that day in front of Lahiere's had been ready at hand because I really did believe that it's body, not mind, which is the great unknown. Noam, of course, is a confirmed antimaterialist. Clearly if a person survives his body's death and decay, if he migrates from body to body, he's not identical with his corporeal lodgings. Idealism doesn't seem an unlikely hypothesis: "It wouldn't surprise me greatly to discover that there really are no bodies." But he finds dualism the more natural view.

In addition to his supernatural evidence, Noam believes that the nonidentity of a person with his body can be argued for on purely a priori grounds. In fact, he claims to have a deductive proof. We had rather a lot of discussions of this proof, its logical structure progressively simplifying so that it finally emerged quite spare and elegant. The overall strategy is to show that the assumption of the identity of a person with his body is conceptually absurd, that it leads to a logical contradiction. I here present a reconstruction.

HIMMEL'S PROOF FOR THE NONIDENTITY OF A PERSON WITH HIS BODY

1. If a person is identical with his body, he would not survive his death.
2. If a person is identical with his body, he would survive his death.
3. So if a person is identical with his body, he both would and would not survive his death.
   Since any proposition that entails a contradiction can't be true, we can deduce from 3 that:
4. A person is not identical with his body.

This proof is logically valid; that is, the premises, *if* true, entail the conclusion. But are the premises true? The first seems rather obvious, but hardly the second (although perhaps it's trivial). So here's another proof that has as *its* conclusion the disputed second premise of the first proof:

First some informal remarks on the strategy used here, which is known technically as a *reductio ad absurdum*. One denies the conclusion to be proved, in this case the second premise, and derives a contradiction. In this way one shows that the denial is false (leading as it does to contradiction), and therefore the conclusion is true.

The conclusion in this case is a conditional proposition, of the form: if xxx, then ——. One denies a conditional by asserting the xxx and denying the ——. So *ex hypothesi:*

A. A person is identical with his body.

B. A person doesn't survive his death.

Now we produce two more premises, seemingly quite innocent:

C. A person's body survives the person's death.

D. If a person is his body, then if his body exists, he exists.

From A, C, and D follows:

E. A person does survive his death.

But B and E contradict each other, showing that you can't assert A, B, C, and D. Since C and D are supposed to be obvious, the inference is that you can't assert A and B; that is, if A, then not B: If a person is identical with his body, then he does survive his death: and that is precisely the conclusion to be proved here, the second premise of the first argument.

I was suspicious of this second proof. One cannot challenge A and B, since they're simply assumed for the sake of the argument. D looks unassailable. Of course, if two things are identical, then if the one exists, so does the other. That leaves C.

"Listen, Noam, maybe a person's body doesn't survive his death."

"Then what are they burying?"

"Maybe it's a different body, not identical with the one that was alive. Maybe there are two different bodies, before and after."

"Do you really want to say that? It's a way of avoiding the conclusion, but think of it. It's crazy. You're going to have to say that at the moment of death the old body just vanishes and is instantaneously replaced with a brand-new one. Quite a trick. And all the physical properties of the brand-new one are going to be spatiotemporally continuous with the just vanished one, which is usually, in the case of other material bodies, sufficient for saying they're identical. Human bodies are going to turn out to be very weird things, quite spooky."

"Look who's talking about spooks."

But I saw his point and turned my critical gaze back to the main argument. If the second premise was okay, maybe the first wasn't as obvious as it seemed:

"What makes it so obvious that if a person is his body, then he doesn't survive his death? Maybe so long as you've got the body, even if it's a corpse, you've got the person."

"Because you don't. That corpse is not a person."

"Why not? Maybe it's just a very quiet one."

"Listen, Renee, I think this is really the heart of the matter. The individual identities of a person and his body, what makes that person that person and what makes that body that body, are just different. The identity of a person has to do with his memories perhaps, certainly his intellectual and emotional dispositions. If you've got a corpse, a thing without memories or conscious dispositions, you definitely don't have a person. But you do have a body, and clearly the same body that you had before. Obviously a lot of its properties have changed in changing from a living to a dead thing, but its identity hasn't changed. It's identically the same, though qualitatively much changed body. The identities of people and bodies just rest on different facts."

"I don't know, Noam, I can't help feeling there's something wrong here."

"Where? Look, you have the possibilities before you. If you're that desperate to escape dualism, then you could claim that corpses are very quiet people or that you've got a simultaneous annihilation of one body and re-creation of another at the moment of death. Now, do those alternatives seem more palatable than dualism?"

"But dualism seems crazy, too."

"Why? I think it's the intuitively natural view."

He would. "I don't even know how to conceive of this disembodied subject you've identified me with. What *is* it?"

"I should think you've had a rather intimate acquaintance with it.

159

When you say you can't conceive of it—that is, of yourself—you're probably conceiving of conceiving in the wrong way. You probably mean you can't picture it, the way you can material objects. If you try to conceive of immaterial subjects in the same way as material things, of course you're going to fail. I have no trouble at all conceiving of the incorporeal, since that's what math deals with. It's the realm I know best."

"There's got to be something wrong," I persisted.

"Why?"

"How can there be an a priori proof for something like dualism?"

"First of all, the proof isn't entirely a priori. It's not a priori that there do, in fact, exist people and their bodies. All that's a priori is that *if* they exist, they're not identical. Secondly, I happen to think that probably most facts about the world are in principle a priori. We're simply not smart enough to deduce them."

Oh.

Noam himself wasn't absolutely confident of his proof. He places much more faith in his supernatural evidence. With Noam proofs are usually an afterthought, even in math. He "sees" things first, then proves them. The brilliant success of his method in math has given him much confidence in its general reliability, even when he extends it beyond matters mathematical. Noam was very confident of his answer to the mind-body problem.

And I must say, I took his answer very seriously. In general I find it extremely difficult, in the presence of Noam's intellectual confidence and established brilliance, to dismiss anything he says. Ava, however, has no trouble rejecting Noam's views, and finds this one —especially resting as it does on his supernatural beliefs—eminently dismissible.

"He's completely nuts on the subject, totally *meshugge*. Just because he's a mathematical genius, that doesn't mean he's a genius in other things as well."

"Are you saying my husband is an idiot savant?" I smiled.

"No, of course not." Ava smiled back. "Of course he's brilliant. He couldn't have his mathematical gift if he weren't. But that doesn't mean his intuitions are always sound. Look at Newton, with his crackpot theology."

"So tell me what's wrong with Noam's argument."

"I don't know what's wrong. I haven't given it much thought and I don't intend to. There's something wrong. Look, it took centuries to find out what was wrong with all those so-called proofs of God's existence, that one that tries to show that God's existence follows from his definition as all-perfect. It took centuries to find out what the fallacy was there. You've got to trust common sense before a priori reason."

Trust common sense. But I don't think common sense has an answer to offer here. What's the common-sense answer to the mind-body problem?

6

MORE REALITY

Perhaps I am no one.
True, I have a body
and I cannot escape from it.
I would like to fly out of my head,
but that is out of the question.
It is written on the tablet of destiny
that I am stuck here in this human form.
That being the case
I would like to call attention to my problem.

—ANNE SEXTON,
"THE POET OF IGNORANCE"

My sister-in-law Tzippy gave birth in December to a six-pound, twelve-ounce boy. The baby was named Reuven, after my father. Reuven Feuer.

My mother's chief worry had been Caesarean section, or, as she put it, "the knife." Tzippy is very slight, "not built for childbearing," my mother repeated throughout the five months she knew of Tzippy's pregnancy. Tzippy had been reading about pregnancy, birth, breast-feeding, toilet training, sibling rivalry—the whole megillah—ever since she felt the first kick in the fifth month and began really to trust in this third pregnancy. She had become a firm believer in the Lamaze method of childbirth, but this required a partner and my brother Avram wanted no part of it. It was *weibeszachen,* woman's business. (Not surprisingly, the Yiddish term has a pejorative connotation.) Miriam Teitelbaum, whose husband also "learned" at Lakewood and who was herself still childless, came to the rescue. Miriam and Tzippy had gone through all the grades of *Bais Yaakov* together. (*Bais Yaakov* means "house of Jacob." There is an international chain of very Orthodox *Bais Yaakov* schools for girls. The high school that had so disastrous an effect on my future religiosity was one.) They went together to the Lamaze classes, and then finally to the birth. The closeness that developed between them shone from their faces at the *bris* of little Reuven. Tzippy's delivery had been a difficult one, seventeen hours in hard labor.

"I could never have done it without Miriam. I can't begin to tell you how she helped me. I was ready to give up. I told the doctor, all right already, put me out. But Miriam and he overruled me." Tzippy was radiant.

"I knew she was near the end by then, " Miriam radiated back. "She was in transition, and people always feel pessimistic then. They had warned us at class."

"Just think, if not for Miriam I would have missed seeing Reuven in those first moments of his new life. Oh, Renee, I still can't get over it. Every time I close my eyes I see it. As soon as he came out and the doctor lifted him up, he turned his head very quickly from side to side, three times: 'Nu, so what's this?' I'm going to see that my whole life."

"Tzippy didn't have any drugs at all. That's why Reuven was born so alert. When we brought him to the nursery, all the nurses commented on how alert he was. He was given a nine-point-nine Apgar out of ten. The nurse told me none of them gets a ten," Miriam bragged. "Already he's getting the best grades."

I regarded little Tzippy with awe. The years of worry over her infertility had lightly written over her sweet face. There was a certain pinched expression that hadn't been there before, and three vertical lines between the eyes. But hers was still very much the face of a child. And this child-woman had passed through the vastness of the experience of giving birth, and now looked back at me from across its great distance. For the first time I felt that she was the woman and I the girl.

Little Reuven regarded everything, including me, with immense dark eyes that spoke of infinite wisdom. He protested loudly at the indignities he was made to suffer at the hands of the *mohel*, but was quickly pacified by a Q-tip dunked in sweet red wine. I searched the little face closely for signs of similarity between the two Reuven Feuers, suddenly quite receptive to the superstition that lies perhaps behind the Jewish naming tradition. Let it be, I kept thinking, let this be my father returned.

Noam had come along with me to the *bris*, after some pleading on my part. He seemed very uncomfortable for the first fifteen minutes or so, standing among the *davening* men. But then he simply tuned out, became involved in his own thoughts, swaying slightly back and forth as he does when unable to pace. He looked like a natural, as I had known he would, the yarmulke perched on his head, *shuckling* in the midst of the *shuckling* men. Several people, I learned, assumed he was one of the *rebbayim* from the yeshiva, and when told he was my husband, those who knew the sad history of my profligacy rejoiced over my return to the fold. My mother was very pleased with this misinterpretation and didn't correct it. Noam remained tuned out.

Two of my mother's three sisters had made it to Lakewood from their homes in the Flatbush section of Brooklyn. The third, a xenophobic, agoraphobic hypochondriac, never travels past Ocean Avenue. They had all been born in Brooklyn. My mother was the only one whom cruel fate had tossed out of that yiddishe paradise into the Westchester wilderness, and from the way she spoke it might have been the Dakotas. She always complained bitterly that of all her sisters she, the most pious, had to live out her life in exile. The funny thing is, after my father died, leaving her free to move where she wanted, she had stayed put in the desert.

My mother was at her peak at the *bris, shepping naches*, presenting to the world at large, and the aunts in particular, her triumphs: her grandson and son-in-law. The expression on her face was pure bliss as she led the aunts over to be introduced to Noam, who greeted them all with his most absent stare and an occasional "hmmmm." To be able to maintain one's inner peace and psychic distance in the midst of that group requires true greatness of mind. They're all thin and under five feet tall, but they take up a lot of space.

Aunt Sophie is a bargain mavin whose life is devoted to the cause of getting shlock for less than half. Almost all her conversation revolves about this one issue, relating the ecstasies of bargaining merchants down below cost, the agonies when she suspects she could have gotten something for less. Hers is a fairly deep gray mattering zone. She feels genuine outrage for those who overpay. And yet I have a warm spot for her; she had been my unexpected ally in the war I waged to go to Barnard.

"How can you not let her accept that scholarship? Do you realize what a school like that costs? Don't you see what a bargain you're getting?" (Can I help it if I come from a family of Jewish-American stereotypes?)

My Aunt Myra was also at the *bris,* and she was really pouring it on for Noam. She's the prettiest of the sisters, managing to look, in her thinness, chic rather than scrawny. She's always smartly dressed, with her hair somewhere or other in the blond-red range. Right now her thin voice was trickling out, in Noam's honor, in her version of an educated accent. Knowing that Noam wasn't Orthodox, she even made some mildly mocking noises about the *bris:*

167

"What did you think of our little religious ritual?" Little laugh, type consistent with accent.

"Hmmmm," Noam answered, his eyes darting about in that way that told me he hadn't heard a word.

"A little barbaric, perhaps"—tiny laugh—"but it's supposed to be hygienic. Even the gentiles do it now." Smile, faded-blue questioning stare.

"Hmmmmm."

The aunts Sophie and Myra exchanged glances.

Aunt Myra apologized to my mother for her daughter Felicia's absence. There was a very important sale at Bloomingdale's today, and even though Felicia "really argued with me, put up such a fight to come to the *bris*, I knew she had been waiting so long for this sale, I just couldn't let her miss it."

My aunt then turned to me and began, in sweet charity, to fill me in on every detail of Felicia's recent goings-on. My infelicitously named cousin is Myra's only child, and as a kid I had spent a good amount of time fantasizing that I was she. (That was before I learned to tame my fantasizing to the possible.) I had never seen a mother so in love with a daughter. (My mother, too, was in love, but with my brother.) Myra's husband, Harry, had a rather limited role to play. He had been required, of course, to make Felicia's existence a reality. After that I'm sure his services in *that* department were never again called upon. The meaning of the remainder of his life has lain in his fur business, which has kept his daughter in the best of everything money can buy. I still remember Felicia's canopy bed, all creamy eyelet embroidery floating on the thick apricot rug in that apricot room. Is this where my passion for the color stems from—from the green envy of those days? How I used to imagine myself in that bed. (You see that my fantasies have involved a bed from the earliest.) We always used to play the princess and her slave when I came over. Very occasionally, she'd let me be the princess.

My cousin is exactly my age, or actually ten days younger, so naturally we've been compared since infancy. (She walked before me, but I was toilet-trained first.) The sole comfort my mother took from my going to Barnard was Barnard's having rejected Felicia. I had always been the better student. One might expect this superiority to have given me the lead in the race with my cousin. Forget it. There's no way I could ever win. She, you see, is described by her mother, whose faith has never wavered, while I am represented by mine, whose attitude is at best lukewarm.

I see I can't probe the old wound, no matter how gently, without the pain bursting forth in full dazzling vigor. In a moment I shall start sobbing that my mother has never loved me, that she cared only for my brother. What a bore; so banal a solution to the mystery of my personality. And yet there it is. I've done what I can. I've transformed the woman into a parody (perhaps you've noticed) in the attempt to dilute some of her awesome strength. But though that's the picture I present to you, it's not the view I naturally occupy. I can maintain it only with great effort before the pull of subjectivity becomes too strong. In the end it is a feeble attempt, as are they all, the pathetically elaborate battlements we construct against the power absolute: the power of the parent. The effects keep on long after the exertion itself has ceased. For they're woven into the very fabric of one's soul. They are one's self. *Can nothing be done?* Must the self that one is, this poor "I" that I am and that I feel myself to be, remain permanently disfigured—encrusted with the oozing scabs of ancient bruises even as the Others are admiring the self-applied surgical dressing? Must the old pain influence every action, as a dull ache shapes a limp?

As a child I was full of schemes for winning her love. Of course my father loved me, but not in the partial way I craved. He loved everybody. He didn't favor me over Avram, as my mother favored Avram over me. He didn't love me *exclusively.* (Thus is a father-fixation forged.) For some reason (perhaps because I'm Jewish) I hooked onto the idea that I had to be smarter. I had always brought home straight A's, so I asked the teachers for extra work and carried home their praise. My fifth-grade teacher gave me a ninth-grade math book to work on. I wrote poems and stories and won prizes for them. And only watched my mother's anger grow. I really was dopey not to catch on, for she could be pretty explicit:

Some friends of my parents were visiting for Shabbos, and we were all sitting at the dining room table, having Friday night dinner. Avram, as was his way, hadn't said a word all through the meal, and I, as was my way, had been chattering throughout, wisecracking and telling stories. My mother got me into the kitchen on some pretext, where her gracious company face instantaneously transformed itself into wild rage. (These transformations were terrifying.)

"You're embarrassing me and your father with all your showing off. You're just a girl," she hissed, trying to pack all the anger into her voice without raising it, for fear the guests would overhear. "You're pretty enough. Why are you always trying to show off how smart you are? Why must you always outshine your brother? Can't you ever give him a chance?"

Avram and me. Felicia and me. Descriptions have always come in pairs, in contrapuntal duets. The good and the bad, the perfect and the problem, the *naches* and the *tsuris*.

But no matter how biased the maternal descriptions, the objective fact is that I got married before my cousin. And my husband *is* a genius. That's on the plus side. But on the minus side, and this must be weighted very heavily, he is *fifteen* years older than I am. Let's not total up the points until we see whom Felicia finally condescends to marry. She's still roaming the Catskills, seeking her intended (doctor) at singles weekends at Grossinger's and the Concord.

There have always been, since the birth of Felicia, states of the world to provoke Aunt Myra's indignation: girls chosen before Felicia to play Queen Esther in the Purim plays; teachers who marked her compositions in ignorance and apathy. But none of this compares to the present singles situation. These young men (especially the Jewish doctors) were spoiled rotten. None of them wanted to get married anymore because these other stupid girls were all giving it away for nothing.

"And they talk about Jewish *princesses*," my mother had sympathetically quoted my aunt quoting my cousin, who—sorry, coz—will for me always present an ostensive definition for that hated term.

My mother always keeps me informed of the aunts' views on my life. They had all been "overjoyed" to learn I was getting married, "except your Aunt Myra, that jealous witch," my mother had chirped in ecstasy. They had been "very impressed" to learn of my husband's prominence. (My mother had found the old *Life* article at the library and sent them all xeroxed copies.) They were also "a little surprised" when their arithmetical computations revealed the age difference between Noam and myself. My mother had never commented directly on Noam's age. She frequently chooses the medium of "the aunts" to make her points. Then, if I react very badly, she can say sympathetically, "Well, you know your aunts."

The morning after the *bris* my mother called with the reactions of the aunts on meeting Noam in the flesh.

"Well, they thought he seemed a little eccentric, but of course that's a mark of his genius, as I told them. You can't expect geniuses to be normal. They were surprised at how good-looking he still is. They all said he doesn't look his age."

I thought often of my little nephew and spoke to Tzippy at least once a week. At three months Reuven began to sleep through the night, and Tzippy, after happily informing me of this, said:

"Now I can finally invite you and Noam for a Shabbos."

Noam absolutely refused. "No, Renee, I couldn't take it. I couldn't take a whole Shabbos. And I certainly couldn't take your brother for that long. I can tolerate the word 'pagan' just about twenty times in one day. That's my limit and it's surpassed in five minutes with Avram."

So I went to Lakewood by myself, after making sure that Noam had invitations for dinner Friday and Saturday.

Lakewood has two identities. It's a pretty little resort community, and it's also the Princeton of *yiddishkeit.* Life there presents Judaism at its purest: the men learning in the elite *kollel,* which is like a graduate department for Talmud; the women producing children and also teaching or running little businesses in their basements to augment the meagre stipends the *kollel* pays their husbands. Some of the families actually live quite well, supported by the wife's father. This is one of the great blessings of wealth, to be able to buy a scholar for a son-in-law and support him in the way of life one couldn't choose for oneself.

Reuven had changed tremendously in three months, as people his age tend to do, I guess. I was initially disappointed to see that he had lost the look of ineffable knowledge, but I soon became enchanted. He was delicate-featured and pale-skinned, and the hair that was coming in was the blond of my father, my brother, and me. He was a real Feuer. He seemed to me to be remarkably beautiful, although I was somewhat skeptical of my aesthetic judgment. I have heard parents of pathetically homely children marvel at their offspring's beauty and debate the pros and cons of a career in child modeling. For all I knew, such creative perception might extend to doting aunts as well.

Tzippy was completely absorbed in her maternity. She was nursing Reuven, and he was a hungry little soul (my mother worried he wasn't getting enough), feeding for about forty-five minutes every four hours. Tzippy, though much larger on top than before, was thinner every place else; especially her little face, which was more pinched than at the *bris*. But she was ebulliently happy:

"I have to restrain myself when he's sleeping not to wake him. I miss him."

I didn't mind the exclusiveness of her concerns. In fact, I enjoyed this glimpse into the maternal world-view. I was rather glad that Noam hadn't come after all.

Avram was also overjoyed in his role as a parent. When I watched him play with Reuven, throwing him high in the air as Tzippy begged him to be careful, making silly faces and noises, I felt for the first time in fifteen years like hugging my holy brother.

Friday night, after the Shabbos meal, Avram sat at the table swaying over a Gemara, and Tzippy and I went into the tiny bedroom so we wouldn't disturb him with our talk. There was a little night light casting a soft glow on the white walls and pink bedspreads. Reuven fell asleep at the breast, and Tzippy looked down at him.

"Ah, Reuven, you have a *tzaddik's shaym*" (a saint's name). "You should only have his *neshuma*" (his soul).

All at once I was crying, and Tzippy silently joined in. She had only known my father in the last year of his life, but a strong and special closeness had developed almost immediately between them. It was she who had shown my numbed family the way when he lay dying in the final days. We had already distanced ourselves from the man lying there, smelling of death and wearing the face of martyrdom. That wasn't my father suffering; my father had already gone. But little Tzippy had shown us who that person was, had walked into the room and straight over to him, kissing him, holding him, talking to him as she always had. How he had smiled at her with that wasted face. Were it possible to feel envy for Tzippy, I would certainly have envied her that last smile. It was four years since my father had died, and still when I spoke or thought of him my eyes often welled up. When I was with Tzippy, her eyes did the same in response.

We didn't speak for a while. The only sounds were the clock on the night table ticking, Reuven's soft breathing, and out in the living room the rhythmic squeak of Avram's chair under his swaying. Tzippy finally broke the silence:

"Oh, Renee, I almost forgot. I'm so absent-minded these days. You have an old friend here in Lakewood, a school friend. Her husband is learning here. She was so excited when she discovered you're my sister-in-law. Her name now is Fruma Friedbaum, but I can't remember her maiden name."

"Not Fruma Dershky? Thin, red hair, great giggle?"

"That's her, but she's not so thin anymore. She's expecting her fifth child, *kayn aynhoreh.*" (This is a Hebrew phrase automatically uttered when any good news is spoken. It's actually an incantation to ward off the evil eye, although now it's hardly ever spoken with that intent. It's like saying "God bless you" after someone sneezes, the original purpose of which, according to Bertrand Russell, was to keep the devil from jumping in as the soul momentarily leaves the body.)

"You're kidding," I said. Again I felt my childishness, felt that I'd been left behind. And left behind by Fruma! We had been best friends in high school, and she had accompanied me, always a step in back, in that heady first flush of doubting. In our schools, as in most yeshivas, the morning classes were devoted to religious studies, taught by rabbis with beards and *rebbetsens* (rabbis' wives) with *sheitels.* In the afternoon we were taught secular subjects by moonlighting public school teachers. Fruma and I called the morning the dark ages, and the afternoon the enlightenment:

"It's like experiencing the renaissance every day of our lives."

We often cut the morning classes and hid down in the lunchroom, where I'd propound the narrowness of Judaism, the naïveté of theism. We read Spinoza and Nietzsche, Freud and Bertrand Russell; and, most glorious of all, David Hume. Oh, what David Hume and his

Dialogues Concerning Natural Religion did for my life.

Imagine the exhilaration of a chronic invalid suddenly transformed into an Olympic athlete and you glimpse my mood of those days. Judged by religious standards my want of belief was a weakness, an ailment requiring therapy. I was always being told to go and speak to this rabbi or that *rebbetsen*. And so I went, like a barren woman wandering from one fertility doctor to another. But barren I remained. They offered me reasons, which I criticized. They told me the criticisms were beside the point because the reasons were really beside the point. They're a crutch for those who need them. The good and the strong get there without them. But I couldn't get there, with or without them.

Can you imagine, then, what it was like to turn from the spirit of religion to the spirit of philosophy, or, as I liked to call it in those days, the spirit of rationality? For here, reasons for beliefs are never beside the point but are the entire substance of the matter. The distinction between the mere belief and the reasoned belief is the distinction that grounds all philosophy. If truth is our end (and what else should be?) we must reason our way there. The leap of faith is not heroic but cowardly, has all the virtues, Russell said, of theft over hard labor. (And we can take his word for it. After all, he was described, in the squabble over whether he should be allowed a professorship at City College of New York because of his book *Marriage and Morals*, as "lecherous, libidinous, lustful, venerous, erotomaniac, aphrodisiac, irreverent" and more; which is recommendation enough for me. Einstein, a habitual scribbler of doggerel verse, wrote him: *Es wiederholt sich immer wieder/In dieser Welt so fein und bieder/Der Pfaff den Pöbel alarmiert/Der Genius wird exekutiert.* [It keeps repeating itself/In this world so fine and honest/The parson alerts the mob/ The genius is executed.] The controversy brought Russell an invitation to Princeton, where he spent the next four years at the Institute. Anyone who is anyone in our world has done time here.)

For me, in those days, the turn from religion to philosophy was like stepping from one ethical system into another, which was the inversion of the first. My moral weakness became my moral strength, the barrenness of my belief was in truth the fertility of my rationality, and I was saved at last.

I had been in the habit since childhood of sending up urgent little prayers: God make me know the answer; make my mother love me; let me not strike out with the bases loaded. The original intent was religious, but over the years the words had simply become a formula for expressing these surges of desire. Now, in high school, the little plea became: God make me rational—even though part of what I meant by being rational was ceasing to believe in the divine presence.

My goal was Barnard, for me the beacon of reason, shining forth on the shores of the Hudson, beckoning to me like a liberation. Smart girls went to Barnard, and I wanted like hell to be one of them. The college's acceptance was not sufficient. I also had to overcome the undertow of religion, in the persons of my mother and the rabbis and *rebbetsens* she enlisted, trying to sweep me out to sea where I would drown. No high has ever quite equaled that first time I took the Seventh Avenue subway uptown and got off in the general exodus at 116th Street, *my* promised land.

And Fruma, whose name derives from the Yiddish-German *frum*, for pious, was there with me at the time of my conversion, sometimes arguing the other side but usually ending up agreeing with me. Finally we were ready to act. We walked into a McDonald's and ordered a cheeseburger each. Not just a plain *trayf* hamburger, you understand, but a *trayf* hamburger with cheese, meat and milk together. We discovered, however, that it's one thing to reach a conclusion and another to act on it. After an hour of sitting and staring shamefaced, we walked out, leaving behind two untouched cheeseburgers.

My friend and I had sporadically kept in touch our first year out of high school, when I was at Barnard and she was going to Brooklyn College at night and the *Bas Yaakov* seminary during the day. ("I have to. My parents expect it.") But we soon drifted apart. The last time I had seen her was at her wedding, when we were both eighteen. We spoke on the phone a few times after, but our increasing estrangement was both annoying and painful. So far as I was concerned, her brief experiment in thinking was over; she had returned to the proper role of the *Bas Yaakov*, the little girl who never questions or challenges, but patters through life collecting little gold stars for good behavior. She had also been, I now learned, accumulating children, one a year since her marriage, not at all unusual in her world.

My first reaction upon seeing Fruma again was shock. I would never have recognized her. She was in the advanced stages of pregnancy and was absolutely enormous, probably because this was her fifth child and she hadn't many stomach muscles left. There had been an all-round thickening of the thin body I remembered: the arms, the neck, the calves and ankles. The gorgeous red hair had been cut off and replaced by a brown *sheitel* with demure red highlights. Only the clear blue eyes were as I remembered them.

But the minute she began to talk in her fast bubbly way, I knew it was the old Fruma.

"Renee, Renee, look at you! You're exactly the same, only better. Tzippy told me you just got married. *Mazel tov!* Look at you. I can't believe it, what a beauty. But why shouldn't I believe it? You were always beautiful. So how are you, what's new?"

We exchanged summaries of our lives.

"I wish your husband was here. I'd love to meet him, he sounds so fascinating. Is he *frum?*" she asked, trying to sound casual.

"No, not at all. I'm his first brush with Orthodoxy. Not that I'm at all observant anymore," I added hastily.

"So you finally tasted the cheeseburger." Fruma grinned. I nodded and grinned back. "Was it good?"

"I don't know. I really don't. Not half so delicious as we imagined."

"None of it?"

"None of it that I can think of. So you're still wondering. You look as if you had put all doubts aside long ago."

"Yeah, I do look it, don't I? I look in the mirror and I can't believe what I see. I look just like our teachers." She grinned. "Our dark-age teachers. In fact, I do teach in the local *Bas Yaakov.* But I'm really a fake. I only look the part. I live a *frum* life, but I don't live it out of my own convictions."

"You don't believe in it?"

"I don't know if I do or I don't. The choice wasn't mine to decide what I believe in. Maybe I would have discovered that I actually do believe in it. I don't know. I went right from my parents' home to my husband's," she said very slowly. "Do you see? Tzvi would be so horrified if he heard me talking like this. I never talk like this."

"I always was your *yaytzah harah.*" That's the evil inclination, dear reader, the snake in the Garden of Eden.

"Yeah." She grinned and then immediately became serious. "Once I said something mildly skeptical to Tzvi and he told me he wondered if I was fit to be the mother of our children. You can't believe what that did to me. More than anything else I want to be a good mother to them, just as I wanted to be a good daughter.

"You know, it's funny my talking to you like this after all these years," Fruma mused. "Don't think that I'm unhappy, that I go around in a blue funk all the time. I'm very happy. It's just that deep down I feel like I'm not really an adult yet, that I haven't reached maturity, because I've never decided for myself how I want to live my life. Someone just handed me the script and I started reading. I don't think I'd even know how to make up my own words, the way you have. I wouldn't know how to decide for myself, to go against everybody else. But you know," she giggled, the same little-girl giggle I remembered, "sometimes I cheat on Tzvi."

"What?" I stared at her, dumbfounded. I thought myself not easily shocked anymore, but I was having trouble assimilating Fruma's words. Was there wife-swapping going on in Lakewood? Was the *sheitel* crowd swinging? Impossible! Fruma looked at me, as if a little puzzled at the effect of her statement. Then she suddenly burst out laughing.

"Oh, Renee! Oh, is this beautiful! Too bad I can't tell Tzvi. Renee, you nut, I didn't mean *that* kind of cheating!" Her laughter was always infectious, and I was laughing, too. The great low belly was bobbing up and down so violently that I feared for the child inside. "What I *meant*—oh boy, is this going to sound ridiculous after what you thought—what I *meant* was that sometimes I don't wait the full six hours between *flayshig* and *milchik,* and once—boy, I thought I was going to shock you with this." She was laughing so hard that she had trouble speaking and the tears were streaming down her face, "Once, Renee, they were offering free samples of a *trayf* cheese spread on *trayf* crackers in the supermarket and I ate one. In fact, it was so good I ate two."

I had planned to leave Saturday night right after *Havdalah,* but

I hung around talking with Tzippy and playing with Reuven until it was quite late. And when Tzippy suggested I spend another night on their lumpy little couch, I happily agreed.

Sunday morning, as I made the trip back to Princeton, I considered for the first time whether I wanted to have a baby. It wasn't a question of whether to have one at all. I'd always taken it for granted that I would someday become a mother. The question was whether this was, metaphorically speaking, the day. Why not? I was a married woman. Noam was already forty. I wouldn't want my child to be embarrassed by a father whom other children mistook for a grandfather. (Would he come with me to Lamaze or, like my brother, decline any involvement in *weibeszachen?*)

I had always pictured myself with a daughter—a golden child, loving the world and herself. And now there was the possibility that she would inherit her father's genius. (I remembered, but briefly, the sorry hopes of Mother Himmel, weeping at her Formica kitchen table.) I could be the mother of a Marie Curie. How's that for compensation for not being a genius oneself? Wife *and* mother of. And if she were brilliant—not that she need be; my love would be unconditional—but if she were, I'd make sure the flames of her creativity were never smothered by self-doubt. It was an exciting thought: Daddy's mind, Mommy's body. And what, Shaw's unbidden ghost whispered in my mind's ear, what if she inherited Mommy's mind and Daddy's body? No matter! She would be loved.

Now, I'm not saying that I was really at the point of taking the step and discarding the remainder of my birth-control pills. I had discovered a new identity to fantasize about, and this was exciting. I don't know if the excitement would have been sufficient to carry me into action. It is, after all, quite a choice: whether to create a person, to take responsibility for another's existence and, to some extent, essence. "Mother" is not an identity one can just try on for size, as I have others. How do all these people do it, I've always wondered, cavalierly *do* it?

But then I have noticed that others don't seem to have quite the problem with freedom that I have, to suffer the burden of choice as I do. Most seem to have their fixed solid natures, cast in one form or another, not this liquefied matter flowing first one way and then

178

another. Fruma wondered whether she had it in her to make up her own words. My problem is, I can think up too many words. Freedom for me is a pain in the Buridan's ass.

And now having a child has been taken out of the sphere of biological determinism and placed instead in the domain of intentional action. Another option to consider and decide upon. And this one qualifies, in the terminology that William James formulated to characterize religious choices, as a momentous decision: not to choose is to choose. I really needed this. Wouldn't I have been better off without so many options before me requiring my attention? I haven't been *bred* to make choices.

Consider my forebears. Consider my maternal great-grandmother, who was married at twelve and lived to have sixteen children and sixty grandchildren before she was carted off, at ninety-four, to Auschwitz. I'm named after her: she was Reine, which means pure. (Fruma and I used to joke about our names: "Pious and Pure, what choice did our parents give us?" But that was the idea, wasn't it?) Since I was her namesake, my grandmother used to feel it was only right for me to hear stories about her. Most of them emphasized her saintliness, but my favorite was this:

It was shortly after her marriage, one Shabbos morning when all the men were in *shul,* and she and her friends were out playing in some mud they made by peeing in the dirt lane that ran through the town. My great-grandmother was using her *sheitel* to mix the mud in. Suddenly the men were spotted returning from *shul,* my great-grandfather among them. And here was his wife with her head uncovered. So she dumped the *sheitel* (after all, what choice did she have?), mudpie and all, on her head and ran.

You know, I think I would have functioned tolerably well in such a world. My energies are considerable, quite equal to sixteen children, I think, if only they weren't being constantly dissipated in making fundamental decisions as to my essential nature.

In any case, this new fantasy of mothering—of mothering a genius —was so exciting that I actually mentioned something to Noam that night at dinner.

"Noam, how would you feel about having a child?"

"A child?"

"You know, Noam, children. You've seen them around. Very young people, tend to be rather short."

"Don't attempt sarcasm, Renee, you haven't the wit. A child is out of the question. A wife is distraction enough." He stared at me coldly for several seconds. "You know, hardly any of the great mathematicians in history were married, and I've come to know why."

That was March; so Noam's hostility had already started by then, that deep numbing anger. When had it first begun? I find it hard to pinpoint, since the change was gradual. There were the walks, I remember.

Noam and I both enjoy walking. We used to love to tramp through the extensive Institute woods where so many great minds have wandered, pursuing so many great thoughts. In the good days, certainly before our marriage and after our return to Princeton as well, we had walked there together often, talking the whole time. Even in the course of our mad Viennese ambulations, when Noam was so preoccupied with his search for personal identity, the conversation had hardly ever let up. I had always loved listening to Noam, talking on a wide range of topics, always interesting and original. But gradually, over the course of that first year of marriage, the nature of the walks changed until they had become almost silent. The conversation had always been dominated by Noam, but now he seldom wanted to speak. On occasions when I'd break the silence with a comment, it would be followed by more silence, during which I'd consider the now apparent absurdity of my remark, whose existence, however brief, I regretted and he ignored. He wouldn't even acknowledge it with his usual absent-minded "hmmmm." And to think that in Rome I had been annoyed by the abundance of Noam's conversation, at least in bed.

Okay, so he was preoccupied with his thoughts. The world inside his head is more interesting than anything outside, I told myself. That's what makes Noam Noam. Perhaps he's working out something very important. Perhaps he's on the trail of something surpassing even the supernaturals. Don't distract him with your petty childish needs.

Think of the two Mrs. Einsteins, I told myself (I had just finished Ronald Clark's biography of the great man): the bad, complex Mileva and the good, simple Elsa. Mileva had been a (failed) physicist herself, bitter and brooding, whereas Elsa is described by Clark as "placid and housewifely, of no intellectual pretensions, but with a practiced mothering ability which made her the ideal organizer of genius." There! That was the description for me to assume. My instructions were clear. And just in case I didn't yet understand, Elsa, good, stolid, contented Elsa, told me again: "When the Americans come to my house they carry away details about Einstein and his life, and about me they say incidentally: he has a good wife, who is very hospitable, and offers a good table." I would have to work on myself until that is what the Americans would say of *me*.

The most persuasive statement of all came from Einstein himself: "I'm glad my wife doesn't know any science. My first wife did." Succinct and clear. Mileva's insistence on her own intellectual identity had doomed her to divorce, while Elsa had ridden out her marriage in relative peace and contentment, sharing in the glory of her husband. Elsa Einstein had not gone mooning around because her husband didn't take her mind seriously. She had mothered him and understood: "You cannot analyze him, otherwise you will misjudge him," she wrote a friend. "Such a genius should be irreproachable in every respect. But no, nature doesn't behave like this. Where she gives extravagantly, she takes away extravagantly." So even Einstein, most noble of men, had had his faults.

Couldn't I be satisfied? I was the wife of a genius, for Godssakes. *I* was a malevolent Mileva with intellectual pretensions and, if not careful, would end up as Noam's first wife. Grow up, grow up, grow up, I chanted to myself as we trampled through the snow. I didn't know what Noam was working on. He didn't discuss his work with me anymore. When I asked him once he said I wouldn't be able to understand it, and I never asked again.

Why didn't I simply stop tagging along on those ever more painful walks? Because I kept hoping, I suppose, remembering and hoping. Noam's natural gait is much faster than mine, really very brisk, and even though I had compromised my vanity and bought some very sensible boots, I had difficulty keeping up with him for long periods. After a while he'd be twenty paces ahead of me, and I'd bleat out: "Noam." Sometimes he'd mumble "Sorry"; usually he didn't say a word, but would just pause a few seconds while I ran to catch up. Then the whole painful process would begin again. It was obvious that he had forgotten my existence, and, dependent as I am on others' assurances that I do indeed exist, this made me wretched. Still I struggled for objectivity: Can't you stop worrying about yourself? Can't you ever get beyond yourself, you petty-spirited woman? Don't blame him because he's different from other people. That's why you married him.

But there was actually very little danger of my blaming him. It was clear whose fault it was. The explanation was ready at hand, because it was the thing I had feared from the first, even before Noam had sat down with me on the dinky. If Noam wasn't interested in talking to me anymore, it was because he had discovered what an idiot I am. How could I have hoped that he would fail to do so? Had I, in my heart of hearts, even wished him to? Fear that p is not always incompatible with fear that not-p. One by one the sacred symbols of intelligence had lost their meaning for me, as I managed, with little effort, to collect them. How many of one's idols can one bear to see exposed?

I believed in genius. Genius that remained duped would try my faith. Noam's infatuation had provided the explanation for his mistaken regard for me. His besotted perception had wrapped me in an intellectual grace and loveliness. His interpretation of my remarks had been generous, often creatively so, making of them something far more brilliant than I had intended, than I ever could intend. I had enjoyed an intelligence of his own making, a little runoff from the great gushing well of his mind. He had finally located the leak.

It's hard to remember the exact timetable of the breakdown between us. I can remember lovely times that first year, when Noam spoke to me as in the old days, the golden spring days when we had first come together, excitement and intensity lighting up his vivid eyes. Sometimes he would come home from Fine Hall full of something to discuss, rushing into the kitchen where I was preparing supper. There was the famous incident I have mentioned of his getting burned when he stuck his head over the pot of soup I was stirring, in an effort to catch my gaze, just as he so often used to place his head over the steering wheel.

But now so many times the face he turned to me was frozen over in anger. That seemed to be the heart of the matter. He was furious with me. It became increasingly obvious that he harbored a very deep and constant rage that would come bursting through with great violence at unexpected moments. When I said something vague, unclear, half-baked, he'd pounce, tearing away with a ferocity that seemed no longer impersonal but vengeful. He wouldn't stop until I was completely broken. Now he's getting back at me, I'd think, for having hidden my membership in the class of dopes he despises.

The attacks paralyzed my mental processes so that I couldn't think, would blather out idiocies, contradict myself left and right; in short, produce ample evidence for his opinion that I didn't know what I was talking about. Once he said to me, it was shortly after our first anniversary: "Now I see why you're having so much trouble hacking it in philosophy."

Noam knew what such a statement would do to me, particularly coming from him. He knew the damage inflicted on my sense of self by my failure to be appreciated by the Princeton philosophers. I had poured out all to him, in the glowing days before our marriage, and he had listened sympathetically, and encouraged me:

"Don't be overwhelmed by this technical turn in philosophy. They're trying to turn philosophy into math, which can't be done. Not that I'm an expert on philosophy, but I know enough about math to know it can't be done. There's a great story about a debate between Euler and Diderot on the existence of God." (Euler, you'll remember, was on Noam's roll call of mathematical minor deities.) "Euler was supposed to take the pro side and Diderot the con. Diderot didn't know much mathematics and Euler decided to trick him. He got up and said that he could prove the existence of God mathematically, that God's being is a mathematical theorem." Noam was laughing. "Then he wrote down some equations, concluding on the last line: therefore God exists, Q.E.D. There's some uncertainty as to how the debate ended. Actually, there are two endings. One says that Diderot walked out in great embarrassment, unable to follow the so-called proof; the other, which I hope is the true one, maintains that Diderot called Euler's bluff.

"Anyway, Renee, I suspect that a lot of contemporary philosophers are playing Euler's trick, probably on themselves, too. Don't let them fool you. Call their bluff."

Noam had made me feel that perhaps the problem lay outside me, in the situation in which I found myself, in the philosophical step-relatives who mocked me. The hero could see through the cinders to the Ella underneath. But now he was spurning me: "Now I see why you're having so much trouble hacking it."

Why this anger that would pour over me at the slightest provocation? Why? I never doubted the answer. Noam despised me. I'd always known he had a low tolerance for stupidity, and had married in full awareness of the risks. Who was there to blame but myself?

Noam and I didn't go abroad that summer. He had deliberated for a while over accepting two of the more tempting invitations, one from the Institute Hautes Études Scientifiques, outside Paris, the other from the Hebrew University in Jerusalem. But in the end he declined, and adventuress that I had proven myself to be, I was relieved. I spent the summer days by myself, tending my little garden and reading about existential despair.

In the evenings there were of course plenty of invitations, but the joy had gone out of them. They were usually flat occasions, and sometimes worse. Noam doesn't have private and public personalities. He is what he is, intensely and always. If contempt was what he showed me at home, it was what he showed me with others. I now welcomed those parties with the invisible *mechitzahs*, the boundaries separating men and women, for I breathed easier away from Noam. The small intimate dinner parties were trying. I could either remain silent throughout or speak and risk Noam's attacks. More and more I chose the first alternative. Much better to be suspected of having nothing to say, than to have repeated the scenes of public humiliation:

The gathering was once again at the home of Adam Loft, the chairman of the math department, where I had met Noam. The invitation was the first in a long time to spark my interest, for a couple I had wanted to meet would be there, Saul and Margaret Kripke. Both are philosophers. He had just recently joined the Princeton department, and his reputation in the field is analagous to Noam's in math (Princeton having once again scored a triumph). The conversation around the dinner table developed, not surprisingly, into a discussion of whether math and philosophy required different kinds of intelligence. Kripke, who himself has done much math, including important work in logic, nonetheless argued that the kind of thinking required by the two fields wasn't exactly alike, although both required much clarity and precision.

"Many very competent mathematicians," he said, "are unbelievably naïve and unsubtle when it comes to philosophy."

"But then, so are many philosophers, wouldn't you say?" Noam smiled.

"I'm afraid I would." Kripke smiled back.

Another mathematician, Herbert Freiburg, argued that intelligence is intelligence:

"The person who can think can think about anything. He may not choose to, he may not be interested in everything. But the potential is there. Intelligence is potential."

"I don't think it's only a matter of differences in interests," Noam had said, agreeing with Kripke. "Even the neurological facts, the differences between the functions of the right and left hemispheres, argue against the monolithic interpretation of intelligence."

"Oh, I'm willing to grant that difference," Freiburg answered. "I was talking only about the functions of the left hemisphere. That's what I mean by thinking."

"But even within the left hemisphere," I said, feeling confident since I was on the side of the gods (or at any rate demigods), "there are differences, aren't there?"

Noam turned and stared at me, the anger already rising in his eyes. I felt the muscles of my stomach begin to tighten. "What did you" —slightly emphasized—"have in mind?"

"Well, the difference between mathematical and philosophical intelligences, for example." I smiled shakily.

"*Are* they different?"

"I thought you said they were."

"No, I didn't. Saul did. And I'm sure he has good reasons. I'd like to know what *your* reasons are."

"You often say how many mathematicians turn to philosophy

when they're unable to do math anymore. Doesn't that show they're different?"

"Not to me."

"Oh," I whispered.

"Oh," he mocked. "Don't you think you owe us an account of your reasoning?"

I was aware of the embarrassed glances around the table. I saw the Kripkes exchange a look of concern. But mostly I was aware of the pounding in my head.

"I don't know, it just seemed self-evident." My voice was pleading. "We always disagree over what's obvious."

"Why is it self-evident?" His voice was a monotone.

"If a person can't do one but can do the other, doesn't that show the intelligence required is different?" I whispered.

"A non sequitur. The topics toward which the intelligence is applied are different. It's possible that the one merely requires more intelligence, not a special sort. A slight decline in powers might incapacitate one mathematically, but not philosophically. Do you understand?"

I shook my head dumbly.

"I think," he said, finally looking around at the others, "that whatever is required for doing math or philosophy has not been very brilliantly displayed just now by my wife."

Noam smiled. I would have welcomed a responding smile or laugh, since silence would only indicate pity for me. And I didn't—have never—wanted that. But unfortunately everyone was quiet for a long moment, until Margaret Kripke, in an obvious, although nonetheless kind attempt to divert attention, began to compliment the hostess on the food.

Our first anniversary passed unnoticed. Noam gave no indication of remembering it, and I thought it better not to remind him of the mistake he had made. I could even sympathize with him, for he must have been terribly disillusioned. I had been, for however brief a time, the one romance of his life, excluding the supernaturals. In some ways he was naïvely romantic, for he had given such matters so little thought (as was consistent with his view of how much thought they deserved). What opinions he did have were simply those most commonly held, those he had unconsciously absorbed from the prevailing attitude. (He was, for instance, always taken aback if I showed any sign of enjoying sex too much. A woman shouldn't be cold, but she shouldn't be a whore.) He had, in those spring days of our courtship, perceived me in impossibly ideal terms. I could sympathize with his disillusionment.

I spent the day of our anniversary alone, crying a great deal, remembering how things had been a year before. Things certainly happened fast with Noam. He had fallen in love virtually immediately and fallen out of love almost as quickly. The "falling" idiom was exactly right. I had little faith the marriage would last. Still, we had made it past the year mark, and now simple annulment was impossible.

Noam seemed to have become much harsher in general. His assessments of others, whether talking with them or about them, were less charitable. I blamed myself for this, too. His disgust with me had poisoned his attitude toward everyone. One incident in particular stands out. It was November, our second. We were discussing which of the several invitations for Thanksgiving dinner to accept. A graduate student who had called earlier in the evening came by to talk to Noam about some ideas he hoped might be developed into his dissertation. Noam acted ferociously, hammering the student over the head again and again with the triviality and emptiness of his ideas. I watched in horror as the student cringed there, stuttering out his answers to the questions Noam kept shooting at him. When he finally slouched out the door, I went up to Noam and screamed into his face:

"*Why? Why* did you do that to him?"

"What are you so hysterical about? I was helping him. He came here to find out if the ideas were worthwhile, and I told him. I did him a favor. I saved him weeks, probably months of wasted effort."

"But the *way* you did it, Noam! Did you have to be so cruel, so relentless? Did you have to mortify him?"

"I assure you, Steve was not mortified. You don't understand these things. Steve was interested in the objective value of his ideas. He's not going to be bothered by the trivialities that concern you so much."

"Trivialities like human feelings?"

"Yes. Trivialities like human feelings." He looked at me for several seconds, considering me. "You know, Renee," he finally said, "you are an essentially trivial woman. You have a lovely face and body, but in essence you are very trivial."

I felt as if I had flunked my final exam, my very final exam.

I HAD BECOME quite frigid by this time. It was my first experience of sex without desire. What a cold, cold thing it is, the bare, dry facts, scraped clean of the film of desire.

On one of my trips into New York at about this time, I overheard a group of pubescent girls, maybe thirteen or fourteen years old, chattering and giggling, and I caught the phrase "making out." It startled me. I hadn't heard the phrase in so many years. In fact, now that I heard it again I was surprised it still had a place in adolescent vocabulary. For the phrase is used by those who are teetering on the brink, approaching without yet plunging in to the inestimable depths; the plunge known in that same vocabulary, at least as it was employed in my adolescence, as "going all the way." I hadn't thought teenagers now hesitated on the other side long enough to have use for a phrase like "making out."

I sat there on that subway remembering the time of my own delicious teetering with Hillel, when each step closer convinced us of the overwhelming power and mystery of what lay beyond. And now I had passed through to that great knowledge, and this was the reality. It was horrible. (How many other mysteries would end this way, were one finally to see through them? How desirable *is* the parting of the mists?)

I was incapable of arousal with Noam. My flesh under his touch was dead, only stirred now and then by a ripple of revulsion. For a while I pretended orgasms, but then I saw that I needn't make the effort. Noam wasn't watching.

He was staring away, and not only in bed. When he wasn't raging, he was absent, at least in spirit. That day he first sat down next to me on the dinky, we had been strangers to one another; and yet he had held my eyes with such direct intensity that I was made uncomfortable by the implied intimacy. And now we were man and wife, and that vivid gaze, which had first settled on me with admiration as I stood in the surrounding circle at Loft's party, that gaze which had directed all its brilliance and enthusiasm at me in the course of the accompanying conversations, that gaze, and all its intensity, had turned away.

Frigidity we call it in women, impotence in men. The terms reflect, I think, the male point of view. But there's coldness and want of power on both sides. I certainly felt impotent, a thing of naught.

I briefly considered masturbation, as (and in much the same spirit) I considered jogging: as something that, no matter how unpleasant, might be good for me. For I thought it possible that my body would go quite dead, become incapable of ever feeling pleasure again; and that, at least according to the collective opinion of the day, couldn't be healthy. But then again perhaps a sexual death, if possible, would be the most reasonable solution. I had once read a former inmate's account of prison life, and he had written that after several months of celibacy all desire had mercifully vanished. Prison had been much easier after that.

But could it all be made to disappear? Despite my respect for Noam's views, and Noam's contempt for Freud's, I couldn't rid my thinking of such concepts as repression. I had an image of molten libidinous matter, seething in the psychical depths, which could be buried but never destroyed. And eventually the volcanic eruptions in personality would come, the lava of the libido spewing forth in geyser-like behavioral aberrations. The best one could hope for would be sublimation (which might, if Freud was right, even make a genius of me). Is it possible to die a merciful sexual death? And where would that leave one?

Sartre says the object of sexual desire is a "double reciprocal incarnation," most typically expressed by the caress: "I make myself flesh in order to impel the Other to realize *for herself* and *for me* her own flesh. My caress causes my flesh to be born for me insofar as it is for the Other *flesh causing her to be born as flesh.*"

But it seems to me that even deeper than Sartre's object lies another: a double reciprocal mattering, the most typical expression of which is the gaze. In gazing with desire on the Other I reveal how he, in my desire, takes me over, permeates my sense of self; and in his gaze I see how I similarly matter to him, who himself matters at that moment so much. It's *this* double reciprocal process that accounts, I think, for the *psychological* intensity of sexual experience. It answers to one of our deepest needs, a fundamental fact of human existence: the will to matter.

Noam had sadly missed the point in thinking the object of sexuality is no more, and no more interesting, than a sensation. His is the solipsistic view of sex, and it leaves out the complexity, the depth, and the reason this part of life matters so much to us. Without the Other and his gaze, the act is little more than clumsy masturbation. And so it was for me with Noam, who now was always turned away, psychically if not physically, like the man in the da Vinci sketch. Making love under such circumstances is hardly the powerful affirmation of mutual mattering it's meant to be.

To matter. Not to be as naught. Is there any will deeper than that? It's not just unqualified will, as Schopenhauer would have it, that makes us what we are; nor is it the will to power, Nietzsche, but something deeper, of which the will to power is a manifestation. (And who am *I*, daughter of a *shtickele chazzen* from Galicia, to argue with the likes of Schopenhauer and Nietzsche?) We want power *because* we want to matter. Neither sex nor power lies at the level of fundamental facts. Beneath are the heaving thrusts of the will to matter. And the will to create? to procreate? These too are expressions of the fundamental will. Deeper even than the will to survive. We don't *want* to live when we become convinced that we don't, can't, will never matter. That is the state which most often precedes suicide—always, I think, when the cause of suicide lies within.

To matter, to mind. Curious to compare the verbs we have formed from the nouns. What we mind is in our power, but whether we matter may not be—and there's the tragedy. Spinoza tried to help us out of it: We can make ourselves matter because of what we mind. No, no, rather: We shouldn't mind that we don't matter. *It*—of which we're a part—matters. Dissolve the individual will to matter in the objective picture of the whole. It's rather a drastic solution, but then perhaps nothing less will do. And does one thereby dissolve the individual? Is this the solution to the problem of personal identity? Is this will our very essence, with which we are and without which we are not? Perhaps. In any case, it's very close to the realization of the self. We no sooner discover that we are, than we want that which we are to matter. In spite of Spinoza.

Can anyone truthfully say, I don't matter and I don't mind? Not I. Of all my many mind-body problems, the most personally and painfully felt has been this: Do I matter as a mind or do I matter as a body? This is the problem that produces the pattern, the pendulum swings of my dangling life. But somehow or other I *must* come out mattering.

And where was I now? I had hoped, like the good fairy tale taught, to save myself by marrying Noam. My mattering to him, who himself mattered so much, was going to do the trick. It had always been a battle against self-hate, and that's a bloody battle. I certainly didn't have the stuff to stand up to Noam's attacks, his palpable contempt. If I have quaked before every idiot's judgment, if the shrug of the shoulders has always been a movement I'm incapable of executing, imagine how it was to be standing before the Highest Judge, the Genius, before whom no invalid inference could be hidden, and to hear the verdict delivered: You are damned, you are dumb.

The sex was the least of it, if that can be comprehended. I am concerned to distinguish my voice from that great chorus of sexual lamentation being sung by women throughout the land, in first novel (the autobiographical one, right?) after first novel. The voices are different. Some sing raucously, some delicately, some with a constant whine. But all are singing the Marital Blues:

> My husband don't please me
> Takes all but don't give me
> In-out and he's done
> And I never come.
>
> I don't say that he beats me
> But the way that he treats me
> Makes me feel old and done
> And I never come.

Then the Love Affair, and the music changes . . . to Rachmaninoff, climax after climax.

> Then he came
> And I came . . . and I came . . . and I came . . .

Till back we go to the blues:

> That bum went off humming
> And there's no second coming.

Women being done wrong, with all the action below the belt. Pelvic drama. I'm not denying the pleasure and pain involved. (Who was it who said bad sex is better than no sex at all? What a blessed sexual existence he must have enjoyed.) Sex that's gone dry and tasteless, that one can swallow only with effort, is one of the more unpalatable experiences life offers. Especially when one is remembering or imagining the cognac-soaked flambé possibilities. But orgasms —weak few or nonexistent—are not the stuff of tragedy.

Nor is my story, although Noam was certainly killing off something more than sexual desire in me. But between my father's tales of Jewish martyrdom and my mother's predictions of catastrophe, I had been brought up with the tragic possibilities of life always before me and I never saw myself as a bowed victim of persecution. If there was one element of the Jewish consciousness my parents had managed to instill in me, it was the true meaning of persecution.

I continued to see much of Sarah and Ava, but I never spoke to either about what was happening to me. Sarah was sunk deep in her own miseries and Ava . . . Well, Ava was exactly the same as always. I could have spoken to her, but I didn't. It was all too painful, and the duplication of the hurting facts inside her head would only have increased the pain. I didn't want anyone inside my head. When I spoke to Sarah and Ava it was usually about their lives, which at this point meant their work.

Sarah and Ava never became friends, as I had hoped they would, for I am always hoping that the people I love will love one another. They thought well of each other but never became close. Each was amused by the other; their respective peculiarities were strengthened to a point just short of burlesque in one another's company. Sarah became purer and starker, and Ava blunt to the point of brutality.

Ava nicknamed Sarah "Reine Vernunft," that is, Kant's Pure Reason. Sarah knew and was amused. Once, when the three of us were having lunch together in the faculty dining room in Prospect, Sarah said something that caused Ava to hoot, to which Sarah replied: "Is that your *Kritik der reinen Vernunft?*"

I saw more of Ava than of Sarah, whose gloomy ancestors would set up a great chorus of whispering accusations if she left her work for more than an hour. Consequently, I often spent my evenings with Ava. (Noam went back to his office after dinner almost every night.)

One night I came very close to telling Ava about my problems, prodded by her own self-revelations. It had started off by her complimenting me:

"You know, Renee, you really look great. You're a damn good-looking woman."

I probably did look particularly good at this time. I had lost all interest in food, something I would never have imagined could happen to me. (But then I would never have thought I'd become frigid, either.) I had lost a few pounds and always look best when underweight and Camille-like. In the past I had only been able to maintain my matter in this form for short periods before my love of food brought me back to my healthy-looking self. (This love, finally acquired sometime in later childhood, is one of my mother's minor triumphs. "If only I live to see my children someday dieting.") But now it was hard to eat, for I always had the feel of cinders in my mouth.

"Look at me, on the other hand," Ava was saying. "I've really deteriorated since college."

Unfortunately, this was true. Ava was about fifteen pounds heavier than she'd been at Barnard and seemed on the whole to take no trouble with her appearance. Her thin hair, shaped like a monk's in college, now drooped unbecomingly down the sides of her too full face. She never wore a trace of makeup (as she had at Barnard) and her wardrobe was confined to jeans, which did not sit particularly well on her zaftig bottom.

"And you know this uglification is intentional, in the sense that compulsive hand-washing is intentional. There's a need behind it. I don't really want to look pretty. I don't want to look feminine. You know why? Because feminine is dumb. Or at least that's how I feel. Look around at the women in academia, the women who make their living from their brains—especially those in the so-called masculine disciplines like math and physics, to take two random examples. They all feel it too. They're telling you with the way they look and dress, the way they hold themselves and speak: feminine is dumb. You've got to stamp out all traces of girlishness if you want to be taken seriously by the others, but more importantly by yourself. I know. I can see it in myself and can't do anything about it. It was okay to be a girl when I was only a student, but not anymore. When I'm attracted to a man and start playing the part of a woman, there's a voice sneering inside me: Dumb. You dumb cunt. You just can't be a cunt with intelligence. You can have a brain and a prick, there's no incompatibility there. 'Brainy prick' sounds all right, but 'intelligent cunt' is ridiculous, a contradiction in terms. We've all swallowed it. I tell you, I think it would be an act of feminist heroism, an assertion of true liberation from the chauvinist myth, to wear eyeliner and mascara. If I ever saw a female physicist dressed to kill and wearing makeup, I'd be impressed.

"But it won't be me," she continued. "I don't care what the others will think; I care what I'll think, what I'll feel like. I can't manage to regard myself as a woman and a physicist, so one of them's got to go. And I suppose being a physicist is more important to me, so goodbye, sex. Men don't have to make the choice, but we do. For us it's either-or."

"Either mind or body," I said.

"Right. Your old mind-body problem again, or a different aspect of it. Ah, well."

I felt close to telling Ava about my own farewell to sexuality and battled with the decision for several minutes. Finally she suggested we get high.

Our dope-smoking was largely a thing of our college past, but occasionally we still smoked if only for old times' sake. While we passed the joint back and forth Ava described some people she had just met at the Institute, using her favored gustatory imagery:

"That guy working with Dyson reminds me of a piece of strudel. Layers and layers, but all of them flaky. And remember that logician

I told you about, the one with the pregnant wife who propositioned me? The husband, not the wife. I finally figured out exactly what he's like. An overcooked Brussels sprout." She added in explanation: "He's English."

"God, Ava, what an awful image that conjures up. A guy with a Brussels sprout for a head. I *hate* Brussels sprouts."

"Me, too. Can't tolerate them. Nor people who remind me of them."

"I've always thought that after the mind-body problem, or perhaps side by side with it, the most important question in philosophy of mind is whether people who like Brussels sprouts taste them the way I do and actually like that awful taste, or do they taste something different?"

"Baffling. Here's another: Do people who don't like chocolate taste it the way I do and not like it, or do they taste something else? Maybe something like my taste of Brussels sprouts?"

"Who can say? The mystery of consciousness and the inaccessibility of the Other."

My memory of the conversation ends here, for the stuff we were smoking proved to be very strong. I have no recollection of what we spoke about. I couldn't even remember then. By the time I reached the end of a sentence, I couldn't recall its beginning. I'd start a new sentence not knowing what I'd just said before, just plunge in blindly. At first such freedom was terrifying, but I gradually adjusted to it . . . and then *exulted* in it. (Why was there the faint suggestion of sexuality, like a softly breathed whisper against my ear? Was it because sex is another analogue for freedom?) I didn't have to be hampered by the requirements of coherence, I didn't have to make sense. I was beyond the bounds of sense.

I had made a monumental discovery, and I struggled to put it into words. It was too big but I tried, for I had to capture it in words if I were to share it with Ava. Finally I had it. I got up on the chair and shouted, "Logic sucks!" and sat down again, very pleased with my statement, my attempt to squeeze the immensity of my intuition into linguistic constraints.

Ava got up on her chair and declaimed:

"Logic is the ladder of pure reason, but alas;

"The ladder's a mere cobweb, and we fall down on our ass."

Oh, Ava! Oh, wonderful, brilliant, incomparable Ava! I was dazzled, overcome. It was too perfect, said it all. She understood. She understood everything. I loved her. Always had. How could I tell her? How could I put all this soaring feeling into words? It was spilling all over, sweeping me away. I fought to get back in. It was important. I had to tell her.

I was dimly aware of various eruptions at the periphery of my visual field, but I was completely absorbed in the problem before me. Suddenly Ava's face loomed up right in front of mine. She was waving a plate of spaghetti under my nose.

"Renee? Are you here? Are you there? Have you penetrated into the womb of the universe?"

"Huh?"

"Renee? Everything okay? You've been sitting there in a trance for almost an hour. You're not hallucinating or anything, are you? That stuff was stronger than I realized. Here, eat some spaghetti."

"Huh?"

"You're repeating yourself, child. Here. Eat."

I ate. Slowly the pieces of my mind began to drift down. I began to remember from one moment to the next. I wasn't sure whether I was gaining or losing something.

Ava had made an enormous quantity of spaghetti, sprinkled with raw garlic, red pepper flakes, and fresh Parmesan. She was busy eating, and so was I. She glanced up.

"You okay?"

"Yeah, sure. I was just trying to figure out how to say something."

"What?"

"I didn't figure out how to say it, so I can't tell you. I'm not even sure now what it was, if it was anything at all."

My friend laughed. "Yeah, it's like that. Only Coleridge could write a work of genius doped out."

But I felt dissatisfied. I still had something to tell her. But the inhibitions and shyness of my unhigh self were imposing themselves on me, together with the bonds of memory and logic. The words "I love you" had seemed too puny to carry my meaning when I was high, but now they seemed too strong. I was afraid. I was afraid of what they might open up before us or close behind us.

I did love Ava, loved her less selfishly, more trustingly, with less hostility than I'd loved any man. As I loved Sarah and Tzippy. But above all, and for the longest time, Ava. And she loved me, I knew, loved me deeply and acceptingly. She would, I think, have taken me that night had I thrown out my arms and embraced her as I longed to do—attracted by her warm receptivity, repelled by Noam's cold anger. There had been times in the past. Always I had been the one to pull away. And if that night I had not? I wonder, dear Ava, I wonder.

You knew I was afraid, as you knew everything else. That was the whole point, the very source of my fear. I was afraid of that knowledge which would be too knowing, that intimacy which would be too intimate, soft skin against soft skin. With men there's never the danger of getting too close. They're too essentially different. They don't know what we feel, we don't know what they feel, and nobody's mental privacy is seriously threatened.

I left a half-hour later, still dissatisfied, and filled with unvoiced longing.

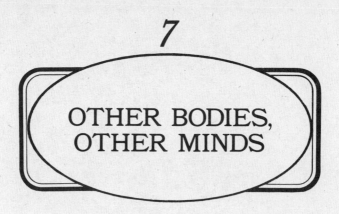

7

OTHER BODIES, OTHER MINDS

Thus the final state of sexual desire can be swooning as the final state of consent to the body. It is in this sense that desire can be called the desire of one body for another body. It is in fact an appetite directed toward the Other's body, and it is lived as the vertigo of the for-itself before its own body. The being which desires is consciousness *making itself body.*

—JEAN PAUL SARTRE,
BEING AND NOTHINGNESS

$\mathcal{T}$he fauna of academe are various. Among the most interesting are the members of the mathematical species. The characteristics found here are very distinctive, facilitating identification. A few times I've described to Noam some unknown creature spotted in town, concluding with: "It's a mathematician, isn't it?" Four times out of five I've been right. (The fifth is usually a mathematical physicist.) The trick is this: If you see someone walking about in the vicinity of a campus who looks as if he's either very backward or very brilliant, then if he's not backward he's a mathematician. There is not another group of people, I'll wager, with eccentricities so pronounced and pure, with personalities so undiluted by the attempt to conform. Why is this so? I have a theory.

(The Other) Himmel's Theory of Academic Types

Observers of the academic scene may be aware that there are distinct personality types associated with distinct disciplines. The types can be ordered along the line of a single parameter: the degree of concern demonstrated over the presentation of self, or "outward focus."

One of the more interesting facts about academic types is that very few fall within the middle range of outward focus (with engineers, geologists, and other very applied scientists perhaps being the exceptions). The majority of academic types are clustered at the two extremes.

At the low end, with outward focus asymptotically approaching zero, we find the pure mathematicians, closely followed by the theoretical physicists (the more theoretical the physicist, the more closely he follows). At the other end, with the degree of outward focus asymptotically approaching infinity, we find sociologists and professors of literature.

The author's special interests demand that she consider the location of the philosophers, which turns out to be complicated.

Philosophy's own ambivalent position between the humanities and the sciences has resulted in a corresponding schizophrenia in the personality type. There are, in fact, two distinct philosophy types, both extreme. Some philosophers approach the pure mathematician's end of the spectrum, while others (probably the majority) rival the members of English departments in their obsessive concern over the impression they make on others.

That philosophy's ambivalent position can result in a split in the philosophy type suggests that the variation in outward focus is itself a function of the nature of the given discipline; and closer examination shows this to be the case. The degree of outward focus is in inverse proportion to the degree of certainty attainable within the given methodology. The greater the certainty of one's results, the less the concern with others' opinions of oneself.

Thus at the end of the spectrum occupied by sociologists and professors of literature, where there is uncertainty as to how to discover the facts, the nature of the facts to be discovered, and whether indeed there are any facts at all, all attention is focused on one's peers, whose regard is the sole criterion for professional success. Great pains are taken in the development of the impressive persona, with excessive attention given to distinguished appearance and faultless sentence structure.

At the other end, where, as the mathematicians themselves are fond of pointing out, "a proof is a proof," no concern need be given to making oneself acceptable to others; and as a rule none whatsoever is given.

Within the walls of Fine Hall, Noam doesn't appear eccentric. There are plenty stranger—some who appear to be straddling the line between sanity and insanity, others who seem to have already taken the step beyond. There is, for example, the much celebrated Phantom of Fine Hall. The corridors of the math building are hung with huge blackboards every few yards, just in case someone is smitten by an intuition on the way to the bathroom. Many of these blackboards bear the legends of the Phantom, complicated equations between political and mathematical terms. At first I used to study them, believing they were sophisticated jokes I wasn't getting. Then I learned they were the work of a former member of the department who had done foundational work in topology before his mental breakdown.

There's a certain degree of danger involved in the life of the pure mathematician, in his intimacy with the inhumanly perfect and the consequent liberation from mortal concerns. Insanity is an occupational hazard, a sacrifice the mathematician risks in his solipsistic splendor.

I suppose the last thing I needed was a mathematician for a lover. But the last thing one needs is often the very thing one chooses, and so it was with me.

SO FAR as I could tell, my buried libidinal lava hadn't produced any publicly observable distortions in the topography of my personality. But there was covert activity, in the form of an igneous fantasy life. Suddenly everybody (with an emphasis on the body) was desirable, with the exception, of course, of my lawfully wedded. I imagined myself with men once known: with Hillel Schoenfeld, my first love, now a physicist at the Weizmann Institute in Israel; with Peter Hill Devon, the epicene musicologist and Wasp *extraordinaire;* with Jack Gottlieb, the sweet mathematician who took me to the party where I met Noam; and even with Leonard Heiss, the cocksure man of letters with unsure sexual tastes, and Isaac Besdin, the menopausal logician.

I didn't only live in the past. I daydreamed about current acquaintances, and sometimes about men I didn't even know: the cheerful blond kid of about seventeen who loaded my grocery bags at Davidson's and always offered to take them right to my home for me, or anywhere else; the muscular man in the tight T-shirts who serviced my Volvo and was also lavish with friendly extra-auto suggestions. (How many men, one wonders, could resist, were attractive women always bombarding *them* with propositions?) I was somewhat surprised by the crudity of my reactions. How could I, with my refined sensibility and overdeveloped mind, respond so violently to those bulging, overdeveloped biceps?

Erotic daydreaming became my favorite pastime. Now it wasn't only Noam who was living inside his own head. Whom would it hurt if I allowed myself absolute freedom of imagination? I could achieve an abandon here—in this disembodied sex, mental and solitary— impossible when it came to the real thing. But gradually my fantasizing began to take on the feel of preparation for action.

I reminded myself often over the course of this winter of my discontent, and the spring and summer that brought no relief, that in Judaism adultery belongs in the same category with murder and idolatry. If faced with the choice of committing any of these three sins or death, one should, and only in these cases, choose death. I tried to feel the awfulness of adultery, but didn't. What a long way I had traveled (backwards or forwards?) from my days with Hillel, when we two had quakingly, achingly perceived the enormity of our actions: tears and trembling, fear and defiance, and the *basso ostinato* of guilt. And then, unlike now, there had been no question of an injured party.

Would Noam be injured? What if he never knew? What if my actions made no difference to his life as he lived it? But no, people can suffer harm even if their experience as such isn't affected. What about a person who is maligned or deceived, even if he never finds out and suffers no ill consequences? Isn't he damaged simply in *being* maligned or deceived? And of course what I had in mind was deceiving Noam. There could be no question of honesty. Noam's views on marriage and morals, as on more romantic matters, are strictly conventional, thus saving him the bother of having to think about these things himself—one of the benefits of conventions in general. He would tolerate no deviations.

So duped he would have to be. Would that constitute the sum of the injury I would inflict? Somehow one feels that more is involved here, a profound betrayal. But that's only if sexual relations have some sort of special significance, if there is a difference that matters between sharing a meal and sharing a bed. "Make love to a pretty woman when you want her, just as you drink a glass of cold water when you are thirsty," goes the French saying. My puritanical husband would never say such a thing, but wasn't some such statement the logical consequence of his trivializing treatment of sex? How could he consistently maintain a difference between sexual desire and other appetites? (Somehow it seemed to matter whether Noam himself could consistently claim damage.) He was the one who thought sex of no consequence. Let bodies do what bodies are given to doing. But what's there to think about? What's there to hold the *mind?* How, I had asked in Vienna, could such a simple appetite be categorized in terms of such distinctions as obscenity, perversity, and sin? So what? had come the answer. So we impose these categories on sex. It's just part of our biologically determined obsession and the delusions thus produced. Think of what the Jews do to the simple appetite for food.

Of course, this was only my mind's own Noam I was quoting, not the paradigm himself. But the words were in character. Noam's opinion was something like this; *exactly* what it was couldn't be known, for it was in the nature of the opinion that it wasn't worth mentioning.

Thus did I work out my rationalization.

LEONARD SCHMERZ WAS an assistant professor in Noam's department, and more and more my fantasies wove themselves around him. By the time I spoke my first word to him, I had already involved him in many of my private adventures. It was the look of the man that intrigued me.

He was tall and thin, with shoulders slightly hunched forward in his worn brown sweater. Crowning the humble posture was a magnificent head, with long black hair, dark complexion, and an uncompromisingly Semitic profile. It was a face, unlike mine, undiluted by the thin bloods of the Diaspora. One could picture it suffering for forty years in the desert sands of the Sinai. It suggested a Hebrew prophet mourning the destruction of his people. Suffering and mourning. Now we get to the heart of it. That was the real attraction: the melancholy depths one read within the liquid brown eyes and downcast full lips. The voice was quiet, low, very somber, with a slightly strained sound to it, as if forced out from beneath a crushing weight on the chest. What was this weight? What was the nature of this sad soul's secret?

It took me three months to unravel the mystery, to diagnose the sickness of his soul, its fear and trembling. Len was an utter bore and knew it. This was what he was mourning. His soul was sickened by its own emptiness; the fear and trembling was that others too might discover its condition.

We would go together to a movie on Nassau Street or a play at Princeton's McCarter Theater, and as the lights came on he would turn to me a face of such unspeakable sorrow that I was pierced through and through. What had he seen that I had missed?

I had experienced such a developed sensibility to sorrow before, in my father. He had been a personally happy man but with great understanding of sadness, seeing it where others didn't. I remember when I was around eight or nine, I was playing by myself in the basement of our *shul* one Shabbos while my father was conducting the evening prayers, and I made an exciting discovery. One of the corridors, which was windowless and led to some classrooms, was unlit on Shabbos, resulting in the thickest, most absolute darkness imaginable. It was thrilling to grope one's way sightlessly, the blackness filling one's eyes, tingling with the delicious fear that somehow one would never reach the end; until finally one glimpsed the pale light seeping under the doors of the windowed classrooms. I couldn't wait for services to end so that I could show my father. Afterwards the two of us walked silently hand in hand down the black passage and back. When we emerged into the light, I saw that my father's face was stricken.

"What is it, Daddy?"

"Perhaps," he said softly, "that's what it's like to be blind."

I had ached with love for my father at that moment, and I ached with love when I saw Len's sad face emerge from the darkness of the movie into the light. What had he understood that I had missed? What had he seen to have caused him such anguish?

He refused to talk, and finally, finally I understood why. Len had seen and understood nothing. Once again he had gone to a movie and didn't know what to think about it, didn't know whether it was good or bad, whether he liked it or not, had no reaction whatever. He would be expected to say something, to offer an opinion, and he had nothing. Once again he stood in danger of having his total absence of taste and personality exposed to the harsh judging eyes of the blessedly opinionated.

If only his physical self didn't promise so much. Wittgenstein said the human body is the best picture of the human soul: *Der menschliche Körper ist das beste Bild der menschlichen Seele.* But here, through some sort of ontological mishap, was a mismatched pair. Len was doomed always to disappoint, never to be able to deliver the depth of which his body spoke. Every relationship was a torment of anticipating that final inevitable moment when understanding would gleam in the Other's eyes, lighting up the vast vacancy yawning within poor Len. His hope was to push that moment off as long as possible, to maintain a suffering silence which the face promised was deep and awful.

This promise is what attracted me to Len, and the attraction ended the moment I penetrated the sad little secret. But the very fact that this had happened made it impossible for me to extricate myself. For this, of course, was the very essence of his tragedy, his knowledge that when others came to understand him they would lose all interest. So I tried to keep the terrible knowledge out of my eyes.

How had it all begun? I had been intrigued by Len for a long time, always aware of his silent presence at parties, *Il Penseroso* lugubriously gazing out at the frivolities of the lighthearted. Whenever I was in Fine Hall I made it my business to pass by his office door, which was usually open. I'd glance in and we'd exchange smiles. The smile on Len's face only deepened the gloom in his eyes. Then one day, it was right after midsemester break, I passed by the office and looked in to see crazy Phil Whiter with his feet up on the desk, his long red hair pushed back behind his shoulders, puffing on his pipe.

"Hi, Phil. What are you doing here?"

"Oh, hi, Renee, how you doing? What I'm doing here is working."

"What happened to Leonard?"

"Leonard? Oh, Len Schmerz. He and I switched offices."

At the next math party I walked over to Len's corner. It was the first time I had ever spoken to him directly.

"Hi," I said momentously. His answering look made me regret the fatuity of my greeting. "I noticed that you changed offices."

"Oh, that." He smiled sadly. "Phil Whiter decided he wanted my office. It has a better view. I never quite understood how I'd gotten such a nice office in the first place. Anyway, when I came back from midsemester break I found all my stuff moved out and his moved in. He had even transferred the contents of my desk, crammed everything in. It was a mess."

"Did he at least ask you first if it was all right with you?"

"No." The sad smile lengthened slightly, increasing its tragic suggestions.

"That's really quite a lot of nerve. Did you say anything to him about it?"

"No." He was made to suffer; I loved him. His face was the history of the Jews: the constant expulsions and wanderings, the forced conversions and blood libels, the pogroms and final solution. My heart went out to him, as it went out to that history.

"It's outrageous! He decides and moves in. It's feudal!"

"Well, I don't know." He glanced nervously at Noam, who was standing a few feet away. It was obvious that he was afraid Noam might overhear this seditious conversation. Len's future lay in the hands of people like Noam and Whiter. If he wanted ever to be in a position of kicking some untenured slob out of a nicer office, he would be wise not to alienate the Himmels and Whiters. "Whiter's a full professor and I'm untenured. He's probably got more right to it."

"He's the mighty lord, you're the grateful vassal." Len's weakness made me feel strong and assertive. His was a pure negativity against which I emerged vividly positive. It had been a long time since I felt this way. "The lord decides he likes the vassal's house or wife, so in he moves." Or the *goyim* decide the yids should go, I thought. But I knew better than to speak analogies like this one, especially to a Jew, no matter how Semitic his profile. "There's no need to talk it over, no need for courtesy. What a hypocrite Whiter is! He passes himself off as such a leftist, but he's sure a friend of the class system when it's to his advantage. Lord, vassal; propertied, unpropertied; tenured, untenured. It's all the same crap. Some people matter and have rights, and some people don't."

"Well, that's the way it is." Len shrugged philosophically, visibly relieved when Noam moved off toward the bar, having never glanced our way.

I had enjoyed my conversation with Len, especially the way I felt about myself when talking to him. Not that it really was myself. It was a role, and I always played it with Len. I stopped by his office the next day and casually asked him if he'd had lunch yet, and we went off to the Faculty Club at Prospect. There I continued to work out the part I would play.

I was the invulnerable adventuress, the remorseless *femme fatale*. I implied that I'd already had many extramarital affairs. Len never found out that it was he who initiated me into the rites of adultery. During our months together each of us worked hard to keep the other away, to shield our respective identities. I finally saw through him, but he never saw through me. When I finally left him it was for another man, the right ending to a polished performance of *La Belle Dame Sans Merci*. I had offered him a pack of lies, a fabricated identity, and unperceptive soul that he was, he bought it all and loved it. Because, of course, I was playing exactly the kind of woman who would fascinate and ensnare a Leonard Schmerz. But that's not why I was playing it. I took on the part because it felt so good. After all the months of being alone with self-loathing and failure, it felt wonderful to step out of myself. And it felt very good indeed to bask in Len's fascination and adoration.

I'm writing about the affair after the fact, with the cynical attitude with which I ended it. But that wasn't the attitude with which it began. It began with wonderful excitement, with born-again ecstasy. My body was alive once again, could give and feel pleasure. Len's melting gaze searched out every swell and hollow. He was worshipful, offering me again and again the highest praise of which the Jewish male is capable: You don't look at all Jewish. Our brothers always expect us to thrill at the words, because of course in their scheme of things there's nothing so desirable as a *shiksa*. I've never understood it. Jewish women seem to me so much juicier and more *betampte* (tasty). It's like the difference between a Saltine cracker and a piece of Sacher cake. The latter may be a bit much at times; but it's moist, it's rich, and it's layered. My symbolic logic professor in college, who regarded himself as a great connoisseur of women, once told me that I was his first Jewish lover and that, judging from me, he had made a great mistake in never sampling from his own kind before. I recognized the compliment, although I was pricked by its suggestion that my qualities could be duplicated in any other daughter of Jacob. And I certainly didn't respect my professor any the more for it. It was as if someone who professed a great love and knowledge of wines told me he had just sampled a Bordeaux for the first time and thought these wines merited further investigation.

Ava and Sarah both knew of my affair with Len. Sarah of the Puritan blood was accepting and sympathetic. I told her a bit about my problems with Noam and she seemed to guess much more. But liberated and earthy Ava was bothered by my infidelity. She likes Noam (one difference between her and Sarah), and she hates deception of any sort. She didn't want to appear judgmental, and never openly voiced the distaste I knew she felt. Her statements artfully sideswiped the issue. She'd come out in her usual forceful manner, only always pointed slightly off target.

"Hell, a person gets married, more often than not he cheats. It's almost become part of the institution of marriage. Courtship, honeymoon, reality, breakdown, affairs, divorce: they could be the chapters of almost any book about the typical modern marriage."

"Thanks, Ava. You're telling me my life is a pulp novel."

"Don't worry, kid. You may follow the general format, but I'm sure you'll do it with panache."

"So you think Noam and I will end up getting divorced."

"No, I didn't mean to imply that. You and Noam could never be accused of being typical."

"But you don't approve of this chapter."

"I don't go around approving and disapproving. I leave that to your religious relatives."

"Call it what you will." Anyone who occupies a mattering zone (and Ava did) approves and disapproves, even if one of the things disapproved of is disapproval. "You don't like it. You're not happy about it."

"I don't like the whole crummy institution. I wasn't particularly happy, if you'll remember, about your getting married in the first place. What I don't like is an obsolete set of conventions that forces people to lie and cheat on each other in order to preserve some empty state of union."

"Oh, come on, Ava. As if lovers don't lie and cheat on each other outside of marriage. It's not marriage that causes the problems, it's human psychology."

"Of course there's dishonesty outside, but not to the same extent. It's just much easier to walk out of an unhappy relationship if you're not legally bonded."

"Is that so good? Maybe if you stick around things can change."

"For the worse. How realistic is it to expect two people to live happily ever after?" Here was one girl who hadn't bought the fairy tale. "Happily ever after isn't human psychology. And also, Renee, you hardly even knew Noam when you married him. You should have expected some surprises." It was the only time she allowed herself to show anything but the most abstract kind of disapproval.

"Hardly knew him? My great-grandmother met my great-grandfather under the marriage canopy."

"Cut it out, Renee, your shmaltzy Jewish shtick. If you want to go back to Babylonia, go already. Just get off that trans-world shuttle."

Now I was an adulteress, in a class with the idolaters and murderers, not nice company at all. (What's a nice girl like you . . . ?) But I breezed along, hardly bothered by guilt. There was no sense of soul-crushing enormity, as there had been with Hillel. The only time I felt like a sinner was when I was forced to make up some story about where I had been or how I had spent my time. I despised the petty deception of those little lies. But about the great lie I was living I was hardly bothered. Just so long as I wouldn't have to make up tales. (Just like the analytic philosophers: the reality didn't matter, just the language.) I tried always to be home before Noam so he wouldn't be there to ask where I'd been.

One night, Len having persistently begged me not to leave, I came home rather late. I walked into a dark house with much relief and switched on the light. Noam was sitting on the couch, his arms folded. I was terribly startled and screamed. He turned to me, his face frozen in his hard, hating anger.

"Where have you been?" His voice was barely audible.

"Oh," I stammered, a lump of fear rising in my throat, "I was with Sarah." I'd call her the minute I got the chance and tell her to cover for me (as friends once had helped me deceive my mother).

"Where the *hell* have you been?" Noam repeated, and the fear spread throughout my body, washing away my strength. I thought I might collapse. All was over, I was finished. He knew. Someone must have told him, or maybe he somehow saw us himself. I was lost.

"What a wife you are! What a wife you've turned out to be!" He was screaming now, standing right in front of me, enraged. I was afraid he might hit me. "Do you know what time it is? Do you ever think about anybody but yourself? Do you ever think about me? I've been sitting here starving for the last hour and a half. You have nothing to do all day. No job, no children, no dissertation. Would it be too much to ask you to have some dinner ready for me when I get home?"

Dinner? That was what he was enraged about? It took a moment to penetrate. I wasn't lost. He didn't know about me and Len. He was angry because I didn't have his stupid dinner ready. The great fear brimming over in me was instantaneously converted into fury:

"Fuck your dinner! So I'm an hour late. Fuck it, Noam! Do you have to make me feel like a murderer for that? You're the selfish one! You're the one who never gives a thought to anybody but yourself! Look!" I picked up one of the lamb chops that had been defrosting on the side of the sink. "Would it have killed you to broil it yourself?"

I threw the lamb chop at him (missing), all the while feeling the absurdity of the situation. This was adultery, a serious business, the stuff of great literature, *Madame Bovary, Anna Karenina.* And here I was throwing lamb chops.

Noam didn't answer. He looked at the meat lying between us, and then walked past me and out the door. Late that night he returned, while I pretended to be asleep.

We didn't talk for a while after that. It's difficult to say for how long; we so rarely spoke these days anyway—just the minimum required to sort out our household and social obligations. We had both taken to reading during meals, Noam his math journals and I the New York *Times* and *The New Yorker.* (Occasionally I'd show him a cartoon I liked or couldn't understand.)

I think we ended up speaking more to one another at parties. For sometimes, when we were with others, Noam invariably at the center,

I saw him once again as I first had, and I would feel a pleasurable stir of warmth.

There are many beautiful and charming and accomplished women circulating through Princeton society. Only last night we were at a party, and I was chatting with two other mathematicians' wives, one a clinical psychologist, the other a linguist, both of them stunning. We were discussing adolescence, which the psychologist's daughter would soon be entering. It happened that we all, but especially our husbands, had been lonely outsiders then.

"And where are they now, one wonders, those popular girls we had envied so much," said the psychologist smiling, while my vision of my mattering map made its appearance.

"And our husbands, so spurned by those girls, now married to such fantastic women," said the linguist, opening her arms to include us.

I always watched Noam to see how, or rather if, he reacted to desirable women like these. It may or may not be hard to comprehend, but I would have been happy to see that he noticed and appreciated their charms. I would have welcomed gladly his eyes resting on them a few moments longer than necessary, as they had at that first party lingered on me. Such attentions would have indicated that this part of him was still alive and kicking, and I would have liked to have known that. But his face never reflected the desirability of the women around him.

As long as I'm on the subject, I might mention that at a party the chances were about one in five that I would be asked The Question:

"What's it like to live with a genius like your husband?" The legend-seeker this time was the quivery, faded blond wife of an assistant professor in Noam's department. By now this question depressed me, with the shiver of the cold wind of truth that only I could perceive.

"Hellishly lonely, if you really want to know," I said savagely.

"Oh, I'm sorry," she mumbled, looking down quickly. Her thin white skin reddened unevenly and unbecomingly (I also happened to know her husband wouldn't be getting tenure), and so I relented and didn't ask her what she was sorry for: her indiscretion or my life.

At home all was silent and cold between Noam and me. I hardly even thought of him as a person in those days; he was just a series of annoyances and complications. And in that gappy form he intruded less and less on my consciousness (which anyway was occupied elsewhere), so that now I can barely even remember him then. Where was he? What was he doing and saying? I have no recollection. I can't even remember any other episodes of anger between us. The great rage within him appeared to have boiled off, leaving behind a dry residue of indifference. He was quiet and resigned, and increasingly absent, in spirit when not in body. (This of course suited me fine. I could be his wife in name and yet be spared having much to do with the man.) The evenings he was home, he stayed either in his study or else in the living room, listening to music. He was spending more and more time with his much beloved Mozart, and had recently taken to listening in the dark, long into the night. A disappointed, but now resigned man. I could just make him out as I climbed the stairs to our bedroom, sitting erect in the center of the couch, his arms folded on his chest, staring into the black. Almost every night I fell asleep with the faint music coming from below.

Sexual relations ceased between us after one attempt when Noam, for the first time, was impotent. I was surprised by the reactions of each of us, for I was hurt and he upset—as if it mattered to either of us. On my part I felt pain that he no longer desired me even sexually. It was a further diminution of the linkage between us—even if this particular link had not in itself ever been very satisfactory.

But what was more baffling was Noam's reaction to his impotence. Why should it matter to him? Yet it seemed to.

"What do you think it means, Renee?"

"I don't know, Noam. Don't worry, you're probably just tired. You work so hard." I couldn't help myself, I felt sympathy. Imagine Noam's being bothered by mere physical impotence. It still touched me deeply when he exhibited any of the lesser mortal emotions.

"Do you think that's all it is?" he asked, for the first time in a long time gazing searchingly into my eyes.

EVERYONE IN PRINCETON, it seemed, certainly everyone in the math department—except, of course, Noam—knew of my affair with Len. And my lover, it was painfully plain to see, was proud of this.

Poor Len. Poor Noam. To be cuckolded by a Leonard Schmerz. Noam Himmel deserved better, At least if his wife's lover were a mathematician of international stature . . .

Len made no secret of his infatuation, not that he told anyone in words. But then nobody expected silent Len ever to use that medium for communication. He made it all obvious enough, always regarding me with a look of hopeless, slavish devotion. (You can imagine how well he did it.) We got into the habit of meeting for lunch, and then we would go to his apartment on Spring Street. (He always trotted a half-step behind me as we walked, like a little puppy.) It was there for all of Princeton to see, and see they did. The only one who didn't was Noam, and that's because he wasn't looking. His wife was of so little interest to him that he didn't even notice her flagrant infidelity. I pitied Noam for his ignorance; but I hated him for it, too.

My affair wilted and withered during the steamy Princeton summer, as I gradually penetrated my lover's interior. The mystery of his personality melted, revealing the core of vapidity. For *this* I had entered the class of idolaters and murderers. (I first began to suspect the nature of his secret when he described to me, in tones of deepest tragedy, how he had walked a block with one of the high and mighty mathematicians at Princeton and all they had spoken of was the weather.) My attitude toward Len became a highly noxious mix of interacting emotions: contempt, pity, and, stronger than either, the annoyance over feeling contempt and pity. The more I scorned, the more I pitied him for being the source. Then, overcome by the urge to comfort, I would lick his secret wound, his (all too justified) sense of inner emptiness. I would invent tales for him, describing how fascinating he was and in which respects. It required the inventive skill of a Scheherazade.

"Len, I really think you're one of the most interesting people I've known." We were in the drab bedroom of his depressing little apartment.

"Do you?" Happiness seemed wrong on that solemn face, but there it was. "How? Tell me how I'm interesting."

Dear God, as if a truly interesting person would ever ask. And now what was I going to say?

"Well, there's your face." I traced it lightly with my fingertips: the high noble forehead and weighty black brows; the soulful eyes and mournful lips and substantial, bravely arched nose. "It's got Jewish history written all over it."

No, he didn't like that. He was frowning. First of all, he identified with that history even less than Noam (whose interest in the subject had increased slightly after his Viennese discovery. Upon returning to Princeton, he had even read Lucy Dawidowicz's *The War Against the Jews*). Len too had been circumcised by a doctor and never bar mitzvahed, although he once offered, in the flow of powerful emotion, to have a bar mitzvah now, for me. Unfortunately, this magnificent avowal of sacrificing love caused me to burst out laughing.

And anyway, Len already knew he had an interesting face. It was his soul he wanted me to describe.

"You have such unusual ways of looking at the world, especially at people. I think you can really see through them, into their secret sorrows, and you suffer on their behalf. You have that capacity to imagine what it's like to be someone else, to see the world as he sees it and to empathize with his reactions, and I think that's probably the most important element in the moral makeup."

There, that ought to make him happy. (It takes more than a good body to be a *femme fatale.*) The poor fellow was all puffed up with satisfaction. Was he so pleased because he thought I believed this tale or had I actually convinced him of its truth? I was once again fighting down contempt, which brought on an attack of pity, and the whole sickening cycle began again.

Now I wasn't only a prisoner of a dead marriage; I was trapped into a dull love affair. Neither identity could save me, neither wife of the genius nor *femme fatale.* Was there perhaps a lesson to be learned? Is there something fundamentally wrong and intrinsically unsatisfying about a woman's attempt to define herself through her relationships with men? Impossible. A woman is who she marries, or—to update my mother's almost timeless wisdom—who she sleeps with. Her essential properties are relational. Besides, what else was there to me? Noam thinks the essence of the individual lies in his intellectual and moral attributes, but I didn't have any of these, not anymore.

THERE WAS MORE than my intellectual and moral decline to depress me that summer. For the first time I heard whispers of the decay of the flesh. I was twenty-five, and it happened like this:

I was in the bathroom, putting on my makeup before the medicine cabinet mirror, and the radio was on in the bedroom. Some item on the news had made me laugh as I stroked on my mascara. And there they were: laugh lines. Or, not to mince words: wrinkles, lightly but undeniably radiating downward from my horrified eyes. It was inconceivable. What truck had I with wrinkles? Oh, I knew the general facts, of course, having to do with aging. But I had never made the deduction to the particular: me. I stood there staring into the bathroom mirror, my mouth creased into a joyless approximation of a smile, taking it in. Time's gifts had ceased. From now on, time would be bringing me nothing but *tsuris*.

How long had those lines been there, this intimate fact about me immediately accessible to others and only mediately known to me? And what other symptoms of aging had already arrived, awaiting my discovery? I hadn't inspected my body for changes in a long time. I had viewed it as having reached a fairly stable condition, except for the fluctuations of five pounds more or less, and I knew exactly where to find them (face and waist). I had regarded my body, for the past few dumbly complacent years, as a finished object, its potentiality realized, its matter formed. Better to have been thinking in terms less Aristotelian and more Bergsonian:

"This reality is mobility. There do not exist *things* made, but only things in the making, not *states* that remain fixed, but only states in the process of change. Rest is never anything but apparent, or rather, relative. The consciousness we have of our own person in its continual flowing, introduces us to the interior of a reality on whose model we must imagine all things. All reality is, therefore, tendency, if we agree to call tendency a nascent change of direction."

My body was no more a fixed thing than my mind. Its very form was a process of change, a becoming. I was mortally afraid of *what* it was becoming.

I hadn't really thought about aging before, at least not in the negative sense. Why should I have? Until now getting older had been a joyfully beneficial process; time was an ally, leading me ever upward. Any afflictions along the way—baby fat, overactive glands—had only to be waited out. Time would heal. But abruptly, quite abruptly, I perceived that the direction of incline along which time was leading me had changed. (Reality is a nascent change of direction. You hit it right on the perpetually moving target, Henri.) The ally had become the enemy, leading me downward to . . . Good God. And these afflictions were here to stay and worsen. Is this, Herr Leibniz, the very best arrangement an omnipotent beneficient God could come up with in the best of all possible worlds? A bare seven or eight years from last pimple to first wrinkle?

I stripped out of my clothes and went to stand before the full-length bedroom mirror. It had been years since I'd made a general canvass, an expedition of discovery. The findings of the past had been satisfying: the gentle undulations of flesh, the delicate swells and tapers. Now the undulations would come in the form of wrinkles and sags.

I first tried to determine whether there had been any sagging of my breasts, viewing them in profile. Had their roundness flattened slightly? Oh, I was vain about those breasts: full, firm, smooth, the nipples golden pale and delicately shaped. But, it suddenly occurred to me, the very generosity of their bulk would hasten their decline. Newton's law of gravity. The force is proportional to the mass. No more running free and braless. I would never again allow nothing to come between my breasts and gravity.

And it wouldn't be only my breasts that were subjected to Newton's gravitational law. Thighs, ass, chin, all would be pulled, would droop and deflate. But the real devastation would take place in the face. Was there no way to fight it? I was dimly aware, in the blithe manner of youth, of a thriving business devoted to opposing these forces of nature. I remembered just that past winter having seen a magazine ad that sent a slight sickening chill of presentiment coursing through me: "If you're over twenty-five, you know that beauty is something you work on." I had just turned twenty-five, and the thought had never occurred to me. I exercised fairly regularly, tennis or squash with Ava about twice a week. (What Princeton matron, even if not so self-respecting, doesn't play tennis?) I played these sports only because I enjoyed them and felt so good afterwards. But *work* on beauty? My attitude toward being pretty had been Calvinist. Some are born blessed, arbitrarily chosen to receive God's love. Beauty is passive, unlike the active powers of the intellect, which is why I would prefer being brilliant to beautiful. But that doesn't mean I was prepared to become an ugly hag. It gave me a fright, this ad, with its suggestion that this aspect of God's universe isn't quite so unfair as I had assumed; but the fright quickly gave way to skepticism. They were just trying to sell products. And what was so special about twenty-five, anyway? They pick some arbitrary age. I was young, young. It was impossible to imagine myself being anything but young.

And so I stood there, naked before the mirror, assimilating such elementary truths as: Youth is not an essential, but rather an accidental property. Nobody is in *essence* young. One either ceases to be or ceases to be young.

Where to go? Instinctively I knew that the people with the facts would be not doctors but women, beautiful and vain women intent on finding ways of circumscribing the relentless laws of nature ruling their bodies, if not their minds.

At the next party I asked an acquaintance, an attractive pale blond woman of no determinate age (but that's the object, isn't it?), wife of a mighty figure in the political science department (my husband and I move with the Princeton powers), whether she knew of a good place for skin. She immediately grasped that it wasn't medical help I was seeking.

"There are quite a few good places in New York," she answered. "The best known is probably Georgette Klinger."

And so to Georgette Klinger I went, a bright honeycomb of little white cubicles buzzing with well-tended women, young and old. The queen bee herself I never saw, although I was told that her complexion, fine-pored and flawless, is a testament to woman's conquest over nature. The cubicle I was ushered into held a chair like a dentist's, a hook for hanging up my dress, a white smock to don, and a very serious, white-uniformed girl with a Hungarian accent who began my treatment with questions, writing down my answers.

"How old are you?"

I told her and she leaned over to probe my skin more closely, gently prodding and stroking it.

"You look very good, Mrs. Himmel, especially considering your age."

That hurt. I just couldn't get used to thinking of my age as a liability. I had always been so *young*.

"Very good elasticity. But it's dry. What do you use to cleanse it?"

"Soap."

"What?" She looked at me in genuine horror, her eyes dilated. Her stare was almost exactly duplicated by the young man—velvet skin, velvet eyes, velvet pants—who later made me up and also asked me what I cleaned with. Their expression was that of a missionary who has just been told by the blithe native that his wife is his sister.

"Ivory soap," I half said, half asked. "I thought it was very gentle." She continued to stare. "Well, what *does* one wash with if not soap?"

"Cream. You don't use soap, you use *cream."* I know moral outrage when I see it. I had stumbled on one more floating region of the mattering map, enclosing a system of perceptions and judgments, values and rules. And I know the spirit of religion when I see it. This young woman ministering to my face was very religious.

The treatment was continued. My face was creamed, steamed over camomile tea, creamed, massaged, creamed, and then creamed. The session ended with a fire-and-brimstone sermon against the pleasures of sunbathing, after I admitted to an occasional indulgence.

"Avoid it. Avoid the sun the way you would a blade across your face. It's your enemy, you especially. You're very fair. Your skin has no protection against the rays. The radiation goes down and breaks capillaries, destroying elasticity. And that means terrible damage, wrinkles. Irreversible."

Irreversible. The word froze my heart.

THIS YEAR not even the coming of autumn raised my spirits. There weren't going to be any fresh starts. Noam and I were sharing the same house but little else. Len had begun to beg me to get a divorce and marry him. But I wasn't going to give up being the wife of one of the world's great mathematicians to become the wife of one of the world's great mathematical bores. Len's absurd chatter about my divorce was unbearable to me. But its very absurdity provoked my pity, making it impossible to get away.

The fall brought as always a great rush of parties. New people are always arriving in September, and parties are given for the more important. Ava was very excited about the arrival at the Institute of the physicist Daniel Korper, on leave for the year from Cornell. She had long admired his work, but found him even more impressive in person.

"I suppose he's not really a *great* physicist. He hasn't done anything revolutionary, he isn't ever going to make the headlines, I don't think. But he's got such a subtle mind, a way of seeing new dimensions to old problems. I don't think anyone appreciates the *problems* more. It's not the kind of mind that ever does shake up the world, but it's fascinating. I'm going to learn a lot having him around this year."

The physicists at the Institute are a very chummy lot, having lunch together every day around a large table, discussing the work each is pursuing. Noam likes to claim that mathematicians are much purer than scientists in their pursuit of knowledge, less prompted by the demands of the petty ego. He claims that this is partly because there's no Nobel prize awarded for mathematics (Nobel specifically excluded mathematicians because his wife was having an affair with one), making the whole profession that much freer from the competitive spirit. But it's never been so apparent to me that mathematicians are particularly successful at keeping clean of the stains of ego. They're a markedly paranoid bunch, reluctant, unlike the physicists, to discuss their work before it's safely in print. One indiscreet word and a result could be known down through the ages as "Linsky's theorem," not Himmel's. Noam keeps both his desks, the one in Fine Hall and the one at home, locked. (What does he fear? A masked mathematical bandit? *My* treachery?)

Daniel Korper's name popped up so often in my conversations with Ava that I began to wonder whether he had succeeded in rousing her from her voluntary sexual torpor. I hoped so, though it seemed unlikely. First of all, she's so frank that I couldn't imagine her not telling me. And anyway, Korper didn't sound like the kind of man my friend finds sexually attractive. He certainly wasn't an elementary particle. Ava likes subtlety in physics but not in bed.

Finally I met him. Noam and I were invited to a party for the new arrival, given by one of the permanent members at the Institute who lived in one of the lovely homes built right on the Institute grounds.

I confess to being distinctly disappointed by the guest of honor. He was good-looking in a cute, boyish sort of way, which isn't my sort. I like a face that's been worked over by life, that shows something of what it's seen and suffered. (I couldn't trust anyone who hasn't suffered.) The imperfections are usually what I end up being touched by, especially if they speak of the soul's activity. But Korper's was a face in which one could still easily make out the boy once there. During the years that ought to have squinted the eyes, sagged the jowls, thickened the lips with desire or thinned them with frustration, the features of this face had preserved themselves, maintaining their small, rounded cuteness. Even his body was rather small and boyish. It was easy to see what a fetching child this had been. The only features that saved the face from succumbing to total juvenility were the very thick black eyebrows ending over the well-formed nose in two closed parenthetical furrows of the skin, testifying to the fact that the man thought for his living. The very thick waves of black hair were sparsely streaked with gray, as another concession to age. But these feeble marks of maturity on the otherwise boyish face produced an overall absurd effect. If Wittgenstein was right and the human body is the best picture of the human soul, then this was not a soul that intrigued me. The voice I found somewhat more provocative: very throaty and somewhat drawled. But on considering it again I thought it most resembled the voice a boy might affect in order to sound older.

Noam knew Korper slightly and seemed to have rather a high opinion of his intelligence and intellectual integrity, which was remarkable considering the man's profession. The two chatted together and I stood with them listening, trying to form an opinion of this physicist who impressed Ava so and whom even Noam grudgingly respected.

I took out a cigarette and Korper, glancing at me as he answered Noam, took out a thin silver lighter and lit it for me. It was then that

I noticed his hands. I suppose that what startled me so was the contrast between the pleasant, wholesome, mute features of the face and the painfully articulate hands:

The nails were savagely bitten down. I couldn't imagine that small restrained mouth performing such acts of self-mutilation. The fingers were very long, perversely so for a man of his size. They seemed at once delicate and decadent. The middle finger of the right hand was particularly arresting, twisted as if it had been separated at the knuckle and then carelessly stuck back on. The obviousness of its ugliness was phallic. These might be the hands of an unusually subtle mind, but these were not subtle hands. There hands would go anywhere, probe any darkness.

I glanced at the pleasant, closed face and then down at the hands, then quickly back at the face. It was extraordinary. I couldn't combine the face and the hands into one conception of the man. Which feature gave the true picture of the soul here?

He had meanwhile taken out a cigarette of his own, and Noam was making outraged noises.

"If you two are going to foul up my air, I think I'll move on."

Korper immediately apologized, his words contrite, his eyes amused: "Oh, I'm terribly sorry. I'll put it out."

"No, it's all right, don't let me interfere with your prolonged suicide. I certainly wouldn't expect Renee ever to put out a cigarette on my account," and he was off.

Korper turned to me. Now the amusement was obvious. "It must be difficult for your husband to live with a smoker."

"It's difficult for me to live with a nonsmoker, a righteously nonsmoking nonsmoker. We've divided the house into smoking and nonsmoking areas, like an airplane."

He smiled. "Marriage is compromise."

"Are you married?"

"Divorced."

"Did your wife smoke?"

"Yes." He was still smiling.

"I take it, then, that's not what broke up the marriage."

"No." The cigarette commuting back and forth between the hands and face created more continuity between them. The face took on more of the look of the hands. "Did you ever try to give up smoking, if not for your own sake, at least for your husband's?"

"That wouldn't be compromise, that would be sacrifice. And besides, I'm philosophically committed to smoking. It's an act of existential freedom."

"Is it? I always thought it was simply an indication of weakness of will."

"For some it is. You see, there are two kinds of smokers, heroic and unheroic."

"I have a feeling I'm the unheroic kind, but go on."

"Unheroic smokers are worried about the health hazards of smoking, which is weakness one, and would like to quit but can't, which is weakness two."

"Yes, I'm definitely cast in the unheroic mold. You, of course, are not."

I smiled my acknowledgment. A couch became vacant nearby and we sat down side by side.

"Heroic smokers don't worry," I continued. "Worry is for little minds. That goes double for worrying about mere physical danger. Fear for the body should never govern one's actions." You, who know my interior too well, are perhaps snickering; however, I was speaking my *beliefs* if not my feelings. "Heroic smokers disdain death. They laugh at death with every inhaling breath."

"So you disdain death?"

"I disdain death."

"What else do you do besides smoke to thumb your nose at the way of all flesh?"

"I drive."

"That doesn't sound extraordinarily dangerous."

"You've never driven with me."

His laugh was deep and throaty, with a far more natural sound to it than the voice. "But you know there really is a serious ethical problem here." His mouth was serious, but his eyes were playful. Now I could see that his was an intriguing face, despite its cuteness. The separate features spoke separate messages. The mouth fit its expression to the situation, while the eyes watched on in amusement. And then in the background there were always the hands, which I kept glancing at. "I feel, against my wishes, the greater sympathy for your husband. How can you balance your desire for the pleasures of smoking against his desire to breathe healthy air? Both are mere bodily desires, and his seems the more valid."

"Validity is a property of proofs, not desires. Desires simply occur, and are acted on or not acted on. To be free is to act on your own desires." Did he think he could throw philosophy at me? I'd give him philosophy.

He smiled. "Spinoza."

"Himmel," I answered, cringing in wait for the inevitable response: I didn't know Noam does philosophy as well. But it didn't come. Instead:

"Yes, Ava Schwartz told me you're a student of philosophy. The mind-body problem, isn't it?"

Why had they spoken about me? Of course I loved it, as I love any suggestion of my mattering.

His eyes had never left my own. I hate to speak to people who keep peering about all the time, as if always keeping an eye out for something more interesting than the conversation at hand. For this reason, I often find partying quite painful. People flit from one conversation to another, always convinced that the really interesting talk is going on elsewhere. I've found myself saying *any*thing (I'd really like to forget some of the things) in such a situation in a desperate attempt to keep the Other's attention on me.

But Daniel Korper was looking and listening to me as if he'd be content to look and listen all night. I got the very strong impression that this is a man who likes and understands women, and there is nothing more attractive to women in general and me in particular.

Haven't you ever noticed how some of the homeliest men (not that Korper was one) can have any woman they choose? It's such a basic difference between the sexes, that in one of them you can have a coupling of corporeal insignificance and sexual irresistibility, while in the other this combination is unthinkable. This assymetry makes me wonder whether *one* account of sexual desire will do for *both* sexes. A unified theory, being simpler, is preferable. The simpler account is, *caeteris paribus,* the better one. But perhaps reality doesn't always accommodate itself to our theoretical tastes. ("Who knows, perhaps

He is a little malicious," Einstein conceded toward the end of his life, after the years of fruitless searching for the unified field theory.) Perhaps my explanation of sexual desire in terms of the will to matter is biased from the female point of view. (Or perhaps its applicability extends no further than myself. This is a problem with introspective psychology: How far can one generalize? To all consciousness? To the human species? One's "own kind" of person? One's self . . . sometimes?)

You'll have noticed that the focus in my account of desire is not directed at bodies but looks past them. What's affirmed in the reciprocal gaze is reciprocal mattering. Bodies are only the means to the end. This is a crucial point, and one that may, I suspect, divide women and men.

One sex's sexiness has to do with the other sex's desires, and what men seem to lust after is a beautiful hunk of flesh, while women crave to feel understood, liked, and interesting. Take heed, all hopeful Don Juans. A handsome exterior is neither necessary nor sufficient. The most physically underprivileged males can be absolutely irresistible. (I speak from experience.) I can't represent the other side, of course. I don't know what it feels like to be a man, to desire as a man. (The inaccessibility of the Other.) But judging from what's desired, it must be pretty different. A woman's sexiness seems to be a matter of her properties as a material object, which is perhaps why she devotes so much attention to this aspect of herself. The men are the ones who have turned her gaze to her integument, for her interiority seems pretty irrelevant to her desirability. But what makes a man sexy or not is his point of view, the way he regards *us*. A man who has that particular manner that shows you he's noticing it all and appreciating it all can pretty much have it all. A woman can burn with desire, but if her matter isn't molded in the right way, she's the only thing that's going to burn up. But a man who really loves women, who genuinely loves them—not with a slobbering, slavish desire, but with a desire that remains in control of itself—such a man will always light our fires. It sounds so easy, but such men are rare. (Again, I speak from experience.) The way Daniel Korper's eyes played over me as we spoke, the way he smiled, made me feel that I'd found one of those rarities, and I began to smolder.

I turned back to his hands, with that secret dark life of their own, and I began to imagine them in various immodest acts. I kept my face down, staring at them, the images vivid, the throbbing warmth spreading and intensifying. We sat for perhaps a full minute without speaking, a violation of the rules of party small-talk I would normally never permit. (Always keep their attention. Don't let them start imagining the fascinating conversations they'll have when they get away from you.)

I made a conscious decision. I lifted up my face to him without rearranging the expression, without blotting out the desire I knew must be there. I had never done anything like that before, offering my desire first, without having received any indication that I was desired. The risk was of the most dangerous sort: the risk of rejection. He met my gaze straight on, his smile gone, the eyes beneath the weighty eyebrows very kind and, mercifully, showing no surprise. His expression told me: I'm at your service. We arranged to meet for lunch the following day.

The next morning I woke up feeling depressed about the previous night and my impending date. Why had I let my face speak my momentary desire, given that man access into my head? All of his ridiculous aspects presented themselves once again to me. I had compromised my precious mental privacy for *him?* His absurdity rendered me absurd.

I lay there in bed, long after Noam left for Fine Hall, remembering the night before with mental groans. I was tempted, even more than what had become the usual these past few months of wading ankle-deep in depression (with its oceanic possibilities), to bury myself under the blankets and go back to sleep, and thus escape the day in unconsciousness.

But I didn't. I got up and dressed, in fact dressed and made up very carefully, all the while feeling ashamed because of the care I was taking. Why should it matter how I appeared for this man? But I changed my clothes several times, unable to make up my mind as to the look I wanted. Should I wear a skirt and sweater in one of the pale beiges or apricots that suit my coloring so well? An image of Daniel Korper's hands floated before me, and I changed into my tightest pair of jeans, stuck them into a pair of high-heeled black suede boots, and wrapped a filmy violet silk blouse against my chest. My beige-apricot appetite I had already indulged in the choice of my panties, lovely wisps of silk apricot and beige lace. Now why, I thought as I put them on, do you give a damn which panties you wear? That man is never going to see them.

I had to call Len and break our standing lunch date. I hadn't thought about it until then. He was incredulous.

"What do you mean you're having lunch with Daniel Korper? He asked you out?"

"Yes. We met last night at a party at Fine's house." I added, feeling gratuitously cruel: "A party given for Daniel." Did Len make, as I did, the obvious comparison: how very unlikely it was that *his* existence would ever precipitate a party, especially up on Mount Olympus?

"Are you going to sleep with him?"

"For Godssakes, Len!"

"I'm asking you if you're going to sleep with him." The voice was choking on its own despair.

"Len, you have no right to ask me that. I'll do what I like." Pity, annoyance, and, like a faint taste of blood, a smidgen of pleasure, of the sadistic variety.

"What do you mean I have no right? I'm your lover."

"You're my illicit, adulterous lover. If anybody has any right to question me, it's my husband." Who of course had no questions because he had no interest.

"I can't believe you're doing this to me." The voice came out with great difficulty, gasping for air. Only a person without a heart could listen unmoved to its pain. But I was hardened by the apathy born of having hung around much, much longer than I had wanted; and I wasn't moved.

Moribund Len had finally passed on to the afterworld, the world after desire. It is a kind of death of the person, a disappearance of the one who once had been. The presence and then absence of desire transforms the perception of him so radically that it's almost like those gestalt-shifts in visual perception, when the duck is instantaneously replaced by a rabbit. Nothing about him means the same. The lines that used to form one picture now group themselves into another, so that one is presented with a quite new object—making claims on one's affections!

I hung up the phone, feeling as if I had managed at last to shake myself free of a tangle of clinging seaweed and grateful to Daniel Korper for, albeit unknowingly, helping me come clean.

But by the time I was driving out to Fuld Hall, where I was supposed to meet Korper, I was feeling only a sickeningly uneasy mixture of excitement and dread. What are you so stirred up about? I asked myself.

I was supposed to meet him at twelve-thirty. At *precisely* twelve-thirty he walked out the door. He must have timed his walk earlier with a stopwatch. Again I was overwhelmed by a sense of the man's absurdity, and felt correspondingly absurd myself. I reminded myself to ask him his ancestry. I'd have bet anything he was a German Jew, a punctilious, tight-assed *Yekky*. (The name Körper is German. They'd probably lost the umlaut in flight.)

I watched him walk over to my car with ridiculously bouncy strides. This man, I thought, is harboring an irrepressible boy inside his body, one who keeps trying to get out. He has consciously devised all sorts of means to restrain the boy: furrows in the brow, drawls in the voice. But the boy keeps popping out. Absurd—not that there was the boy, but that the man was fighting him.

I watched him bob his way over to the car and had the impulse to switch into drive and press the gas pedal down to the floor. I could just picture the ridiculous look on his ridiculous face as he watched me speed away. Dear God, I moaned, as I fought my impulse, what am I *doing* here?

He smiled at me. "Do you want to drive or shall I?"

"I will, of course," I answered shortly. Out of what dark chauvinist cave had he just stumbled?

"Then at least let me pick the restaurant."

"Be my guest."

"No, you will be mine. On that at least I insist. Let's drive over to Bucks County. I know a nice inn there overlooking the river. The foliage should be wonderful now."

I love that drive over to the Pennsylvania side of the Delaware River, especially in the fall and spring. So even though the long drive there meant extending the date, I agreed.

"What's your ancestry?" I asked as we made our way out of town.

"German Jewish," he said, surprised at the question.

"Both sides?"

"Yes. My parents came over in 1937. I was born in transit."

Bull's-eye! I can spot them anywhere, even the assimilated ones. The German Jews and the Hungarian Jews have the most extreme of the nationally defined Jewish personalities, and the ones that have survived the homogenization of America most intact. Hungarian Jews are materialists, in the economic, not metaphysical sense. They have a deep devotion to *things*, especially wall-to-wall plush carpeting and crystal chandeliers. (The Orthodox sometimes even have carpeting and chandeliers in *succahs*, the little temporary huts, built for the harvest holiday of Succoth.) The women are very devoted to themselves as women. (Georgette Klinger and many of her employees are Hungarian Jews.) It's they who have won the characterization Princesses for the whole class of us. None of them has ever been known to wear eyeglasses. Any who are cursed with bad eyesight get used to contact lenses or to not seeing.

And the German Jews? They're very devoted to themselves as German Jews, at least the first few generations of them. It's a holdover from Europe, where there was complete agreement, at least among the German Jews, on their superiority. They suffered from a (as it turned out) tragic sense of pride in the German *Kultur*, in which they played some part, once they were finally released from the ghettos in the nineteenth century. In the relatively short period from emancipation to destruction, there was a great flowering among them —producing, at the end, the finest bloom of our species, the man who demonstrates the human possibilities. I mean, of course, the hero of my heroes (true in both senses): Albert Einstein. He, however, was one German-born Jew (he renounced his citizenship early on) who detested all things Prussian. His was a repugnance that germinated in the ruthlessly, but typically disciplined atmosphere of Luitpold Gymnasium, where he was educated in his youth, and intensified at the end of his life, with the experience of what the Prussian spirit could produce.

Einstein had absorbed little or nothing of this spirit into his own. In fact, his personality formed in large part in reaction against the detested *Geist*. It was his active suspicion and even contempt for authority that allowed him to challenge the fundamental premises of classical physics. In later life he replied to a young girl who had sent him a manuscript: "Keep your manuscript for your sons and daughters, in order that they might derive consolation from it—and not give a damn for what their teachers tell them or think of them."

But many other German Jews bear the traces of some of the more innocent aspects of Prussianism. I remember one summer my parents and Avram and I spent the week of my father's summer vacation (needless to say, he wasn't given very generous vacations) at a hotel in the Catskills whose clientele was almost exclusively *Yekky*. My father spoke a perfect German, and at first they assumed he was of their own kind. When he mentioned he was from Poland, and his wife's family from Czechoslovakia, a distinct chill was perceived, softened by a little pity. That hotel was the only Jewish establishment we ever visited where everything started precisely on time. Dinner was at seven. At six fifty-eight, the dining room was empty. At seven, everyone was seated. Talk about anal compulsive. Which brings me back to Daniel Korper.

As we got past the Princeton traffic, I accelerated sharply. The road became a narrow, hilly, curving country road, the kind of surface I like best. Let's see if this anal little *Yekky* has any balls, I said to myself. I kept a peripheral eye on him and the speedometer, watching to see if he stiffened or gripped his seat as we approached eighty. (Noam was always my most relaxed passenger. No matter how crazy I got, he never noticed.) But Korper's body remained relaxed, his expression slightly smiling. There was a sharp turn in the road and I accelerated madly around it, wheels screeching. He turned to me with a little laugh.

"You really do drive like a philosopher."

I didn't like the sound of that. "What do you mean?"

"Didn't Plato say that to philosophize is to prepare to die?"

"Are you nervous? Do you want me to slow down?"

"No, I'm rather enjoying it. Perhaps you'll make a heroic smoker of me yet. Although I would hate to lose my life precisely at this moment, just when it's looking somewhat interesting."

"Meaning me?" I usually shrink from being so direct, but the speed was making me reckless.

"Meaning you."

I felt that he too was being unusually to the point. "I take it that's supposed to be a compliment. But 'somewhat interesting' isn't my idea of high flattery."

"But it *is* high flattery. To affect the interest with which a middle-aged man regards his life is a remarkable achievement. But you understand that."

"Do I?"

"Yes. I have an unreasoned belief that you understand it all. We're parallel lines, you and I." His voice was light and playful. So was his face when I glanced at it, an act of daring at the speed at which I was driving. (I see I'm showing off to you.) He was only flirting.

"Parallel lines never meet."

"Who wants to meet? One infinitesimal point of convergence, followed by ever widening distances. Parallel lines can travel along side by side forever."

The perfect metaphor for Noam and me, I thought. Two straight lines that converged briefly one spring, and now could only continue to separate. But I didn't say it. I knew the script: revelations of marital disappointments and disillusionments, listened to with inexhaustible sympathy and understanding. *Prolegomena to Any Future Adultery*, by Emmanuelle Cunt. I could hear the whole scene unfold in my head. Not that I was such a seasoned adulteress; I'd only played that particular role once. But the scenario had a familiar feel to it. My Columbia College professor-lover, Isaac Besdin, had begun by complaining to me of his wife—a real *shiksa* Saltine cracker, from what I could discern from his description and the photo of her on his desk.

Yes, I could hear the scene play itself out in my head, and so I said instead: "But who says our lives have to be straight lines? Who says we can't change direction?"

"Oh no, straight lines we are. We can never change direction, never turn back."

"A strict determinist."

"Of course."

"Why of course? I thought you physicists had decided we live in an indeterminist universe."

"I'm one of the last holdouts, sympathetic to Einstein's view that quantum mechanics can't be the last word." So that's why Noam could tolerate him. "Anyway, indeterminacy, if it's a fact, exists only on the level of elementary particles. On the human level the appearance of indeterminacy is only a function of our ignorance of the true causes."

"Spinoza."

"Truth," he intoned solemnly, and then we laughed.

"I won't reply to that one. I like discussions that end in one-word proclamations, like 'Truth,' 'God,' 'Existence.' "

"Then this discussion is ended. Shall we begin another or simply hold our peace?"

"Let's hold our peace. I love this stretch of road."

We had crossed the Delaware River into Pennsylvania and driven through the tourist quaintness of New Hope, and now we were following the old Delaware Canal, which runs side by side with the river here. It's a very beautiful road. We didn't speak except for Dan's directions to his inn, which was in a woodsy area about a quarter-mile back from the river, up on a hill. The river could be seen, framed by the peaking autumn leaves, aglow in the sunlight. We sat at a table beside a windowed wall, admiring the scene.

"Tell me," Dan suddenly asked, "what's it like to live with Noam Himmel?"

Dear God, The Question. It shattered my feeling of easy contentment like a rock sent through the glass beside us.

"Do you really expect an answer to that? Shall I give it to you while standing on one foot?"

He, of course, would not understand the allusion: to the mocker who asked the great and gentle rabbi Hillel to summarize the Torah while standing on one foot, to which Hillel replied: "That's easy. What you wouldn't have done to you, don't do to others. As for the rest, go and study." And the mocker became a disciple.

Korper's expression was immediately transformed, all the features, even the observing eyes, pulled into an expression uniformly solicitous.

"I'm sorry, it was a very stupid question." He paused, looked at me and then toward the window. "It's just that I imagined it must be rather lonely."

I pretended to read the menu. Instead of feeling happy about his intuitive plunge into the essence of my life, I felt put off. I didn't want anyone inside my head. He was invading my most private privacy in a way that Leonard never had done in all our months together. I did what I often do when I feel my interiority threatened by invasion. I lied.

He asked me about my background.

"Oh, I come from a family of academics, very enlightened and rational people. My father was a chemist and my mother a psychologist."

"Clinical?"

"Yes, she has a practice and also teaches. Her specialty is neurotic housewives. She discovered an interesting syndrome, and published several papers on it. Many women, she found, fill the emptiness of their lives by creating all sorts of things to worry about. It's a substitute for confronting their own inner void. She's been able to explain a lot of behavior by positing this as cause."

He didn't say anything, just nodded slightly. Then:

"Where did you grow up?"

"Manhattan. East Seventy-second Street." Always give as much detail as possible, to encourage the illusion of veracity.

I continued to lie my way through the meal, dwelling lovingly on the closeness between my older sister and me, and the great care my parents took in encouraging our intellectual self-fulfillment. There. Let him try to get into me now!

We finished the meal and returned to the car. I told him he could drive if he wanted. (I was feeling dispirited. The soul pays for defending its secrets in this way.)

When we were almost back in Princeton, I turned to him and said: "You know, Dan, I've been lying. Hardly anything I've told you is true."

"I know."

I couldn't believe my ears. God, I prayed, let this be a nightmare from which I'll be awoken.

"How?"

"Ava told me about your background."

was a moment I wish never to have repeated. ("My original fall existence of the Other," says Sartre in the chapter "Shame" in *Being and Nothingness*.) The lack of accusation in his voice and face made it all the worse. He had listened so quietly, all the time knowing I was lying. I hadn't put a thing over. If anything, I had made myself only more transparent, exposing how thoroughly pathetic the scene from inside is. How could I ever return to the role of *femme fatale*? I certainly never wanted to see Korper again.

But this was Princeton, and I couldn't avoid him for long. And by the time I finally did see him, I was anxious to. It was about three weeks later, at a very noisy party with too many people in too small a house. If Dan had tried to get in touch with me in the interim, I would have been annoyed and uninterested. But since he hadn't, I found myself, in accordance with the deviant logic of the emotions, wanting him to.

When I saw him walk into the party, I felt my heart give a vigorous push against my rib cage. He walked over to the bar and fell into a conversation with Ned Solo—or an approximation of a conversation. Poor Dan, I thought. Talking with Ned is like falling down the rabbit hole into a Leibnizian universe. The man is a closed system, a self-determining entelechy. His conversation is governed by the internal laws of his own nature, each comment following from a previous one and not subject to external influence. He sometimes gives the *appearance* of responding to something someone else has said. But that appearance is just illusion, the result of the principle of preestablished harmony. Ned is a monad, and monads have no windows.

The first time I spoke to Ned, I of course didn't know he was a refugee from Leibniz's ontology. He asked me what I was working on (remember, the preestablished harmony), to which I responded, "The mind-body problem," to which he responded: "Oh, do you know any gauge theory?" I did not, and I listened carefully to Ned's ensuing soliloquy, trying to make out the connection between the mathematical theory he was lecturing me about and the mind-body problem. Though I believe that my pet philosophical obsession weaves its way in and out of far-flung topics, I was surprised—and disturbed—that I might have to learn gauge theory. I hazarded a few more remarks and observed that they made no difference at all in the flow of Solo's conversation. It was impossible to have any effect on the man.

I saw that Ned was now rambling on, Dan watching and sipping his drink. I wasn't particularly blessed by my partner-in-conversation, either. Nora O'Shea is one of the few female members of the Princeton math department and she's so awfully pleased with herself, but not in any honest, straightforward manner. She's an example of the more obnoxious sort of peacock: a closet peacock. Once you get the dictionary to her private language, you understand that everything she says translates into self-praise. But it takes a little insight and lots of experience in the varieties of peacocking to acquire the dictionary. And of course once you do, the annoyance is sharpened by the fact that few other share it. On occasions when I exploded over Nora's obsessive egotism my listeners, including Noam, always expressed wonder.

Outwardly she's a drab little figure, with a bony Irish face crying out for makeup. (I'm only a bitch when provoked.) But Nora would never dream of putting a frivolous blusher to her aggressively intelligent features. Femininity is beneath her. She disapproves of all its manifestations. At parties where I knew she would be, I always tried to remember to wear particularly low-cut clothes for the sheer pleasure of watching Nora—whose chest is concave—stare in thin-lipped severity at my cleavage.

Right now she was complaining to me about the *enormous* size of her classes and her need to procure a second graduate student to help with the grading. Translation: "I'm such a *popular* teacher." It would be at once an act of self-help and altruism to free myself and Dan of Nora and Ned, neither of whose self-involved sicknesses was contagious, but one didn't want to get too close.

I interrupted Nora's gloating lament. "Oh, look, there's Daniel Korper. I have a message to give him. I hope you find another preceptor."

As I left her for Dan, I felt suddenly magnanimous. After all, would large classes ever satisfy her longing for large breasts, or a second preceptor approach attracting a lover?

"It's your own fault, Nora," I called back. "If you weren't such a terrific teacher, you wouldn't have such big classes."

As I moved off in Dan's direction, I could see Nora pinking with pleasure, the chest, which would never be in any danger of revealing cleavage, rising up in exultation.

Dan smiled warmly when I reached his side, extracting himself skillfully from Solo's monologue.

"I was hoping you'd be here," he said after Solo had moved on.

"Why don't we escape outside?" I answered. "The noise is so awful."

The silence and slight chill of the night fell on us like an old friend. I was slightly drunk, my body feeling as if it enclosed an inner warmth that no cold could penetrate. We walked down the quiet streets toward the lake.

"I'm sorry about lunch the other day."

"Why?"

"I'm sorry I kept lying. I'm even sorrier that you knew I was lying."

"Why did you? It doesn't fit the heroic mold."

"I was afraid you saw through me."

"Is that so bad? Are you such an awful person?"

"I think so," I said softly, for only the night to hear.

But he heard. "I don't," he said just as softly.

We had reached Carnegie Lake and walked along it for a while. I discovered we were holding hands. When had he taken mine, or had I taken his? The night had such an old-friend kindly feel to it.

"Noam and I made love for the first time right here, this very spot. It was spring. We'd been picking wild asparagus."

"It sounds very romantic."

"It was."

Dan kissed me. "How sad your voice just was," he said. "So wistful and sad. I'm sorry."

I wasn't sorry. I only wanted him to kiss me again. He did.

"Come." He took my hand and we began to walk again. "This spot already has enough memories for you."

We walked farther upriver to a soft, grassy hillside almost under the Harrison Avenue bridge. We moved slowly. I was right about him, I remember thinking, he does love women. Someone was moaning softly in the night. For a moment I thought it was the night herself, and then realized it was me. He was playing with me, bringing me to the edge and then away. But then he couldn't hold me back any longer. How long did it last? I don't know. The internal observer, with her play-by-play descriptions, her stopwatch and her scorekeeping, was silenced.

When I opened my eyes, Dan was looking down at me. He stroked my cheek and said, so softly, so deeply, like the voice of the tender night hugging us:

"Are you back yet?"

"From where?"

"From where we both were just now."

"Were we in the same place? How do you know?" Ever the skeptic.

"Knowing that is part of being there."

We lay together for a while, neither of us wanting to move, kept warm by each other's body.

"Come to me tomorrow morning," he said. "Come to me early. Can you? I want to see your body in the daylight."

I went to him early the next morning. He answered the door in his bathrobe.

"I was afraid you wouldn't come."

"Why?"

"Because I wanted you to. And you want people to want you desperately and then can't stand it when they do."

"Did Ava tell you that too?"

"No, you did. I must tell myself never to want you too much." He kissed my hair. "Come, let me see what you look like in the harsh glare of an October morning. I've been lying here thinking the moonlight must have been flattering."

He led me into the bedroom, lay me on his bed, and undressed me. Then he stood back and smiled.

"You're a lovely woman. That curve from the waist out to the hips." He sat down and traced my outline with his open hand. "It's the most moving curve in a woman's body. And yours is so particularly lovely."

"Are you going to sit there and admire me like a piece in a museum?"

He shook his head slightly and turned me over. "Such a lovely ass." He ran his hands over it. "What fine food must have gone into the perfect marbling of this flesh. It was all the finest food, wasn't it?"

"I'm afraid not all. I have a weakness for pizzas and all kinds of chocolate."

"Ah, I'm going to forget the pizzas altogether. As far as I'm concerned, this firm flesh was built of galantine of duck and pâtés de foie gras with fresh white truffles."

"I very much doubt if truffles build marbled flesh."

"No? Then rich, runny Bries and deep, dark, lascivious Swiss chocolates. If I didn't want you for your subtle philosopher's mind and gentle Madonna's face, I'd want you for your ass alone."

And I'd want you for your hands, I thought, but I didn't say it. I was afraid of saying anything that might interrupt the wonderful things those hands were doing. I could not believe their genius, their knowledge of what it's like to be a woman. How did they know to move in just that way in just that place for just that long? His hands worked their way back under me, never pausing in their certainty, as he entered deep inside me. How could a man know a woman's body so well?

We lay in bed afterwards, smoking his cigarettes. I was pursuing my preorgasmic thoughts, marveling at the knowledge of Dan. Did he really know what it's like to be a woman? How could he? I don't know what it's like to be a man, what it's like to have a penis and enter a woman. It must be very different for them, for Dan. I longed to know. If an angel of God were to appear at that moment and grant me any knowledge I desired, that's what I would have asked. What does it feel like to have a man's body, to have Daniel Korper's body? What does it feel like to be he? It was the question that most mattered that moment.

There it was once again: the ineradicable separateness of consciousness. The world he inhabits is his alone—with precious few of its details expressible in language and thus accessible to us Others. How I would have loved to slip into his world and see things as he does, to merge our two worlds like two drops of water. That would be to become one with him—for we *are* our worlds, just as Leibniz said. (But *windowless?*) Of course, one bumps into the metaphysical facts. How close can we get? One penetrates, the other is penetrated, but we never break through. Sex is a battle against metaphysics.

"What are you thinking about?" Dan turned to me.

"Oh," I answered, "an aspect of the mind-body problem."

"I am as well, a very practical aspect. Come, let's get dressed, have some coffee, and we'll discuss it."

We sat at his kitchen table, sipping his Melita-dripped coffee from Institute mugs (they provide everything).

"Now," said Dan, "here's the problem. You make a very strong argument for the body, so strong that I'm afraid my purpose here will be forgotten. This year in Princeton is very important to my work, and I'm afraid of getting hypnotized under your power. Oh, but I'm assuming that you feel as I do, that you want to continue our relationship. Am I assuming too much?"

"No."

"No, of course not. It's too good, we both know that. Look, here's my proposal. I hope it won't sound too brutally practical. I propose that we arrange a kind of schedule as to when to meet. Since you're married, you have more restrictions, so I'll fit my hours around you. What times are good for you?"

"A schedule? A schedule for fucking?" The tight-assed little *Yekky* with his stopwatches and schedules. My first impression of him had been the right one. "Are you going to write it down in your appointments book: Monday, Wednesday, and Friday, nine to ten, fuck Noam Himmel's wife?"

"You're very angry." My God, the man had powers of penetration. "I'm sorry. But I really don't know any other way. Affairs will fill up all available time if you don't draw rather rigid boundaries around them. You're angry. I'm sorry."

I damn well *was* angry. I got my jacket and left. Damn brainy prick. The trouble with you, Renee, is that you think the male sexual organ is the brain. Why do you keep fucking around with these great minds? Go be an intelligent cunt, paradoxical as it may sound, and find yourself a nice blue-collar lover. Stop trying to be a combination of Jean Paul Sartre and That Cosmopolitan Woman, and find yourself a nice simple mind with an ever ready erection. Yeah, fat chance in this town, this princedom by the turnpike, with its puny demigods on stilts. Effete, effeminate, impotent, prickless pricks. Fuck you, Daniel Korper. Fuck your fucking schedule for fucking.

I cooled down after a while. Why was I really so angry? I wanted Daniel to fill up my life, and he didn't want me to fill up his. For me, there was nothing else. My former loves—philosophy and Noam —now both reproached me with my failure and inadequacy. But there was more than me in Daniel's life, things that were important and that he didn't want displaced. And he was right, of course. I would have wanted to make his life as empty as my own, so that I could fill his void as he would fill mine. But that would be wrong. It would be unforgivable to take out what was already there. Len Schmerz, of course, had begged me to do that, but such was his weakness and I had despised him for it. You can't have it both ways, kid. I called Dan at his office.

"I'm free any day, all day. Nights are harder. Sometimes Noam works at his office, sometimes at home. And we have a lot of social engagements."

"Why don't we spend every morning together? And I'll work afternoons and nights. And come as early as you possibly can. It will never be too early. That way it's almost like waking up to you in my bed."

I was nervous about telling Ava. I knew how she felt about cheating in general, and now it was with Daniel Korper, about whom I wasn't sure how she felt. I went over that evening. We sat on her couch and listened to the Zuckerman recording of the Tchaikovsky violin concerto.

"Ava, Daniel Korper and I are lovers."

"When?" Her head was back, her eyes closed, as they had been while listening to the music.

"Last night. We wandered away from the party at the Searles'."

She nodded. "You don't seem surprised."

"I'm not. The morning after Fine's party Dan talked to me about you, asked me questions. He wasn't prying or anything. He didn't ask me anything I couldn't tell him. But it was obvious you had captured his fancy. He told me you two were having lunch—a few weeks ago, wasn't it? Actually I expected it would happen sooner."

"And you're not angry? Or unhappy or whatever?"

"No. It's your business, yours and his." And Noam's, I knew she was thinking. "And anyway, if you're determined to have affairs, which it seems you are, let it at least be with a Daniel Korper. That kind of temptation I can understand."

So it was as I had suspected. "Ava, did you want him yourself?"

She didn't answer right away. Then: "Yeah, I wanted him. But that was all it was ever going to be: wanting. If I'm going to draw a line around sex in general, I'm going to draw a double line around Dan. He's a professional colleague. And not just any colleague. He's important to my work, and I can't afford to have any other kind of involvement with him." She leaned her head back against the couch again and closed her eyes. "I guess I even feel a little vicariously happy about you and him." She grinned. "It's the next best thing." I grinned back. Her eyes were open again, and she was viewing me sideways. "I'm not going to go panting and drooling over the details, but just tell me. Is he good?"

"He's good." We were both still grinning.

"Good. Good for him. I'll take your word for it. But you know what? No matter how good he is, he can't be as good as my fantasies of him." She laughed. "It's just as well. He could never have lived up to those fantasies."

"Well, feel free to go on fantasizing," I said generously.

"Oh no. I couldn't do that. Just like I could never fantasize about Noam."

Fantasize about Noam? What a thought. "You know," I said, "I haven't exactly swept Dan off his feet. He wants us to keep a fucking schedule, mornings only."

I expected to hear her familiar hoot, but instead she nodded seriously. "Good," she said. "I'm glad. He has important things to do here this year. His work is very significant, Renee. Always remember that."

I was terribly shamed by her words, and the concern they revealed. She seemed to sense my shame, and smiled, trying to wipe out the solemnity of her tone.

"In other words, kid, you can have the body. Just leave us poor beggars his mind."

I got both. I went to Dan every morning. I'd never known a man could love as he did. I was at long last in the hands of someone who knew what he was about. The men I had known before, being highly educated, were all adequately informed on the technicalities of female sexuality. They all knew about the clitoris, knew it required some stimulation, etc., etc., and conscientiously gave it and the other memorized anatomical facts their due. That was just it, though. It was all done out of conscientiousness, out of their enlightened commitment to equal rights, prodded by the internalization of their mother's voice of long ago, chanting: Now, don't be selfish.

But Dan was so different. He loved the body. And I loved his. I loved its feels, its smells, its tastes. And always the wicked genius hands.

I got his mind as well—a mind supple, and subtle, and inexhaustibly rich. Its special brand of intellectual enthusiasm, the playful seriousness of its constant questions, made it the only place in him in which I still perceived the boy. Only the boy wasn't ridiculous (impossible to believe I had once thought Dan so), but wonderful. I enjoyed the qualities of his mind all the more because they were in such contrast to the tyrannical purity of Noam's intellect, always intent on the purge of the trivial. Nothing was ever dismissed by Dan as too trivial for consideration, and nothing ever was trivial when he considered it. His mind enlarged and deepened everything: Why can't we tickle ourselves? What is the sexual significance of breasts? He had a way of turning over any topic and revealing its deep side. He too liked to stare at simple facts, but unlike me he didn't get lost in confusion. He pushed ahead, got a grip, made connections, spun out theories. Not that he would drop a theory on your head, like a block of cement. (I've known such theorizers.) His method was delicate, open, questioning: Why is it jolting to consider the naked body beneath the undesired clothed body? How did it happen that we evolved hairless? Human beauty—actually beauty of all kinds, but particularly human—was a passionate interest of his.

His former wife, by the way, was not beautiful. I saw a picture of the two of them of long ago, together in Harvard Yard. The pain of discovering that he still carried the damn picture with him was almost counterbalanced by my relief at seeing that she was no contest as far as looks went: short, dark, stocky, looking much more a daughter of Israel than I, although she's only half Jewish. But still she had been incredibly powerful. I was awed by the strength of a woman who could walk away from Dan.

Curious that she wasn't beautiful, when my looks were so important to him, a continuous topic of conversation and analysis. Which was the better profile? (The right.) Did my breasts fit Arthur Koestler's characterization of the perfect breasts as shaped like the cups of champagne glasses? (No, but Koestler had been wrong.) Dan was interested in my looks, but, unlike most of the others, he wasn't fooled by them. This too was a favored topic, the power-duality of beauty, enslaver and slave of others' desires; beauty, the iridescent carapace with the soft, unprotected belly.

"A beautiful woman is more of a person and less of a person. We don't really believe in her suffering. How can the beautiful suffer? Certainly not in the grimy ways of the unlovely. Can a goddess have hemorrhoids, worry about mortgage payments? How can we presume to reason by analogy from our interior to hers?"

"If you prick us, you pricks, do we not bleed? If you tickle us, do we not laugh? If you poison us, do we not die? And if you wrong us, shall we not seek revenge? If we are like you in the rest, we will resemble you in that." I ran my nails lightly down the length of his thigh.

"You're welcome to more than a pound of the flesh," he had answered, in that deep drawl which had become the sexiest sound in the world to me. That voice was but one of the many entrances he provided into the dark and musty cave, D. H. Lawrence's "blue-smoking darkness, Pluto's dark-blue daze." Let him speak in that drawl, look at me and slowly smile, sip wine with a concentrated look, smoke—any of these and more, countless more actions, and I went immediately under. I must have trusted him, to have allowed him to lead me so far down. How could I not have trusted? He was the father-lover incarnate (because he never expressed any need?).

Then perhaps I wasn't really in love, since my passion was the progeny of my infantile sexuality. But the inner-world-transforming attachment to a person is an abnormal response. Something is going wrong—and not only in the thoroughgoing distortions of perception. One isn't simply reacting to the objective lovability of the Other. The explanation has got to lie partly in the quirks of the inspired. The image I have now when I think of such attachments is the one I also get when I think of the biological mechanism of certain poisons: the key jammed in the lock. And it's true that now, as I write, my life has the feel of a convalescence, although I'm not sure what I'm recuperating from.

Strange doubts these, for one who has believed so religiously in the salvation of romantic love. I've always conceived the solutions to my life in terms of "true love." When it became apparent that my marriage wouldn't yield the right answer, my mind immediately began to play with other possibilities (and my body soon followed), but always of a romantic nature, always developed around the repeated theme: someday I'll really fall in love.

But perhaps romantic passion is a pathological response, as Freud interpreted the love of God. And what future has *this* illusion? It too is soul-wrenching to renounce, for, like the other, it provides a division between the sanctified and secular, colors and differentiates the drab and monolithic space and time of experience, and drenches one's life with significance.

That year was a winter of many dark days, "Ithaca days," Dan called them. The bleakness outside gave sharper contrast to the lambent warmth of the rooms on Einstein Drive, lighted by a fire in the grate. The word "cozy" comes to mind, but it is far too mundane to do justice to the atmosphere of those rooms. "Cozy" is for children tucked in bed, the night light on, and the low murmur of the grown-ups' voices nearby. Perhaps it is the right word, after all.

Dan had been divorced for nine years (at the time that he was divorcing I hadn't yet had my first date). He had met his wife, Eleanor, when he was an undergraduate at Harvard, she a student at Radcliffe. They had gotten married the June of their graduation, Dan continuing at Harvard for his Ph.D. They had tried for two years to have a child. There wasn't anything physically wrong with either of them, it just didn't happen. So Eleanor enrolled in Harvard Law School. She changed tremendously in her three years there, growing in self-confidence and becoming increasingly restless in the marriage.

"She felt she had gotten married too young. She wanted to know more about life, about other men. We decided to continue being married, but we would allow each other the freedom of other relationships. I didn't really want it. I went through agonies of jealousy. I was just trying to hang on to her."

But he couldn't. She finished law school and he got his degree the same year. She went off to a prestigious New York firm and he went to Cornell. Still, they stayed married.

"I kept trying to get a job in New York. Finally there was an opening at Columbia. I didn't tell her about it until they offered it to me. When I called her she told me that she wanted a divorce, that there was someone else with whom she was in love."

"And do you still love her?" I forced myself to ask him.

"I don't know. I think she'll always be the most important woman in my life."

It hurt even more than I had expected.

"She married the other man, by the way. He's a lawyer. They have two daughters."

He *did* sound sad when he said that, I didn't imagine it. But he had laughed when he looked at me.

"Don't waste your sweet pity. I'm quite glad we failed in our procreative efforts. I don't think I would have made a good father."

This time I kept my face under better control. I didn't let him see what his words meant to me, the dreams they were negating. My golden daughter, now with Daniel's fertile theorizing intelligence. Our daughter. So he no longer saw children as a possibility. Why not, for Godssake, why not? A young woman could give him children. I could. Why was it not a possibility? And which of the other propositions I was daily, nightly, hourly fantasizing about were not alive for Dan?

It was always a challenge I could rarely resist (and very rarely succeed at) to get him to stay longer with me, to violate the time limits he had imposed. Did he realize the nature of this game for me? Once, half aroused, he leaped out of bed and started for the shower, then turned back, contemplating me and smiling.

"I saw pale kings and princes too,/Pale warriors, death-pale were they all/They cried—'La belle Dame sans Merci/Hath thee in thrall!'" Keats' poem became a running joke with us.

Always I was straining against the boundaries of our relationship, trying to extend Dan's presence, corrode the self-containment of our mornings, which flew by so quickly.

"What do you think sex is the best metaphor for?"

"Sex."

"No, come on, Dan. Sex is the best metaphor for . . ."

"Freedom. The focused surge of what-the-hell freedom. And you?"

"Transience. The ephemerality of ecstasy."

"Poor dear, you concentrate too much on the orgasms of life."

My longing to spread Dan out in the rest of my life first prompted me to invite him to our house for dinner. I was very nervous—not because of the need to dissemble before Noam, for I was confident of Dan's and my abilities in that sphere, as well as Noam's obliviousness. What I feared, rather, was having to cook for Dan, who is an excellent cook himself. I spent hours planning the menu for that ill-conceived, overambitious first dinner, a disaster from soggy soufflé to unflammable flambé.

But I got over the fiasco and my fear, and often had Dan to our house, usually together with Ava, their professional relationship providing the excuse for our socializing with him. The four of us could be very funny together. Ava and I tended to one-liners, Dan to word play and funny stories—many of which presented brilliant men in their ridiculous aspects. (For instance, the mathematician who's stopped by a colleague and asked whether he's eaten yet. He stares in abstraction for several moments and then finally answers: "I don't know. Which way was I headed when you stopped me?") I wondered about Dan's having so many such stories to share with us. Noam's funniest bits were a kind of soft slapstick. He frequently displays a physical humor, acting out things with a body whose awkwardness makes his movements all the funnier. For example, once the four of us were discussing brain bisection and Noam suddenly jumped up and demonstrated how a person whose corpus callosum is severed, leaving each of his hemispheres with a mind of its own, would walk down the street, each hemisphere opting for a different direction. The three of us howled as Noam shoved his body first to one side and then the other down the length of our living room.

Did Noam never suspect? Only once did it occur to me that he might. Ava and Dan were again over for dinner. I walked into our dining room from the kitchen, carrying the food. Noam was smiling and saying (I have no idea what had led up to the odd remark):

"It's very uncommon to believe something that one thinks untrue." He looked at me, still smiling. "Renee, can you think of anything you believe that's not true?"

I smiled back. "No, but I can think of things that *you* believe that aren't true."

Everyone laughed and then Noam asked: "What are they?" And then immediately the smile vanished and his face took on a look I'd never seen—fright, perhaps—and he said quickly, "No, no, don't tell me."

I felt slightly ill. What was he asking me not to tell him? And I also felt touched, as I always did when Noam appeared vulnerable, when he exhibited a raw emotion, although I wasn't sure how to identify this fleetingly present one.

Was there anything else from then to notice about Noam? If there was, I didn't see it, for I had given up watching. I was living in another world, where the only thing that mattered was Dan. (I had relocated on the mattering map. I lived no longer in a zone, but on a point. No wonder I'm left homeless now, uncertain of what matters. I'm in the market for a new world.) Noam is absent in my memory. He intruded on my consciousness only now and then with his explosions of annoyance over some minor domestic mishap, some chore or other I had forgotten to perform. (My unconscious was rebelling against our domesticity. Food was constantly burned, milk spilled, bills forgotten.) I have no notion of his version of this story I'm telling. I'm only trying to describe how it all seemed to me—then, when it was happening.

But while I tell you that version, several others keep clamoring in my head—the same story, only different, describing the same actions, only different. No, perhaps not even the same actions. One changes one's view of them and they transmute. Is there a right way of looking at them—the *objective* way? The view depends, once again, on what matters. I set down one picture and stand back to look at it, and instantaneously it shifts, turns itself inside out and looks every bit as good. I've no clue as to which is the right view, and growing despair over whether there *is* a right view. Is all this mattering business a feature of our subjectivity—and *nothing more?* Is the fractured mattering map, with its floating isolated regions, all there is? Is *that* God's view? Isn't one of those regions the right one, God's very own? If not, then no thing and—since who matters is a function of what matters —no one really matters. The will to matter burning within reduces us all to ashen absurdity. (I think what I am asking is that philosophically disreputable—in fact, slightly scatological—question about the meaning of life. The Princeton philosophy department totally failed with me.)

One of the dinners we all shared at our house was a Shabbos meal. Or in any case it was a meal of traditional Jewish foods consumed (but not in the spirit of Shabbos) on a Saturday afternoon in December. My idea for it was prompted by my reading Isaac Bashevis Singer's "Short Friday"—the beautiful tale of marital devotion, enclosed within the larger love of the Jewish way of life. In the extreme longing the story inspired I ran out and bought Jenny Grossinger's *The Art of Jewish Cooking*. (Typically, I already owned the cookbooks of almost every other cuisine.) I did all my cooking before sundown on Friday, as the Orthodox do. I even managed to find WEVD on the radio, and listened to the Yiddish program that featured the *chazzanes* my father had so loved, as I prepared my challahs, gefilte fish, potato kugel, and cholent (for which I didn't go so far as to buy kosher meat).

"What are these?" Ava asked when she saw the two twisted bread loaves on the table.

"Challahs."

"I know, dear heart. But what are they doing on your table?"

"For Godssake, Ava. We've had plenty of French and Italian loaves on this table. We've had Arabic pita, Irish soda bread, and Southern spoon bread. Why the hell can't we have challahs?"

"Okay, okay, we'll have challahs. What else are we having? It smells good."

"That's the cholent."

"Oh shit," Ava groaned, sinking her head into her hands.

"Okay, we'll call it a cassoulet. That will make it acceptable to you."

Dan and Noam were sitting at the table, too. Noam was engaged in his fervent atavistic *shuckling*, oblivious to it all. Dan was smiling as he watched Ava and me, and now asked:

"What is this cholent that smells so good and provokes such passions?"

"It's what Orthodox Jews eat on Saturdays, especially in the winter. It's a mixture of beans and potatoes and meat, but mostly beans, that's put up to cook before sundown on Friday, when the Sabbath starts, and cooks slowly in the oven until it's eaten for lunch the next day."

The cholent happens to play a prominent role in Singer's story, being responsible for the death of the loving pair through asphyxiation. It wouldn't have been the first time, I'm sure, that Jews have been killed by a cholent.

"That *is* something like a cassoulet," Dan answered. "Minus the pork butt and sausages. What kind of meat do you use?"

"We Jews call it flanken. I think it's beef short ribs. In any case, that's what I used."

I could have called my mother and asked her. But her powers of deduction being what they are, she would have put an ad in *The Jewish Press* announcing that her daughter was returning to the ways of her foremothers.

"And don't you like cholent, Ava?" Dan asked.

"It's just that I don't fully trust Renee," she said, and then a brief look of panic crossed her face and she glanced quickly at Noam. He, however, was still *shuckling* and oblivious. She turned back to Dan. "Renee can't shake off the hocus-pocus she was raised on. You never know what's going to send her shuttling back again. And I choose my directional deliberately, Renee. It *would* be back, you know."

"Oh, fudge off, Ava. It's just a meal."

That was one of the last things I said at that meal. I listened silently to my companions, my husband, my lover, and my best friend—to Dan's witty comparisons between the gefilte fish and quenelles, between potato kugel and pommes dauphine. I had never felt quite so separate.

I stared out at the winter-stripped elms and remembered Shabbos at home. I could hear my father's singing, the sweet warm tenor rising up in his love. Beside it the secular chatter of the Jewish *goyim* I had surrounded myself with, circumcised by doctors and not knowing what it is to yearn for the coming of the Messiah, sounded insignificant and despicable. But I had despised the religiosity of my past. How could I expect anyone to share my outlook, contradictory as it is? And I'm probably no different from anyone else in this respect. How can *any* of us expect others to share our world, particular as each of ours is? One is alone, alone, alone, alone. Alone in one's own world.

LEONARD SCHMERZ HAD offered to have a bar mitzvah. And Noam—though not for love of me—had begun to identify more with his Jewishness as a result of discovering who he was or once had been. But there were no soft spots to chip through in Dan's cynical armor. Like Ava, he never doubted his doubts. And he was much more successful than Ava in detaching me from the pull of my past:

It was about two months into our affair. The month before, during the two days of menstruation (the artificially light period induced by the pill), I had declined being made love to, concentrating just on satisfying Dan, and I planned to do the same on this day. We were both undressed, Dan lying beside me on his bed.

"Unstop yourself," he said, giving the string of my tampon a gentle tug. "And I mean that in all possible senses."

"My limited intelligence can only determine one," I said quickly, pushing his hand away, and yes, blushing.

"You're all stopped up, my poor child, with Jewish tampons, with the Jewish distaste for the body."

"Distaste for the body? That's Christian, I think. It certainly isn't Jewish. God, don't you know anything at all about your own heritage? Why does your vigorous curiosity pick its way so daintily around that one area? If you were really rational and objective about it, you'd at least know as much about its basic tenets as you do about psychoanalysis and the Upanishad. Jews are not ascetic. They don't believe in celibacy. Distaste for the body is not a Jewish value at all. Quite the contrary. It's actually a *mitzvah* to make it on Shabbos."

"That's probably worse," Dan said. "Koshering sex the way they do meat. Soaking and salting it to get out all the blood. Do they salt and soak their women before throwing them into the *mikvah?*"

I had to smile at the image. "I went there once, you know, to *mikvah*. Hillel wanted me to." (By now I had told Dan all about my previous lovers.) "It was a place on the Upper West Side, not too far from Barnard, with a sweet little *mikvah* lady all dressed in white, with a white babushka on her head. First you took a bath, then showered, and then you had to go before her while she checked to make sure your nails were cut short enough"—it had killed me to cut my long nails—"and there were no tangles in your hair, no loose strands of hair on your body. And then you go into the little *mikvah* room, with a pool about four feet deep and four or five feet square. You go under, legs open to make sure the water penetrates the entire surface of the body. It was absolutely imperative that all my hair go under. The poor little *mikvah* lady was so concerned. So much hair, so much hair, she kept moaning. And then you make a blessing, on the *mitzvah* of dunking, and—you're not going to believe this—she gave me a washcloth to cover my head while I recited it. For modesty's sake. There one is, naked before one's God, with a little washcloth on one's head for modesty's sake. I couldn't help it, I started laughing."

"Good for you. Why don't they all start laughing, I wonder."

"Oh God, why do I encourage you in your cynicism? I ought to be advocating the other side."

"Why?"

"Because there *is* another side, and you're too narrow-minded to see it."

"If it's narrow-minded to exclude some possibilities as too remote for consideration, I suppose I am narrow-minded. Rationality demands it."

"Is it so remote?"

"I've never heard of anything to suggest otherwise."

"The survival of the Jews?"

"If you want to explain their survival by hypothesizing supernatural favoritism rather then the somewhat special sociological conditions prevailing throughout their history." He shrugged his naked shoulders.

"Their history? *Their* history? You would have been gassed along with the rest of them. Their history. You're just like the evil son in the Passover Seder service. There's the evil one, the intelligent one, the stupid one, and the one who's too young to ask any questions. The evil one asks, 'What's all this to you?' dissociating himself from the proceedings."

"Sounds intelligent to me. What's the answer he gets?"

"He's told that all this is because of what the Lord God did for us when he took us out of the Land of Egypt. For us, and not for him, because had he been there he wouldn't have been saved."

"And you, poor dear, are wondering whether you too would have been left unredeemed in the land of the strangers."

"Oh, there's no question. I'm an adulteress, in a class with the murderers and idolaters."

"And me. Don't forget me."

"Some consolation for paradise lost."

"Look, I have a request. If you're going to undertake my Jewish education today, I would prefer our getting back to the *mikvah* lesson. That at least is somewhat titillating. Only let's make the *mikvah* lady young and voluptuous. That's a lovely picture, her checking you over for loose strands of hair. Did she stamp you kosher on your lovely ass?"

"No, I wasn't stamped. But when I finished with my dunking, two more times after the blessing, she pronounced me kosher. She really said it, 'kosher.' It was funny, of course, but it did make me kind of happy, being pronounced kosher."

"But you are, my dear child, even unsoaked and unsalted and dripping with blood, you are kosher. *I* pronounce you kosher."

The hand moved back, gave a harder tug at the string between my legs, and then moved inside me. I was horrified, my muscles tensing.

"It's all kosher, Renee," he whispered, his mouth against my ear. "It's all okay. Bodies and sex and blood. Bloody sex, sexy blood. Relax."

I did relax, losing myself in the world of his hand and my body. But I was brought abruptly out of it when he pulled his hand away, bloody. I looked quickly into his face, searching for signs of his disgust. Here it comes, the male revulsion at the state of being female. How could he not be repelled by this uterine debris, the uncleanliness at the heart, or rather the womb, of womanliness? But his face showed anything but disgust.

"Relax, relax," he whispered as he entered me and we began to move through territory that was totally new to me. How to describe the feeling rising in me? It was very intense, joyful, revelatory. A feeling of acceptance. My eyes were oozing tears, my womb blood, and he was embracing it all. And when we finally parted and I saw my blood on his body, I felt clean.

BUT NOT EVEN DAN was totally devoid of the love of God, the "intellectual love of God" of that pious *apikoros*, Spinoza. Only Dan called it "objective reality," or sometimes the "out yonder," recalling Einstein's remark: "Out yonder," Einstein had said, "there is this huge world which exists independently of us human beings and which stands before us like a great, eternal riddle, at least partially accessible to our inspection and thinking. The contemplation of this world beckoned to me like a liberation."

Dan is, as he himself said, one of the dying breed of physicists. He believes in objective reality and, like Einstein, sees his job as one of description. Not Ava, though, with her nothing-is-but-theories-make-it-so line. Hers was always the cynical voice cutting in when the rest of us got fired up with the romance of objective knowledge (Ava mistrusts enthusiasms on principle), with getting a glimpse of the world-as-it-is, in itself, unconditioned by the forces of subjectivity. We all felt the romance of it—Noam in math, Dan in physics, and me (dear God) in philosophy. (Philosophy has long suffered in comparison to math and science. So too here, in her representation in our little triangle.)

This attitude of Dan's was the basic reason Noam didn't subject him to the dismissing glance he directed at most other currently active physicists. And of course Dan has the highest respect for Noam, for he too resides in that region where the genius is hero. When we four sat around the table, discussing science or math or philosophy, then the lines of force were centered around Noam. It was he who would hold forth most freely, with we others questioning or arguing, but never rivaling his position of supremacy. One could dismiss him at other times, but not when we came together as minds.

But otherwise my husband receded into insignificance so far as I was concerned. Most of the time, as I've said, he hardly even seemed a person anymore. He was just a series of annoying events, and the fewer the better. Not that he presented too many obstacles. He was the most obliging of cuckolded husbands. Even when he was there, he usually wasn't there. I certainly never thought of him when I was with Dan.

And even away from Dan my mental processes were saturated with thoughts of him, my thinking an internal dialogue between us: What would he say to this? How could I answer him? All day long he spoke to me. The vaporous intellectual goals I once held were now condensed into an attainable one: to be of interest to this one man. That was all that mattered. His appreciative laughter at my remarks or excited response to my thoughts sent a shaft of satisfaction penetrating deeper than any that had flickered forth from the scholastic praise and awards of the past.

No one but Dan seemed real. The others, even Ava, enjoyed reality only to the extent that they related to him. People who had before meant so much to me now took on a shadowy existence. My sister-in-law, Tzippy, for example, the mother of the child who carries my father's name. Little Reuven was almost two and a half; in fact, Tzippy was pregnant again. If this was my nephew's "terrible two" stage, he has the makings of a saint, for he is a sweet-natured, loving child, with a precocious appreciation for music. He started carrying tunes in his infancy, and sits entranced listening to classical music on the radio. "More Mozart, please!" he cries out when Tzippy tries to turn the radio off. I would speak to Tzippy, though not as often as I used to. I only saw them twice in the past year. (They have no car and so can't visit us. And anyway, their coming would create an embarrassing situation since they wouldn't eat anything in my *trayf* house.)

My friend Sarah was also pushed aside. She wouldn't presume to intrude herself on others' lives unless called upon; and I wasn't calling. It couldn't be helped. My time with Dan was all-absorbing, crowding all else out. In this respect, as in others, this period had the sustained qualities of orgasm. I had finally achieved it. All the rest was foreplay. But, as my lover himself admonished, one shouldn't place all one's focus on the orgasms of life.

8

SOLUTIONS
and
DISSOLUTIONS

All these considerations, said Socrates, must surely prompt serious philosophers to review the position in some such way as this. It looks as though this were a bypath leading to the right track. So long as we keep to the body and our soul is contaminated with this imperfection, there is no chance of our ever attaining satisfactorily to our object, which we assert to be truth. . . . The body fills us with loves and desires and fears and all sorts of nonsense, with the result that we literally never get an opportunity to think at all about anything. . . . That is why, on all these accounts, we have so little time for philosophy. . . . It seems, to judge from the argument, that the wisdom which we desire and upon which we profess to have set our hearts will be attainable only when we are dead. . . . It seems that so long as we are alive, we shall continue closest to knowledge if we avoid as much as we can all contact and association with the body, except when they are absolutely necessary, and instead of allowing ourselves to become infected with its nature, purify ourselves from it until God himself gives us deliverance.

—PLATO,
THE PHAEDO

Philosophy has succeeded, not without a struggle, in freeing itself from its obsession with the soul, only to find itself landed with something still more mysterious and captivating: the fact of man's bodiliness.

—NIETZSCHE,
THE WILL TO POWER

*I*t was spring, and I was growing more and more desperate. Dan would be going back to Ithaca at the beginning of June, and I had no thought but going with him. But he said nothing and I said nothing. I did talk more and more of leaving Noam. I longed for Dan to encourage me in this at least, but he never did, just quietly listened. Was he acting out of scruples, not wanting to affect my decision? Or was it that he didn't really want me? He had never said he loved me, never, not even at those moments when the phrase just naturally slips out. For my part, I couldn't imagine life without him.

It was a cold spring and this gave me the illusion of having time. When the weather turned hot in May, my desperation mounted. I had to speak. I'd test my power over him first, see if I could get him to break our schedule, to give me a whole day. If I could get a day, perhaps I could get a lifetime.

I got my day. He granted it freely, willingly, with no hesitation. We debated where to spend it, whether at the beach home of a friend in Avalon, New Jersey, that was available to us, or in New York (I fancied the Plaza), or just on Einstein Drive. In the end we decided on New York.

"I'll get us a room at the Plaza, parkside. And I want to spend the night there with you, Renee. Do you think you can manage it?"

I'd manage it. But whom to ask to cover for me? My best friends, Sarah and Ava, were in Princeton. With whom could I be going to stay? Tzippy? I could never ask her to be an accomplice to my adultery. And if my brother Avram ever found out, he'd stone the three of us.

I finally just went to Noam without a story at hand and told him I was going to New York and would spend the night with a friend. He never asked me the name, or how I could be reached. I don't know what I would have said if he had. Maybe I would simply have told him the truth. I was tired of covering up.

· · ·

We had a parkside room. The first thing I did was take off the bedcover to see if there were satin linens. I was very disappointed to find the plebeian polyester blends.

"The Plaza's not what it used to be."

"Nothing is." I was surprised at how serious he sounded. Then he smiled. "You like this, don't you? This sort of luxury."

"Oh, I don't know. It's fun, but probably only because it's so different. Luxury is not something I've ever really lusted after. It was never my dream."

"Yes, I know. Perhaps you would have been better off if it had been." He stared at me a moment, again serious. Then he smiled again. "Anyway, you look very good in this setting. You look the proper part of a princess."

Then make my story end happily ever after, I felt like crying out. No, not now, not yet. First I had to make him feel my power. I lay back on the bed. There was still so much I didn't know about Dan. A year of exploring and there was still so much to discover. I could never exhaust all there was to him.

I had never even asked him one of my favorite questions. But there would be time, there would be time. Or would there?

"Dan, if an angel of God were to appear to you right now and offer to answer any question, what would you ask?"

"Oh, I don't know. There are so many questions. Right off the top of my head, I'd probably ask why the electron has the particular charge it does. That's a classic unsolved problem in physics. We have no idea of the answer, none at all. What would you ask?"

"For the solution to the mind-body problem," I answered promptly.

"Ah yes, of course."

"You've never really told me. What do you think? Are you a body?"

"No, I certainly am not. But everybody else is."

"That's the most improbable answer I've heard yet."

"Yes, but I think it's what we all unreflectively and inconsistently think. It's unnatural to identify yourself as a mere body, but it's natural to identify anybody else with his."

He sat down beside me. I was wearing a yellow sundress, which he slipped off over my head. I had to admit the man had a novel approach to the problem.

"This is you, Renee Feuer Himmel."

He put his hands on top of my head and then slowly ran them down, tracing the outlines of my body: down the outside of my shoulders and arms, up under my arms, and then down again, down my legs and around my feet, and slowly up the inside of my thighs, where they finally rested. I had never known the mind-body problem handled in such a wonderful way.

"You are flesh," Dan whispered. "That's a presupposition of lust."

"Not very logical," I muttered.

"Lust is more absolute than logic."

"Good God, Dan. What sacrilege. If Noam could hear you."

He laughed. "Somehow I think your husband would be more outraged at the moment if he were to see me."

I wasn't so sure. Which would have infuriated Noam more, a violation of his wife or a violation of logic?

We stayed in the room for several hours and then went out walking —window-shopping and visiting several galleries. (Dan knew more about art; he knew more about everything.) In a boutique window on Madison Avenue we saw a glorious little silk number in my shade of apricot, which Dan insisted that I go and try on, and then insisted on buying.

"You'll wear it tonight at dinner."

The gift made me feel like a kept woman, an expensive courtesan, and this was fun, too, as it is always fun for me to slip into another identity. That evening I wore the dress to Lutèce (my first time there), where we shared a rare rack of lamb, a raspberry soufflé, and two bottles of Taitinger champagne. (What were we celebrating? I was afraid to ask.) I can still remember every taste and texture of that meal.

Dan, of course, is very interested in food, as he is interested in everything. He was always intrigued by my gustatory experiences, conditioned as they are by my Orthodox unbringing.

"I just can't imagine what it's like to regard certain portions of inanimate matter as not only edible but evil. It's really fantastic that food can be perceived to have moral qualities. I'll never be able to experience that, the delicious thrill of ingesting the forbidden."

I described for him the period of my life when I first began to break the laws of *kashrut*, the weeks of frenzied fressing in which I tried to experience all the sapid sensations of which I had been deprived in my previous seventeen years. I wouldn't take a bite of meat without spreading it with butter, just for the perverse pleasure of mixing *milchik* with *flayshig*.

After years of *trayf* living, the sinful pungency has of course faded. But there are certain foods that can still evoke the moral dimension for me. As a child I had been taught to read labels to make certain that the ingredients included only pure vegetable shortening, so I still feel a kind of moral shock at the sight of a pure, unashamedly naked hunk of lard. And after learning at age four to first break an egg into a glass and then search to make certain there are no blood spots before scrambling it (ironic that the Jews should have been accused of *blood* libels), I am drawn with repulsed fascination to blood sausage. I don't know if I'll ever be able to regard even a simple pork chop as morally neutral.

We had had only a salad for lunch, in order to be properly hungry for dinner, and now we felt stuffed.

"You'd think drinking all those stars would make you feel like floating instead of like this," I said.

"Let's walk until the heaviness wears off," Dan said, slipping his arm around me.

We walked and talked. There was a wall of tears rising in my chest, and I kept laughing to force it back down, as I remember doing as a child. There was the pervasive feel of an ending, subtle but unmistakable. The champagne had been to celebrate the end of our affair. I won't let it happen, I thought, I won't let him go. I'll use all my power.

Dan had kept his arm around my waist. In the Plaza elevator he slipped it up under my arm so that his fingertips were just resting on my breast. I was very tired and silently doubted that I would be able to make love. But Dan's power over my body had only grown over the year. It was like hypnosis: the more times you go under, the easier it is each time to fall into a deep state. At the very first touch of Dan's hands or tongue (which was as brilliant as his hands) I would go under. I couldn't let him go.

I reached orgasm in the flood of tears that had threatened all evening. Dan switched on the lamp beside the bed.

"My God, Renee! What is it? What's wrong?"

"I love you, Dan, I love you. I love you. I want to stay with you. I want to leave Noam and stay with you. Don't you want me?" I sobbed.

Dan closed his eyes and leaned back against the headboard. He didn't speak.

"I'm sorry, Renee," he finally said. "I can't do it for you. You would like a passion to sweep you away beyond decision, beyond responsibility. You won't find such a passion, at least not in this bed." He paused, and then went on. "I won't be distilled into the essence of your life. I don't have the taste for such things, not anymore." He got up and pulled on his pants. "If you want to leave your husband, leave him. But don't do it for me. Don't do it for any man."

A voice was screaming in my head· He doesn't want me, he doesn't want me. When I spoke, my voice sounded so strangely quiet alongside that other hysterical one.

"What was I for you? Just a good lay?"

"You were all a woman could be for me at this point in my life."

"Which is a good lay."

"Well, yes, if you like. But you're a good lay because you're very beautiful and very bright and very, very sweet. You're a good lay because you're a wonderful woman. And if I were anything but a very tired and burnt-out middle-aged man, I'd feel differently."

Eleanor, I thought, still the power of Eleanor. He had told me how he felt about her: "I think she'll always be the most important woman in my life." But I was so arrogant in these matters, I couldn't believe any woman could defeat me. And now I was defeated, not even by the woman herself, but by her memory.

There was nothing more to say. (A woman with a father-fixation meets many burnt-out men.) I too got up and dressed, and we sat there waiting for the morning. Dan had already left me.

I can't remember the next week very well. It was the closest I've come yet to suicide. When I couldn't stand the quiet of my home anymore, when the chanting in my head became unbearable, I'd go out walking. Every passing car tempted me. I could see it so vividly, the leap that would place me smack against the hood. Why not? What did it matter now? What did I matter? Death is God's way of dealing with adulterers, death by stoning.

And not only God's. The two greatest heroines of fictional adultery, Anna Karenina and Emma Bovary, with whom I had dared to compare myself, both took their lives, Anna by throwing herself in front of a train and Emma by nibbling on some household poison. (Emma's death, prolonged and excruciating, was a how-not-to lesson for all us would-be suicides.) Perhaps the only thing that held me back was the small doubt Noam had planted as to whether death would end it all. He had told me in Vienna, when speaking of those who had died and been revived, that the only returnees to report bad experiences were the failed suicides. "They had a sense of cosmic disapproval." That's all I needed.

I didn't see or speak to Dan, and he didn't try to get in touch with me. The deepest wounds of the past had come from words—rejecting, dismissing, belittling. But no spoken signs had hurt as their absence now did. *Any* word would have been better, would have left me feeling that I mattered somewhat to the man who alone mattered to me.

I agonized over his silence, in the stillness of my home or walking the streets, trying to torture out its meaning. Did it signify ignorance or indifference? Either he didn't know my state or he knew but didn't care. For knowing and caring he wouldn't have held back all words. Both interpretations implied betrayal. Either his understanding or his kindness had betrayed me. And I had believed in both with the perfect faith of a child.

I went around in a daze, unable to eat or sleep, barely able to breathe. (Poor Len, I thought, suddenly sympathetic.) Noam didn't notice. I had run through the gamut of emotions this past year and the man I was living with had never noticed. One thing at last emerged clear and distinct. I had to get out of this marriage. I had to get away from Noam. Our marriage was dead, dead. It had to be disposed of.

It was about two in the morning. I had gone to bed early, about nine, dizzy with exhaustion. But then, of course, I had been unable to sleep, had lain there hour after hour, the voices chanting, until finally the truth had broken over me. Get out, leave him. There's nothing here.

Noam hadn't come to bed yet. He was in the bedroom we had converted into his study. I got out of bed and walked into his room. He was sitting there at his desk, a pencil in his hand, bent over a yellow pad with blue lines. He looked up in surprise.

"You're still awake."

"Noam, I don't want to live with you anymore. I don't want to be married to you."

He put the pencil down on the pad, carefully, right between the two centermost lines, holding it there for a few seconds to balance it.

"Noam, did you hear me? I'm leaving you."

He didn't look up from the perfectly poised pencil. "Tonight? Are you going tonight?"

"Yes. Tonight."

"I see." He still hadn't moved. "Yes, of course. It all fits. I didn't predict it, but it was predictable. Of course I would lose you, too."

His voice was very quiet. I had to strain to hear it. It was a voice I had never heard before and it disoriented me. Something about it didn't make sense, but I couldn't identify what.

"What are you talking about, Noam? What else have you lost?"

"I've lost everything. I've lost everything. You might as well know now. There's no reason why you shouldn't know."

He finally lifted up his face to me and it too was new. I didn't understand. What was going on here?

"I've lost my mathematical powers." His voice broke. "I don't have it anymore. I never knew what it was when I had it, and now I don't have it anymore."

Tears were streaming down his face. So that was it! Noam was suffering! It was too much to take in. This was sadness, the deepest sadness I was hearing and seeing. I had never seen Noam sad. I had seen him excited and triumphant, disgusted and raging, but never sad. I was completely bewildered.

"But you're working, Noam. You're always working."

He laughed, a dry, hard laugh I'd never heard. "Do you want to see my latest results?" He held up the pad, which had been covered by his arm. There was an intricate geometrical doodle. "I sit at my desk. I just sit. Nothing comes. The only thought in my head is: It's gone, you're old. I never knew what it was when I had it, but it was wonderful. It was power. But mathematics is a young man's game. Here, listen."

He unlocked the top desk drawer, where he kept the results he was so jealous of, and took out a thin little paperback, *A Mathematician's Apology*. There was a photograph of a man on the cover, leaning back in an easy chair, elbows resting outward. He peered out at the camera over his specs, brow furrowed, a very interesting young-old face.

"This was G. H. Hardy. He was a first-rate mathematician. This book was written after he lost his powers." Noam laughed, that same eerily new laugh. "Obviously after. A mathematician *with* his powers doesn't have any interest or time to write a book like this. But it's a very fine little book. A justification of the life of pure mathematics. And the joy," he added softly.

He opened the book and quickly found what he was looking for.

" 'Mathematics is not a contemplative but a creative subject,' " he read. " 'No one can draw much consolation from it when he has lost the power or the desire to create; and that is apt to happen to a mathematician rather soon. It is a pity, but in that case he does not matter a great deal anyhow and it would be silly to bother about him.' "

He closed the book and looked up at me, the intense stare of old.

"Hardy was really quite lucky. He kept going until he was sixty, which is very unusual. Even Newton gave up entirely by fifty, and he had discovered around forty that it was gone." (Noam was forty-one.) "Hardy was very lucky. But you know what he did when it finally deserted him? He tried to kill himself. It didn't work, he botched it. But he didn't have to live much longer anyway. Unfortunately, I'm a much younger man."

The sound and sight of him was so strange, I still was having trouble taking his words in, trying to give them sense.

"How long, Noam? How long has it been like this?"

"I'm not sure when I knew for certain. I had suspected it for a long time. I began really to suspect it soon after you and I were married. But I still had work to do. I was working out some ideas I had had a long time ago, ideas I never had time to develope. Compared to the things I was doing they were insignificant. But then I was grateful for them. I finished with them about a year and a half ago" (when I had started up with Leonard, I thought). "And since then there's been nothing."

I tried to think of something to say. But none of this fit. He looked up at me.

"I was angry at you, I blamed it all on you, at least at first. I kept telling myself you were distracting me, that you were draining my powers. I remember when you suggested our having a child." I recalled the incident. I had returned from Lakewood after meeting Fruma, who was big with her fifth child, and I was big with the fantasy of mothering a child with the genius-gene. "That's the whole trouble, I told myself. She's stifling me in the ordinary. I know I've been terrible to you, Renee. I haven't been able to control it. I'm so angry all the time, at least I was. And not only with you. I've been terrible to the younger people, the students, the ones who still have it. They have it all ahead of them, and it's all behind me."

Stop it, I told myself, don't start seeing him as a person.

"But it wasn't their fault and it wasn't yours," Noam was saying. "It wasn't our marriage, Renee. In fact, the marriage wasn't a cause, it was a symptom. At the height of my powers I wouldn't have married. I couldn't have fallen in love." He smiled and said softly, "Not even with you. You see, I didn't have room in my life for two passions."

This stranger was my husband? My view of him, like everyone's, was dominated by the fact of his genius. What was he, who was he, stripped bare of this fact?

"Why didn't you tell me? Why didn't you ever talk to me?"

"Because I knew you loved the genius. I know that all I've ever been to anyone, including you, including myself, for that matter, has been defined by my mathematical gifts. It was all anyone ever asked of me. It was my justification."

The urge to comfort overwhelmed me, in spite of myself. "You always talk about people's justifications," I said. "People don't need justifications. They're people. That's enough."

I said these words without really thinking, moved by the desire to offer him something. And I've been staring at them ever since.

"No, it's not enough," Noam answered. "Most people are worthless. I wasn't, but now I am."

"You mean you're no better than anyone else. Is that so terrible?"

He turned and looked out the window. The sky was still dark.

"No, Renee, I don't think I have to tell you that I'm less than other people. It's not as if I used to be like others, only with something extra added. So that you could take away that extra and there would be a person like others. That extra was my whole being, my substance. It didn't leave room for anything else. But that was okay. If I was less of a person, it was only because I was more of a person. That's the way everyone thought of it, including me, including you. No. Of course you'll go, of course."

He stood up abruptly.

"This self-analysis is disgusting me. I shouldn't take myself so seriously. If I don't matter, it doesn't matter that I don't matter. Look, you stay here tonight. I'll spend the night at the Nassau Inn. We'll talk tomorrow, figure out how to arrange things. Good night."

He walked quickly out of the room. I heard the front door close a few seconds later. I went downstairs and sat there in the dark until daylight, shifting through the layers and layers of shock, trying to understand and absorb it all. Boom ba boom ba boom, one thing after the other, taking the breath away, as Noam on the train into Vienna had described his heights.

I hadn't understood the nature of the story I was living, had misperceived my role in it and misidentified the victim. My own soul-sickness had absorbed my full attention. All else had come to me filtered through it. I had consistently misinterpreted Noam, from the angers of the first part of our marriage to the air of resignation he had borne the last year and a half. I had taken it for granted that *I* was the focus of his discontent. And I had been so angry at him for never looking at me! He had been living in torment for most of our married life and I had never guessed. It had been so long since I had even thought of him as a person.

I called Dan around eight in the morning. I knew he got up around then, for it was then that I used to go to him. Aside from everything else, he was the person who understood everything better than anyone. He listened quietly as I told him the story.

"Poor Noam," he said softly. "How terribly alone he is."

Dear God, yes. The full extent of his isolation suddenly opened up before me and I cried out at the sight of it. I got off the phone, ran up to the bedroom and pulled on some clothes. I ran out to the car and drove over to the Nassau Inn. But the man at the reception desk said that no Noam Himmel was registered there.

My mind froze over in fear. I fled from the place, dreadful images before me: Noam's bloated body pulled out of Lake Carnegie, Noam leaping from the tower of Fine Hall, the tallest building on campus. Fine Hall! Noam's turf.

I drove my car around Ivy Lane, parking in back of the building. Noam's office is on the twelfth floor. I didn't knock. When I walked in he was sitting near the window, staring out at the Princeton beneath him. I went over to him and put my arms around him and we held each other, crying.

THAT WAS several months ago. It's autumn again, my sixth in Princeton. The undergraduates have returned, the classes have resumed, and the leaf-strewn lawns are trod with a more purposeful step. We had spent the summer here again, Noam once more turning down invitations from around the world. Now I understand. It would be like an arthritic former tennis champion looking on at Wimbledon or Forest Hills. And Noam is still so young. He just turned forty-two. What will he do with his life?

He still has teaching, of course, but that aspect of his profession never mattered much to him. It was all in the discovery, all the joy and meaning. Teaching was a nuisance. How little of it would be demanded of him was always a bargaining point in the days when schools were competing to get him. (And they'd still fight.) Besides, I suspect he still harbors bitter feelings of envy toward the mathematically young and vigorous. There's still a very deep anger in him, but now I understand its nature. I know it's not directed at me and I can deal with it.

Once Noam suggested, half in jest, that now it was time for him to turn his attention to philosophy. He had always called my field the pastureland for old mathematicians and scientists. I remember his making some rather brutal remarks about a Princeton physicist who had just published a book on philosophy and the natural sciences. It was the first year of our marriage, so Noam must have been suspecting the failure of his powers. We were at a party, and a physicist named Vince Fonti, a rather lovely man, asked Noam if he had read Price's book. Noam had laughed.

"Poor Frank. I guess this means he's over the hill. When physicists start writing about the philosophical consequences of their former work, you know they've had it. That's the form their senility takes, they start spouting philosophy. It's a real problem with philosophy of science, philosophy of math, too, for that matter. Either you have philosophers doing it, and they don't really understand math and science, they don't have that intimate knowledge that comes only from working in the fields themselves. Or else you've got the has-beens, the nearly senile. And if they don't have the mental energy to do their real work, what makes them think they can solve the problems in philosophy? No wonder no progress is ever made there. A scientist or mathematician in full command of his powers has no interest in or time for philosophy."

"I don't think Price is in his dotage," Vince had answered. "I enjoyed his book immensely. He may not be an active physicist anymore, but he's written a very interesting and maybe even important book." Noam shrugged. "You know, Noam," Vince smiled. "Perhaps you ought to be more sympathetic to men like Frank."

"Why?"

"Getting older is not some sort of disease that only certain unfortunate people catch."

"What's your point?"

"My point is this: Even you will find yourself getting older someday. That is, if you're one of the lucky ones."

I cringed, waiting for the avalanche of fury. But Noam had simply stared at Vince for a few seconds, and then turned and walked away. Vince looked down at the drink in his hand and then at me.

"I'm terribly sorry, Renee. I didn't mean to upset him."

The memory of this conversation and others like it made us both smile when Noam first said, "Maybe I should take up philosophy of math." But Noam has been talking of it more and more of late, and I think he's even written up some of his thoughts. The problem is, he's so terribly young—not young for a mathematician, but for a man whose life is over, or who believes it is. This time Noam really has survived his own death.

It was like living with a stranger, especially in the beginning. Often I'd look at him, thinking, He's not a genius. Is he even the same man? By his own criterion of personal identity it's dubious that he is. He always said his mathematical creativity was his essence. The old Noam would have sooner identified himself with some unknown Viennese schoolboy than with a man without the power to create.

But the power is gone, and sometimes I still feel that the person is, too, that this is a stranger. But unfortunately for him, the stranger has the other man's memories, and those memories torment him. It's funny, especially considering my reasons for marrying in the first place, but it's of course the stranger I've known for the longer time, the stranger with the genius's memories. I don't know if I ever even met the genius.

MY OWN FEELING of mourning has passed by now. At first it was intense, at times approaching what I felt after my father died: a cried-out numbness, occasionally breaking out into something so much worse that one welcomes back the numbness. At its peak I sometimes forgot what I was mourning, believed myself to be grieving the loss of my father. But no, it wasn't my father this time, I'd remind myself. It was Noam's genius that had gone, and Dan, and Ava—I lost her, too—and something else as well. Perhaps the illusion that we need not be alone.

Just in case we in Princeton forget the inescapably transitory nature of life, there is the Institute for Advanced Study, with its stream of temporary visitors flowing in and flowing out like the river of Heraclitus. Nothing remains the same. Dan left in June—I never saw or spoke to him again. There is a very serious-looking economist occupying Dan's former rooms. I've seen the man quite often, for somehow or other all my walks seem to take me down Einstein Drive. The economist is fortunately not a very observing man; he never seems to recognize me, even though he must have seen me staring up at his windows.

Ava left Princeton soon after Dan did, for California of all places, to accept a position at Caltech. Not only did my best friend abandon me to go off to that despised land of alien values; she went off happily, exclaiming about Caltech and the people she would work with there. Her happy chatter about the virtues of California—the *weather*, for Godssake—pelted me like stones. Her eager acceptance of the yoke of banishment betrayed me and the New York existence we had shared. My closest and dearest friend, is there anything we share anymore? I don't even know how to picture you. Has your unwholesome pallor been burned away by those banal sunny skies? Are you still bitingly honest, or is that prohibited there? Oh, Ava, have you lost your Bronx accent?

Our last conversations were painful. She saw my misery, she even sympathized with it, but she would not share it. Our situations were so completely at odds, how could our viewpoints fail to be? Ava had chosen her goals and depended on no one but herself to carry her to them. She felt sorry for me about Dan, but she wouldn't immerse herself in my sorrow. It wasn't just her own happiness. It was her view of me and my misery, how I must have seemed to her in her strength of her own making. "Sometimes, Renee, I regret having ever taught you to say 'fuck,' " she told me.

Ava is gone, Dan is gone. Now it's Noam and I alone with each other. But if I've come to regard him as something of a stranger, I've also come to view him with something new and comforting, with human sympathy. He's on the mortal sphere now, the sphere of suffering. Beneath the iridescent carapace—in his case the mathematical genius—lies the soft exposed underside. And he looks at me differently, too. He regards me as his friend. I think I'm his first.

I haven't gotten him to accept the words of comfort I offered on the night of his revelation: that people don't need justifications, that they're people and that's enough. Noam has always occupied a single region of the mattering map, where the people who matter the most are the geniuses. That this is so was taken for granted, as was his own privileged position. I don't know if it's possible to get him to change his perspective, not to relocate on the mattering map but to turn from it altogether. I've been trying hard to do so myself, to see the map for what it is: a description of our subjectivity and nothing more. From which region does God look out on us? From none, of course. Not because people don't matter objectively, but because they do. They simply do. Any view that confers degrees of mattering, that distinguishes between those who matter and those who don't, has no objective validity. We all count in precisely the same way. That's the view from nowhere inside, the view from out yonder. And its contemplation beckons to me like a liberation.

There's nothing philosophically new in all this. I'd even written it out on exams: "In Kant's ethics the term "person" is not merely descriptive but normative. Persons are ends in themselves and sources of value in their own right." So the words were there, ready to offer that night, even if not backed by belief. (One of the advantages of an education.) But I've been staring at them ever since, and I've watched them as they began to stir and then to leap up and dance. There is that difference when the knowledge is formed from the matter of experience and written in the soul's own blood.

The view beckons like a liberation, and I try to keep my gaze steadily on it. But the pull of subjectivity is so strong—the tug backwards into the muddle, where some people matter more than others and we must constantly be figuring out who they are, sick with the worry of whether we are among them.

People don't need justifications. They're people and that's enough. I wonder if someday these words will be able to do for me all that the old words once did, shouted out in unison by the congregation of Israel. They are shouting them now, for it's the Ten Days of Repentance. My father always prayed beautifully, but his voice took on a new dimension during the holy days of autumn, especially at the *Kol Nidre* service that begins Yom Kippur, when the very gates of heaven are said to open. "Is he singing or crying?" some little friend would always ask me as my father implored on behalf of his people. He felt the enormous responsibility of his position. Wrapped in the purity of his special white robes, he was the messenger of his community, their lives hanging in the balance:

"On Rosh Hashanah their destiny is inscribed, and on Yom Kippur it is sealed, how many shall pass away and how many shall be brought into existence; who shall live and who shall die; who shall come to a timely end, and who to an untimely end." His eyes were shut and he was raised on his toes, his soul straining ever upwards as the chant continued.

And then had the congregation responded, in one great thundering voice:

"But repentance, prayer, and charity cancel the stern decree!"

Long after I ceased believing in these words, the sound of them had caused my spine to tingle and eyes to tear, as there is often a lag between one's rationality and emotive responses. I'm not even confident that today the words would entirely fail in their effect were I to put them to the test.

People and their suffering matter. Noam suffers, and his suffering matters no more nor less than anyone else's. The only difference for me is that I might be able to make a difference for him. I would like to. Dear Noam, I would like to.

But so far I haven't succeeded in getting him to accept my new words.

"Why do people matter particularly, just because they're people? What makes them and their suffering of any more consequence than that of any other living creature? We just can empathize with them more, because they're more like us."

"You think the suffering and death of a person is on the same level of significance as the slaughter of a chicken?"

"No." We both smile. "But only because we're capable of excellence, of scaling the heights. Only because our kind can occasionally produce the Mozarts and Einsteins."

"Okay, that may be. But then we all do matter, we're none of us nobodies. We don't have to justify our existences. The Mozarts and the Einsteins do it for us, by demonstrating our possibilities."

"Perhaps. But even so, Renee, it's a difficult thing to go from being one of the sources of significance to being a mere receiver."

"But you're *not*, Noam. You'll never be merely that. It was you who scaled the heights, up beyond all the others, to the transinfinite realm, to the numbers bigger than all others."

"Yes," he answers softly, smiling at me, his eyes, their most brilliant blue, gazing into mine. "I did do something. The supernaturals."

THE OTHER INHABITANTS of our little world don't seem to have caught on yet to the fact that the spirit of genius has taken leave of Noam. And perhaps it won't matter too much to them. The fruits of its former presence, the supernaturals and all the rest, will always be with us, and perhaps a grateful world will feel that this is enough for one man. Perhaps they'll continue to respect and cherish Noam, not for what he is doing but for what he once did.

But so far, at least, I can tell that even among Noam's closest colleagues the truth isn't known. They are waiting to see what he will produce next, what he will take out of his locked desk drawer. The attitude is still worshipful here in Princeton, where Noam Himmel is a living legend. And often I still see that question hovering on someone's lips, as he debates with himself whether it would be too personal a demand, too much of an intrusion, to ask the wife of the great man: "What is it like to live with him, to live with a genius like Himmel?"

FOR THE BEST IN PAPERBACKS, LOOK FOR THE

In every corner of the world, on every subject under the sun, Penguin represents quality and variety—the very best in publishing today.

For complete information about books available from Penguin—including Puffins, Penguin Classics, and Arkana—and how to order them, write to us at the appropriate address below. Please note that for copyright reasons the selection of books varies from country to country.

In the United Kingdom: Please write to *Dept. JC, Penguin Books Ltd, FREEPOST, West Drayton, Middlesex UB7 0BR.*

If you have any difficulty in obtaining a title, please send your order with the correct money, plus ten percent for postage and packaging, to *P.O. Box No. 11, West Drayton, Middlesex UB7 0BR*

In the United States: Please write to *Consumer Sales, Penguin USA, P.O. Box 999, Dept. 17109, Bergenfield, New Jersey 07621-0120.* VISA and MasterCard holders call 1-800-253-6476 to order all Penguin titles

In Canada: Please write to *Penguin Books Canada Ltd, 10 Alcorn Avenue, Suite 300, Toronto, Ontario M4V 3B2*

In Australia: Please write to *Penguin Books Australia Ltd, P.O. Box 257, Ringwood, Victoria 3134*

In New Zealand: Please write to *Penguin Books (NZ) Ltd, Private Bag 102902, North Shore Mail Centre, Auckland 10*

In India: Please write to *Penguin Books India Pvt Ltd, 706 Eros Apartments, 56 Nehru Place, New Delhi 110 019*

In the Netherlands: Please write to *Penguin Books Netherlands bv, Postbus 3507, NL-1001 AH Amsterdam*

In Germany: Please write to *Penguin Books Deutschland GmbH, Metzlerstrasse 26, 60594 Frankfurt am Main*

In Spain: Please write to *Penguin Books S. A., Bravo Murillo 19, 1° B, 28015 Madrid*

In Italy: Please write to *Penguin Italia s.r.l., Via Felice Casati 20, I-20124 Milano*

In France: Please write to *Penguin France S. A., 17 rue Lejeune, F–31000 Toulouse*

In Japan: Please write to *Penguin Books Japan, Ishikiribashi Building, 2–5–4, Suido, Bunkyo-ku, Tokyo 112*

In Greece: Please write to *Penguin Hellas Ltd, Dimocritou 3, GR–106 71 Athens*

In South Africa: Please write to *Longman Penguin Southern Africa (Pty) Ltd, Private Bag X08, Bertsham 2013*

84, different plane